*Vicky,
Clay just did
San[...]*

CLAY

A Leaving Marks and Undercover Crossover Story

T.A. MCKAY

CLAY

Copyright © T.a. McKay, 2018

ALL RIGHTS RESERVED

Cover art by Kari March designs - www.karimarch.com

Formatting by T.a. McKay

This is a work of fiction. Names, characters, places and incidents are either the product of the author's imagination or used factiously and any resemblance to actual people, dead or alive, businesses, establishments, locales or events is entirely coincidental. Any reference to real events, businesses or organizations is intended only to give the fiction a sense of realism and authenticity.

All right reserved. No part of this publication may be reproduced, stored in a retrieval system, or transmitted by any means – electronic, mechanical, photographic (photocopying), recording or otherwise – without prior permission in writing from the author.

Pirating an author's work is a crime and will be treated as such.

DEDICATION

To the staff at Blackburn Starbucks, Aberdeenshire. Thank you for the never ending supply of coffee that got me through this book.

INTRODUCTION

This book is intended to be read after the Leaving Marks series and after the Undercover series.

The Leaving Marks series is a two book MF series.
    The Undercover series is a two book MM series.

This book should be read as the final book in both series.

AUTHOR NOTE

Even though I have tried to stay true when it comes to Sam's job, there are some things he does that I know aren't possible in real life. This book is fiction and to make the story possible, the lines had to be blurred slightly.

PROLOGUE
Clay

SIX YEARS *Before*

I raise a bottle of beer to my lips as I listen to Gabe try and convince me he doesn't like Rhys. Does the guy honestly think that I'm buying any of the shit he's trying to sell me? I have spent the last six months watching him trying not to drool every time she walks past, but to be fair, I'm not sure he's aware that he's doing it. It all started with little looks that he hid quite well, but recently I can see him watching her whenever she's around. He can't seem to look away when she's in the same room as him. As he keeps talking, I wonder if he's trying to convince himself more than me.

I put the bottle on the table and pretend to sneeze. I need to get this guy to realise his feelings sooner rather than later. "Sorry, I'm allergic to bullshit. There must be some around here somewhere."

Gabe scowls, looking like he wants to reach over the table and punch me in the face. Never going to happen, my friend. Gabe knows that in a straight-up fight between us, I'm handing his arse to him in a bag. Not trying to sound big headed, but I can kick most people's arses. "Fuck you, Clay. I've told you before that I'm just friends with Rhys. I don't want anything more."

I swear he should record this shit and replay it when we talk, it would save him a lot of time and trouble. "Yeah yeah, so you keep telling me. The only thing you aren't doing is convincing me." I never thought I would see the day when Gabe would show any interest in a girl. He's never had anything past a one-night thing the whole time I've known him. I think everything with his mum and dad has jaded him towards any relationship. I know that feeling, but with Gabe, he deserves someone special. He is a great guy, and I think Rhys would be perfect for him.

"I might have said this before, but just in case I haven't. Fuck you, Clay." I try to hold in my laughter, but it's difficult. He really is too easy to wind up when it comes to Rhys, and now I think it's time to have some real fun.

"Well that's cool, I just needed to check before I give Rory the green light." I put the beer bottle to my lips taking a well-timed drink. I know what I just said will piss Gabe off and I don't want to be able to give him an answer too quickly.

"What fucking green light?" *Bingo*. I knew he'd bite.

I keep drinking, letting the seconds drag out. With every beat that passes I swear he gets redder. When I'm sure he's about ready to explode, I lower the bottle to the table. "Well it's just Rory asked me if I thought it would be okay for him to ask Rhys out. I wasn't sure before, but now I know that you're just friends, I can tell him that he's good to go. That's not a problem is it?"

I see him struggle for words. It's clear he wants to tell me that I can't tell Rory to ask Rhys out, but if he does, he'll need a bloody good reason. "I'm going to the loo." That's the only response he gives before storming away from the table. I finally let my smile out knowing the poor fucker is gone. He has a serious boner for Rhys and nothing will change that.

I look around the bar and take in who's sitting around us. It's a Wednesday night so it isn't too busy, a few new faces, but most are regulars. My eyes stop on a guy who's leaning across the bar talking to the owner Roxy. I know I shouldn't stare, but he has on tight-fitting jeans, and my attention is entirely on the curves of his arse. I lick my lips as I stare a hole in his jeans, but I don't move from my seat. If he had been female, I would have been buying her a drink before she had the chance to find a seat to put that cute arse on. He's not though, so I will stay in this seat and enjoy the view like every other time. Looking is fine, approaching isn't.

My eyes widen with panic when he turns and looks straight at me. It can't be possible that he felt my stare on him, but when Roxy points in my direction, I want to vanish under the table. I pick up my beer to try and distract me from looking back over at the guy. The last thing I need is to be caught again, even when my curiosity needs me to know if he's still looking. I ignore the fact that Roxy had pointed at me, nodding as she spoke to the stranger because my nerves are already on edge without wondering why she had. I don't notice Gabe returning to the table until he sits across from me, but I give him my full attention, trying to calm my breathing as he stares at me.

"What's wrong with you?"

I swallow deeply and force a smile onto my lips, trying to hide the fear I'm feeling.

"Well, that's even scarier. Don't do that smiling thing. It doesn't suit you."

I growl at his smart arse response. If the guy wasn't my best friend, I'm sure I would hate him. I'm about to explain how much I dislike him when a shadow falls over the top of the table, big enough to cover both Gabe and me. I don't have to look up to know who's standing there, but I send up a silent prayer that I'm wrong.

"Clay Wilson?"

Gabe looks at the owner of the voice, but I can't seem to find the courage to turn my head. I'm scared that something will show on my face, something that I want to keep deeply hidden.

"Clay?" I look at Gabe who's giving me a strange look. I know if I ignore this stranger it's going to set off alarm bells.

"Sorry. Yeah, I'm Clay Wilson."

The stranger holds his hand out, and I reluctantly place mine into it. His hands are huge and warm, and there seems to be a direct line from them to my dick. My heart starts to race as the same old fight occurs inside me. I tell myself I'm straight, that checking out a hot guy doesn't mean I'm gay.

"Niko Reeves. I was told you might be able to help me."

Thinking of working with this guy stresses me out. Makes me feel that some of the secrets I've been trying to hide for so long might be found out. I would turn him down in a second if it weren't for the look in his eyes. He looks like he's fighting a battle between falling apart with grief and taking someone's life due to anger. I've seen that look before, and it tells me I need to agree to this, no matter what comes of it.

1
Clay

PRESENT DAY

"I need your help, brother."

The voice on the other end of the call makes me want to weep with relief. After three months of worry and no contact, to hear Niko's voice is like a balm for my nerves. The last I heard from him he mentioned that things were going down at his job, and then nothing. I kept the faith, believing that Niko was smart enough to dodge any drama, but there was always that part of me that worried, especially since I knew where he worked.

Blue Diamond was advertised as a legitimate escort service, but I knew there was more to it because no escort service would need Niko and his particular skills. The fact that Niko never explained what his role was in the company led me not to ask questions. I went with the *if I don't ask he won't need to lie* scenario. I think part of me didn't want to hear what he actually did, the job that made him vanish for months at a time without any contact. My friendship with Niko isn't exactly the kind of relationship that we spend a ton of time together, but usually, he checks in periodically, unlike the last few months. None of that silence matters now, he needs my help, and that's all that's important. "Anything."

I'm met with silence, but I let Niko take his time. He's always been the quiet type, and if you push too hard, he will close down completely. It was one of the first things I learned about him, if you give him a little time, he will tell you everything. It doesn't take long before he speaks, and even though it's only a few words, I'm instantly on alert. "Someone I love's in danger."

"Can you get to me?" I have no idea where he is right now. The last time we spoke, he was living in Scotland, but that's probably changed since then, especially if he went off grid enough to dump the mobile number he had before. I have no idea who he's with or what trouble he's in, but before he vanished he promised to call and fill me in as soon as he could. It's taken three months, and that makes me worry. What made him go dark for so long, and who is in trouble?

"It will take me a couple of days. I need to sort some things out first."

"I'll be here." I hear a gentle exhale over the call and I know that I've just eased some of Niko's burden. The man is his own worst enemy. He takes every single problem and makes it his own, the need to protect everyone around him so deeply ingrained, it makes him a little crazy.

"Thank you, Clay."

"Like there was ever any doubt. Just get here, and we'll get this sorted." I'm met with silence again, and before Niko can hang up on me, I speak. "And Niko?"

"Yeah."

"Be safe, brother." There's a grunt before the call ends and I throw my mobile onto the stack of papers on my desk in front of me. Leaning back in my chair, tilting it so I can put my feet up on the desk, I scrub my hands over my face to try and get rid of the sudden tired feeling that's seeping into my bones. Turning Niko away when he needs help would never happen, but he picked a shitty time to call. *Two days.* That's how long I have to try and tie up three jobs that are nearing completion. Thankfully two of them are just typing up the official reports and meeting with the clients to explain my findings. Simple. The last one, well that's going to take a little bit more work.

I drop my feet to the floor and reach into the bottom desk drawer, taking out my camera case and extra telescopic lens. I probably won't need the expensive lens, but I'd rather have it with me to get the evidence required for Mrs Aspill. If her husband is slipping his dick where he shouldn't like she suspects, then I'm going to need to prove that to her. Standing slowly, I reach my hands above my head and stretch until my back cracks in a satisfying way. I've been in the office far too long, and even though I'm about to be stuck in my truck for god knows how long, at least it's outside in the fresh air and not within these four walls that I'm getting sick of looking at.

Making a mental checklist, I grab everything I think I might need including the camera and my laptop. If the man in question isn't there when I arrive, at least I might get some of the reports written up while I wait. I pack up my bag and grab it before making my way out to the reception area. Margaret is busy on the phone, but she looks at me, mouthing something that I can't make out. When I shrug my shoulders at her, she gives me an eye roll that any stroppy teen would be proud of.

Margaret joined the CW Investigations team not long after I bit the bullet and rented this office space. It's not large, but it's a lot bigger than working from my spare room where I started the business. Gabe had spent months telling me I needed to move to a proper office, that it would look more professional to clients, and now that my business is booming, I'm glad he pestered me. Margaret has been the most valuable member of my staff, and as much as I would love to claim I hired her after an impressive interview, she pretty much told me she was working for me. I had no intention of hiring a front office manager, but she'd saved my arse, and she's been here ever since. She'd been walking past the front window when I had lost my shit at the photocopier, screaming while beating the crap out of the side of it because it wouldn't stop printing sheets of client information forms. The phone had been ringing off the hook, and my stress levels were about to make me say fuck it and walk away. She didn't even speak before she picked up a few of the forms from the copier, read over them quickly, and answered the phone. That was the day I knew I couldn't live without her.

She finally hangs up the phone and takes a moment to write something on her ever-present notepad. When she's finished, she turns her full focus on me, her glare making me shrink back a little. There are very few people in this world that can make me feel intimidated, but the small five-foot frame of Margaret is one of them. She's an older woman, and she treats me like her kid. When I mess up, and she gives me that disappointed mother look, well, it makes me want to beg for forgiveness.

"What did I do?" I can't help but ask her because whatever I did to piss her off, I don't remember it.

"Did you forget that it was Thursday?"

Apparently being Thursday is important, but for the life of me, I don't know why. I wrack my brain to find anything but nope, there's nothing. I shrug my shoulders again, and from the look on her face, I'm sure if Margaret were tall enough, I would be getting a slap to the back of the head.

"You have a meeting tonight with Mr Rogers. Do you have all the files sorted to give to him?"

Fuck. I totally forgot about meeting with the lawyer that is dealing with a domestic violence case, one that I've been doing background checks for. He needs to get the files tonight so he can work through them before the court case. If I don't get them to him, he won't have enough time to plan his argument. The files are ready to go, all the information for the sick fuck I've been looking into written up and highlighted to make it easier for Mr Rogers, I just forgot about meeting him. Now with Niko coming, I don't have the time to go.

I smile sweetly at Margaret, and she shakes her head. "Nope. I'm not meeting with him, Clay. You do remember part of your job is actually talking to people?"

I ignore her dig. I meet with every single client, even if I hate it. I'm more a do the job kind of guy, not so much a people person. "But he likes you, Maggie. I can see the glint in his eye when he looks at you."

There's a blush to her cheeks, but she catches the smile that's threatening to grace her lips. "Don't call me Maggie. And this isn't my job."

"I know, but you're so much better at it than I am. You and Mr Rogers don't need me. I'll even spring for dinner." I give her the sweetest smile I can muster. I'm not sure how sweet it looks, but it works.

She sighs deeply before holding her hand out. Knowing exactly what she's waiting on, I reach into my back pocket and pull out my wallet. Grabbing the company credit card, I hand it over to her, and she glares at me again. "I'm ordering the lobster and then the Wagyu beef."

I lean down and kiss her cheek. "You order anything you want. The files are in the meeting room. There are two of them with the case name on the top. I owe you one." I make a mental note to send flowers to her ... again. Margaret was sent from the angels that first day, and she's been saving my arse ever since. Not wanting to push my luck too far, I leave before she changes her mind about going to the meeting for me. Honestly, I think that Mr Rogers will prefer having Margaret there because I wasn't lying when I said that he always looks happy to see her. There is that look in his eye when she appears in the room, the one that tells me he wouldn't mind seeing her outside of our meetings.

"Be professional, Clay."

Her words meet my ears as the door close behind me, and I smile to myself. It's always her parting comment when I'm about to leave on a job. I would love to say that her statement isn't needed, but since she's had to come to bail me out of trouble with the police more than a dozen times, it's always handy to have the reminder. As I say, she's sent by the angels.

When I reach my truck, I put my bag into the passenger seat before moving to the boot to check that I have my back up camera. It's not as good as the one I keep safely locked up in my office, but it's good enough to take pictures if something happens to my main one. After being caught with a broken camera more than once, I decided that a backup is always handy to have, especially if you are missing the important shit you are being paid to find out. Once I've double-checked my supplies, I get into the driver's seat and programme my satnav. I need it today because the sleazy hotel that Mr Aspill is meant to be meeting his mistress in isn't one I've been to before. Turning on my music I ease my truck into traffic, starting the hour-long journey to get me to my location.

WHY ARE THINGS NEVER EASY? These are the words I've repeated to myself over and over again while trying to balance on the top of the large bin around the back of the dive of a hotel. I use that term hotel loosely because this place looks only a step above a condemned building. Why people pick these sorts of places to get their freak on, I'll never know. When I bang someone, I don't want to have to worry about what I might be rolling in.

Shudders go through me at that thought, and I put my full focus back on what's happening inside the window in front of me. I'd hoped that when Mr Aspill and his *friend* had arrived, they would get into it before getting inside the room, making my job easy, but they hadn't. They hadn't even arrived together, and I thought this job was going to become longer when the woman I had been watching for had never come. The bigger shock had occurred when an older gentleman had knocked on the door my mark had gone into, and when he vanished inside, I knew that my report was going to cause a lot more pain to his wife. Mrs Aspill had explained that she was convinced that her husband had been seeing another woman, not once had she thought it might be a man. Now I'm sitting on top of a bin trying to get the evidence for her because I'm sure without these pictures she won't believe me.

The curtains are open slightly in the middle, and I lie on my stomach so I can keep the camera as steady as possible. Zooming in, I get a clear shot of the two men inside. I watch them interact, taking pictures as I take in the scene in front of me. Both of them are sitting on the couch, their hands entwined as they smile at each other while chatting. The moment looks intimate, and I feel like an intruder. If I didn't know that one of them was married, I would think I was watching a happy couple spending some time together. They look in love, and the look that Mr Aspill is giving the other man is nothing short of adoration. My heart clenches as I watch then, a slight trickle of jealousy seeping into my bones.

I shake my head and return to the job at hand. I'm not here for anything other than to get the pictures that my client asked for. The men move from the couch to the bed where they spend time savouring each other. Again, this doesn't look like two men who are meeting for a quick fuck. These are men with feelings for each other that can be seen clearly even through the camera. My heart goes out to his wife because I'm not sure that he's going to give up his lover, and that means nothing but heartache for this group.

When I feel I have enough evidence for my file, I turn away from the men, giving them their privacy for the rest of the night. This might be my job, and cheating on someone is a lousy thing to do, but there are a few times when I feel for the people I'm investigating. It must be hard when you fall for someone you shouldn't. Like falling for a man when you are married to a woman. I don't know if that will make it worse for Mrs Aspill, knowing that her husband has fallen for something she could never give him. Would it have been easier if he were with a woman, something that she could actually contend with? Nope, not going down that line of thinking. I'm doing my job here and nothing more. The fallout from her husband's actions isn't my problem. I present the evidence, get paid, and then walk away. Job done.

I pack my camera away, getting to my knees, so it's easier to work. The night has darkened without me noticing, and as I lean back I misjudge where the bin ends. I struggle to distribute my weight as I slip to the edge of the bin. I know what's about to happen, but I'm utterly powerless to stop it. Being a big guy is handy in this job as very few people try to start trouble, but at times like this, I wish there wasn't so much weight to me because when I go over the back, I know it's going to hurt like a motherfucker. My only hope is to try and roll when I hit the ground, but when I go over backwards, that hope is dashed. *Fuck it to hell.* That's the only thought I manage before my back connects with the ground with a thud. I lie and blink up at the sky while struggling to breathe. A few seconds later something hits my chest making me grunt, and it takes me a moment to realise that it's my bag falling from the top of the bin. At least I don't have to go back up there to retrieve it. Instead, I lie where I am, the rotten smell from the bags of rubbish turning my stomach, but I can't get my body to move. It's like it's given up and even the feel of something brushing against my neck can't make me move. Actually, the thing against my neck tells me I need to get the fuck up. As soon as I'm sitting up, I scrub my hand against my neck, the tickle of whatever bug had been there still making me shudder. I can deal with many things, but creepy crawlies are way out of my comfort zone.

Grabbing my bag, I rush across the street and head towards my truck, which I left parked in the car park outside a small shopping area. There'd been other cars there when I arrived in the afternoon, so I'd blended in nicely. Even now there are still a few cars parked, so I know no one will be concerned about me still being there so late. I press the keyless entry button and open the door, thankful that I thought ahead and turned off the overhead lights before leaving earlier. I slip into my trucks dark cabin and instantly start the engine. Common sense tells me to check the camera to make sure the pictures I took are adequate, but with the feeling of the insect still making me shudder, I say fuck it and race towards home. I need to get into the shower and quickly.

The garage door rises as I approach it and I slow my speed to allow it time to open fully. I expect to be able to drive straight in, but I'm met with the large brooding figure of Gabe standing with his arms crossed, just inside the door. I ease the car forward until it's just about touching him, refusing to lose this game of chicken. He's my best friend, and I enjoy the constant dick measuring competitions we have, even if Gabe's slightly ahead when it comes to not giving in, and I need to claw some points back. I rev my engine, my truck bouncing as the tyres fight against the brake I have pressed down. I can see the smirk on Gabe's face because the fucker knows that I would never actually touch him with the car. I finally relent, opening my window so I can shout at him. "Fine, you win. Now move your arse so I can get into my own fucking garage."

Gabe looks far too happy when he takes a few steps to the side to give me space. I park my truck in its spot, pressing the button to close the door behind me. Grabbing my bag off the passenger seat, I ignore Gabe as he follows me into the kitchen. I don't acknowledge him at all as I head to my bedroom, dropping my bag in my spare room as I pass it. The need for a shower is still there, and the cocky fuck I can hear in the kitchen will just have to wait on me.

2
Clay

"So, who were you so desperate to wash off your cock?"

I ignore Gabe as I walk to the fridge to grab a bottle of beer. I continue my silent treatment until I've finished the whole bottle, and only then look in his direction. He doesn't seem fazed by my silence, and that pisses me off more. It's bad enough he got the better of me in the garage, he could at least pretend that I'm annoying him by not answering his questions. "I was working."

Gabe's eyebrows raise, and he looks like he doesn't believe me. "Yeah, I'm sure it was work."

"Fuck off. I was following someone, and it ran late. These pictures don't take themselves."

The knowing look leaves Gabe's face, and confusion takes its place. "Then why the sudden need for a shower?"

I feel the tips of my ears burning in embarrassment. I'm one of the lucky people who doesn't blush for the world to see, and I'm thankful every fucking day for that. There's no place in my job for being embarrassed, especially if a client is giving me intimate details of the situation at hand. There's also the fact that if Gabe ever realised that he could make me blush, I would never live it down. "I fell off a bin. There were insects."

It's clear that Gabe is fighting hard not to let his laughter escape and I make a silent promise to myself that if he laughs out loud, I'm going to clock him. Taking a deep breath, he seems to get himself under control. "Ah, that explains a lot."

I growl before pushing off the kitchen cabinet to replace my empty bottle. I pop the cap as the laughter finally escapes Gabe. "Laugh it up, fucker."

He bends over and rests his hands on his knees, his body shaking as he laughs so hard no noise comes out. It takes a few minutes, but he finally stands upright and lets out a deep breath. "Sorry. I was just picturing that. Was it like the spider incident? Oh god, please tell me it was like the spider incident."

I can feel the threads of fear spread through me even at the memory of that night. I try as hard as I can not to think about what happened, but Gabe loves to bring it up whenever he can. It had occurred at one of Gabe's client's houses, at a party that we'd been invited to. The whole night had been fantastic, and I was close to getting into some hot redheads bed when we decided to start the night early by slipping into a bedroom. She was so fucking hot and demanding, and as soon as I got her inside the room, I had her pinned up against the wall. She had fought back, setting my blood on fire, and after nearly tumbling over when she wrapped her legs around me, I gripped the top of the closest piece of furniture to keep me upright. That's when the whole night changed from a perfect wet dream to a fucking nightmare. Something had tickled my hand, but I hadn't put much thought into it since my focus had been entirely on the redhead. That was my mistake and one I will always regret. The tickle turned into more pressure, and that's when I started to focus more on that than the woman in my arms. The weight continued past my hand and up my forearm, and that's when the real worry started. I used my other hand to search the wall to locate a light switch, hoping that since we hadn't moved far from the door, there would be one close. Finally finding it and turning it on, it took a few minutes for my eyes to focus in the sudden glare. When I could finally see clearly, I looked down at my arm and my heart about stopped. There, sitting happily on my arm, was the biggest fucking spider I'd ever seen.

I would love to pretend that I carefully picked the obvious pet tarantula off my arm and put it back into his open terrarium like the strong man I like to portray, but none of that happened. The reality is that I screamed louder than anyone I'd ever heard, waving my arms in the air like a lunatic while scratching at the door to escape. It took too long for me to notice that the woman I was with had scooped up the spider and was placing it gently into the tank, and it took me even longer to see that she had the door open in front of me. I should have calmed down and said thank you, but that would mean focusing on anything other than the abject fear coursing through me. Instead, I just got the fuck out of there, shouting abuse at anyone who dared get in my way. To this day I'm still trying to live that night down, and my best friend seems to have great delight in bringing it up over and over again.

"Why are you here annoying me?"

"I wanted to see when you're free in the next few weeks." A look of uncertainty flashes over Gabe's face, but it vanishes just as quickly as it appeared.

I'm about to tell him I'm free anytime he needs me, but after the call from Niko, I know that I'm not. I hate not being there for Gabe whenever he needs me. He's been my best friend since the morning I found him sleeping in the doorway of my brother's record shop, his small frame freezing as he tried to stay out of the cold wind. My brother warned me not to take him in, that I didn't know where he came from or what sort of trouble he was bringing with him, but one look into his eyes told me everything I needed to know. Gabe was a kindred soul, a man who life had screwed over, and I wanted to help him.

He's been through so much recently, and even though I got rid of his biggest problem, that doesn't mean my job is done. "I'm busy, but depending on what you need, I might be able to clear some time."

"It's nothing really. It's just I get my cast off soon, and I'm nervous about working again."

My heart goes out to Gabe. His life imploded over the last year, and he is still dealing with the aftermath of it all. Rhys may be safe now that Paul is gone, but the injuries that Paul inflicted are still healing. Now I can see that it's more than just the physical that Gabe is trying to recover from. Apparently, his confidence took a knock too, and that might be harder to come back from. "I've been thinking about getting my rib piece reworked. I need to add more colour to the lettering because it's too dark for me. Or possibly something new, I need to decide."

"Any ideas who you want to do it?"

"There's only one man who gets his hands on my body. You know this."

The relief on Gabe's face is clear to see. I've given him what he needs without him having to ask. Gabe is never one to ask for help, and even when he does, it's difficult for him.

"Just let me check my schedule and get back to you. I have something I need to work on first, then I'm all yours."

The next half hour is spent catching up after a busy week, just the two of us shooting the shit without any other worries. No matter how stressful things get at work, I can rely on Gabe to chill me out. We've been friends for so long that he knows how I work. I might look like a beast on the outside, and most of the time act like one, but I still need some moments to relax and give myself a chance to regroup. That's what Gabe is, even though I see him less now that he's with Rhys. I don't begrudge him happiness for a single second, even if there is a steady ache of jealousy when I see them happy together. They have this love that I've never seen before. Even my own parent's relationship had seemed to be based on tolerance and habit, and I learnt everything I know from them. They taught me how to be distant from the people around me, so I don't let those pesky feelings get in the way. No, I'm not destined to find the love of my life, but I'm more than content to watch my family be happy since they allow me to be part of their lives.

"How did the meeting with Mr Rogers go?" Margaret puts my coffee cup down on my desk, and I look up from the file I was giving a final read through. Struggling to sleep last night found me arriving at the office in the early hours. I'd managed a couple of hours of sleep before my mind took over and all I could think about was Niko and being ready for him to arrive. That brought me into the office while it was still dark, but at least every case is now up to date and ready to be signed off. I just need to meet with the clients and give them their file.

Margaret stays quiet for far too long, and I raise my eyebrows in question. She brushes some imaginary lint from her trousers before clearing her throat. "The meeting went fine. He was happy with all the information I presented him with, and he said that it would make his case a lot easier."

"And?"

Her eyes flicker from mine for a fraction of a second and I know that there's more to last nights meeting than she's letting on. Part of me thinks that I should respect her privacy, but then the bigger part of me wants all the juicy details. "And nothing."

"Oh, does Maggie have a crush on the nice lawyer man?"

"Call me Maggie one more time, boy." She doesn't say anything else before leaving my office with a slam of the door.

Chuckling, I turn my attention back to the file in front of me. Teasing Margaret is far too much fun, but now I need to be prepared for retaliation. She will get her own back, of that I'm sure. A knock on the door has me raising my head again as Margaret pops her head around the edge of the wood.

"There's a courier here with a delivery. He says I can't sign for it, only you." She appears confused, but I'm not. I've been expecting this since the day I spoke to Niko. I knew that he wouldn't arrive without giving me a chance to have a look over what his problem is.

"It's okay, M. Send him in." She lets in an older gentleman who hands over a large brown envelope. I sign for it and wait until he leaves before I rip it open. It's filled with sheets of paper, printouts of emails, and I feel my stomach clench with anger. It's like history is repeating itself as I read through the first few emails that I unpack. Hate and anger in written form cover the pages, and it takes me back to several years before when I was up against the same thing. Only that time I was too far behind and Niko ended up losing someone important.

Emptying the envelope out onto the table also gives me a password for an email account, and I don't hesitate before I sign in to check it out. I'm met with dozens of new emails, and as I read through them, I can feel the anger building in the words. Email after email I can sense the deep underlying hate for Niko and Corey. I've never met Corey personally, but Niko mentioned him in passing when he called me a few months back. He'd told me he'd rescued a guy from Blue Diamond, and it didn't take a psychic to realise that Niko had feelings for the guy when he spoke. His call a few days ago just confirmed that fact. *Someone I love is in danger.* Now I know for sure that it's Corey and I will use everything in my power to find this sick fuck.

Reading over every email once takes longer than I'd anticipated, and by the time I get to the final one, I get a horrible sense of déjà vu. I've read emails like this before, but I know it can't be the same person. It's just a coincidence that this person has chosen to send emails. It can't be the same person, that person's dead and rotting in a shallow grave.

"I'm leaving, hun. Is there anything you need before I go?"

Margaret's voice makes me jump. I've been so focused on the emails that time has gotten away from me. It's the first time I notice that my office has become dark and only the light of my computer is illuminating it.

She turns on the overhead light, and I blink at the sudden brightness. "Wow, I didn't realise the time. I'm fine. You get home."

She slips her arms into the jacket that she'd been holding, and buttons up the front. "If you're sure?"

"Go home, woman. I don't want to have to pay you overtime, so stop trying."

She smirks but ignores me completely. "There's some salad in the fridge, try and eat that instead of takeaway. I've also set up meetings tomorrow so you can close up the outstanding cases. Mrs Aspill seemed particularly interested to see what you found out. I managed to get them all before lunch, so you'll be free and clear by the afternoon."

"You're a gem, Maggie. I don't know what I would do without you."

I see her chewing the inside of her cheek, and it takes everything in me not to laugh. I found out really early on that she hates being called

Maggie, which means I have to do it whenever possible. "I don't know why I put up with you. I'm sure I could find a better paying job somewhere else."

"You love me and don't pretend you don't."

"Hmmm. I'll see you tomorrow."

I smile at her as she closes the door behind her, leaving me alone for the night. I go back to the beginning of the emails, this time reading them carefully to pick up any hidden markers. People tend to focus entirely on the words that people write, but I have learned to look past that, to see what they are telling you without actually meaning to. Even in the first read through I noticed some interesting things. The fact that the writer is making broad threats is good, it says that he doesn't have a focus for his anger yet. He might have used Corey's name, but it's a general threat against something that Niko loves. That bodes well for Corey's safety. What isn't a good sign is that the language is becoming more disjointed, less calm. You can see his anger building, so the messages are ranging from calm and collected to angry rants about Niko and his friends. The writer is losing his cool, and that has me worried.

Taking page after page of notes keeps me busy for more hours than it should have, and even though I have found out enough to profile the person who wrote the emails, it isn't enough to help me identify them. It's a start, but I want to find out who this fucker is. The things he's written, the threats that he's made against Niko and his man, that shit needs to be dealt with, and I'm just the man for the job.

I WATCH Niko as he sits across the desk from me. He swirls the alcohol around his glass as he stares at it. Since coming back to my office from the bar, Niko has given me small snippets of information about his sister's disappearance, but it's not enough. If he wants me to help, he's going to have to open up. The silence drags on, and just when I'm about to give up hope of him answering, he starts to give me more. "I've been getting emails." He downs the Jack in one go, a hiss coming from between his lips as he swallows.

"What kind of emails?" I can make an educated guess on the types of emails

because getting shitty spam doesn't leave you looking as distraught as Niko looks right now.

"He says he has her. That he's hurting her. Fuck!" The restraint that Niko's been holding onto all night is slipping, and I see the tears building in his eyes. I can't even imagine how that would feel. A stranger taking someone I love and then torturing me with the knowledge. It was hard enough dealing with my brother's condition, and I knew he was safe where he was.

Niko gets out of his chair and leans across the table, grabbing the bottle I left sitting there. He doesn't even look at me as he tops up his glass before downing it in one gulp.

"I'm going to need to see those emails."

Niko lets go of the bottle as he reaches into his pocket, and I use the opportunity to slide the bottle back to my side of the desk where I put the lid back on. Something lands on my desk, startling me, and I pick up the memory stick before looking at Niko.

"It's all on there. There are too many to print out."

Fuck. That must be a shit ton of emails. I place the memory stick on the top shelf of my filing tray so I'll be able to find it when I need it. My desk is always such a chaotic mess that anything of importance gets lost in the loose papers. The mess drives Margaret crazy because I won't let her clean it, but the chaos helps me concentrate. She might make this whole place run like fucking clockwork, but my desk is the one thing she isn't allowed to touch. "I will check them later, but give me a rough outline of what they say."

"That he has her and he's hurting her. That her screams are such a turn on and he can't wait to make her bleed …" His sob cuts off his words, and I can do nothing but watch as Niko falls apart across from me. The sounds coming from deep in his chest sound heartbreaking and agonising, and I want to go to him, give him some comfort. I stay seated though because I'm not sure he would want a stranger touching him. "I'm sorry … I should…" He abruptly gets up from the seat and rushes towards the door. He struggles with the handle before bracing his arms on the wooden door and dropping his head. His sobs get harder, and that has me moving. I don't care if he doesn't want my comfort, he can easily push me away if he needs to.

When I reach him, I wrap my arms around his chest from behind and hold him. I can feel his chest heave against mine as he lets out everything that's trying to break him. I don't know how long we stand like that together, but he eventu-

ally calms enough to lean back into my body. He rubs his face with his sleeve and takes a couple of deep breaths. "Thank you."

I start to ease up on my hold but his hands gripping my wrists still my escape.

"And I'm sorry. It's just ... it's been hard. This whole thing is screwing with me."

I can only imagine how this shit messes with your head. It's bad enough to have a loved one missing but to know that some sick fuck has them and you don't know where, well that would send me over the edge. "I promise to help any way I can."

"Thank you."

I WAKE with a start when my phone rings on the table next to the sofa. I don't remember falling asleep, but the crick in my neck tells me I've been here for a while. I stretch out my neck, groaning when the tight muscles protest against the move. I check my phone, throwing it back on the table when I see it's just a text message from my bank. It's far too early to worry about authorising an incoming payment. I scrub my hand over my face trying to dislodge the memories of the dream I was having. Not just a dream, but memories from when I first met Niko. Going through the emails last night must have stirred up the past, making me relive that time over again. I just pray that this time we have a better outcome because I'm not sure that Niko would survive losing another loved one.

3
Clay

*F*UCK *ME*. *She's crying*. I sit and watch Mrs Aspill sob, feeling completely fucking awkward. I want to rush from the room, but Margaret tells me that might come across as slightly unprofessional to the clients.

"A man?"

I've already explained a dozen times to her that it wasn't a woman her husband was with, but she can't seem to get her head around that bit of information. "The only person I saw him with was a man. I didn't get an identity of him, but you didn't ask for that. I could still run his picture to see if I can find out who he is-"

"No! I don't need that." The panic in her voice makes me wonder if she's going to talk to her husband about this. Maybe she can see in the pictures what was obvious to me even at a distance. The love between the two men was shining clearly for anyone to see, and there is no way she could miss it unless she wanted to deny it. "Thank you for all of this." She motions to the pictures lying over the desk, her eyes stopping briefly on the photo that most of her attention has been on since she opened the file. It's not one of the ones where her husband is naked in bed, not even one where he's kissing and touching his lover. It's the one that clearly shows both men simply holding each other. They look like the rest of the world doesn't exist, that it's faded away around them and they aren't in a hurry for it to return. It's a look that I've seen between Gabe and Rhys, and there is no denying what that look is. Pure and utter love.

"It's what you paid me for." It's a detached answer, but the last thing I want is for Mrs Aspill to feel she can get emotional support from me. I barely give my friends that sort of support, I'm more a give me an enemy to fight type of friend, so I would be completely hopeless if she got really upset. I start to gather the pictures and typed up notes into a pile so I can slip them back into the manila file, hoping it will be a sign to Mrs Aspill that the meeting is ending. The only thing that's outstanding is the payment, but since I don't deal with that part of the contract, our business in here is done. Getting her out is now my only priority.

She seems to take my subtle hint and scrubs at her eyes before picking up her handbag. She rummages inside for a few minutes and produces a cheque book from inside. "Yes, and you did a great job. Let me settle the bill, and I'll let you get back to your other jobs. Who do I make this out to?"

"I don't deal with that. If you see Margaret in the front office before you leave, she'll sort out a receipt for the payment." I push the file towards her, and she looks at it like it's an unexploded bomb. Her fingers twitch, and it's clear she can't decide if she should take the folder or not. "Just so you know, the only copy of the evidence is inside that file. I don't keep anything as back up so there's no way to request a replacement. " I've seen many clients refusing to take the evidence I give them, but then days or weeks later decide that they need what I found out. By then its too late, so I like to make it clear to them that this is their only chance. My words apparently make her decision for her, and she pulls the file towards her.

"Okay. Thank you, Mr Wilson."

I stand and wait while she gathers her belongings. My eyes flicker to the clock on the wall while she's focused on putting the folder inside her bag. This was my last meeting of the morning, and once she leaves, I will be able to give Niko's problem my full attention. I have queries from a few potential clients, but I told Margaret to mark me off on holiday for the next few weeks. The news had made her happy because she's always telling me I need to take more time off from the business. I didn't have the heart to tell her that I'm only taking time off so I can work harder with Niko on his problem.

Mrs Aspill coming to a stop beside me brings my attention back to the room. She's standing close to my side, too close, and when she rests her hand on my wrist, it takes everything in me not to flinch back. She's a gorgeous woman, and I usually would welcome the obvious come on, but I'm not feeling it. I want to pretend it's because she's a client, but the truth is I've been feeling out of sorts for the last few months. I can't quite explain what is wrong, all I know is that there's an emptiness growing inside that I can't seem to fill. I tried to fuck it out of me, but after taking a new woman home nearly every night for a fortnight, I knew that it wasn't working. That's when I decided that I needed to take a step back from any relationship, even the one night stand kind until I could get my head sorted.

"Thank you again, Mr Wilson. If there's any way I could repay you for all your hard work, just let me know." She licks her lips, and again, a month ago I would have been all over that shit. Not today though. Today I want to find out where Niko is and then have a drink.

"If you just pay Margaret that would be fantastic." Her face falls instantly, and I can see my rejection has been more obvious than I intended. I ignore the hurt look in her eyes and open the door, holding it open for her until she leaves. Thankfully Margaret is waiting for us in the reception, and I give Mrs Aspill a nod before retreating to my office. This job would be so much better if it weren't for the whole talking to people thing. I know my aversion to people makes Gabe laugh, especially when he says I'm the friendliest guy he's ever met, but truthfully, that's changed recently.

I collapse onto the seat behind my desk. Six months ago I wouldn't be sitting in here alone after a beautiful woman flirted with me. At the very least I would have had her bent over my desk while I ploughed into her, or if she had pleaded her case, I would have followed her home so we could spend the afternoon in her bed. None of that interests me now, and I can't work out when it started losing its shine. That's actually a lie, and one I've been trying to convince myself for far too long. I know when everything changed, I'm just not ready to admit that to myself.

My mobile phone rings and I smile when I hear the ringtone I've set for Niko. Heathens by Twenty One Pilots plays loudly throughout my office, and I think it's a shame that he'll probably never hear it. I answer the call, my smile still on my lips. "Niko, my brother. When will your arse be here? I have stuff to show you."

"I'm on my way. I can't fly so I need to drive. That's gonna take a little longer."

I'm glad that Niko is being smart and making sure that he isn't leaving evidence of his movements. If the writer of the emails can track him, leaving proof of his travelling could put Corey in danger. Not wanting to get into things on the phone, I keep the conversation as light as possible. "What are you driving these days? Please tell me it's something manly and not one of those environmentally friendly pieces of shit. I'll grow old before you get here."

"I don't even know why I like you."

"My arse looks good in jeans."

My smile grows as the banter flows. I've missed this fucker, and the quicker he gets here, the better I will feel.

"Yeah, that's the reason. But to answer your question, I'm driving a pretty nice Beemer, so it won't take me long to get there." I laugh at his comment, remembering back to when he blew the engine in the shitty Corsa he'd driven when we had been looking for his sister. He swore it was because the car was old, but I knew that it was more likely that he had been going far too fast for the small car.

"Well, let's not get a ticket. It's easier to fly under the radar if you don't get pulled over for doing stupid shit."

"Oh ye of little faith. When have you ever known me to do illegal shit?"

This makes me laugh even harder. I don't know everything about his time with Blue Diamond, but after taking the time to look into the company, I know there was nothing remotely legal about it. Getting past the innocent looking façade led me into a world where human life was sold for money and control. Now is not the time to get into that, but maybe once he gets here, I can ask some questions. For now, I just want to get Niko here. "And at that, I'm going to bow out before I say something that will earn me a punch. Drive safe, my friend, see you soon."

I hang up and start to tidy up the files on my desk when there is a knock at the door. "Yeah."

Margaret pops her head around the door and smiles when she sees me finally tidying. "Don't let me interrupt you, but just wanted you to know that I'm heading home."

"Okay. Remember I don't want to see you for at least a week." I haven't given an official length of time that I'm going to be absent for, but I've made sure that Margaret will take the whole week off. She complains about how much I work, but truthfully she does more hours in the actual office than I do. Everything in the office falls on her shoulders, and where I get to leave to ease some of the stress, she's stuck here until her day is over.

"Yeah, yeah. Of course that means you won't be in the office at all in the next few days."

Margaret knows me better than nearly anyone in the world, and she's right on the money when it comes to this. I might be taking time off, but I will be in the office every day until I get to the bottom of Niko's problem. Not that she knows this, so it's better to plead my innocence. It's not like she'll believe me anyway. "I will lock the door and throw away the key just as soon as I make this place spotless."

This makes her laugh hard, her cheeks reddening with the effort. "Pull the other one, it has bells on. I'm not sure which one of those things is the bigger lie, but I will leave you with the illusion that I believe you."

"Thanks, Maggie. Make sure you relax and enjoy your time off."

She smiles sweetly. "If you need anything-"

"Leave, woman."

This gets a small huff of laughter from her before she closes the door gently behind her. I give her a few minutes to leave before I head through to the reception to make sure everything is locked up for the night. The last thing I need is for a potential client to come walking in and ask for help. I want to take time off, and there would be no way for me to turn someone away if they needed help. It's the reason I got into this business, the need to help others deep in my soul, but that doesn't mean I have to do it every single day.

A NOISE PULLS me from my sleep, and it takes me several moments to become aware of my surroundings. I blink a few times and try to focus on what had woken me. Falling asleep on the couch in my office has become a regular occurrence, and I'm sure I sleep here more than in my bed these days. Another noise has me instantly alert and before I have a second to react an arm wraps around my throat and tightens. Instinct takes over, and I grab it, throwing my head back to connect with my attacker. A hand lands on the back of my head halting the movement and laughter reaches my ear.

"Not often I can get the jump on you, old friend."

Niko sounds like he's smiling and that makes me want to continue my attack on him, maybe spill a little of his blood to make me feel better. Instead, I wriggle until he lets go of me and I'm off the couch in seconds. I growl before taking off around all the obstacles between us, and Niko laughs as he backs away.

"Don't do it. The last thing we need is you pulling something important again."

His comment has me slowing, my laughter bubbling up inside. He's talking about the time that we were out running together, and I'd told him that I could easily outrun him even though he's younger than me. He got a gleam in his eye before he took off sprinting and in my wisdom, I took off after him. I lasted for about a hundred yards before my thigh muscle ripped and I dropped to the ground with a thud. "Part of me thinks it would be totally worth it."

"Missed you, brother."

Three words and I'm striding across the office again, but this time for a very different reason. "Come here." I grab Niko by the shoulders and pull him into a bone-crushing hug. The minute his body connects with mine I feel all the tension drain from my muscles. "Fuck me. I missed you."

Niko holds me tightly, and I sink into his embrace. I keep him there far longer than is probably considered acceptable, but I'm so glad to see him alive and safe that I don't care. All too soon I need to let him go, and I let him slip from my arms, but I look him over. It's the first time in close to two years that I've seen him, and he's changed more than I thought possible. Niko was always toned and fit looking, but now he looks like he spends hours a day in the gym. He's still not as big as me, but a fight between us would be more evenly matched. "Where was the weak spot?"

"Window at the back, second floor up. Was surprised you let that one pass."

"I don't rent that floor, so I didn't think to look. Most people would take the locked door as a hint to stay out."

"Amateurs." He smirks and winks at me.

"Drink?" Niko nods and I walk to the back cabinet to pour us both a glass of Jack Daniels. I have beer in the little fridge in the meeting room, but tonight feels like a hard liquor type of night. Handing Niko his glass, we both take a seat on the sofa that's slowly becoming my bed. Before I can get comfortable, Niko downs the generous measure I'd given him. I stay quiet, just raising my eyebrow at him, before getting up to grab the bottle and bringing it back with me. "That bad?"

"Worse."

I sip at my drink and wait for Niko to be ready to share. He refills his glass before he's finally ready to speak. "I hate lying to Core. I swore that when I got him out of that place, I would never treat him like this, but I need to keep him safe. I can't let him be hurt again."

So many questions run through my head, but I don't know if this is the time to ask them. I want to know why Niko took a job in a place like Blue Diamond, what he actually did there, but then there's a part of me that doesn't want to know if he has blood on his hands. I would never judge him, I couldn't after the things I've done in the past, but I don't understand how he could work there. There was no part of that company that was legitimate, and I can't get my mind around a guy like Niko wanting to work there, not after his sister. So I keep my questions for later, instead focusing on Corey. "Is he safe just now?"

"Safer than if he was with me. I need to find out who's doing this and why."

"Do you think it's connected with ..." I don't even know how to describe his last job, but he can apparently read my mind.

"To do with being a bodyguard for a gangster who ran a prostitution ring?"

I can't help but laugh at how open he's being about it, but I can't hide the bile that rises in my throat when I hear him finally admitting the truth about the company he worked for. My laughter dies, and I finally ask him what has been burning in my gut for far too long. "How the fuck did you do that, man?"

"I didn't care about anything. I was numb, and the job seemed so black and white. I knew the shit that Ryden was doing was illegal, but all I saw was the fact I was keeping his men safe from people who might hurt them. I didn't care about anything else other than protecting them."

"What changed?"

"Corey." Niko's face changes when he says Corey's name and I feel that tug of jealousy I feel when I see Gabe and Rhys together. The love is clear on his face, and even though I'm happy he's found someone special, I can't help but wonder why everyone else seems to get that except me. Not that I want to find that special person, or at least that's what I always tell myself.

"He's a lucky guy." I mean those words. Niko is genuinely a fantastic man, and even if there are now things in his past that are on the wrong side of the law, he's loyal and loving.

"Nah, I'm the lucky one. To have Core loving me is like a dream come true, and I can't imagine being happier than I am now."

"Apart from the fucker who's harassing you?"

Niko's demeanour changes instantly, darkness appearing in his eyes and it's something I've only seen on him once before. That time he didn't let the focus of his anger walk away, and I know that the outcome this time will be the same. There's only going to be one perfect ending for Niko when it comes to this threat against Corey, and it's going to take bloodshed before this whole thing is over. I just pray that it's not the blood of someone I know.

4

Sam

I CHUCKLE GENTLY to myself as I watch the line of code in front of me become corrupt. The sense of power is addictive, and knowing that you're fucking up some low life scums plans feels even better. The change in the code isn't invisible because I want them to see that someone knows about them, that someone is watching them, but it will take them a long time to sort what I fucked up. The temptation to sign my work, leave a visual link for the world to see what I can do, is always there, but being invisible is too important. I need to stay off the grid, no matter how much my ego tries to convince me otherwise.

My mobile rings and I glance over before picking it up and answering. "Speak."

"Bite me."

I feel the edges of my lips twitch up at Grant's rebuttal, and the sound of his voice makes a tingle spread through my body. I've only met Grant on a few occasions, but there is no way to deny he's fucking hot. There's a part of me that wants to bed him, but the bigger part of me knows that it'd be a huge mistake. He's the closest thing I have to a friend, and I don't want to mess it up. "What can I do for you, officer?"

"I found Corey, or at least I think its Corey. I'm going to try and get close to him, put the phone in place. I might be offline for a few days, but I'll let you know when I'm back."

Grant has been searching for his missing friend for several months now. He's a police officer, but he walked away from his job when his friend, Drake, went missing after a raid. Drake had been working undercover to try and take down an illegal prostitution ring, but when it came time to get him out, he vanished along with the man who ran it. Grant is determined to find Drake to make sure he's safe, and if he is, to finally get some answers from him.

"Okay. Remember to get it within a foot of a computer or system network and dial seven-two-six."

The phone I gave Grant isn't actually a functioning phone. From the outside, it looks like a plain old iPhone 6, but if you were to open it up, you would find a transmitter that'll allow me to gain access to any computer it's placed next to. Hopefully, if this is the Corey we are looking for, there will be information on any computer he has. It might not be the right guy, or if it is he might not know anything, but it's the only connection to the company, Blue Diamond, that took Drake I could find. Frustration gathers in my chest as I think of all the hours I searched to find something connected to Blue Diamond but came up empty-handed. I've gone after a lot of illegal companies, but this was the first time they'd gotten the better of me. Even purging a system usually leaves information, but there was nothing.

"I remember. I just need to find a way to get close."

"Good luck with that. Stay safe, Grant, okay. Any problems use the phone to call me. It works like a radio so you can leave me messages, I just can't reply. If you need help, I can get it to you."

Grant is silent for a few beats, and I wonder what he's thinking. The last time we spoke, he was nervous about doing all this. Quitting the police force had thrown him for a loop, and even though he had a plan to follow to try and find Drake, when we got a big fat zero on the leads front, he started to panic. His frustration and worry were understandable, as was the way he grabbed on to the Corey lead with both hands. Thank fuck it panned out because I'm not sure Grant could have coped much longer with no information on Drake. He was close to losing all his faith in finding his friend, and my frustration at hitting so many dead ends was driving me insane. Now Grant has something to focus on while I try to dig deeper into Blue Diamond. I'm hoping that I'll be able to tell him something at some point, but I refuse to mention it to him in case I get nothing.

"Thank you for everything, Sam."

My eyes dart around the room before I catch myself. Hearing my name over the phone makes me instantly alert, and it's a crazy response when I'm in my own home. I know I'm secure, but it doesn't stop the old worries from rearing their head. "You're welcome. And I say again, stay safe."

There's a grunt on the other end of the phone before the line goes dead. I put my phone on the desk and bring my attention back to the screen in front of me, my smile returning when I see the person on the other end of the screen trying to fix the code I just messed with. *Good luck with that, my friend.*

I CRUNCH DOWN on the Tic Tac I'm eating and enjoy the burst of cherry across my tongue. I stare at my computer screen, reading the email over and over again. It's pretty similar to the other messages I get pleading for help, but this one has warning bells sounding in my head. That's why I'm confused. In the past, if there'd ever been anything that made me concerned I would delete it, but this time I can't seem to press the button to remove it from my inbox. The email had arrived into my encrypted account, the one that can't be searched for. You can only get the contact details from others I've worked with previously, and any suspicious accounts are instantly blocked. The security on this account is triple fire-walled with an intricate spider web of fake backdoor entry points that lead straight back to my tracking system. If someone tries to hack or piggyback onto this account, I'll know who they are before they even realise they're being tracked.

Ninety percent of the emails were trashed as soon as I gave them an initial read. One day people will realise that I can't be hired to trace lost gambling money or lost cars. Tons of lower level hackers can work on that shit. My time is too precious for that sort of job. The remaining emails are from bigger companies trying to trace stolen money and individuals looking for information on particular people. These are the jobs that pay the bills, and they pay well. My rates are steep, but I have a never-ending list of potential clients who are willing to pay whatever I ask. Yes, it costs a lot to hire me, but I'm fucking good. I'm not bigheaded, just honest.

This email is making me pause for far too long though. I reread it before moving it to my possible folder. I have no intention of following up on the message, but for some strange reason, I can't bring myself to delete it. I sit back in my chair and think about what I read. A missing person that they want help to find. They didn't mention if it was family or not, just a few details that might help me find this person. I don't do missing people. There are far too many emotions involved, and I know how stupid that sounds when I'm currently working on a missing person case for Grant. He's a friend though, or at least he is now. Even when I helped him when he was still part of the police force, there was something different about him. He was relaxed and focused, and I thought that if circumstances were different, there would be a good chance we could be friends. Thankfully luck was on my side, and he contacted me after he left the force, giving me that chance to get to know him better.

A horn outside pulls me from my thoughts, and I'm up and out of my chair instantly. I press the panic button next to me once, and I hear all the shutters on my windows coming down. It's only visible from the inside meaning that whoever has turned up without permission won't know that anything is happening. It was the first thing I had installed when I moved into my small cabin, and I have never regretted the cost. Knowing what is out there looking for me, my safety is the only important thing.

I move quickly to the screens at the front of the cabin, my eyes scanning over the different security cameras I have set up around my perimeter, making a mental note to add an alarm to the front gate. It's usually locked, but apparently, I need something more to alert me to visitors. I relax instantly when I see Kelly pulling up in front of the house. He isn't due today, but I know there is no danger from him. I quickly type in a code to the main panel by the front door, and the shutters over all the possible entries start to rise. I'm at the front door before they are fully open, but I have enough room to get past them and outside to meet Kelly on the bottom step.

He smiles as he approaches with a white bag held out in front of him. "I thought you might be hungry?" He shakes the bag, and it's only then that I notice the name on the front.

"Sliders from Jerry's?"

He looks at me as though I'm losing my mind, his forehead scrunching up as he speaks. "Would I bring you anything else?"

Laughing as he takes the last few steps, I grab him into a hug that lasts a few seconds too long. When I pull back Kelly's cheeks are red, and his eyes are shining with something more than happiness. "Why don't we eat outside? The weather is a lot nicer than I thought it was and I could do with some fresh air." The truth is I'm running a system sweep on one of the big oil companies, and I don't want Kelly to see anything. I don't want to risk him being able to read something that's confidential. He doesn't know what I do to make my money because I keep him in the living room area of the cabin, and I want to keep him in the dark as much as possible. It's nice to have a friend who doesn't know that I'm RedDragon, the name I use to do all my online transactions. To Kelly, I'm just Sam that lives like a hermit in a cabin in the middle of nowhere. He delivers my groceries so I don't need to leave my property, and after a few months of general chit chat, we started to build a friendship. He's never asked me why I live so far away from anywhere and I'm thankful for that. I want to be able to keep my lies to a minimum with Kelly, so I don't mess up and lose his friendship.

"Sounds like a good plan." He walks to the small table I have sitting on the wooden decking at the front of the house. There isn't a garden as such on my property, just this seating area that gets the sun all day. He takes time to spread out the sliders and drinks he brought, and by the time I sit down across from him, my stomach is rumbling. I didn't realise I was so hungry until the smell of the food hit my nose, and now it's clear that my Tic Tacs weren't filling me the way I thought they were.

My stomach rumbles again, and Kelly laughs as I reach for one of the sliders, not even waiting until he has everything out of the bag. "Hungry?"

I nod because my mouth is full of hot chicken and jalapeños. I groan when the flavour explodes on my tongue, and I become acutely aware of Kelly staring at me, his cheeks heating more than before. My dick takes notice when he licks his lips, his tongue making a slow slide across them and leaving them wet. *Shit*. I might need to go out and get some action if I'm looking at Kelly with anything more than friendship. It's not that he isn't attractive, because he is, but he's a friend and fucking and running isn't on the cards. Except he's looking at me like he would be totally up for that idea. Maybe a friend with benefits type arrangement would work, it's not like we see each other all that often.

Kelly must realise that he's staring because he clears his throat before handing me the bottle he was holding in his hand. "I got you iced tea." He blushes and won't make eye contact with me when I take the bottle.

"Thanks. For all of this, I didn't think about eating."

"I figured. You tend to get stuck in your head when you're working on something." Apparently, I've been letting Kelly see more of me than I usually show. Has he been around that much that he's noticed something like that?

It's my turn to stare, wondering why I let him come around when I hide away from everyone else. It doesn't take me long to realise the reason, and it's pretty simple. *I get lonely*. I like to give off this persona of being a loner, of being happy with my own company, but the truth is I get sick of being on my own. I've been hiding away so long now that I've forgotten what it's like to hear someone's voice that isn't on the other end of a phone. When Kelly arrived to deliver my food from the local supermarket, his happy smile was contagious, and I found myself talking to him longer than I probably should have. When he turned up the next day with an excuse of a missing clipboard, I should have chased him away and told him not to come onto my property without permission. Instead, we ended up chatting for hours about nothing, and it was everything. I shouldn't have let him come back again and again, his safety is an issue if he's around me, but I can't seem to tell him to stop coming.

"What? Do I have something on my face?" Kelly rubs his hand over his face, but there's nothing there. That's not what I'm staring at.

"I'm really fucking horny."

MY BACK HITS the wall just inside my front door a fraction of a second before Kelly attacks my mouth again. I've always worried about the lack of filter between my brain and mouth, but this time it worked out just fine. The words had barely managed to escape my mouth before Kelly was over the table attacking me. We haven't spoken since I declared that I was horny, but I think we're both on the same page since I wasn't the one that dragged us inside and pinned me to the wall. I give Kelly a few minutes of being in control before I swap our positions, his back thudding gently against the door as he tries to keep control. It's not going to happen, and he soon realises it, melting into my hold and letting me take over. It's my turn to claim the kiss, enjoying the feel of his tongue brushing against mine. I can't remember the last time I was with someone, and if I didn't have Kelly in my arms, that thought would be a lot more depressing.

Grabbing his t-shirt in my fists, I drag him with me as I walk backwards across the cabin towards my room. I'm hoping it will keep his focus away from my office that's open for him to see inside. All the computers are on show from here, and I don't want him to notice them. I keep pulling him until he's safely inside my bedroom, and I kick the door closed behind me. As soon as it clicks I relax and focus on getting Kelly naked. He shudders when my palms connect with the skin of his chest, his skin pebbling as I run my hands over him, taking his t-shirt with me until I can pull it over his head and throw it behind us. His jeans and boxers follow behind that, and I groan when my fully clothed body grinds into his. There's something incredibly sexy about being dressed when your partner is entirely naked, and I take my time to enjoy the sensation.

Kelly's turned into a quivering mess, and I'm convinced it's only me pressing against him that's keeping him on his feet. A surge of lust goes through me, and I have the very sudden need to see how crazy I can drive him. Dropping to my knees, I run my tongue along the length of his cock. It jumps against my tongue, and I grip it in my hand to keep it still. I bite his foreskin gently, savouring the gasps and groans from above. Giving head is one of my favourite things to do, and Kelly's cock is beautiful. Not too long but nice and thick. There's something to be said for a guy who doesn't have a huge cock, especially when they know how to make the most of what they have.

"Oh shit, Sam." Kelly's hands grip my hair as he tries to thrust into my mouth. Not willing to give him the chance to move again, I use my hands to pin his hips to the wall behind him. His moaning becomes louder when he realises he can't move. To reward him I finally suck him deep into my throat. I can take him fully, not stopping until my nose is buried in his pubic hair, and his resulting cry is like music to my ears. I pull back, letting his cock slide along my tongue, and a burst of precum covers my tongue. I swallow it and moan, the taste making me want more.

"If you come will you still be able to take me?"

His eyes are dazed as he stares down at me and I'm not sure he heard me.

"Kelly?"

He blinks, and his eyes focus.

"If you come, will I still be able to fuck you?" I desperately want inside him, but I want to taste him first. If he's too sensitive after coming to have sex, then I will taste him another time. Getting my cock in him is the only thing I need today.

"Yeah. God, yeah I'll be fine."

"Good answer." It's my only response before I swallow him again. With his grip pulling the hair from my scalp and nonsense being shouted down at me, I let him see how horny I really am.

5

Clay

I STARE at the wall in front of me, the one covered with every single email that's been sent to Niko, and I know I've missed something. I have this feeling in my gut that when we go to the address that Porter managed to locate, something is going to go wrong. Maybe not covering his tracks hadn't been a mistake, what if he's drawing us in so he can get his hands on Niko, or perhaps it's nothing more than a distraction? While we're looking to locate where the emails came from, the culprit is heading in the other direction behind our backs to grab Corey. I'd feel better if I had enough people to have eyes on Corey, but I don't have that sort of manpower. No, I just have to go with the hope that Niko's location hasn't been found and that his man will be safe.

My mobile rings and I absently answer it, my focus still on the wall in front of me. "Hello."

"It's me. I'm outside the house." My stomach drops when I hear Porter speak. He's been driving a two street area since we pinged a general area, trying to find the house of the sender.

"You sure?"

"As sure as I can be. Clay, there's something you need to know before we go in." If I wasn't nervous before, the tone of Porter's voice has me on edge. He's worked for me the last seven months, and he has one of the coolest heads I know. To hear him off kilter is unusual, and a little scary.

"Shit. I have a feeling I don't want to know this but tell me."

"I managed to get a look around the house, and there's a room in the back."

Hundreds of different visions flash through my mind about what might be in that room, and none of them are pleasant. "What's in it, Porter?"

"Photos. Hundreds of them. I suggest you don't let your man in there when we go in."

"Noted. Let me know when you're ready for us."

"Will text you when I'm in place."

The line goes dead, and I slip my phone into my pocket. Staring at this wall isn't going to help anything, and it's probably a better idea to tell Niko what's happening. On the way back to Niko I make a couple of mugs of coffee, and just as I'm entering my office, I hear Niko ending a call with Corey. His voice is soft, but there's an edge to it that shows how close he is to losing his shit. I've seen it build over the last few days. With every hour of missed sleep, every new email, and every extra day spent away from Corey, his nerves are becoming frayed. Part of me wants to keep him away from the house we found, but I don't want to get between him and any vengeance he might need.

"I know you, Corey. I can almost hear what you're thinking so let me make something very clear. If you leave, I will tear this world apart looking for you. Have you taken a second to think that all this might be about me? *I'm* the one getting emailed. *I'm* the one they found. They're using you to punish me because they know what you mean to me. They know you are the only thing I can't handle losing."

His words make me pause, the ache inside my heart becoming obvious. To hear him talk with so much love makes me see how much I'm missing by not opening my heart to someone. Niko was always like me. He was a loner, a guy who wasn't looking for anyone to fill an empty part of him, but he found that anyway. He's fallen in love just like Gabe did, and it's cutting deeper than I thought possible. What happens when they move on with life and leave me here, still in the same place as always? Is love the thing I'm missing from my life, the reason I've been feeling so out of it the last few months?

Pulling myself from my darkening thoughts, I plaster a smile onto my face and walk into the room. Niko keeps his back to me and ends the call with I love you, but the air becomes thick with the tension seeping from him. I swallow down my stupid feelings, deciding that I need to get a grip and focus on Niko and his actual problems. "How's the little lady?"

Niko turns and glares at me. I would like to pretend it scared me, but he wouldn't be convinced in the slightest. There have only been two times that I've gone fist to fist with Niko, and both times he came off worse. Granted, the first time wasn't exactly a fair fight since he was holding a gun to his mouth attempting to eat a bullet, and I took him by surprise. Since I saved him that night, I'm not going to feel bad about it. That was the day I saw how far Niko had fallen, and less than two months later he was gone, working for the types of men that you wouldn't want to get on the wrong side of.

"Don't start. I don't have enough caffeine in my system to deal with you right now."

I take a seat at my desk and can't help the smirk that his words bring. He really is a grumpy fuck when he goes too long without coffee. "Lovers tiff?"

"Did I speak a foreign language? Shut the fuck up."

Winding Niko up is one of life's little pleasures, but I don't get to do it enough. I've had to fit months worth of shit talk into just a few days, and as much as I would love to continue, I can see that Niko is on the edge of losing his composure. It's obvious how much he's worried about Corey, so I take pity on him. Instead of giving him more grief, I push his coffee towards him. "Finish that one, and I'll get you more. I want you in a better mood when it's time to leave."

His face changes at my words and I can see more tension building in his shoulders. "When do we leave?"

I take out my phone to buy myself some time. I need to find a way to broach the subject of the room, but I don't know how to. I need to keep Niko calm, or he'll become a hazard to the raid, and I refuse to get anyone hurt. We need to get information, and we won't get that if

Niko goes in ready to kill. I've seen the damage he can do when he lets the rage take over, and I need him to keep a lid on it today. This isn't the same as the last time. Corey isn't dead. "We'll head out in about thirty minutes because I want to give Porter enough time to run a full security sweep of the area. I know you want to dive right in, but I need to make sure it isn't a trap." I wonder if now is the best time to tell him what we found, but he takes the decision away when he growls.

"I know you're right, and that's the only thing keeping me in this seat. All I can think though is protect, crush, kill."

Laughter bursts out of me, and I stare at him. Apparently, Corey brings out the protective side of my friend. Again he reminds me of Gabe. When Rhys was in danger, I swear he would have ripped apart anyone with his bare hands if they'd gotten in the way. The only reason Paul had managed to hurt Gabe was because he got the jump on him. My stomach sours as I think of my inability to protect Gabe and Rhys, but feel better knowing that Paul won't be able to hurt them again. "Holy shit. Paint you green, and I swear you'd be the Hulk. Anyone ever tell you that before?"

"Actually, you aren't the only person to tell me that."

I sit and watch in fascination when Niko's cheeks turn red. No way, this can't be happening. "Holy shit, are you blushing? That makes me not want to know why... apart from the fact I kinda do." I'm dying to hear Niko's response, but my mobile goes off, bringing my attention back to today. I glance down and see Porter's message telling me the property is secure and he's waiting for us. I take a deep breath to settle my building nerves before looking up at Niko. "We're up."

Niko is out of his seat instantly. He nods as I grab my gun and tuck it into my holster, watching as he does the same. Neither of us voices our concerns, but since we've both decided to carry a gun, it tells me we're on the same page. I just hope that I can get Niko to stay calm, but I'm not sure even I can manage that.

I COLLAPSE onto my bed and let out a huff as I connect with the mattress. My body is screaming at me to get some sleep, but my mind won't shut off.

I keep going back to this afternoon when we arrived at the house. I should have known that Niko wouldn't wait to be told what to do, but the memory of his face when he saw inside the room that Porter had mentioned, well that will live with me forever. It started as shock, but it quickly changed to pain. I can't imagine how he felt seeing his intimate moments with Corey being invaded by some unknown person, to know that someone was that close to them and could have hurt them at any given time. The pain left quickly and in its place was left pure, red-hot rage. The last time he looked like that was when we entered the cave where we found his sister and her kidnapper. That day I walked away and let him vent his fury on the guy, today I left him to destroy the room while I questioned the guy we had found in the house. The poor guy had had no idea what the fuck was going on when he walked in the door. Any sane person would be scared shitless with three huge men grabbing them as they entered their own house, and it didn't take long for Barry to give up everything he knew about the man who was renting his room.

We let Barry go with a warning to call us if his roommate came back. He promised that he would, but I'm not holding out hope of that happening, and it's frustrating as fuck. The man behind the emails was there, right within reach, but he slipped through our fingers. Porter has set up camp outside the house, but I think the fucker has gone underground. He's always been one step ahead of us, and I can't think of how to win this fight. "Fuck!" I scream the word at the ceiling before sitting up, groaning as the movement makes my body protest. There's no point in lying here for hours trying to sleep when there's no chance it's going to happen.

Changing clothes is the first thing I do, putting on a pair of shorts and a vest before heading to the kitchen to check what there is to eat. I don't hold out much hope that there's anything edible, but I still check, hoping that maybe I stashed something the last time I went shopping. A search of every cupboard and the fridge brings up nothing, and I give up, my energy waning with even this simple task. I'm just closing the cabinet when my eyes catch the bottle of Jack Daniels at the back of the shelf. Without even thinking I grab it before heading to my living room and collapsing on my lumpy couch. I open the bottle and take a large swig straight from it. The burn is welcomed as it spreads down my throat, and I follow it with another large swallow.

Relaxing back into the sofa I close my eyes and let my mind drift. I don't try to stop thinking, and I don't try to force my thoughts in any particular direction. I just relax and let go. I continue to down the JD as my mind wanders. I think about Gabe and Rhys, the pain they've been through recently and the fact that instead of ripping them apart, it just brought them closer to each other. I didn't know love like theirs existed, especially after everything I witnessed between my parents. They taught me what love between couples looked like, but it's nothing like I'm starting to discover with my friends. Ten years I've known Gabe, and now that he's with Rhys, it's the happiest I've ever seen him. I thought he was content in his life before, but talking to him now shows that he was missing a part of him, a part that she fills perfectly. I see the same thing with Niko. After he lost his sister, he seemed to turn into himself, so much so that I never thought he would let anyone else in. He did though, and Corey changed him in a way I didn't think possible. He's still the same guy I knew - determined, strong, and loyal beyond belief, but Corey makes him more. Fuck. This isn't what I was taught about love. The love I knew destroyed and hurt, made the people involved fade to the point that they lost who they were. That's all I saw with my parents, right up to the point my father left and the real pain started.

Hissing in pain as I down more Jack, I blink at the ceiling as my thoughts head in a direction I don't want them to.

Cameron.

As soon as my brother's face flickers in my head, I can feel the tears building. Even sixteen years after losing him, picturing his face can make me break down. I lost everything I had the day he died, and nothing has ever been able to fill the void. Not that I've ever tried. He was too young to die, too good. He should be the one that's here now, living the fantastic life he would no doubt have had. Instead, it's me that's here, wasting the days until I take my final breath. I love my friends, class them as my family, but there are moments like this when

I feel so fucking alone. There's no way to love the people around me more, but every night I go to sleep alone. I don't even come home most of the time, preferring not to feel the emptiness in this house. And that's precisely what this place is. It's a house, nothing more.

"Is that you all ready to go?" I take a large mouthful of coffee and try to chase away the hangover that's threatening to make me puke. Drinking on an empty stomach was an epically bad idea last night, and as soon as I woke this morning, I regretted it more than I've regretted anything in a while. I'm now on my fourth cup of coffee, and I can feel it make my stomach churn with acid. It's clearing my head though so I keep going, ignoring the sloshing feeling.

"Yeah, I want to get on the road early, so I miss rush hour. It's gonna take long enough to get back, and I don't want to be sitting in traffic for hours."

I stare at Niko over the rim of my mug. There are so many questions I want to ask him, but I can't seem to find the right words.

"Out with it."

I put the mug down on my desk and drop my feet to the floor. I lean my elbows on the table and watch Niko as I finally voice what I want to know. "I'm just wondering if you're gonna tell Corey what you found in that room?"

It's Niko's turn to watch me, and I can see the uncertainty in his eyes. I don't like to see him so conflicted, but this is a decision that only he can make. "I thought I should, but then I changed my mind. I hate keeping things from Corey, I do, but since the evidence no longer exists, will the knowledge really be that helpful to him?"

"That was a pretty impressive destruction job you did. I'm thinking of hiring you if I ever need a room cleared for redecorating." When I had returned to the room after leaving Niko on his own to seek a little vengeance, there had been nothing left to show what had been there before. All the photos had been ripped down, and the sparse furniture that'd been there was broken to pieces. He'd been standing over the pile of debris like he wished he had something to set fire to it with. I'm glad he didn't have anything because I'm sure the house would have gone up around us. It doesn't remove the fact that it was there in the first place, and maybe Corey should know to watch his back. "Seriously though, you don't want to keep this from him. If he finds out, he'll be pissed, and you're the one who keeps telling him there should be no secrets between the two of you."

I don't want to put pressure on Niko, but I also don't want this to come between him and Corey. I've been trying to get Niko to open up more to Corey, to tell him what they're both up against, but he refuses to. "I know, and I'll think about it on the way home. Keep me up to date with anything you find out. I'd rather not leave Corey again but I will if you need me." Niko grabs his bag from the table and turns to face me. I feel the loneliness start to shadow over me, and he hasn't even left yet.

"Leave it with me, Niko. You know I have your back. Now go see your man. It might improve your mood. You don't do well going so long without getting your dick sucked." I give him my most convincing smile, which I think he buys, especially when he retorts to my comment.

"Are you offering for next time?"

"Fuck you, Niko."

Niko bursts out laughing as he grabs me in a hug. I hold on a little longer than I should, but I worry that I might not see him again. Every time Niko leaves my company there's a chance he will go AWOL, and it will be years before I see him again. He presses his lips against my ear as he speaks, and I swallow back the emotion that's invading me. "Thank you for everything. I wouldn't trust anyone else with this."

"Any time. I'm always here for you." All too soon he breaks away, smiling before leaving me standing in the doorway. "Stay safe friend. Please stay fucking safe."

6
Clay

I CHECK the clock on my dashboard again and see that it's time to get moving. I promised Gabe I would come into the remodelled Virgin Ink so he could practice on my skin. He got his cast off about a week ago, and he's nervous as hell about putting needle to flesh after his injury. I've tried to tell him he's overthinking it, that there's no way he's lost his gift, but he isn't hearing me. So I'm here to get some new ink on my neck, and I've been looking forward to it for days. There's nothing quite like the feeling of that needle piercing your skin and the burn it creates as it vibrates against you.

With that in mind, I get out of my truck and head to the front door of Gabe's tattoo shop. I knock lightly, not giving in to the urge to bang on the door loudly. Up until about six months ago, I would have done just that, but Gabe has been through too much to frighten him merely for my amusement. I will give him a few more months before I fuck with him. I need to make sure he's back to his old self before I do it. Gabe smiles as he opens the door and steps back to let me inside.

"Hey." He's pale, and I can see his hands shake as he plays with the leather cuff on his now plaster free wrist.

"You look like you're about to shit yourself. You're not filling me with confidence here, man."

"Fuck off." Gabe pretends to look pissed, but I can see the tension easing from his shoulders. Hopefully, he'll relax more before he gets me onto the couch because the way he looks just now, I'm not risking letting him near my neck.

Following him to the back of the shop, I look towards the reception desk that looks strange without Rhys. "Where's Shorty today? Thought she might be here for moral support."

Gabe grabs a wipe and goes over the couch even though I can still see damp patches on it, telling me he cleaned it not that long ago. "She doesn't know I'm here. I thought it'd be better if I did it without her watching."

He'd hinted before that he hadn't told Rhys how he was feeling, but I'd hoped that he would change his mind and spill it. *What is it with my friends keeping important shit from the people they love?* Maybe they just seem happy, but my mum and dad were right, and this is the beginning of the secrets and lies. "Why are you keeping this from her? She'll understand that you feel nervous."

Gabe throws the wipe in the bin and spins to face me. His face has lost its nerves, and it's replaced with frustration and anger. "Because I'm fucking sick of being weak. She saw me get beat down by the guy who was after her, I couldn't even protect her, so I refuse to show her that giving a tattoo is fucking making me sweat."

I stand for a beat just staring at Gabe with my mouth open. I can't believe what he's been thinking all this time. "What the actual fuck, Gabe?"

"Look, let's just get your tattoo done."

"Forget that." I move closer to him but he refuses to look at me, so I grip the back of his neck and pull him towards me. He fights against my hold, but I don't give in and let go. If he wants to hide from me, he's going to have to work a hell of a lot harder than that. "Look at me."

It takes a few moments, but eventually, Gabe relents to my demand.

"You stop thinking that shit right now. Do you honestly think that Rhys thinks you are anything less than her fucking hero?"

I see moisture building in his eyes, so I keep talking, not letting him argue with me. There are a lot of things I'm shit at in this world, but making Gabe see the truth about who he is, that I can do.

"No one could have protected themselves against Paul that night. He took you by surprise and knocked you out like the fucking coward he was. You have nothing to be embarrassed about."

"You don't see it because you're like Captain America. That would never have happened to you."

I growl in frustration. Gabe has been thinking this crap for so long he actually believes it. I let go of his neck and spin him, pushing against his back until he's in front of his work chair. "Sit." Crossing my arms across my chest, I wait patiently for him to sit. When he does, I take a deep breath, not quite believing that I'm about to admit to any of this. "I'm going to tell you something, and you aren't allowed to say anything. Once we're done, we will get on with my tattoo and never speak of this again."

Gabe's eyes glitter with excitement and I know I have his full attention.

"Do you remember about a year ago when I had to get stitches over my eyebrow? I'd been working on the stolen pedigree puppies case."

He nods but keeps blessedly quiet. If he'd commented I'm not sure I would be able to continue.

I sigh again, wanting to change the subject but knowing that I need to share this with him. "Well, I might have lied a little bit about how it happened."

"You did?" Oh yeah, I have his full attention now.

"A little. So I didn't exactly fall while escaping over a fence when the thieves came home. I was attacked … but by a seven-year-old."

Gabe bites on his lips, and I can clearly see the humour in his eyes. God, I'm a really good fucking friend admitting this.

"She came home and thought I was trying to steal her puppy, so she grabbed a plastic baseball bat and smacked me with it. And not just once. Many, many times."

The snort is hard for Gabe to hide, but I let him have it. Anything to keep the smile on his lips instead of the pain from a moment ago.

"So now that I've told you that I ended up in hospital after losing a fight with a seven-year-old, you will stop thinking all that stupid shit about yourself. Now pick up your tattoo gun and fucking mark me." I don't wait for a response before I get settled on the couch. I close my eyes and relax into the cool leather as I listen to Gabe get his gloves on and test his gun. I flinch when the cool cleaning liquid splashes against my neck. "Arsehole."

The next few minutes pass in silence as Gabe works to put the transfer on my neck and hands me a mirror to check the placement. I don't even check before giving the mirror back to him, trusting him entirely in this. There's no one else that I would allow to mark me permanently, but Gabe has my full faith. I get settled again, tilting my head to the side so he can get full access to the area. I'm facing away from him, and just before he starts working, he speaks.

"Thank you." His voice is quiet, but it sounds more confident that it had when I arrived.

"Any time. But just so you know, you need to talk this shit out with Rhys, or I'm telling on you." I hold in my laugh, not wanting to test Gabe's patience when he's about to tattoo me.

"Arsehole."

I don't disagree with him in the slightest.

Just over an hour later I'm leaning in closer to the mirror so I can see my new tattoo clearer. My throat closes as emotion fills me when I take in the intricate feather that runs from behind my ear and down to my shoulder. I brush my finger over it as I stare in awe. The thing looks so fucking realistic that even though it's on my own skin, I need to touch it to confirm it's not real.

"Don't touch it with your grubby fingers. You know the routine, Clay."

I do know, but I couldn't stop myself.

"Is it okay?" There's a layer of vulnerability in Gabe's voice, and I want it to vanish.

"It's not bad." A sponge smacks me on the side of the head, and I turn to face Gabe, a huge smile on my face. "It's fucking amazing, my friend. It's ... stunning." The design is a tribute to my little brother Cameron, not that I told Gabe that, so for him to make it as perfect as he did, well it means everything.

"I had to make it amazing, just like he was."

I stare at Gabe for several heartbeats before I can talk through the lump in my throat. "What do you mean?"

"It's for Cameron, right?"

I merely nod, wondering how the hell he guessed that.

"You talk a lot when you're drunk. I remember one night you picked up a feather and told me they made you happy, that it was your brother looking over you." He gives me such a gentle smile, and it breaks my composure.

My mum used to tell me that when we found a feather in the garden is was our Nana Monroe, her mother who had died before I was born, watching over us to make sure we were safe. The story always stuck with me. When I lost my brother I lost my way for a little while, drinking more than I should have and fucking any woman who would let me, then one night I noticed a large white feather lying on my bed. All windows were closed, and I couldn't work out how it got there. That was the night I decided I needed to get my life sorted. I was wasting the time I'd been given, and I was dishonouring Cameron's memory by doing it. I'd spent most of my adult life making his years the best I could, and when I lost him, I lost my path.

It's a story I've never told anyone before, or so I thought, but Gabe has kept it close to his heart like I do my brother. To try and hide the tears that are close, I grab him into a hug and hold on tight. He returns the fierce grip I have on him, and we stand there as I try to get control over myself. I don't often show my emotions to people, but when I do finally give in, it tends to be Gabe that sees the cracks. "Thank you."

"Any time. For anything."

I release him and scrub at my eyes, trying to hide the fact that I was crying even though it's really fucking obvious. "Right, let's get this thing covered so we can go get something to eat."

Gabe humours me and cleans over the tattoo before covering it with cling film. We don't talk again as we close up the shop and approach our vehicles.

"Where do you fancy eating?"

I unlock my truck and lean against the door while Gabe waits for an answer. We go through this every time we decide to eat out, and we always end up at the same place. "Not doing this again. I will see you there, whoever arrives first gets a table." I get into my truck with the sound of Gabe's laugh in my ears.

"Is everything all right with you?"

Looking up from the pizza crust I was playing with, I give Gabe my full attention. I didn't realise I wasn't listening, but since he looks at me expectantly, I think I may have missed something. "Sorry, what?"

Gabe rolls his eyes before leaning forward and resting his elbows on the table between us. "I asked what was up."

"Nothing. Everything's good."

Apparently, that isn't the right answer because he glares at me hard enough that I wriggle in my seat. "Okay, so let's pretend that I don't believe you and think you're full of shit. Fancy telling me the truth?"

Gabe has been by my side for years now. He appeared in my life by a stroke of luck, and I decided to keep him. I saw something in him that I could connect with, and it didn't take long before we became best friends. Cameron was worried when I first met Gabe, telling me that a random guy sleeping in the doorway of our shop isn't exactly the person I want to take into my home, but I have never regretted it for a second. When I found him at the door of my record shop, he was cold and hungry, but I could still see the pride in his eyes. I wanted to know his story, and after feeding him a warm breakfast, he was completely honest with me. Well, not entirely, but it was enough to know he wasn't a danger. It was only a few years later that he told me the truth about his dad and what he'd done, but never did I judge him because of it. There was no need to. Gabe had proved himself as a trustworthy and loyal friend, and I was lucky to have him in my life.

Now for the first time ever, I wonder how much to tell him. How honest to be? Should I explain that I feel like I'm going insane? That my emotions are fluctuating between feeling nothing and feeling too much. Do I reveal that the last few months I've felt lonely and empty, almost like my soul is missing something, and I don't know what it is?

Or do I just figure that I might be losing my fucking mind and tell Gabe that everything is fine?

"Clay, seriously, what's wrong?"

"Honestly? I don't know. I'm just feeling ... numb. It's like–"

"There you both are. How did I guess you'd be here?" Rhys leans down and kisses Gabe on the lips before taking the seat next to him.

I smile at her, hiding the fact that I don't want her here. I was about to finally open up to Gabe about how I'm feeling, but now that I've been interrupted I'm not sure I will ever get that courage again. "Hey, Shorty."

Rhys returns my smile before grabbing a slice of pizza from Gabe's plate. "Did I miss anything exciting?" The words come out around a mouthful of food, and I realise that's why she fits in around here. Her manners are as bad as mine.

"Nothing exciting." Gabe raises his eyebrow at me but doesn't bring attention to the fact I've just changed the subject. I'm sure he'll bring it up again at a later date, but for now, I'm safe from spilling my feelings in front of Rhys.

"Surprised to see you here, Clay. You've been so busy recently."

I pick at the label on my bottle so I can avoid looking at her. I don't want her to see the truth that I'm only just now admitting to even myself. I've been using work as an excuse for being absent, but the real reason is that seeing Gabe and Rhys together is difficult. I want them to be happy, but watching them has shown me that my life is missing something. The lie is an easy one to justify to everyone, including myself, so I keep it going. "I finally took some time off, much to Margaret's approval."

"Wow, time away from the office? I didn't think you could survive not working." She winks as she teases and I pick up my scrunched up napkin and throw it at her.

"I said I was taking time off. I didn't say I wasn't working." I tip up my bottle and empty the last of the cider from the bottom, wincing as the warm liquid fills my mouth.

"You didn't mention that earlier. What're you working on?" Gabe looks really interested now, but I see Rhys look at him when he mentions spending time with me. I wonder what excuse he used to get the afternoon free to tattoo me. I decide to give him an out with his woman.

"Remember Niko?"

Gabe nods.

"I've been helping him to find someone who's causing problems for his boyfriend."

"Is everything okay?"

"Don't know yet. Hopefully, we will find what we need before anything happens."

"Who's Niko?" Rhys' voice pulls my attention from Gabe.

"An old friend. I met him years ago when I took a case to find his missing sister. Been friends ever since."

"So I've not met him?"

Gabe leans in and kisses Rhys on the head. "No, sexy. And you won't."

I laugh, and Gabe glares at me, but apparently, Rhys misses the exchange because she keeps asking questions. "Why not?"

"Because he looks like a better-looking version of Clay. Not as tall but yeah, he's pretty hot." It's the first time I've heard Gabe sound like he's intimidated by anyone, and if he didn't seem so serious, I would take the piss out of him. Actually, this is probably the best time to take the piss.

"Oh come on, Gabe. If Rhys was going to fall for anyone that's better looking than you, it would be me."

"Fuck you." His rebuttal has me laughing hard, and it only takes a few moments before Rhys is joining me. To ease the sting though she leans into Gabe and kisses him gently on the cheek.

"You know you're the sexiest guy I know. I'm a very happy woman, and no other man compares." She brushes her lips against Gabe's again, but when she tries to move away, he grabs her by the back of the neck to keep her right there. The kiss deepens, and I grab my wallet from my pocket, throwing a twenty pound note on the table. Neither of them notices when I stand and put my jacket on, only finally separating when I cough. When I have their attention, I smile.

"I'm gonna head out. Got some work to do on Niko's case. You two behave." I can see Gabe is about to speak, probably to ask if I'm okay, so I cut him off before he has a chance. "I'll call you."

"Come for dinner soon?" Rhys takes my hand and squeezes it.

"I will, short stuff." I nod at Gabe before leaving the happy couple behind.

7
Sam

"You want me to hack his email?"

"No. Will you stop typing for two bloody minutes and listen to me."

Grant sounds frustrated, and it brings my attention fully to him and away from the security system I'm trying to navigate around. "Sorry. Start again."

Grant gives me an exasperated sigh, but there's no real anger behind it. He's used to me getting caught up on other things when he's trying to talk to me, so him calling me out is par for the course. "I need you to try and get some information on who is sending Niko emails. Anything you can find."

"Niko?" The name rings a bell, but I can't place it.

"Fuck sake, Sam. Niko and Corey, the guys I've had you searching for for months. The ones I'm living with."

Okay, so maybe I need to give Grant a bit more attention. I can remember what he's told me now about both Niko and Corey, and the information that I'd helped him get. My mind has been so filled with this latest job that it took me a minute for everything to come back to me, but now I'm up to speed again. I remember when Grant first mentioned Niko, Corey's boyfriend because we were both shocked by his existence. Nothing we had found had pointed to Corey being attached to anyone, and that could have put Grant in a lot of danger. I'd told Grant to get out of there, but he said he was safe, that he wanted to stay to try and find out more. I knew there was something Grant wasn't telling me, but I hoped that he would open up when he felt comfortable. "Sorry. I'm with you now. What's up?"

"Niko's been getting emails that are threatening Corey. I told him I would get you to work your magic on the account."

"Send me the details, and I'll get on it." I stop talking for a few seconds, wondering if I should ask all the questions I have running through my head. None of them have to do with what he just asked me to do, but all of them are about his current situation, since he isn't forthcoming with whatever he's hiding.

"Out with it." Should've known that Grant would know instantly that I had something to say. We might not have met a lot of times in person, but the last year we have gotten to know each other well. After he left the police force, it was like he needed someone on his side and I was more than willing to be that person. Grant helped me so much in the beginning that it was nice to be able to repay the favour. I haven't seen him in years, but I'm hoping that now he's closer that we will be able to meet up. He has become a proper friend to me, more than just a guy I'm trying to help, and he probably knows me more than anyone else in the world. Even Kelly only knows limited shit about me, just the stuff I'm willing to share. There is only one thing I'm keeping from Grant, but I do that to keep him safe. That information is dangerous to anyone who knows it, and I'm not willing to put anyone at risk.

"How does Niko know about me?"

Pause. "I told him about you."

"Why? I thought your past was meant to be a secret?"

Another pause, this one slightly longer. "It was, but Niko found out."

My heart starts to race with worry for Grant. We know next to nothing about these guys apart from the dodgy background they came from, and if they've found out who Grant really is, then there's a good chance he might be in danger. "Shit. Are you okay? Do you need me to come to get you?"

"No, it's all good. Apparently, he's known for a while. His only concern is protecting Corey, and since he knows I'm not a danger to him, he wants my help." Grant has a strange tone to his voice, making him sound softer, and I'm not sure what to make of it. I decide to ignore it because my only thought is to keep Grant safe.

"Are you sure? What happens if he suddenly changes his mind?"

"He won't. He's not that kind of man."

I'm trying to get my head around all this. All the information we have about Corey and Niko points to the fact that they were both probably involved in Blue Diamond, an underground prostitution ring. In what capacity I don't know, but it wasn't exactly a company registered with the better business bureau, so I can't imagine that either of them did anything legal. "Not dangerous?"

Grant laughs, the sound relaxing me slightly but not completely. "Oh fuck no, he's dangerous, but ... at the same time, he's not. He's loyal and keeps his word." There's that dreamy sound again, the one that makes it sound like Grant has feelings for Niko. Shit. He can't be that stupid.

"Grant, you haven't slept with him have you?"

"God, no. He's in a relationship with Corey." That might be the truth, but he can't hide the way his voice slips away towards the end of that sentence, and my mind is struggling to catch up. Why does he sound ...shit I don't even know how he sounds. It's not exactly sad, more like he has a longing that he's trying to hide.

"Do you want to?"

"I'm not having this conversation with you. I'll send you the information you need in the email. Thanks for helping again, Sam." He doesn't even wait for me to say goodbye before he hangs up on me.

That doesn't stop me wondering what the fuck is going on, in fact, it makes my mind go into overdrive thinking about it more. Maybe I'll be able to get more background on this Niko guy when Grant sends over the email details. There must be some clues if he opened an account. What most people don't realise, is even if they don't use their own information to set up a fake account, they usually use something that's connected to them. A relative's birthdate or an old address. In my experience there's always something, so maybe I'll be able to get something on Niko or Corey. I've been worried about Grant since he came up with the insane idea of trying to get into that bloody cabin, but now that I know they know who he is, well now my worry is off the charts.

Getting up from my chair, I leave my office and head to the kitchen. Now that my attention is away from the firewall I'm trying to break through, I decide that it's probably the best idea to eat. I'm always forgetting, and it's usually only when I start getting a migraine that I remember that food is just as important as coffee and Redbull. Opening the fridge I search inside, trying to find something that's easy to make. Unfortunately, it's nearly empty. Shit, this means I'm going to have to put in a grocery order, and that means seeing Kelly again. My stomach sours at that thought. Sex with him had been a one-time thing, a way to scratch an itch and I thought he understood that. We're friends, and I felt that we were merely doing the added benefits thing. The way we'd parted ways afterwards tells me that maybe he wasn't on the same page as I was. The smile and lingering looks, the talk about seeing me again soon, that shit proved that we had very different ideas about what we did. Now having to see him again is going to be awkward as shit. Groaning I slam the fridge door and head to the small freezer that I keep on the back porch. I barely glance at its content before grabbing a pizza. It's not the most nutritious of dinners but it's easy and filling, and it will save me from having to put in that order for food. Anything to put off the inevitable, even if it's just for a few more days.

BILE RISES up my throat as I read another email that was sent to Niko. The things that this sick fuck is saying about the guy's boyfriend are horrendous. No wonder he's willing to overlook the fact that Grant is an ex-cop, especially if he can help catch this guy and protect Corey. I've spent far too long reading the emails since I got into the account, but it's like a car crash you can't look away from. I wasn't even planning on reading them, I didn't need to to help, but then curiosity got the better of me, and I opened the first one. After that, there was no way I couldn't read the rest, even if I'm trying to convince myself it's to see if there's anything I can pick up while my tracing programme searches for an IP address or location.

A ping sounds on my laptop, and I spin in my chair to see what's been found. I search over the website that's come up, wondering what the hell I'm looking at. It's a blank page, one telling me that the page I'm trying to find no longer exists. *So why the hell did my computer highlight it?* I start nosing around, trying to find a way behind the blank page. It doesn't take long, and as soon as I gain access, window after window opens, bringing up pictures of men in various poses. All the men are different in their looks, but there is a common theme running through each picture, and that is they're cuffed and have a letter tattooed on their chest. I have no idea what I'm looking at, but the images keep coming, covering my whole screen with erotic pictures. They eventually stop, and it gives me a chance to have a proper look at them. The men all look young, though not young enough to be illegal, and they're all wearing the same thing. Which is they aren't wearing anything other than a letter. All the letters are different, like a way of identifying them, but they're all large and black, covering the left side of their chest.

Clicking through them all takes a while, but there's one picture that I keep coming back to. It's of a younger looking guy, one with blonde hair and the letter J on his chest. I have this feeling of recognition like I've seen him before, but I can't place where. I close over all the other pictures, but I keep that one open because it's starting to really fucking annoy me. *I know him from somewhere.* I grab my can of Redbull and sit back in my chair, staring at the guys face. I need to place him, or it's going to drive me insane. I go through everyone I've worked for but that's not it, he hasn't hired me for anything in the past. My mind then drifts to the actual jobs, is this someone that I've tried to find or I've investigated. I take a mouthful of my energy drink just as it hits me, making me choke on the liquid. *Holy fuck.* The guy I've been staring at is Corey. As in the guy who Grant is staying with.

There have always been suspicions that Corey was one of the prostitutes that Blue Diamond hired out, but this is the first time that I've seen the evidence of it. But why have I suddenly found it? I spent months trying to get any scrap of information about him, and there was nothing, now suddenly I see something concrete and very condemning. I trace back over my programme trying to find what had alerted me to the website, and it points me to a backup email that was used by Niko to open his new one. It's not something that would point to him in an obvious way, especially since it's only linked to him through five other email addresses, but the link is enough that I found it, or more accurately, my programme found it. The reason it opened this website is one of the email addresses is linked to an account set up to log into the main site. It's been purged, but there is still the evidence there underneath the missing page.

This new knowledge leads to only a few possible scenarios. It could mean that Niko was a member of Blue Diamond, which is very unlikely, or it says he worked for them. This has been the probability the whole time, but this is finally some hard evidence that he did. I open another window on my screen just as there's a knock on my front door. Initially, I groan, but soon the reality hits me along with the panic. *Someone's at my door without any of my perimeter alarms going off.* I want to rush to the monitors on the back wall to check what's happening out there, but fear has me unable to move. Fuck. There's no reason for anyone to be here and that's never a good thing. I take a deep breath and try to think rationally. If someone was here to hurt me, would they knock on my door to get my attention?

That's what finally gets me moving towards the door, albeit very slowly. The people I'm hiding from are dangerous, and I wouldn't put it past them to put a bullet through the door if they suspected I was standing there. And that's the thought that has me stopping again. What if someone dangerous is on the other side? What if they're trying to distract me while they surround me? My eyes flash to the windows, the noticeably uncovered windows that give straight access into my home. The urge to puke becomes strong, and so does the urge to collapse to the ground and hide from the world. Another bang on the door has me jumping, my pulse racing as tears fill my eyes.

"*You won't ever escape me, Sam. I will come for you one day.*"

Damien's words echo through my head again, kicking my panic up to epic levels. I knew that he'd find me, I just thought I would have noticed that he was coming. I've spent the last sixteen months being a ghost so I couldn't be found, but apparently, I didn't hide enough. I stare at the panic button by the front door, the one that'll lock down the house and put off the inevitable, and if I could build up the courage to press it, I can try and plan my escape. That's where the problem lies. I can't get my feet to move. I need to though, or I'm going to make myself an easy target. Confidence bolstered enough to finally move, and I tread quietly to the console and type in my code. I'm about to put the house into lockdown when someone speaks from the other side of the door.

"Sam, are you in there? It's Kelly. Sam?"

The sudden loss of fear has me dropping to the floor in relief. *Holy fuck*. I feel like crying now that I know I'm safe. I don't think I've ever felt fear like that before, and now that common sense is returning to me, I realise how stupid I've been. Of course it wasn't Damien's men at the door. There's no way in hell that they'd knock before taking or killing me. When they finally come for me, I won't know anything about it. Leaning my back against the door, I take deep breaths to let my heart rate return to normal. I don't plan on opening the door to Kelly, because that's a headache I don't need just now, so I sit and calm down. Closing my eyes I try to escape to my happy place, the part of my mind where it's comfortable and safe, but the adrenaline instantly takes me to the memory I don't want. The one that changed my entire life.

"Sam I don't think you understand what I'm trying to say here."

"Oh, I understand." I try not to shuffle my feet as nerves threaten to make me collapse to the floor. In the six months I've been working for Damien, I've never refused to do anything, but this time there's no way I can do what I'm told. I look at the little boy who's sitting in the corner, his silent sobs breaking my heart.

"If you don't do it someone else will. Is it worth losing your life over?"

I bring my eyes back to Damien and steel my back, putting as much force into my words as I can manage. "Totally."

Damien growls and stands up abruptly, slamming his chair against the wall behind him. "Take him away."

Two sets of hands grab my arms and start to pull me from Damien's office. My gaze flicker back to the little guy in the corner, his fearful eyes meeting mine. "I swear, Damien. Do not touch him."

Damien's only response is to laugh, the sound mocking me as I'm dragged away.

"I'll get you out, okay?" These words are purely for the kid, and when he hears me, he nods his head.

"Wait!" The controlling hands drop instantly from my body as Damien walks around the table to stand in front of me. His eyes burn into mine, burning anger clear to see. "That was a cruel thing to do, Sam."

My mind scrambles to work out what point he's trying to make. I pictured lots of things coming from him, threats or intimidation, but this has me confused. "What?"

His chuckle sounds evil, and it has the hairs on my arms standing on end. "Well, promising that poor boy that you'll get him out. Why would you get his hopes up like that, especially when you know what's going to happen to him?" He leans in close, his voice dropping low and sinister. "The only way he's getting out of here is to the highest bidder, and I doubt that it'll be a happy experience for him."

I swallow down the bile in my throat. How did I ever think that Damien was a decent person? When I started working for him, I thought he was a real businessman, that he only took me on to help him garner information about the other companies he was trying to bid against. For the first few weeks, it seemed legit, and that's why I stayed until now. It didn't take long for the jobs to become a bit sketchier. Like hacking into peoples email accounts to plant fake emails, or crashing companies servers to leave them struggling. This time though he's let me see behind a dark curtain, and I'm now no longer willing to take part. Selling kids is sick, and I will take him down. I just need to get the kid out of here before I do anything. I designed his computer system so getting into it remotely won't be a problem, meaning I can take his company down from anywhere in the world, but I will do that from a distance when I'm safe. Once I know he's safe, I'll collect evidence of what Damien's been doing and send it to the police.

"I will stop you."

"Good luck with that." Damien looks back at the men behind me. "Take him out back. You know what to do."

I'm grabbed and dragged backwards again, but my eyes don't leave Damien. I refuse to give him the satisfaction of seeing the terror I'm feeling inside. Instead, I stare him down while my head goes through all the horrific scenes of what is probably coming my way. I've seen some of the beatings that men have taken at the hands of Damien's men, and I'm just hoping I can survive one.

8
Clay

THIS IS the part of any investigation that drives me insane. The quiet time when you're pretty much just waiting for something to happen so you can deal with it. I've exhausted every tool in my arsenal to get any lead, but there's nothing new to find. It means I'm on the back foot and I fucking hate that. I don't like it when someone else is in control of a situation, but there's nothing I can do about it. There's no way to move forward until this fucker emails us again.

I grab the bottle of beer from my desk and take a swig as I open the last email that Niko received. I've already read it close to a dozen times tonight, letting each word sink in deeper to see if I can catch something that I missed the other hundred times I've looked at it. The phone on my desk rings and I absently answer it, my eyes not leaving my computer. "CW investigations."

"Get the fuck out of the email account."

My eyes widen at the words that are growled down the phone at me. I don't know who the hell is talking to me, but the fact they know about the emails, and that I'm reading them now, shocks the ever-loving fuck out of me. "What?"

"You heard me, get the fuck out of the emails. You are messing with my investigation, and I want you to stop."

"Who the fuck are you?" My mind is still trying to catch up with what the hell is happening here.

"Sam and this is now my case. Stay out."

I'm left with a dead phone at my ear when the fucker hangs up on me. I put the handset back on the table slowly, staring at it as my anger starts to grow inside. My mind can't get off the burning question I have. Who the fuck is Sam?

I don't have time to ponder the answer to that because there's a knock on my office door. I look up to see Gabe standing there with a six-pack in his hand. "Am I interrupting?"

"Of course not." I get up and walk around my desk to greet Gabe with a bro hug. I motion for him to sit on the couch, and I follow him down onto the cushions. "To what do I owe the pleasure? Can't normally drag you away from Rhys this often."

Gabe hands me a bottle of beer while he pretends to glare at me. "Bite me, Clay. I just thought I would drop in since our last night out was cut short."

I take a long pull from my bottle as I stare at Gabe over the bottle. I knew when I left that he wasn't finished talking, but I'd run like the chicken I am. I hate talking about my feelings to anyone, even Gabe, but tonight it looks like I've used up all my excuses to avoid it. "You and Rhys looked cosy. I didn't want to intrude."

"Wow, you really wanted to avoid the conversation we started."

I take another drink to drag out time before I need to answer. When I can no longer avoid it, I lower the bottle and try to act innocent, which is difficult for me. "I have no idea what you mean."

This makes Gabe laugh hard. "The innocent thing isn't working for you. Not once since I met you have you worried about being in the way. You usually enjoy being a pain in my arse. I've known you for too long to know when you're bullshitting me, brother. Now, out with it. What's eating you?"

Picking at the label on the bottle, I take a moment to try and work out what to tell him. Everything will come out eventually because I can never keep anything from Gabe for too long, but there's usually a lot more alcohol involved before I'm relaxed enough to talk about shit like this. Being truthful is probably the way to go here, now if I could just work out what that was. "Honestly? I don't know. I've just felt off. I don't know how to explain it." I laugh, putting as much effort as possible into it to convince Gabe that the whole situation isn't affecting me like it is. I don't want him to worry about me because that's my job in our friendship. I worry for everyone and hide all my own troubles. I've always found it easier to focus on others, because the last time I let life dictate my emotions, I nearly lost myself.

"Try hard."

I glower at him, but it doesn't deter him, his gaze never leaving mine even for a second. Fuck me. I'm going to have to try and work out how to put my feelings into words for the first time. I've not even tried to sort out the feelings in my head, so to tell Gabe is going to be fucking difficult. "Shit man, why not ask me to do something easy like getting my dick pierced?"

This gets a laugh from Gabe but doesn't distract him enough to let me off the hook.

"Fine. There are just moments when I think, maybe, that I might want ... something else. Something more. I don't know what that thing is. I feel -"

My sentence is cut off when the main office doorbell rings. I check my watch and see that it's nearing four o'clock. The closed sign on the door should deter people from trying to see if anyone is here, but apparently, that doesn't matter to the person ringing again. I look at Gabe like he might know who's there, but he shrugs his shoulders. I get up from the couch and move slowly towards my office door, hoping that if I take my time, the person wanting my attention will give up and fuck off. The door's locked and all the lights are off, apart from the ones back here in my office, but those can't be seen from the street outside. Actually, that raises an interesting question. "How the fuck did you get in here? The door's locked."

Gabe chuckles as he leans to the side so he can slip a hand into his pocket. When his fingers re-appear, he's holding a key, one I know for a fact I didn't give him.

"Arsehole." I leave him laughing on the couch as the bell rings again. I head towards the door because whoever is on the other side isn't giving up any time soon. When I turn the corner into the main reception area, I can see a dark shadow through the frosted glass door. It looks like I'm going to have to deal with this, even though it's tempting to call Margaret and make her come in. Not that I would ever do that, especially since it's Saturday, but it's nice to entertain the idea.

When I reach the door, I unlock it and open it wide, standing in the doorway so whoever is on the other side doesn't think I'm inviting them in. When I'm met with steely grey eyes, I know that this isn't a possible client. I cross my arms over my chest, making sure that I use my extra few inches of height to my advantage. The man in front of me, wearing a dark blue suit, screams police and they usually don't bring anything useful to the table. The only reason I tolerate them on any level is because I have to to keep my investigator's license and gun permit. I need to keep them sweet or risk losing both of them.

"Mr Wilson?"

My only response is to nod my head.

"I'm detective Archer. I was wondering if I could ask you a few questions?"

I let my gaze travel the length of the detective, taking more time than I would normally, hoping that it might annoy him. Since I can't tell him to fuck off, pissing him off is the next best thing. He looks slightly older than me, and his hair slightly grey around the edges. He's a few inches shorter than me, but his body is slim and lean, making him look taller than he is. I should be put at ease by this fact, but his eyes are what have me worried. There's determination in them, like he's used to winning any battle he goes up against. I step back and motion him into the reception area, not wanting to discuss whatever he is here for on the street. "What can I help you with, detective?"

He steps inside, his eyes roaming around my business, taking everything in. "I believe you know Gabe Ryan?"

I'm instantly on full alert. There's only one reason this detective is here asking about Gabe, and I hope to fuck Gabe stays put in my office. I can handle this guy and lead him away from anything he wants to know about Gabe, as long as Gabe stays hidden in the back. "You already know I do or you wouldn't be here."

My non-answer doesn't seem to faze the detective, and he carries on like I haven't spoken. "When Mr Ryan was in the hospital, did you know the whereabouts of Paul Clark?"

The mention of Paul has me grinding my teeth together. No other name on the planet makes me want to kill as much as that one. Not even my father creates the same rage, and that man is the poster child for a shitty human. "I try not to think about him when possible." My answer is vague, and I'm hoping that I'm not showing any outward signs of nerves. I know nearly every step that Paul made while Gabe was in hospital. I also know the current whereabouts of Paul, but I'm not planning on telling this guy.

I loosen the grip of one hand that is holding Paul's jacket. My grip is the only thing that is preventing him from tumbling over the side of the bridge and ultimately, to his death. I can see that he is fully aware, his eyes full of fear. He tries to grab my arms, but he's struggling due to his angle. When I followed him this afternoon, I knew that it would be the last time. I needed to end this shit for Gabe's sake, and I needed to do it while he still had an alibi. Being in the hospital is about as good as it comes when it comes to proving you didn't do something illegal.

"Tell me why you went after Gabe, and then I might let you walk."

Paul relaxes slightly in my hold, his wriggling becoming almost nonexistent, and he laughs. "Do you think for one second that you'll let me go? I'm not fucking stupid you meathead."

"You're right. Let me rephrase that then. Tell me why you went after Gabe and most of you can walk away." *He glares at me, but I stay silent. I can see the indecision in his face. He wants to say some shit, but he's worried about what I will do. I should probably tell him that his answer won't change what is going to happen, but having him on edge is my aim. To help with that I relax my grip again, letting him slip further from my hold.*

"Fuck! Okay, I went after Gabe because I wanted to. He's always been a cocky fucker, acting like he was better than me."

I gape at Paul. All this is because of jealousy? He broke Gabe's arm because he was fucking better than him? "He might never tattoo again."

Paul laughs and even upside down, hanging over the edge of a very tall bridge, I can see the happiness on his face. "I can only hope."

I'm done. Even if my mind wasn't made up as soon as he said those works his fate was sealed. "You know, you're right. Walking away isn't one of the options I'm giving you."

I let go of Paul's jacket and watch as he starts to slip over the edge of the bridge. The only sound Paul makes is a small gasp as he realises that his life is about to end. It's too late for him to do anything, though it doesn't stop him from trying to grab at something to prevent his fall. There's nothing he can do though, and I watch as he tumbles through the air towards the ground.

That wasn't his final resting place, but that location will go to the grave with me. No one knows what happened to Paul or where I buried him, and I'm happy to keep that secret

"You're probably aware that Mr Clark is currently a missing person."

"And my heart breaks every second of the day."

The detective ignores my sarcasm outwardly, but I can see his mind working behind those cold eyes. "We're retracing his last few days again, see if we can gather anything new. Rechecking all the CCTV cameras around his home." He says that last bit differently, like he's trying to make a point, and fuck me does it work. I didn't know there was CCTV around Paul's shitty little apartment, which is why I didn't hide any of my movements. I spent days parked up across from his place, not even attempting to stay in the shadows. I didn't think I needed to.

"Well, I hope that it gave you something interesting." I can hear the strain in my voice. Anyone who knows me might notice, but I'm hoping this detective won't pick up on it.

"Oh, it did. Some very enlightening viewing." He goes silent and watches me. He's looking for a reaction, and I refuse to give him one, even if my stomach is threatening to empty. He must have seen me on those videos, and it makes me wonder why I'm not being dragged to the police station for questioning.

"That's fantastic. Well if that's all you wanted?"

"For now." He turns and heads to the door, stopping before he reaches it and looks over his shoulder. "Forgot to ask. Does anyone else drive the black Ford Ranger that's registered to you?"

"No one." My answer is automatic, and it's not until he grins that I know I've probably just made a colossal mistake.

He nods and leaves, closing the door with a final thud. I stand and stare at it, wondering what I just set into motion.

"Are you okay?"

I jump at Gabe's voice, spinning to face him with a fake smile. "Yeah. It's all cool." He watches me as I walk past him, his eyes burning a hole in my back as I make my way to my office. Collapsing onto the couch, I grab my bottle of beer, downing the remainder before taking a new one and half finishing it. By the time I come up for air Gabe is next to me, his fingers playing with the loose edge of his bottles label. "You look like a constipated elephant. Out with it." I was trying to make Gabe laugh, but he barely reacts before speaking.

"What happened to Paul?"

"I don't know."

Gabe finally looks at me. "Don't lie to me, Clay. Not to me. Not after everything we've been through. I know that Paul didn't just go missing, and now the police are asking questions."

The whole reason I've avoided telling him about what I did to Paul is that Gabe is a gentle soul and that knowledge would drive him insane. To know that I took someone's life for him, he wouldn't be able to live with that without making it right. That means he'd throw himself on any sword that he felt was aimed at me. I can't let that happen. His life is perfect now, and I refuse to let him lose Rhys again, especially when they've only just found their way back to each other. "I'm not going to tell you, but know you and Rhys are safe. Paul won't ever hurt you again."

"Why won't you just tell me?" He sounds pissed, but there's no way I'm going to give in on this one. I will not put Gabe in danger by telling him the truth.

"Plausible deniability."

"You are full of shit, Clay." He gets up from the couch, the anger rolling off him in waves.

I quickly follow him up, getting close enough to him that I can grab him by the back of the neck and hold him close. I make sure his eyes are on mine before I speak, and when I do, I make sure he's hearing me clearly. "I did what I needed to do. You are my family, Gabe. The person who means the most to me in this world, so I did what I needed to do to keep you safe. I won't explain what I did. You don't need that in your brain. The only important thing to me is that you're safe, and I would do it again if I had to." My voice gets thick as I near the end of my little speech because Gabe's eyes start to fill with tears.

"What if you go to jail?"

"I don't care. You'll still be safe, and that's all that matters."

A tear breaks free and runs down Gabe's cheek. I don't say anything and just pull him in for a hug. I hold him tight, the empty feeling that has been haunting me fading slightly as Gabe hugs me back. Maybe this is what the problem has been. I've been feeling guilty because I've been keeping secrets from Gabe all this time. It's not emptiness inside, a need to find someone to be mine, it's just the unknown feeling of guilt. That makes more sense than being lonely, because I've spent such large chunks of my life alone, and it's never bothered me before.

Even after Cameron died and I had to tell my dad. I had turned up at his door to tell him his youngest son had passed away, but the news was met with a blank stare. My dad had asked if I needed anything, and when I said no, he'd looked awkwardly at me before telling me, he needed to go to his son's parent's evening. I had just told him that his son was dead, and he was only worried that he was going to be late for something with his new family. That was the day I realised that my dad had checked out of my life, and wasn't willing to be part of it any more.

9

Sam

I STRETCH my hands above my head and release a sigh of relief when my spine cracks. I've been sitting in front of my computer screens for far too long, and for me to admit that is huge. I can spend days there, just napping with my head on the desk occasionally, but today I needed to walk away or risk a severe migraine. Taking a deep breath, I let the cold fresh air fill my lungs. I very rarely come outside but my minor panic attack the other day has shown me that I'm becoming a nervous recluse. It's not exactly the life I'd envisioned for myself when I moved to Scotland, but sadly it's become my reality.

Eighteen months and six days I've been here, and not once have I ventured to the village a few miles over. Driving through the gates at the edge of my property seemed to trigger something inside me, and I found it difficult to leave the safety that my perimeter seemed to offer me. It only got worse when I added all my security measures. Those were what finally helped me sleep at night, but even that's changing. I can feel the panic start to build inside and I don't know why. There's been no evidence that Damien is looking for me, but my brain won't let me relax. It's continuously worrying, letting the fear of being found dream up scenarios that lead to my death. The last time I got a trace on Damien, he'd caught a plane to Norway, and there's no paperwork to say he ever returned.

The fact that's he's able to leave the country is frustrating, especially since I thought he would be in a jail cell rotting away by now. He's not though, and I can't find his name attached to any police investigation. I risked everything to send the police the information they needed, but nothing has come from it. I've tried to resend it a few times, but every email or file I send seems to go missing before it reaches the people that need it. I have no fucking idea what's going on with it, and I'm scared to search too deep in case I get seen by the people I'm hiding from.

Taking a deep breath, I listen to the birds overhead and enjoy the peace of the moment. I need to have more times like this when I relax and enjoy the day. I'm being really bloody stupid over this whole thing, but knowing it and being able to change it are two very different things. I've been stuck indoors for so long that I'm allowing every little noise to make me freak out when it isn't needed. Shit. Even Kelly coming to the door the other night had me thinking I was about to die. If I plan to live the rest of my life in constant fear, I may as well have let Damien take me out. I didn't though, I fought back to get away so I could live, but this isn't living.

I stroll down the little-overgrown path that leads around the edge of my property. I walked this path so many times when I first moved in, the need to continually check the perimeter fence driving every step. The six-foot wire fence was barely enough to keep the wildlife out, and soon that knowledge was too much to deal with, making me call in a security company to cover my property in cameras and alarms. My imagination was my worst enemy, and all I could picture was being grabbed or killed as I made my way around my garden. The thought of someone watching me, getting to know my routine so they could take me out made me stop my hourly walks, and soon I was unable to move much further than my front decking. Now I barely leave my cabin, and if I do go outside, it certainly isn't past the end of my driveway.

Scrubbing my hand over my face, I finally realise how insane I sound. I haven't left my house in over a year, and even walking around my garden is enough to give me a panic attack. *Fuck*. Who even lives like this? Well, apparently I do now. I've let Damien dictate my life even when he's not attempted to find me. The only alert to someone searching for me online was just after I ran, but there's been nothing for the past fourteen months. Unfortunately, that seems to have made me even more paranoid, like the unknown is what will eventually get me. I stop walking and stare at the trees around me, letting the peace spread through me for the first time. I picked this place because it's out in the middle of bumfuck Scotland. No one will ever be able to stumble on it, and there's no paper trail that leads it back to me. My name doesn't show anywhere on the deeds or any of the utility bills. There's nothing that would bring anyone here, but still, I spend my whole time hiding. Well, no more. I refuse to live like this.

With more determination than I've ever had, I head back to the cabin. I need to keep moving because if I falter, I might not do what I'm planning on doing. Now is the perfect time to drive to town. I don't want to order a food delivery because facing Kelly isn't on my list of happy experiences, so unless I plan on starving to death, then I need to go food shopping. I reach my front door but barely step inside. I only need to grab my keys and set the alarms. I'm scared that if I go too far inside, the safety net of my four walls will stop me from leaving again, and I need to do this now. I key in the code to arm the alarm and close the door with a confident thud. I will do this. I don't think as I get in my car and start the engine. My head is clear as I use the remote to open the gates at the end of my long drive, but as the wheels hit the main road, I can feel the first tendrils of fear spread through me. I ignore them, pushing the accelerator as I put more distance between me and my haven.

I PUSH the trolley down the chocolate aisle and look at the shelves in front of me. I've been in the small supermarket for longer than I thought I would manage when I first arrived. I've no idea why I haven't done this sooner, I mean it's not like Damien or his goons will follow me into Tesco to kill me. Every step I've taken today has made me feel even stupider than the one before. I've spent too long locked up inside four walls that I thought would keep me safe, and there's been nothing scary on the outside of them. I've built up this whole scenario where people are after me when the truth is that I'm safe here in Scotland. Smiling to myself I continue grabbing things from the shelves, finally able to get the things I want to fill my cupboards with. Getting my groceries delivered meant that I ordered the same old basics, but now I have a chance to look before choosing. It's such a simple thing, but it felt like a mountain climb to get here.

My mobile vibrates in my pocket, and I absently grab it while trying to decide between mint and orange chocolate. I see Grant's name on the screen and answer with a smirk. "What's up?"

There's a rustling noise on the other end of the line before Grant answers. "Hey, how're things?"

"Do you really want to know or do you want to know if I found anything about the emails?" I can hear Grant audibly sigh and I chuckle at the sound. He's easy to wind up, so I try to do it as often as possible. I have very little in my life that gives me joy so I have to take the chance when I can.

"Fuck off. How are you?"

"I'm good actually. Just out doing a little shopping."

I'm met with silence, and I know that I probably just shocked the shit out of Grant. He knows how I feel about being out in public, or having anyone on my property, so this must be a bit of a shock. "Well, that's... huge."

"Tell me about it. Thought that maybe it was time to grow my balls back and finally go explore."

"So you went shopping?" It's now his turn to laugh.

"Small steps, Grant. Teeny, tiny steps."

"I still wish you would tell me who you're hiding from. I could help, you know, return the favour for everything you've done for me."

I bite my lip. Grant has told me before that he knows I'm hiding and wants to help me. I've never given him any information before, but the urge to finally let someone in hits me hard. I wish I could, but I don't want anyone to get hurt because of me. I will keep my secret, not wanting someone's pain on my conscience. "It's all good, nothing I can't handle on my own."

"I know you *can* handle it. I'm just saying you don't *need* to do it on your own."

I stare at the floor as his words find a crack in the wall that surrounds my secret. How I wish I could let him in, to see the darkness that's chasing me, but I won't. I'll stay strong so that Grant will remain safe. "Thanks. There's nothing on the emails yet. I plan to run another search feature this afternoon, and hopefully, that'll give me something to work with."

"I really didn't call about that. I was checking on you."

My chest tightens at his declaration. I didn't have any real friends in my life, but that's what I feel Grant is. He seemed to creep under my cocky attitude and stuck around to get to know the real me. I put up a convincing front, one I constructed after years of bullying at school, and no one usually takes the time to see behind it. I'm not a little guy, but since I'm what people would consider a nerd, I've always been fair game for them to push me around and harass me. It's one of the main reasons I concentrated so much on computers. Online I could be anyone I wanted to be, and the more I taught myself, the more powerful I became. The cocky attitude came after I left school when I made my bullies pay for what they did to me, but it was that attitude that got me into trouble with Damien. I realised far too late that I wasn't untouchable, and life has been shit ever since. "Thank you, but I really am fine."

"Not completely convinced, but I'll let it go for now. Take care, Sam."

"You too." I hang up, and for the first time in a long time, I feel at ease. I don't know if it's that I'm finally out of my self-appointed prison, or if it's having Grant care for me, but whatever it is, I'm happy.

I WATCH the screen as it runs through the programme I constructed to try and find the location of the email sender. It took a while to tweak an older application I had, but since it seems to be working, it was completely worth it. The circle on the map is getting smaller, so hopefully, soon it will point at an area to start looking. It's possible he's using a remote server, but if he is, I'll cross that bridge when I come to it. I'm taking any small step forward as a positive and I will work from anything it gives me.

My vision flickers over to the other screen that's working on something completely different, but just as important. My moment of bravery this afternoon led me to run another search on Damien. I haven't done a manual check on his movements recently, relying entirely on the alerts that I have set up. There are a few hits on his name, but nothing that is causing concern. Most of them show movement within Norway, which is precisely what I would expect since that was his last known location. Still, I track the notifications as they come up.

An alert from my central computer has me pulling my eyes from my own problems and back to the screen working on Grant's investigation. My programme has done what I hoped it would, and it's given me a location of the email fucker. It's not a full address, but it's enough that I can start a search on the street to get information. Twenty minutes later I'm looking at the website for the PI I called the other day and cursed out. I didn't think to search for any information on him earlier, not after Grant had told me that he was Niko's friend who was also looking into the guy. Now I'm hacked into his computer servers and reading every report he has on the suspect. I really should tell this Clay guy how shit his firewall is, but since that would hinder my access, I decide not to bother. His reports are pretty good, giving me information that I'll no longer need to find myself. I copy over his files, my focus going straight to a sketch he has of a possible suspect. I take that too, automatically running through the facial recognition programme that the local police don't know I have access to.

While that runs, I decide to check out this Clay guy who runs the business. I've spoken to him on the phone, or more accurately I've cursed him out, but I didn't see the need to find out who he was. He was just some random guy who was getting in my way, and I needed him to stop. Now curiosity has me searching his name. I get a few hits that can't be him, but when I finally stumble onto the right guy, I stop instantly, my jaw dropping open when I see what he looks like. *Holy shit*. I didn't know men like him existed in real life. The dude is fucking huge, like bigger than anyone I've ever seen huge. Damien and his guys liked to think that they were badasses, but they're nothing compared to this guy. His dark hair is cropped short at the side with a little more length on top. Not enough to be long, but enough to grab hold of while he sucks your cock. *Fuck*. Just that thought has my dick twitching in my jeans.

 I continue my thorough inspection of his body until his piercing eyes draw me in. I can't see the real colour of them in the picture in front of me, but the intensity of his stare oozes out from the computer screen. This is a guy who doesn't ask for respect from people, he demands it. I can't imagine that anyone wouldn't instantly give this man what he wants, and again that thought has my dick trying to get involved in my internal conversation. My dick wants to know what Clay would demand if he was here, and I'm sure that he would be more than willing to give him anything.

 I drag my eyes away from the impressive visual in front of me and start to read the important information. Clay began his business seven years ago and almost instantly became a well-known name in the community. He's worked some pretty impressive cases, but nothing too high profile that he's become publicly known. He seems to keep himself on a pretty low profile, which I suppose is a good thing for a private investigator. There would be nothing worse than your mark knowing who you are. There's more of the usual information about him, but my attention is soon pulled back to the picture. I'm glad I didn't know what he looked like before I called him or I probably wouldn't have done it. I'm not usually easily intimidated by a pretty face, but this guy looks like he's much more than that. He's intense and powerful, and really fucking gorgeous. Yeah, there's no easy way to get past that fact.

 I close down the window with Clay's picture because there's no way in hell I'll be able to get any work done while his eyes are staring at me. No, it's better if I forget about how the guy looks, well, maybe just until bedtime tonight. That's another thing I decided today while I was changing my life. I'm actually going to use my bed to sleep in, no more falling asleep on my computer chair or the couch in the living room. I have a perfectly good bed in my room, and I have no reason not to use it to get a good nights sleep. I have no open cases that need my attention, well apart from Grant's one, so I can safely take some time away to get a full nights sleep for a change. Today's been the day for stopping all the shit in my head that's trying to drown me. I've already proven to myself that it's safe to leave my property, so sleeping in an actual bed shouldn't be such a big step.

All my good intentions are derailed when an alert comes through on Damien, and I read the notification that tells me he was seen on a security camera in London. He's back in the country, and I'm not sure how that's possible when he hasn't flown back. I'm instantly typing away on my keyboard searching through all the recent flight manifests for Damien's passport number, but I'm right, there's nothing that shows he got on a plane. A sudden thought hits me, and I spin in my chair to check over the outgoing flight information I have on him. I bring up the passenger information and search the airport security log for the day he flew. When I get the screenshot of Damien as he passes through security, I instantly feel sick. I didn't think to check this, and now my mistake is going to bite me on the arse. The man in the picture looks like Damien, like almost identical, but I know it isn't him. I spent far too long looking at his face to see one glaring difference. About a month before I left his property, he was attacked when he went to do a business deal. The altercation left him with a scar that ran from the corner of his eye down to his mouth. It was thick and pronounced, but since it probably wouldn't be on his passport photo, the security officer wouldn't know to question him about it being missing.

Shit. Damien never left the country, and now he's a ghost, just like me.

10
Clay

I SWEAR the rain starts as soon as I cross the border into Scotland. It's not heavy, but after the heat of the last few hours driving, it's a huge change. The windscreen wipers move slowly keeping my vision clear, the rubber squeaking quietly as the window dries. I turn the music up slightly to block the noise, my fingers tapping as I listen to Imagine Dragons. I hadn't planned on making the drive to see Niko, but Gabe mentioned it a few days ago, and the suggestion stayed with me until not making the journey felt wrong.

Thankfully Margaret was only too happy to take an extra few days off before heading back into the office to hold down the fort. Since there are no currently active cases, she'll only have to field new requests, and she can do that in her sleep. I swear that woman was made to be my assistant. She can deal with clients like a pro, but she can also cope with me, and that shit isn't easy. I'm a fucker to work with, and I'm not ashamed to admit that. Margaret doesn't think twice about calling me out on it though, and I think I respect her more for it. There are very few people who're willing to go against me, and the ones who do are the ones I will trust with my life. Gabe, Niko, Margaret, and more recently Porter, are the only people who have the balls to tell me I'm being an idiot, and are able to take the wrath of doing it. None of them cower down when my anger takes over, meeting me toe to toe with their own.

This thought leads me straight to Sam, the little fucker who called me out before hanging up on me. I don't know who the hell he thinks he is, but he didn't think twice about ripping me a new one. He's been stuck in my head since his call because I suddenly want to meet him so I can punch him in the face. I need to talk to Niko about the little shit, possibly find out where he lives so I can pay him a visit.

My phone rings over the hands-free and I answer it with the button on my steering wheel. "Hello?"

"Hey, boss. You okay to speak?"

"Yeah. What's up?"

I left Porter to work with his contact in the police to try to get an identity on our suspect. He hadn't heard anything when I checked in earlier, but hopefully, this is some good news. "I have a few mug shots I'm going to send you. There isn't one person that fits the description perfectly, so I have taken the closest few to see if Niko recognises any of them."

It's more than we had this morning so I'm willing to accept any sort of lifeline. "Fantastic. Did you get anything from the fingerprints?"

"That was a dead-end. Whoever's doing this doesn't have a record."

It was a lot to ask, but I'd held a little bit of hope that it would go in our favour. Wrong again. "Would have been nice, but I'm not shocked. Just send me what you have, and I'll get on it as soon as I arrive at Niko's."

"No problem. Drive safe, boss."

I hang up, and music fills my truck again. Part of me wants to pull in and check my messages from Porter to see the photos he sent, but it won't make any difference right now. Niko's life has been so secretive these last few years that I don't know anyone he has come up against. I wouldn't even know what Corey looked like if it wasn't for the photos we found taped to the wall in that room. I managed to see enough to positively identify Corey in the future before Niko destroyed everything. No, the only person who might be able to identify the suspect from the mug shots is Niko, so the sooner I get to him the better.

AFTER CHECKING myself into the only guesthouse within a fifty-mile radius of Niko's cabin, I call him to tell him that I've arrived. It's late afternoon, but he agrees to meet me in the local coffee shop. I don't know why he doesn't want me at the house, but I'm not going to question him about it. This is his shit show, so he gets to run it. Now I'm sitting here waiting on him to arrive in a cafe that sells pretty good coffee, but it's also full of other stuff. There are bookcases of books along the walls, making it look a little like a library, but there is also the café area and a row of computers. It looks like one of the Internet cafes that were on every corner a few years ago, but apparently, this village didn't get the memo that they're no longer in fashion. Not that I think that's the look they're going for, I think it's more to do with function than anything. There are barely any shops in this little place, so this café covers a lot of services, including a post office and local coffee shop.

The bell over the door goes, and I see Niko look around the café. When he sees me, he heads in my direction. I chose the table in the back corner since I don't want anyone to overhear what we're talking about. When he reaches me, he pulls me from my seat, his arms wrapping around me for a brief hug.

"Good to see you, brother. I didn't expect you to travel this far to help."

I glare at him. "Liar. You know I'd travel anywhere to help. I can investigate just as easily here, and then I'm on hand in case you need me."

His smile looks relaxed, which is a massive difference from the last time I saw him. A waitress approaches, and we both order a coffee, waiting until she's gone to start speaking. It's actually Niko that starts, his relaxed demeanour vanishing as he talks. "Did you find anything important? Is that why you're here?"

I do have things to show him, but I don't want to jump straight into business talk. Since Niko reappeared in my life, I haven't really had a chance to speak to him. The whole time has been taken up by protecting Corey, which I'm totally okay with, but I want to chat with my friend. "I have a few mug shots, but nothing that's pressing. I just thought I would come to catch up. You were gone for a fucking long time, my friend. I want to know where you were."

The waitress returns with our coffees but leaves quickly. "I was working."

"No shit. What were you doing? How did you meet Corey?"

Niko looks nervous, like he isn't going to tell me anything, but a few minutes later he starts his tale. "I was working for a guy called Ryden. He was running a ... let's just call it an escort agency."

"It was a prostitution ring." Niko doesn't seem shocked that I know about Blue Diamond. He actually looks relieved that he doesn't need to go into too much detail.

"Yeah, it was. It's not as bad as it sounds though."

I raise my eyebrows at his comment. I'm not sure how he can defend his job and what he was involved with, but he's my friend, and I will let him speak before I fully judge.

"It wasn't. The guy's knew what they were signing up for. They were looked after, and most of them had a better life in the business than they did before. We looked after them, made sure they were safe."

"You trying to tell me no one got hurt?"

Niko bites his lip while spinning his coffee mug. It isn't a positive reaction, and that in itself gives me the answer I was looking for. Still, I give him the benefit of the doubt and listen to his response. "We lost a few boys, but it wasn't us. Some customers got overzealous, and we weren't quick enough to save them. We didn't want to lose them, we did everything we could to get to them. Ryden made sure that he protected them."

"Why did you leave?" This is one of the main questions I've wanted to ask. I had a suspicion about what Niko did for Blue Diamond, so nothing he's said has surprised me, but the whole company just vanished. I can't work out what happened, and my mind always goes to the worst-case scenario.

"Ryden closed the company and vanished. He called the police and gave them the location of the compound. He let them rescue everyone."

"But why?"

Niko smiles and shrugs his shoulders. "He fell in love."

My mouth drops open at the reason behind a criminal mastermind giving up everything. I know that Gabe went to prison because he fell in love, and now Niko is putting his life on the line to protect his man, but a criminal giving up his power for love? I didn't see that coming. "Seriously?"

"Seriously. He took the wrong man, and it spelled the end for Ryden and the life he knew."

Okay, now I'm confused. "Please explain."

"He fell in love with a policeman who was working undercover trying to bring down his company."

My mouth is still slack as I listen. I never once imagined that two people could fall in love in such a fucked up situation. I'm the biggest sceptic when it comes to love, but I believe that it can happen if the people are meant to be. But a cop and the man he's trying to bring down? Shit, never saw that coming. "That's fucking crazy. How could he trust him once he found out about his lies?"

Niko gets a funny look on his face, like he's upset at the question. "Drake was the guy he was meant to find. Sometimes love hits you when you aren't looking for it. It isn't always as straightforward as you think."

"Love is never straightforward, mate. Love brings people to their fucking knees and makes them weak." I've seen too many people being destroyed because they fell in love, and even though Gabe and Niko appear to have found their soul mates, I can't believe that they will live happily ever after. I wish them all the luck in the world, but I'll also be here for them when it all goes to shit.

"You're wrong. It doesn't make you weak, it makes you strong. Meeting Corey changed my life. He makes me want to be a better man, makes me want to spend the rest of my life making him smile."

"And you're saying there's not another guy out there that you're meant to be with. No other man who you might need to make you whole?"

Niko drops his eyes from mine and stares at the table. He's taking too long to answer, and I wonder what the hell I just made him think about.

"It wasn't meant to be a trick question, Niko."

His mouth opens to speak just as his mobile rings. He answers it after a few rings and has a conversation with the person on the other side. I think it might be Corey, but I'm confused when Niko growls and tell him not to let Grant leave. Niko hangs up and is instantly on his feet. "I'm sorry, I need to go. I'll call you in the morning and let you know what's happening." He starts to walk away, and I follow him after leaving some money on the table to pay for the coffees.

I'm outside by the time I catch up, grabbing him by the arm and spinning him towards me. "Is everything okay? What the fuck is happening?"

"It's fine. I'll explain later, but there's no danger here. This is... personal." He nods briefly before slipping his arm from my hold and vanishing across the street and into his car.

I'm left standing on the pavement watching him driving away, wondering what the fuck just happened.

I FOLLOW the satnav as it leads me up a narrow dirt track. I would've driven past the road if it hadn't been for the directions as it's well hidden behind some bushes and trees. The overgrown edges of the track make it look like no one's been here in a while, and that makes me feel more confident for Niko and Corey's safety. I still take my time as I drive along it, taking in the surrounding areas and making a mental note of the layout. Trees surround the whole area, which is both a blessing and a curse. The foliage gives fantastic cover for us if we need it, but on the downside, it also provides other people coverage if they're hiding and watching.

The road soon opens up into a drive area that holds a few cars, one of them I recognise as Niko's BMW. I scan the area ahead of me quickly before turning my eyes back to the cabin. It isn't huge, but it has a homely feel to it, which is nice. It reminds me of the cabins I would go to on holiday with my family when I was younger, and there's one I remember vividly. I think it was the last holiday we went on as a family before the shit hit the fan and our world broke apart. It was a cabin near York, and it was a magical place. I'd spent my days searching the forest for animals and hidden secrets, and at night we sat as a family around a small campfire and told stories. It was the perfect holiday, and the last time I ever went away with Cameron.

Pushing those thoughts from my mind, I get out my truck and head up to the front door. I knock but keep my head moving, scanning the area in front of me. There's a large open area that helps to prevent people from sneaking up to the cabin, but the tree line is thick and full of shadows. I need to get people out here to keep an eye on things and set up a proper perimeter. I'm just wondering if I could get Porter and Joseph to drive up to take care of security when the door opens behind me, pulling me from my musings. I turn fully expecting to see Niko standing in front of me, or possibly even Corey, but there's someone I don't recognise standing there, and it makes me wonder if I have the wrong place. No, I know it's the right place because Niko's car is in the driveway.

"Can I help you?"

I stare at the guy in front of me, letting my eyes scan over him as I try to work out who the hell he is. He isn't as tall as me, and his build is a lot slimmer, not that he looks skinny though, and going by the muscles on his arms he could probably hold his own for a while in a fight. "Where's Niko?"

The guy blinks slowly but doesn't move, or answer me and that's beyond frustrating.

"Seriously. Where's Niko?"

"I asked you who you were?"

I should be happy that this guy is questioning me without telling me anything about Niko, but again I'm a step behind, and it's starting to piss me off. "I'm Clay, and I want Niko."

My name sparks recognition in the guy's eyes so at least I now know he's a friend. "Wait here."

"Seriously? You could just let me in instead of being a fucking idiot." The guy doesn't let my outburst faze him, and I can't help it when the edge of my mouth quirks up into a smile. "But I approve of you keeping me out here. Tell Niko to get his ugly arse outside or I'm gonna put a knife through all the tyres on his beemer."

Unknown guy nods before shutting the door on me, leaving me standing there pretending to fume, even though I'm perfectly content now that I know that Niko's surrounded by people with a level head.

The door opens a few moments later, and I'm met with Niko who's glaring holes into me. "You honestly threatened my wheels?"

"Anything to get you to move your arse. I wasn't sure if the butler would pass on my message."

Niko burst out laughing at my comment before giving me a brief man hug. "You're such an arsehole." He turns to pop his head back inside the cabin. "You two come meet Clay." He watches as two guys approach. One I recognise as Corey, and the other was the guy who answered the door.

I watch them as they come to a stop in front of me, my attention entirely on the fact that the two of them are holding hands. Not a strange thing, apart from the fact that Corey is Niko's boyfriend.

"Clay, this is my boyfriend, Corey. And you've already met Grant."

I look between the three men, and I can sense something is going on between them. It's like there's an invisible connection that binds them all, and it's evident in the way they look at each other. Corey and Grant may have been the ones holding hands, but Niko's eyes drink in everything about both men, and it leaves me wondering what the fuck is going on here.

Niko smiles at Grant, his whole face softening when Grant smiles back, and that's when the obvious answer hits me. These three guys are fucking. Okay, maybe not the three of them, but Niko is definitely fucking Grant. I get even more confused when Niko leans in and kisses Corey on the forehead, his eyes never leaving Grant as his lips connect. "I'm going to the office with Clay. I won't be long."

Both men nod as we walk past them and into Niko's office. I stay quiet as I take a seat across from Niko, my mind going crazy with all the information it's trying to process. There is so much I want to say, so much I want to ask.

"Spill it."

I just stare at Niko wondering where the fuck I start. I came to show him the mug shots from last night, but now the only thing I can focus on is the apparent relationship between him and the other two men. I run my tongue over the front of my teeth as I try to work out what the hell to say.

"Come on, Clay, don't leave me in suspense."

"Shut up. I'm just thinking where to start. There is so much I want to know, and I think I should find that out before we talk shop."

Niko glares at me, apparently oblivious to what's actually going through my head. "Don't make me hurt you."

This makes me laugh because there would be no way that Niko would ever beat me in a fight. "Please. Like that would ever happen."

Niko rubs his temples as his frustrations start to show. He wants me to hurry up and talk to him, but I'm not sure how he will react when I finally ask the burning question I have. "I'm getting old sitting here, Clay. For the love of fucking god spit it out."

Fine fucker, if you really want to know. "How are you getting away with fucking both guys?"

11

Sam

I PURPOSELY IGNORE the new alert that's come up about Damien's whereabouts. I made the decision the other day not to allow myself to be ruled by my fear, and I refuse to give in so quickly. Damien hasn't actually moved far from London, possibly hiding until he knows there's no one after him, so I'm determined not to obsess over him. Finding out that he'd never left the country shocked me to my core, but once I looked into it deeper, it was apparent that he wasn't becoming a ghost completely, not recently anyway. I think he just wants the authorities to believe he's out of the country, so that shows me that there maybe is some heat following him after all.

Pulling my attention back to the file that's open on the screen in front of me, I smile when I see Marc holding his new baby sister. There are very few things in my life that I'm proud of, but Marc is the one glowing beacon that tells me I did something right. Knowing that he has a fantastic life makes everything I'm going through worth it. Marc was the petrified little boy I found cowering in Damien's office, waiting to be sold to the highest bidder. It's the first time I'd seen anything like that from Damien, but it was enough to change everything. I knew that I needed to get Marc out of there, and I did it. He's now safely back with his parents, and thankfully, has very little memory of what happened. I'd been horrified when I found out he had been drugged, but I realised it was actually a blessing when he reported to the police he only remembered missing his mum. It all worked out okay in the end, and seeing him smile is all the reward I need.

Closing down all the open windows on my monitors, I get up from my desk. I've fallen quickly back into old habits, and it's frustrating as hell that I have. I was determined to get out daily to take a walk and enjoy the weather, but I've been hiding inside again. I need to change that, but first I need some liquid courage. I take a detour through the kitchen to grab a Redbull. The sugar and caffeine hit should settle my nerves, so I drink a whole can before putting the can in the recycling. Once I can no longer put off going outside, I saunter to the front of the house, stepping out onto the small porch into the sunshine. The weather hasn't been great recently, the rain causing some massive flooding in the river that runs along the edge of my driveway, but today seems perfect. I love it when the sun is shining, and the temperature isn't too high. My pale skin doesn't lead to me being a natural sun worshipper, making me want to hide out, so I don't get too many freckles over my nose. I have spent my life looking younger than my twenty-seven years, but when I get a face full of freckles, I look even younger, and not in a cute way.

A car engine pulls my attention to the double gates that block the road to my cabin. My heart starts racing, and everything screams at me to get inside, but only a few minutes ago I was telling myself to not fall back into being scared. I force myself to stand my ground and watch as the car stops, the engine turning off before the driver's door opens. A huff of relief escapes as I see Kelly getting out of the car. The comfort is very short lived when I see his smile even at this distance. This isn't going to go well. Kelly leans on the gate as I slowly approach, practising in my head a way to get out of this whole conversation. Can I fake a phone call? Maybe I could have if I actually had my mobile on me, but it's sitting on the desk in my office.

"Hey, good looking."

I hold in the groan that's building, but only just. "Hey."

Kelly leans his arms on the top of the gate, his eyes drifting down over my body. I shouldn't have slept with him. I should have just kept him as an acquaintance, even a friend, but I had to go ruin it by going there. It was a stupid fucking mistake and one that is going to bite me in the arse now. "How're things? I haven't seen you in a while."

"Good. Just been busy, you know how it is." In my head, I'm screaming at him to leave. I just need him to get in his car and drive away. Nothing good can come from him being here, and I'm certainly not revisiting the mistake I've already made.

"Oh, right. So ... um... I was wondering-"

An alarm goes off inside the cabin and I nearly fist pump the air at its timing. It gives me the perfect excuse to interrupt what he was about to say because I have a feeling that he was about to ask for a repeat of what we did. "Sorry, I need to go check on that." I back up from the gate but keep my eyes trained on Kelly. I wish he would take the hint and leave, but he continues to watch me.

"Is everything okay?"

"Yeah, just work calling. See you around." I finally turn my back on him, but I can sense him standing there staring at me. I'm really fucking glad my gates are locked because I'm pretty sure that Kelly wouldn't think twice about following me up the dirt driveway.

I quickly slip inside my front door and lock it securely behind me, arming the perimeter alarm just to make myself feel better. Kelly's not a danger to me physically, but he is a danger to my peace and quiet. The last thing I need is for him to push for something I'm not willing to give him. I force myself not to watch the security cameras to make sure he leaves, instead moving into my office to silence the alarm. It's louder than is technically needed, but I set it up that way so I can hear it wherever I am, awake or asleep. Sometimes I leave my computers searching for stuff while I'm sleeping or eating, so I never want to miss things they find.

I sit and start typing, turning the alarm off and leaving the room in silence. My eyes scan over what's been highlighted, finally stopping when a picture appears on the screen. I've been running facial recognition over the Internet since the police network gave me nothing. This picture is from a missing person post in a lower level chatroom, and it was from nearly six years before. I click on the post, reading over how this guy's brother had gone missing and he was looking for him, and he was willing to pay for any information. I copy the photo on the post but don't see the connection to it that my programme obviously found. I suppose if I squint they might look a little similar.

Nothing else on the advert seems relevant, so I spend the next hour tracing the person who posted it all those years before. *Daniel Gallagher.* The name means nothing to me, but I keep searching just in case it's helpful to Grant and his new friends. There's not much to find on the guy, and that in itself is telling. He posted a shit ton of stuff around the time his brother went missing. There are pleas for help and rants about what he was going to do when he found the person that hurt David, the guy he named as his sibling, but suddenly it all stops. After that there are only a few things on him, but nothing that would set alarms going. He paid his bills and went to work on a daily basis like a good little taxpayer. I'm about to stop the search when his online buying history suddenly takes a turn. Where he wouldn't buy anything out of the ordinary, he suddenly starts purchasing an arsenal of equipment. So he either decided to get into the BDSM game, or he's preparing for something. Rope and handcuffs, actually restraints of every kind, along with a selection of drugs that could knock a horse out. Digging a little deeper shows me the path to a hidden website, one that would give any serial killer a boner.

These operations think they're slick. They've put up all these barriers that they believe hide them from the typical online user, and I suppose they do. For me though, their safeguards are nothing more than a distraction for a few minutes. Before I have a chance to focus my full skill on the problem I'm in, my eyes widen in shock. I've seen a lot of depraved websites in my life, and I've taken more than my share of them offline, but this is more than I've ever witnessed. It's like a perverts safe place, and I vow to make it vanish once I've got the information I need. Page after page of instructions and recommendations for getting as much fun from hurting people as possible. From the best knives to use, to what chemicals to add to the skin to make people scream. It's all there on the screen with people liking and approving of that shit.

My stomach revolts when I open up a picture and realise very quickly what a mistake I just made. Reading about this stuff is terrible, but to see the evidence of what they're doing goes beyond what I can handle. Concentrating on Daniel's screen name, I only open things he's commented on, carefully reading just his words so that I don't accidentally read something I'll never be able to forget. I'm not far into my mission when I realise that this Daniel is his own kind of twisted. He doesn't seem to get the same sexual satisfaction out of what he's learning as some of the other evil bastards, but he's fully invested in hurting someone in the worst way. The thing is I don't know what to do with all this information. I don't want to go to Grant with it because it doesn't really help him with his search. This guy might be the one sending the emails to Niko, but he might not be, and all it will do is stress Grant out more and I don't want that.

My eyes flicker over to the notepad where I've written the information on someone else who is a stranger. Someone I actually stole some of this information from. *Clay.* I could send him everything I've found, but if I do, then he'll know I was in his computer. Is it worth the risk of admitting what I took from him to give him something that might help? I'm not sure, so I'll keep searching, and if I feel there's anything that screams a direct threat, I'll let him know. Until then I will just keep searching.

LEANING BACK against my car I watch the numbers change as the fuel gauge counts up. I've been getting out and about more recently, so I finally had to fill my car with petrol. It's only maybe the fourth time since I arrived here that I've needed to fill it, but I feel that this is a little win. I wanted to get out more, and this is proof that I've done just that. Now if I could build up the courage to actually leave the town, then I would feel more empowered. Small steps, Sam. Teeny, tiny, baby steps.

"I thought it was you."

I yell as I jump away from my car, coming face to face with Kelly. Fuck me, is this guy following me? I plaster a fake smile on my face and try to calm my racing heart. Kelly doesn't scare me, but his presence does make me feel really fucking awkward. "Oh, hi."

Kelly walks around my car, and I step back to keep the petrol pump between us. "How have you been?"

I'm getting really sick of that question from him, but I smile and shrug my shoulder. "Good. Busy." It feels like the conversation we had the other day, and I have nothing new to say to him.

"You haven't been ordering your groceries for delivery. I thought I might have seen you." He smiles, and his eyes sparkle, telling me exactly what he was hoping.

Shit. I need to learn to keep my dick in my pants. For the first time in well over a year, I finally sleep with someone, and I choose the one guy who won't accept that it was only a one-time thing. "Nah, trying to get out more. New me and all that."

Kelly takes a step closer, and it takes everything in me not to step back to keep the distance between us. "I like the old you."

The fuel pump clicks in my hand, and I thank the Lord for giving me a reasonable excuse to look away from Kelly. He's starting to push, and I don't like it. I never once promised him anything other than a fuck, but he's looking for something more than that. I return the nozzle and take my time closing up the fuel cap, hoping that Kelly will get bored being ignored. Apparently, my good luck hasn't kicked in because when I turn around, he's still standing watching me.

"So, do you have plans for the rest of the day?"

God this is it, this is the moment I'm going to have to tell Kelly that he needs to back the fuck off. "Work is hectic, so I need to go straight home to get on with it before I fall behind." Okay, so I'm officially a chicken shit.

"I could give you a hand?"

I take a deep breath, bracing myself for the conversation I'm going to need to have. He won't even listen to my excuses, so I can't put off being a dick any longer. "Look, Kelly. I know that we did a thing, but-"

His eyes go wide before I have a chance to finish my sentence and he finally puts some space between us. "No. Um, I'm sorry. I just thought ... shit." He doesn't say anything else before he spins and almost sprints away from me. He's muttering, and I swear I hear him say something about not doing his job correctly, but since I have no idea what he's talking about I just put it down to the embarrassed rambling from him.

I continue to watch him as he gets in his car and drives away, his focus never coming back to look at me. No part of me feels good about what I just did, not that I really did anything. I didn't have to fully spell out what I was about to, but he knew. Maybe he's smarter than I thought. I just wish he'd gotten the hint before I had to do this. Never once has the urge for a blowjob ended in such an epic failure. Actually, that is a huge fucking lie. Fat raindrops hit the top of my head, and I rush around to the driver's side of my car, thankful for the pay at the pump function. Especially when the heavens open barely a second later, soaking everything in a matter of moments. There're no other cars in the small petrol station, so I sit for a few moments and let my mind drift to the last time my sexual urges had nearly ended in disaster. It should make me cringe, but a smile crosses my lips at the memory.

"Dude, seriously. If you suck it any harder it's gonna come off in your mouth." My hoover mouthed date looks up at me from his position at my feet, and the glint in his eyes tells me that he's taking what I just said as a compliment, not the warning I'd intended. My thoughts are proven right when he closes his eyes and goes right back to sucking ... really fucking hard.

I close my eyes and try to focus on the little bit of pleasure he's giving me, but when his teeth come into contact with my dick, I can't concentrate on anything but that. My body goes tight and ...the guy —shit, what was his name again? – purrs around my cock. The only problem is its fear that has my body tensing, not the pleasure he's trying to give me. My eyes scrunch close as I repeat to myself to relax, to let the guy give me the release that I so desperately need, but when his teeth catch the edge of my tip, I know it's pointless. I actually feel myself starting to wilt in his mouth, but instead of him noticing and asking what's wrong, he starts sucking harder, his teeth scraping more.

Reaching down I grab his hair, pulling on it as I try to ease myself from his mouth. It's now that he doubles down his efforts and it elicits a scream from my throat. This finally stops —I really need to remember his name- him, and he looks up at me, and that's the first time I notice that the saliva running down his chin is tinged with red. Reaching out I wipe it from his skin and bring it closer to my face. I want to make sure what I'm looking at is real and not just the shadows from the dark room. Nope, that's blood. Whatever his name is stands up, brushing his erection into my now very flaccid cock.

"Why did you stop me?"

My eyes go straight to his mouth because I want to inspect that fucker to see if he has a bleeding gum or cut lip. If he doesn't that means it's my cock that's bleeding, and I'm not sure I will be able to keep calm if it is. I try to feel anything that might be wrong with my dick, but I swear the thing is numb. I can barely feel the pressure of the guy's erection against it, even though he's trying really hard to come from just rubbing off. "There's blood." I hold my fingers up in front of the dude's face, and he scrunches up his eyes as he stares at them.

"It's only a little."

Four words are all it takes for my dick to pretty much hide inside my body. I gently push whatever the fuck his name is away by the shoulder and reach down to tuck my scared cock inside my jeans. This night hasn't gone the way I wanted, and I should have just walked away when I turned up and saw the guy standing outside his house. He said he couldn't have sex inside because the spirits weren't feeling it, then he led me towards this shed at the back of his garden. I should have just gone home, but I thought I didn't need the guy to be sane to get good head. It's been weeks since I came with something other than my own hand and that's led me here, with a bleeding cock and a guy that doesn't look bothered by the fact.

"You're leaving?" He's shocked, and that only shocks me more. Who would think that blood after a blowjob was a good thing?

"Uh, yeah. It's been...fun?"

He pushes against me again, his lips brushing against my ear as he speaks with a growl. "But you didn't come. I want to eat you all."

That was when I pretty much ran screaming from the guy's property. I ran like the hounds of hell were chasing me, only stopping once I reached my car and locked the door behind me.

Okay, so compared to that this whole clusterfuck with Kelly isn't that bad, but I still should have kept it in my pants. As I start my car, I vow that I won't be having sex with anyone for a long time, especially with someone I need to see on a regular basis.

12

Sam

"Whatsup?" I expect many possible answers from Grant. A sigh, sarcasm, even a pissed off rant about using that word he hates more than anything, but what I get is very different.

His voice is tight, and if I didn't know better, I'd say he's been crying. "I need somewhere to stay."

I get up from my computer and leave my office, giving Grant my full attention like he deserves. My worry is off the charts, especially since I know that Niko is aware of who Grant is. "What happened?"

"I can't, Sam. Not just now. I just need somewhere to stay."

I don't even think twice before I speak. "Come here. Do you have a way to get here?" The last time I talked to Grant, I felt that something more was happening, but he'd assured me that there was nothing wrong. Now he's leaving his only link to Drake, and that can only mean that something huge is wrong with this picture.

"I can get to you, but it will take a few hours."

"I'll be here. You know that."

"Thanks, Sam." He hangs up, and I stare at my phone for a few minutes.

This will be the first time in nearly four years that I've seen Grant, and I wish it were under better circumstances. It's not though, and I need to get shit sorted, so he feels welcome. It takes longer than I'd have thought to get my spare room sorted out, but by the time there is a knock on my door, it looks liveable. It couldn't be classed as five-star accommodation, but there's a bed and a place to keep some clothes.

The second knock has me rushing to the door, and when I answer it, Grant is standing there in the flesh. Holy crap, he looks like shit. It's obvious he's been crying and is struggling not to now, and the urge to hug him hits me hard. I haven't been physical with anyone that I wasn't fucking for a long time, but tonight, with Grant, I just want to make him feel better. Without giving it another thought, I step forward and engulf him in a bone-crushing hug. He stills for a moment before he wraps his arms around me, his body shaking as he gives in to the tears he was trying to keep at bay. I don't know how long we stand there just holding each other, but it's Grant that pulls back first.

"Sorry. I was trying not to be a lunatic when I first saw you."

"Shut up and get in here." I step back, and Grant enters, his eyes flitting around the living room as I take the huge bag he has over his shoulder. He staggers slightly, and it's the first time it registers that Grant smells of vodka. "Please tell me you didn't drive here drunk."

Grants eyes are glazed over, but he shakes his head, finally making me relax. "I've been outside for a while."

I want to take him through to the kitchen and sober him up, ask him what happened and why he's here, but I think the best place for him is in bed. He needs to sleep some of his aches away. "Good, because I would hate to have to punch some sense into you."

This gets a laugh from Grant, and I lead the way down the hall to the spare room. "Do you want to get cleaned up before sleeping?"

Grants stricken eyes meet mine, and I feel the pain bleed from inside him. "Forget that. Come on, bud. Let's get you to bed." He lets me lead him to the mattress where he collapses, muttering shit about being alone and stupid. I watch him for a few minutes, not surprised when he falls asleep almost instantly. He'll probably have a shitty hangover when he wakes up later, but going by the way he looked when he arrived, that will be the least of his worries.

I HEAR Grant before I see him, his groan meeting my ears before he enters the kitchen. It's nearly four in the afternoon, and it's the first time I've seen him since he arrived early this morning. I had a suspicion that his hangover would be epic today, but from the sound of things, it's worse than I imagined. "Afternoon, sunshine."

"Meh."

I laugh at his response and pour him a cup of coffee, putting it on the table in front of him. Grant grabs it quickly and drinks nearly the whole cup. "Regretting getting drunk?"

"Regretting being sober."

I tilt my head as I stare at him. The pain isn't gone from his eyes, and I realise that his sleep hasn't helped him as much as I thought it might. Sober isn't helping Grant, but maybe I can help with that. "Okay, let's get drunk."

Grant smiles at my suggestion. "That sounds like a great fucking idea."

Getting up from my chair I start a search in the cupboard to try and locate some sort of alcohol. I don't drink much so I'm not sure what's there, but I'm sure I'll find something. I push a few cases of Redbull away from the front of my bottom cupboard, and I instantly see the bottle of tequila sitting at the back. I'm not sure where I got it or how long it's been there, but it seems to be calling out my name. I grab it and hold it up in front of Grant. "I don't have lemon or salt, but will this do?"

"Anything will do. Seriously, I just want to forget this week."

And with that, I grab two shot glasses before we head out to the porch. It doesn't take too many shots to get Grant talking, and when he does my heart aches for him all over again.

"I didn't want to fall for them, but it was so easy. I just wish I'd realised what a stupid fucking mistake I was making." He downs the tequila in his glass before refilling it, instantly downing that one too.

"So it was more than just a *holy shit two men are sucking my cock* thing?"

This earns me a glare from Grant, and I hold back the laughter that's threatening to escape. Things are getting heavy, and I want to make Grant feel better, and the only way I know how to do that is with inappropriate questions.

"Yeah, it was. I thought I was special. I thought that maybe I was part of their relationship." Tears build in his eyes again, and I want to hug him. He's been fighting them for a good hour now, and nothing I've said has made him feel better.

"But I don't understand what happened. What made you leave?"

"Nothing specific."

I fill his glass as he tries to avoid my stare. "Liar."

"How would you know?"

"I've spoken to you enough to know when you are talking shit, Grant. I know you better than you want to admit, and I'm calling bullshit right now."

He slams his glass on the table after emptying it, his eyes still not meeting mine. "You don't know a fucking thing. This isn't some online shit that you think you're an expert about. This is real life. Grown-up feelings and everything."

If I didn't know that Grant was hurting, I would take his words as a personal attack, but since I can see his heart is breaking, I take them as they're meant. A distraction from his pain. "Wow. Like real feelings? I'm not sure what they are, but you might want to talk slowly, so I understand."

This gets Grant looking at me, shame added to the pain that was there a minute before. "Sorry." He scrubs his hand over his face and leans forward, his elbows leaning on the table in front of him. "I'm being a dick."

"You are, but I forgive you since you're pretty to look at. Now, want to tell me what happened?"

"Not really." He looks at me hopefully, but I wait patiently for him to speak. "Fuck. Fine, but know I'm doing this under protest." Another shot. "The emails I've had you tracing are being sent to Niko. He's worried about Corey, and so am I. Shit hit the fan the other night, and Corey went missing"

"Went missing?"

"Was taken by someone."

Holy shit. Suddenly I have the urge to get on my computer to try and help with the search, but I know that Grant needs me more. There's very little I can do on my computer that the men around Niko can't do since they can physically search for him. That doesn't answer the one important question though. "So if Corey is missing, why the fuck are you here? Why aren't you helping to find him?"

Grant looks down at the table and rubs his nail over the wood grain. "He doesn't need me. Niko will find him. He's all Corey needs." The pain is back in his voice, making me push him more to get him to open up.

"You just left?"

Grant grabs the bottle from the table and swallows deeply from it. He hisses, and I can just imagine the burn he's feeling. "I had to."

"Why?"

"Because Niko said I was a mistake." I expected him to scream at me, but I barely hear him.

"Shit." It's the only response I can give him because I can only imagine how much that fucking hurt. To fall for someone only to be told that being with you was a mistake. Yeah, that shit must sting.

"Exactly. Not really something that makes you want to hang around. The last thing Niko needs is to look at me while he's dealing with finding Corey. He doesn't need that stress."

Grant might be saying the words, he might even believe them, but I can tell they are cutting him deep. This is why I don't do relationships. Well, this and the fact that I've never met anyone I wanted anything more than a quick fuck with. I don't think there's a man out there that I can see myself settling down with, and with my past, I suppose that's a good thing.

"I'm really fucking sorry, Grant. I don't even know how to help you just now."

"Just let me drink the rest of this bottle, and that will go a long way to help."

I knock my glass against the neck of the bottle and smile at Grant. "That I can do."

"I'M HEADING OUT FOR A RUN." Grant is standing just inside my office door putting his earphones in.

"I'll be here when you get back."

He nods and disappears. I'm still worried about Grant, but at least he's sober now. He spent far too long trying to drown his sorrows in a bottle, but he's now spending his time running. At least this crutch is better for his liver.

Ignoring my need to fix Grant, I focus on the screen in front of me. I've been working hard on Niko's emails since Grant arrived. Knowing that Corey's missing is fucking with my head. I don't know either of the men who Grant was involved with, but I can see how much they mean to him. Hearing Grant talking about them, seeing how much he feels for them, it makes them seem more real, and it makes the need for information more critical.

An alarm sounds and I roll my eyes, knowing exactly what it is without looking. I open up the email and see that Niko's trying to sign into his email account again. When will these guys just fucking stop? I've had enough, so I dial the number for Niko that Grant gave me in the beginning, listening to it ring a few times before it's answered. I don't give Niko a chance to speak before I let my frustrations out. "Stop trying to get into the fucking email account!"

"What?

I roll my eyes, wondering how Grant thought this was the guy who could find Corey on his own. "I said stop trying to get into the email. What part of don't sign in did you not understand? When there is something I want you to see I will let you know. Fuck, all you tough guys are the same. There's a reason I changed the password. Stay the fuck out." Okay, so maybe I've let some of my Grant frustrations come out on Niko. He's hurt my friend, and I don't like to see him like that, but I'm honestly getting sick of him and Clay getting in the way. Clay has spent the last three days trying to get into the email account, even though I sent him a message to tell him to stop. He might be big and hot, but he has no idea what he's doing so he needs to back off. Now Niko is trying my patience, and even though I understand his need to do something to help, he's getting in my way.

Thankfully there isn't a new alarm, so Niko has apparently taken my phone call seriously. I'm just about to sign out when a new email arrives. It's the first one today, and I'm instantly in it, my stomach dropping when I see nothing more than an address. I could pretend it's something different, but I know that it has to be the location of Corey. Whoever is sending these emails to Niko is trying to lure him to this location, and that screams trap. I should send the information straight to Niko, but I spend a few minutes looking into the sender. He's changed how he usually does it, this time leaving himself traceable, and the second I get a location I know why.

Shit, shit, shit. This can't be happening.

I'd promised myself that if I thought the information about this Daniel guy was needed, I would send it to Clay. Well, I have a feeling that some of it might be useful, so as I redial Niko's number I send an email to Clay, attaching everything I've found on the guy. As the call is picked up, the email is marked as read, and I imagine Clay reading over what I've sent.

"Hello?"

"You got an email. It doesn't say anything except an address that's about forty miles west of you. But we have a problem." I sense movement, and I spin in my chair to see Grant standing inside my office door. His eyes are fixed on me as I speak to Niko, and I know he realises who it is on the phone.

"What's the problem?" Niko sounds excited by the knowledge of having a location for Corey, and I hope that Clay can get him to slow down and realise that this whole thing is probably a trap. That's not why I called though, and that's not the problem I've found. "The problem is it came from your computer."

Grant's eyes go wide as he listens to what I'm telling Niko. This psycho has managed to get close enough to Niko to gain access to his computer connection. I don't know if it means that he has a remote access point like I had with my fake mobile, or if he's piggybacked onto his connection from outside of the property. Either way, the guy has been close enough to do it.

"What?"

"The email. Came from. Your Computer." I slow my words down to let Niko's brain catch up. I might be a dick, but I can understand that he's going through a lot just now. The man he loves has been taken, and he's lost Grant as well. I don't think he's as unaffected as Grant believes, but now isn't the time to dissect that inkling.

"Send me the message." Niko hangs up, but his voice changed when he spoke, and I wonder what the hell I missed.

"What happened?" Grant steps into my office more and he looks over the screens in front of him. He stops when he sees the email open and the address sitting there.

"We got a location."

A small sob escapes Grant before he takes a deep breath. "It's a trap."

"I know." It's so fucking obvious that something terrible is going to happen when Niko arrives to get Corey, and I just hope that he spends a minute to get some help.

"Fuck." That's all Grant says before he vanishes from the office. I sit there for a few seconds wondering what the hell happened, only rushing after him when I hear him hitting the shower. By the time I reach the spare room he's already out of the shower and scrubbing his body dry with a towel. The fact that he's naked in front of me doesn't seem to faze him, and he grabs clean clothes and starts getting dressed.

"What are you doing?"

"I'm going to help." He doesn't even pause getting dressed.

"Grant. I don't think it's a good idea. You've already said it's a trap, so going is dangerous."

He slips his feet into big boots and leans down to tie them. He doesn't even acknowledge that I'm speaking to him, making me growl a little in response.

"Grant?"

He gets up from the bed and grabs his jacket, and I finally step in front of him and put my hands on his shoulders. He stops and looks at me, his eyes frantic as his mind works overtime.

"I don't think you should go."

He takes a deep breath. "I know, but I have to. I can't stay here when they're both in trouble. They might not want me, but I can't let them get hurt. I can't, Sam."

I stare deep into his eyes, and I see the determination there. I'm not going to be able to get him to change his mind, but hopefully, I can make him act cautiously. "Fine, but please don't go racing in. Take your time and stay safe."

A little smile graces his lips when he realises I'm not going to try and change his mind. "When have I ever raced into something that's turned out to be a bad decision?"

I groan as I pull him in for a hug, hoping with everything I have that I will see my friend again.

13

Clay

I watch Niko approach the front of the building from my position to the South. Everything inside is telling me to storm in with him, but a soft approach is a better option. We have no idea what's happening inside that building, but we have clocked a few men checking the grounds outside it. Usually, this wouldn't be a problem, but they're armed, and that makes me more cautious. I expected Daniel to have people helping him, there was no way he could do all this shit on his own, but they seem very organised, and their planning is paying off so far.

Fucking Daniel Gallagher. Not a name I knew before a few hours ago, but one that will stick in my mind just like his lowlife twin brother. I could have spent my lifetime looking for someone who would want to hurt Niko, and I never would've pointed in his direction. I thought we'd seen the last of that family when Niko had killed David, the brother that had taken and murdered Niko's sister. I didn't even know he had a brother, and that fact has now come back to bite me on the arse.

"Check in." I release the two-way mic attached to my ear and listen as my own team answers me.

"Echo two in position." I look towards the back of the building and see Porter nod at me before vanishing around the corner again.

"Echo three has visual inside the building." Calum's lying on the high ground to the right. He has a direct line of sight into the building, and he's the only one who knows what's happening.

"Echo four in place."

"Echo five in position."

All my men are where they need to be, but my attention is still on Calum. "Echo three, what can you see?"

There's a slight delay before a response. "Four hostiles. No ... three hostiles and one captive tied to a chair."

So three outside and three inside, making a total of six men we need to take out. I have five men in my own team, plus Niko who is now inside the building. "Can you see Niko?"

Another pause before the line crackles and I get my answer. "He's inside. There are a shit ton of boxes blocking the area, but I can see him."

I wonder if the boxes are covering more men, but I know that Calum knows his job, so the thought is short lived.

"Echo one, we have a problem." Porter's voice comes over the line, and I'm instantly alert.

"Go ahead."

"We have one of ours on site."

He confuses me because all my men are on site. "Explain."

"It's Grant. He's here, and one of the hostiles have him."

Shit. This can't be happening. I hadn't added Grant into the plan we'd made because I wasn't expecting to see him. I thought he was a safe distance away from all the action. I should have known there'd be no chance he'd stay away if there were a chance that Niko and Corey were in danger. And of course, he knows. It's obvious that Sam was the one who sent me the email about Daniel. He saw a connection when I missed it, and I fucking hate that I didn't see what was in front of me. Granted the description that Barry gave us didn't lead to a perfect photo fit of Daniel, but I should have seen it. If Sam had seen the connection, then I should have. I won't even get into the fact that the little shit had hacked my computer to get the information in the first place, because if I think too hard about that, then my anger grows, making me want to track the little shit down.

"Shit! Echo one, we have one of ours in danger. I suggest we move in ... quickly."

I blink to clear my mind of Sam, focusing entirely on the shit storm in front of me. "All teams move in now! Silent entry unless needed." I'm moving before I've finished speaking, trusting my team to know what to do. My only thought is getting inside and saving my friend. That also means protecting the men he loves, because if either of them gets hurt, then I'm going to lose Niko forever. He might like to pretend that he doesn't have feelings for Grant, but the damn idiot is fooling himself.

My back hits the wall, but I don't stop, running along it and towards the door that Niko entered through. It seems to take forever to get inside, and my nerves start to build. What if I end up being too late? This thought has me pushing harder, making my feet move faster. I slip in through the door, checking quickly to make sure that I'm alone before taking off down the hall. When I reach the next door I still while I listen carefully, making sure that I'm not about to walk into danger. The coast is clear, and I enter the main warehouse, using the boxes as cover as I get closer to the action. Reaching the final one I can use, I peer around it just as Daniel's attacked by Grant.

I want to take a moment to take stock of what's happening, but there's a guy with a gun moving in behind Niko. I don't think twice as I rush the guy and put a bullet in his head. He drops instantly, and Niko's moving before I get a chance to blink. He rushes straight to Corey. He doesn't make it though as Daniel attacks him. An arm around my neck stops me going to his aide, and I'm pulled back away from the main action. I allow myself to be dragged, and as soon as I get my feet below me, I snap my head back, savouring the feel of the guy's nose breaking under my attack. The guy grunts before he loses his hold on me, and when I spin, I can see that he knows it's over. The panic building in his eyes is obvious, but I don't let it stop me, and I attack him with all the frustrations I've been feeling recently. I use his face as a punch bag, relishing every bit of blood that flows from his face.

A hand on my wrist stops my attack, and I look over my shoulder to see Porter standing there.

"It's finished, boss."

Looking down at the guy on the ground I see that Porter's right. His face is a mess, and as I concentrate on his chest, I see there's no movement. Yeah, it's finished. The shit thing is I don't feel any better. I still feel that uneasiness inside me, the one I thought I could get rid of by purging my anger.

"Let's go." Porter walks away, and I follow his lead, noticing for the first time that the whole warehouse has gone eerily quiet.

Daniel is lying on the ground, a quiet moan coming from him as he tries to move. That's not going to happen though. Niko has left him a bloody mess, so he isn't going anywhere any time soon.

Gentle speaking has me turning to look at the three men behind me. Niko is holding Corey close, but it doesn't erase the pain on his face. He was so close to losing him, I can only imagine the pain that's still rushing through him. Grant is watching them both, standing slightly back like he's trying to give the two of them privacy, but Niko isn't having any of it. Niko grips Grant by the back of the neck and pulls him close, their noses touching as he speaks quietly to him. Even in this moment, they look at each other like their hearts are connecting. There's no one else at this moment, and I wonder if there will ever be anyone who's soul speaks to me like that.

Shaking my head I turn away from the men, my chest aching enough that I rub a hand over it. *What is that shit about?* I distract myself by leaning down close to Daniel, finally taking in the face of the guy who has been torturing Niko. The description that Barry gave us really isn't anything like this guy, and I use that as a good enough excuse for not joining the dots before. If I'd seen Daniel's face properly, I would have recognised him instantly. Not for being Daniel, but he's David's identical twin, and I will never forget that fuckers face as long as I live. The last time I saw David's face, it actually looks a little like Daniel does now, and that fact has a small chuckle coming from me.

Daniel's attention latches onto me, his face scowling before he coughs out some words. "Laugh all you want, fucker."

"I'm sorry, that was rude. I was just thinking though, you look just like your brother did the last time I saw him." I know it's low, but the reaction I get from Daniel is totally worth being a dick. As he growls I lean in closer. "And I think that Niko might have just as much satisfaction ending you as he did your brother. But to make you feel better, I promise to bury you next to him." I don't wait to see his response before I stand, taking my attention away from him.

"Clean up, boss?" Porter comes to a stop in front of me, and I nod at him.

"Yeah. We need to get rid of all the evidence and then get the fuck out of here."

STARING AT MY MOBILE, I try to talk myself out of calling Sam and yelling at him. I actually want to thank him more than anything, but I refuse to give him the satisfaction. He's been a fucking thorn in my side since he was asked to help us investigate, and even though I've only spoken to him a few times, he is stuck in my head. Something about his cocky attitude has me wanting to smack him upside the head, and it's a feeling that's strange. I can usually brush off attitudes like his, but he's like an itch inside my body that won't go away. I know from speaking to Grant that Sam is staying not too far away from this cabin, so if I want to give in to the urge, I should do it before I travel home. Grant's actually the reason I have Sam's number, but I don't think he expected me to use it. I want to call him just to show him he isn't the only one who can get details on other people, anything to prove to the little shit that he isn't as good as he thinks he is. Laughing at my own wayward thoughts, I put my mobile down on the table in front of me. I need to clear my head and get the fuck out of here. I have a business to run, and the sooner I get back to it the better.

Grabbing my phone again I call Margaret, planning on letting her know I'll be back to work tomorrow. I don't need her in straight away, but if I'm cutting her holiday short, she should know about it. I try the office first, thinking that she's probably in trying to catch up with messages. I told her not to come in, but she never fucking listens to me.

"CW Investigations. How can I help?"

I smile as I hear her sweet voice, thankful again that she walked into my office that day and told me she was my new receptionist. "Hey, good looking."

"Oh, Clay. Thank god."

Okay, so the sudden worry in her voice when she hears it's me doesn't set my nerves at ease. My mind goes through a hundred different scenarios of what's happened. "What's wrong?" I match her worry because I'm starting to think that my business has burnt down.

"There was a Detective Archer here. He said he needs you to go to the station, that they need to speak to you urgently."

My stomach churns at the news, almost wishing that my business had been levelled. At least I would have a way to deal with that, but not knowing what this fucking detective has on me is a problem. "Did you tell him where I was?"

She scoffs like she is insulted. "You seriously just asked me that? I know how to do my job, Clay."

"I'm sorry, so what did you tell him?"

"I said you were undercover on a job and I wasn't sure when you'd be back."

This settles my nerves enough that I can breathe easily again. This buys me some time to form a plan, and I have a feeling that I'm going to need a really fucking good one. "Thanks. I was calling to say I'm heading back, but I might stay a few more days now."

"Understood. Just take care."

This isn't my first brush with the law in connection with a case, but this is the first time that depending on the evidence they have, I could end up going to prison. Shit. I really need to find out what they know and what they're going to charge me with. I bite my lip and think about Sam again. He's someone who could help me with my problem, I just need to have the balls to ask him. That's the problem right there. I don't want to give the fucker the satisfaction of knowing he's better than me, especially since he's already one up on me after hacking my fucking computer. The only problem is I don't think I have any other option. As far as I can tell Sam is the best hacker I know, and I'm sure I've not seen all his skills yet.

Swallowing my pride, I bring up the number I have saved for Sam and press to connect the call. My stomach churns as I wait for him to answer. Shit. I don't think I've ever been this nervous making a call, and I have to wonder why I am now.

"What?"

One word and I want to reach through the phone to grab the little shit. He has this attitude that oozes from his pores, and I can feel it even across the miles. "It's Clay."

"I know that. What do you want?"

I close my eyes and take a second to breathe deeply. I won't let him get to me. He's trying to get a reaction from me, and I won't give him the satisfaction of giving it to him. "I was calling to say thank you for sending that email. It helped a lot."

"I thought it might."

I crack my neck and take another lungful of air, letting it out slowly. "I take it you had fun in my computer."

"Your security system is shit. I swear a toddler could get past your firewall."

My mouth drops open. I paid a small fortune to get my system protected, and here is this guy I don't know talking down to me about it. He has a fucking cheek because I didn't ask for his opinion on anything. The purpose of my call is suddenly forgotten, and I think I need to make a few things clear to Mr Samuel Leighton. "I don't know who you think you're talking to-"

"Clay Wilson. Owner of CW Investigations and driver of a Ford Ranger. That's a big car there, Clay, are you trying to make up for some sort of shortcoming? Thirty-four, two hundred and twenty pounds, six foot five...yeah, big guy, I know who I'm talking to. So do me a favour and stay the fuck out of my way if our paths cross in the future. You were messing with things you didn't understand, and you just made my job harder."

I don't know who this little punk thinks he is, but he's pissing me off. I was fine when he was helping us find who was after Niko and his men, but now he's just annoying me. "Don't understand? I know you think you're some kind of expert-"

"I don't think. I know. There's a huge difference between those two things."

I grit my teeth together until my jaw is aching. I want to reach through the phone and grab his scrawny little neck. Okay, so I don't know what he looks like, but in my mind, he's a little nerd who is too pale and jumps at the slightest thing. "I swear to god I'm going to find you and when I do, we'll see who's the big guy."

"Good luck with that. No one finds me if I don't want them to, and I've hidden from better men than you."

The phone goes dead in my hand but not before I hear a muffled arsehole from Sam. I throw my phone on the desk, cringing a little when it bounces with a sickening thud. I would worry more if my anger wasn't filling me to the point of exploding. That little shit hung up on me. *He hung up on me.* No one does that and gets away with it. I'm out of my seat before I click off the call and I go in search of the one person who can help me. Grant is sitting at the front of the house when I find him. I march up to him, and his full attention is on me instantly, and I wonder if he can feel the anger radiating off me.

"Is everything okay, Clay?"

"Tell me where he lives."

Grants forehead scrunches up in confusion for a few seconds before a light bulb goes off in his head. I expect him to tell me to fuck off and leave his friend alone, but instead, a small smile graces his lips. "Wow, he's really got under your skin." He tilts his head and looks at me.

I stumble in my anger, not liking the way that Grant's suddenly assessing me. I don't know what he thinks he sees, but I want him to stop. "I want to kill him. Just a little bit."

That smirk never leaves his lips, and it's starting to annoy me. "I think you might be just what he needs."

What the fuck is Grant talking about? What who needs? Is he talking about Sam, because if he is, the only thing Sam needs is a beating? Except I won't actually hurt him, I just want to show him that he shouldn't prod an angry bear because it might fight back. "Just tell me where he is."

Grant looks unsure for the first time, his teeth biting into his bottom lip. I think he's going to deny my request when he asks me an important question. "You're not going to hurt him, are you? Not really?"

I let out a sigh, knowing that as much as Sam riles me up there is no way I would hurt him. If I felt he was a threat to anyone I loved then maybe, but I doubt that's the case since he's one of Grant's good friends. "No. I might just throttle him a little. Just to make myself feel better."

Grant stares at me, and I release another sigh.

"Fine. I need his help with a personal problem. I think he might be able to help."

"Is there anything I can help with?"

It's sweet of Grant to offer, but the truth is I don't want anyone important connected to this shit show of mine. I can ask Sam to help and then walk away, never having to see him again. I refuse to let my family get involved with my problems, and I have a feeling that Grant is going to become an important part of my family. He's Niko's man, even if he believes he isn't at the moment. "No. This is something that only Sam can help with."

"Fine, but I swear, Clay. You hurt my friend, and I will have your balls."

I laugh at Grants response. This will be a quick visit. Get Sam to see what the police have on me and then leave. As simple as that.

14

Sam

THE HOUSE HAS BEEN REALLY quiet since Grant left. He was only here a few days, but I got used to him wandering around making the place feel less empty. Being on my own has never bothered me before, but I think having him here brought back memories of spending time with my family. I look at my tablet and smile at the pictures my mum posted of my new baby niece. I've avoided looking at their social network profiles, knowing that it would be painful to know how much I'm missing, but I gave in to the urge this afternoon. I didn't know my baby sister was pregnant, and seeing her beaming from the picture, her beautiful new daughter in her arms, breaks my heart into a million pieces.

My family spent a long time looking for me when I vanished, but now they've gotten on with life, just like they should, but seeing it is both great and painful. I wonder if they still miss me or if they've just accepted that I'm gone and have forgotten all about me. Does that happen when someone vanishes without a trace? Does their family give up on them and forget to ease their pain? The shitty thing is I don't know what option I prefer. Common sense tells me that my family not living in constant worry and sadness from my vanishing is a good thing, but then there's a massive part of my heart that doesn't want them to give up. I'm hoping to go home one day. Once I know the danger is gone and I can meet that beautiful little girl in the picture without worrying that I will get her hurt.

I collapse back into the wicker chair and stare at the blue sky. Holy shit, I'm an uncle. The smile that covers my lips just happens as my heart momentarily fills with joy. There was no name attached to the picture so the little one is nameless until I can go searching, but knowing that there's a baby out there that shares part of my family's DNA, well that shit blows my mind. When I get to meet her, she's going to find out how much her Uncle Sam loves her. That's the thought that finally has my excitement fading. There's a chance that she won't ever know her Uncle Sam and I hate that. This is a time I should be celebrating with my little sister, but because of Damien, I'm hiding out in the woods, hundreds of miles away from anyone who loves me.

Sudden restlessness attacks me, and I need to move. If I keep sitting on that chair, I'm going to start having a panic attack, and that's not an option. I've managed to keep them at bay the last few months, well apart from the one the other day when Kelly turned up, but that one was entirely warranted. I take long strides down the mud path that leads to the trees behind my house. Moving is the only way to keep the panic from taking over, and if I let that happen, there is a good chance I will collapse and not get up again. The last time I let the darkness in I ended up drinking more than I should have and then had the idea that the world would be better off without me in it. It was the first time those thoughts had ever entered my mind, and when I woke up with a killer hangover in the morning, I was really fucking glad I'd passed out before I could follow through with the stupid plan.

Stopping in the middle of the path, I tilt my head up to face the sun, closing my eyes as I let the heat caress my skin. I try to clear my mind from everything that's threatening to hit me in a rush, focusing entirely on the sounds around me. I listen to the birds, letting out a deep breath as I try to get the muscles in my chest to relax. Deep breathe in ...hold for five seconds ... breathe out. I repeat the action several times, and a smile graces my lips when I feel my heart rate start to return to normal. This is my lesson on why I shouldn't go spying on my family. I need to learn that having no information is a good thing because then I don't feel like I'm missing a huge part of me. I need to strengthen the walls I've built up inside, pretend that nothing can get inside and hurt me again. It's easier to pretend that I don't care about anyone in this world, because then if I lose them, it won't hurt.

Turning back towards my house, I realise that the biggest mistake was letting Grant in. I was happy inside my lonely little box, doing jobs and making lots of money. Then along he came with his infectious personality, and eventually his sob story. I should have hung up the first time I spoke to him, but since it was helping with a police case, I thought I could keep him at a distance. I should have just done the job and hung up, but I spoke to him, and that was when he got under my skin.

"Why do you keep calling me?"

I hear Grant laughing over the line, and I can't help but smile. I don't want to enjoy his calls as much as I do, but Grant is growing on me, like a fungus. "You miss me, don't try and lie."

"I plead the fifth."

"We don't have that in the UK." *There's humour in his voice showing he loves the banter just as much as I do.*

There are very few people that can hold my attention as much as Grant does, and there's a small part of me that hates when our cases together are finished. Okay, so our work isn't exactly official and on the books, but I've helped Grant with a few things now, and it's been fun working with him. "Okay, Mr Policeman. You could've just let me go with it."

"Where would the fun be in that?"

"Did you call me just to annoy me or is there another reason?"

"I need your help to find a car that was involved in a hit and run."

This isn't the sort of thing Grant usually has me trying to find for him, and I'm pretty sure that the police have a direct link to the DVLA. He could easily find this out himself. "Um ... did you forget your password or something? I'm sure you have someone in-house to do this."

I first came into contact with Grant when he caught me hacking into the video screens at Piccadilly Circus in London. I'd planned to stream the video of two men dancing together followed by a video protesting the lack of rights for LGBTQI+ partners. It was my way of sticking it to the man, and one that would be seen by a lot of people. I hadn't noticed Grant as he stood close by watching me. He'd waited until I was just about to push the button and had placed his hand on my shoulder, leaning in close to my ear and telling me that I was about to make a terrible decision. Usually, I wouldn't have listened to anyone when it came to the ideas I had, but there was something in his voice that made me falter in my choices. Thankfully Grant hadn't been on duty so there wasn't much he could actually do to me. Add in the fact he'd stopped me from actually doing anything, so there was no crime committed. He still took my details, and a few months later I got his first call for help.

"Fuck off. I need your help because it wasn't a British plate. We know it's Polish, but we can't run it. That's where you come in."

"So what you're telling me is that I'm your bitch?"

"Pretty much, but you love it."

Yeah. Letting Grant into my life was the start of my downfall, but I just continued perpetuating that mistake when I went on the run. I should have cut all ties with him, but like a fool, I gave him my new mobile number in case he needed to contact me. I never imagined that he would need the help he has, or how important he would become in my life. I don't know how much the email I sent to Clay helped in the long run, but I'm glad that there was something I could do to help my friend. When Grant had called, he'd sounded sad, but when he told me that they had gotten Corey back, there was genuine joy in those words. I'm not sure what's going to happen with him and his guys now, but he promised to fill me in soon.

The whole situation with Grant and the two men still makes my head spin. Who would have thought that when Grant went to find his best friend he would find men he would fall in love with instead. I don't even know how that works. Having two guys at the same time must be really fucking confusing. Sex would be easy, but the emotions must get all tangled up. Do they get jealous of each other if they show too much attention to one specific partner, and do they only have sex as a threesome? Okay, so the image I have of Grant with two men isn't exactly a turn-off, but I couldn't do it. There's too much drama with just one bloke in your life, I would hate to live with the minefield of more. Not that I even want one guy, but there was a time when I imagined it. Long before I was old enough to realise that's just not for me.

My head is full of images of the three men together when I turn the corner that leads me to my front door. I'm not ashamed to be thinking about Grant and his boyfriends since my mind would fill with pictures of Clay if I let it. I've found that if I stay away from work too long my head fills with icy blue eyes and that usually leads to a hard dick. I can't help it, the man might be the biggest arsehole to walk on the face of the earth, but he's really fucking hot. I'm a young guy with eyes so I have no problem with admitting that Clay ticks a lot of boxes for me, and I can also be honest about the fact that getting under his skin is also fun. God, I'm pretty sure if I ever met the guy he would knock me the fuck out. Especially after that last phone call. I could feel his irritation as he spoke and that only encouraged me more. I said things I would never be brave enough to say to his face, having way too much fun prodding the bear.

A noise has me raising my head, and I swear my stomach drops to my feet. Blinking a few times to make sure I'm really seeing what's in front of me, I groan when I realise that it's not a mirage. Like my thoughts have magically pulled him from my head, Clay is storming up the driveway towards my house. His eyes connect with mine, and I can see the rage burning deep inside them even at this distance. Why the fuck is he here? How is he here? No one knows where I live except… fucking Grant. I'm going to kill him … or kill his credit score …or all of the above. First I have to escape from the really pissed off looking giant that's getting closer.

I take off at a sprint towards my cabin just as Clay picks up his speed. I get inside and slam the door before engaging all the locks. I'm tempted to press my panic button to close the shutters over all the windows, but sitting in here in the dark wouldn't do my nerves any good. I'm sure that Clay isn't a real problem other than he promised to find me and show me what a big guy he was. And holy shit, he's a huge fucking guy. Even across the distance, I could see how enormous he is. His muscles flexed as he moved with purpose, making a glorious image as he came after me. Damn, if the guy didn't want my blood, I would be completely willing to bend over for him. I can imagine how much power that body contains, and what he could do to make me scream. Fuck, now so isn't the time to get the horn thinking about the hot guy that I'm hoping is going to vanish from my property.

A loud bang on the door I'm leaning against has me screaming in shock. I didn't really expect Clay to just give up and go home because I came inside, but I was kind of hoping he would. Of course, I'm not that lucky.

"Open the door, Sam."

God, that voice. It's so much clearer through the door than it had been on the phone. There's a growl that's making the short hairs on my arms stand on end, and since today isn't going to end well for me, I really shouldn't enjoy the sound as much as I do.

Another bang on the wood.

"Sam?"

"Sorry, Sam's not here right now. Please leave a message and fuck off." I cringe. Why can't I get my sarcasm under control? I'm not making this situation any better by speaking.

"God damn it. Open this fucking door before I knock it down."

The wood vibrates under my back, and I step away from it like I'm expecting Clay to come crashing through it at any second. I stand in the middle of the entrance hall and stare at the door, not sure what the hell I do now. I doubt Clay is going to leave before he actually gets to say his piece, but I really don't want to answer the door and face the crazy man. I don't know him, and even though I'm sure Grant wouldn't give my address to someone who is a real danger, I don't want to test the theory.

"I'm not going anywhere, Sam. You'd be better opening the door and getting this over and done with."

I can't help the laugh that spills from me. "Yeah, that's just what to say to get me to open the door. Why not just describe in multicolour how much you're gonna hurt me?"

I expect some angry response or at least another bang on the door, but when there's only silence, I worry more. At least when Clay was making a lot of noise, I knew where he was. Why the hell did I have to get enjoyment out of pissing him off so much? When the silence stretches out I approach the door slowly, fully prepared to run at the first sign of Clay being there. I lean my head against it and wish to fuck that I had a peephole or at least a window that I could see the front porch area, but no, I thought that it would be safer not to have one. I'm tempted to go check the cameras, but that would mean leaving my position.

Standing straight, I steel my back and decide that I'm going to face the nightmare that's standing on the porch of my house. There's no way to avoid this, and I was the one who wanted to be the big man and start an argument. Now I just need to keep my courage long enough to not collapse into a nervous heap at Clay's feet. With a deep breath, I grab the door handle and pull, only to laugh at myself when the fucking thing doesn't open. I eye up the locks that I forgot to disengage, feeling really stupid as I unlock them now. My bravery is starting to waiver, so I don't think as I grab the handle, pulling the door open and bracing myself for what's about to happen. I expect Clay to be standing on the doorstep, but there's no one there, making me feel anxious as I move forward, stepping over the threshold onto the porch. I search the area, but there's no evidence that anyone was ever here, well except the car that's still parked on the other side of my locked double gates.

Turning to face the house, I look along the length of the building fully expecting to see Clay appear around the edge of it, but he's nowhere to be seen. This is actually scarier than having him in front of me because right now he could be anywhere and doing anything. A scuffing sound has me spinning and standing directly behind me is Clay. He's on the bottom step, and even though I'm firmly in the top one, it's clear he's a lot taller than me. I'm not a short guy, but Clay makes me feel like I'm tiny.

"You."

Okay, I lied. Not knowing where Clay was wasn't scary. This is scarier. Seeing him up close, his eyes shining with anger and determination, his immense size dwarfing me as I stare at him. I start to back up without conscious thought, but as I move, Clay matches my steps to keep a constant distance between us. With each step he scales, he grows more massive and much more intimidating. His glare never leaves me, and I'm stuck in it, not able to look away even if I wanted to. Shadows cover his face as we enter the house, but it doesn't steal anything from his presence. In fact, I think it makes him appear more menacing.

My back hits the hall wall, and a gasp leaves me. It's not the startled gasp I expected, it has an erotic edge to it. Clay crowds me, and I feel a shiver spreading through my whole body. *Holy shit.* This guy is so fucking intense, and even though my mind is screaming to run away, my body is screaming at me to push closer. When Clay's eyes drop to my lips I hold my breath, my tongue flicking out and running over my bottom lip. I have no idea what the hell is going on now, but I know I don't think I want it to stop.

15

Clay

I STARE at Sam's lips for far too long. I can't seem to get my eyes to move anywhere else. I finally force my stare away, fully taking in the guy standing in front of me. He isn't how I pictured in my head and its kind of throwing me a little. He's much taller than anticipated, only a few inches shorter than me, and even though he's slim like I thought, he looks as though he could give anyone a run for their money. His dark hair looks soft and falls over his forehead in waves, skimming just above the most unusual eyes I've ever seen. As he stares at me, they look cool grey, but when he blinks they suddenly look bluer. They are mesmerising and adding them to high cheekbones and full lips, he's fucking beautiful.

Whoa. That thought has me stepping away from Sam because I've no fucking idea where it came from. I've always been open in my own head about how handsome some men are, I mean I have eyes, but not once have I ever thought a guy was beautiful. *Hell no.* I've admired them, felt that they had a body that took a lot of hard work, but those things are normal. Those things are thought by all men. The way I'm staring at Sam isn't normal. Neither is the fact that I can feel myself harden in my jeans. *Fuck, what the hell is going on?*

"Clay?"

I blink a few times as Sam's voice breaks through my fogged up mind. I've put distance between us, but it isn't stopping the strange need I have to touch him. Shaking my head, I pull my focus back to what I came here to do. I need to tell him that he's a cocky little shit and he needs to watch who's he's shooting shit off to. Except when I open my mouth that's not what comes out. "I need your help."

Sam's as shocked as I am by my words if his suddenly widening eyes are anything to go by. A heartbeat later his teeth bite into his bottom lip, and it takes everything in me not to moan at the move. *What the fuck is happening?* I take another step back to increase the distance between us, and the movement seems to wake Sam from whatever daze he was in. I can see the change in him instantly as he stands up straighter, and I can see that I'm about to get more of the Sam patented attitude. I just wish that didn't excite me so much.

"What makes you think I want to help you?" There's that cocky tone he gives me on the phone. It makes my dick twitch in my jeans, confusing me even more.

Common sense is screaming in my head for me to get out of here, to return home and try to get the information some other way. I'm sure Porter knows someone who could get some sort of answer for me. I don't need Sam. The biggest problem with that idea is I can't get my feet to move. There is something in Sam that makes me want to stay, like a fear he's trying to hide from the world, but I can see it. Sam might come over as confident to everyone else, but there's something in his eyes that screams for help. I recognise that look. It's the same one that Gabe gets when everything gets too much, and it's something that I can't turn away from.

Fuck. Why couldn't he just be the arsehole I thought he was? "Because you aren't the dick you want me to think you are."

He scoffs at me, but he doesn't deny my words. "So what is it you think I might want to help you with?"

I run my hands through my hair because there's no way that Sam isn't about to judge me for what I'm going to ask him to do. He already looks at me as though I'm nothing but a huge dumb fuck, and this is only going to make him think less of me. "I would like you to find out what information the police have on me."

This gets his attention, and one eyebrow rises. "The police? What makes you think I can do that?"

"Because you're the best, we both know that."

I'm hoping that praise will get him on my side, and the colour heating his cheeks shows that it's affecting him a little. "How do I know you aren't a criminal and I'll be helping you get off with something?"

I cross my arms over my chest and stare at Sam. He's getting his confidence back, and that brings a glimmer to his eyes. He knows he holds the power here and I need to convince him to help me. "How did you know that Niko wasn't a criminal?"

"Because Grant vouched for him. I trusted Grant's judgement."

"Who do you think gave me your address?" I think I have him with that fact, but the sneaky fucker just won't give in.

"As I said, I trusted it. Not sure about now, only time will tell." He mimics my stance and crosses his arms over his chest. He takes a step forward, and it takes all my effort not to step away. I don't want him getting too close because he seems to make my body react strangely and I don't want to have to examine the reason why too much.

"Fine. You have my word. I'm not a criminal, and I'm not trying to hide a crime. Actually …" I don't know how to finish that sentence because that's exactly what I want him to do. I want to hide killing a man, and I don't think you get a worse crime.

He sticks out a hip, his eyebrows rising as he waits for me to continue. I give up my posturing and run my hands over my face. I've been through too much recently to give a fuck now. I've spent weeks trying to help Niko, and this whole shit storm is happening because I wanted to help Gabe. If Sam isn't going to help me, then fuck it. *I'm done.* "You know what? Forget it. I'm sorry I came, I should have fucking known no one would be willing to help." I turn on my heels and storm out of the door. I'll just go back home and work out what the fuck to do. I should have just done that, to begin with. This detour was a stupid fucking idea, and I'm now paying for it with confusion and frustration.

I've just made it to the bottom of the steps when Sam appears in front of me, his hands held up as he tries to stop me. I still and glare at him, waiting to see what he wants.

"I'm sorry. I'm just ... I'll help."

I need to walk around him and go back to my car, but his eyes are pleading with me not to go.

"How about a truce?" He smiles sweetly, and my laughter comes automatically.

"A truce?" My brain is screaming at me to leave. Just get in my car and get the hell away from here, but I ignore it. I never claimed to make the best decisions.

"And a beer?" There's that smile again, the one that makes my stomach tumble. I push the feelings away and go against my better judgement.

"A beer would work."

Sam doesn't say anything as he circles around me, he keeps his eyes on mine as he walks backwards to the cabin behind him. It's like he's scared that if he looks away I'll vanish. I follow him back inside, finally looking around the room as I walk through it. From the outside, I expected it to look like a hunting cabin you would see in the movies, but it looks more like a bachelor pad. The furniture is mismatched but looks homely and comfortable. Heading into the kitchen behind Sam I see that it's small but functional, everything a young guy on his own would need. He grabs two bottles of beer from the small under cabinet fridge and hands me one. I twist off the top as Sam leans against the sink unit. He bites his lip and twirls his own bottle in his hands. When the silence carries on, I decide to start the conversation.

"Are you going to help me?"

Sam looks up through his lashes. "Yeah."

"Thank you."

He unscrews his own cap and takes a small sip from the bottle. "I'm going to need some information, so I can do my job."

I merely nod because that goes without saying. I would be stupid if I thought he could sort out my shit without me telling him what happened. I could try to keep it a secret, but as soon as he starts his search he's going to find out everything, and I think it's better for him not to suddenly find out I'm a murderer.

"The more you can tell me, the more I can find out."

I nod again before taking a large pull from my bottle. Silence surrounds us, the only sound is Sam's thumb ring clinking against his bottle. I stare at the piece of jewellery, fascinated by it and the way the black metal looks against his pale skin. Sam moves suddenly, pulling my attention away from that sexy black band. *Sexy?*

"Come with me."

He doesn't hang around to make sure I'm following him, and I end up trailing behind him down the hall to a door I missed when we walked past it earlier. He opens it and enters the room, my eyes going wide as I step in behind him. I've seen Porter's home office, and I often laugh at all the tech that he has there, but it's nothing compared to what I'm faced with in Sam's office. There are a dozen screens around the room, covering nearly every flat surface, and they all seem to be doing something different, the letters and numbers on each of them moving as they scroll. There's only one seat in the room, and it's placed in front of the two biggest screens and also a laptop.

"You said my truck was overcompensating for something, I think maybe you are too?"

Sam looks over his shoulder, and the smile he gives me makes my heart stutter. It's the first of me seeing anything other than disdain on his face, and I wish I hadn't seen it, because now that I've seen it, I have a feeling I'm going to try harder to see it again. I drag my gaze away from him and focus on the screen in front of him. I need to get my head sorted and do what I came here to do. Only once it's done can I go home, and I need that more than anything. I need to finally take that holiday that I've been lying to Margaret about. I need to get away from it all and sort my head out before it fucks with me more.

Sam's grip on my arms pulls me back to the room, and I flinch out of his hold. He holds up his hands in surrender and takes a step back. I swallow hard and try to calm my racing pulse. "Sorry. I was just going to get you a seat so you didn't have to stand. I need to grab one from the kitchen."

I nod as he leaves the room and I take the time to have a firm talk to myself. I'm acting like a fucking idiot in front of Sam, and I'm probably not improving his opinion of me. I need to pretend I'm not insane so he doesn't throw my arse out. I check my watch and see that's it's later in the afternoon than I thought it was. It's getting close to five o'clock, and that means it will be acceptable to get pissed soon. The beer that I got from Sam is still in my hand, but it's not doing the job at relaxing me like a bottle of Jack would.

A noise from the hall has me looking over my shoulder, and I see Sam enter with a chair that I hadn't noticed when I was in the kitchen. He gives a small smile as he places it within reaching distance, his gaze never leaving me. I don't blame him. The way I keep zoning out and losing my shit, he must think I'm one moment away from murdering him.

"Have a seat, and I'll get some info."

I put my bottle on the desk and drag the seat closer to Sam. When I get settled and look towards him, he's glaring at the bottle on the desk. I gingerly pick it up again, and when his stare turns to me, I try to give him an innocent smile. "Sorry."

"It's okay. Just ... well, beer and expensive equipment don't mix."

"Noted." I give him a small salute with the bottle, and he smirks.

He turns his attention to the computer in front of him, bringing up several new windows before asking me a series of questions. Most of them are what I expect, like what police force and any details I could give him about the detective involved. The answers come easily until he starts to dig deeper. Now my heart starts to race, and for a very different reason than before. "I need to know about the case. I could search forever without finding anything. It will be quicker if you tell me." His voice gets quiet as he finishes his sentence. I wonder what he's thinking about me because for some reason, I don't want him to think anything horrible.

"It's a missing person case. Paul Clark. He's been missing for about three months now."

Sam stares at me for far too long, and I turn away before he does, hating the fact that he seems to be able to see deep inside me. When he starts clicking away on his keyboard, I risk a glance at him. He's biting his lip, and I can almost hear his brain working.

"Ask it."

His fingers still but I don't look up at him. "Is he actually missing?"

"Depends who you ask. To his family and the rest of the world he is."

"I'm asking you."

I pick the label from the bottle in my hand, the paper coming away easily with the condensation wetting it. "I know he's not missing."

"Clay?" Sam's voice is quiet but level, but there's still a power in it that makes me finally look up at him. "What happened?"

This will be the first time I've ever admitted to anyone what I did, but as Sam looks deep into my eyes, I suddenly want to tell him. Actually, it feels more than that, I need to tell him. I need to share my burden with someone. "He was threatening my friends. He'd already hurt my best friend, and I knew he would come back to finish the job once he toyed with him some more. Gabe was vanishing before my eyes. He was changing because of the fear." The words thicken in my throat, and for the first time, the emotion of what Gabe went through hits me. I've had to be strong for Gabe and Rhys, making sure that they were both okay, and now, having to explain everything, it hits me like a freight train.

Sam reaches out and takes my hand, gripping it tightly on top of the desk where it's resting. The warmth from his skin spreads through mine like tiny little tingles, and I stare at our connection. He's a stranger, and the fact that he's touching me should bother me, but it doesn't. His touch is soothing, and I can feel my scattered emotions start to settle, and that shocks me. Gabe has been the only person in the past that has managed to calm my racing thoughts, but a simple touch from Sam is all it's taking to clear my head today.

When Sam removes his hand from mine, I finally pull my attention away from where we were joined. I can still feel my skin tingle, and I miss his hold. "What did you do?"

"I protected them."

I can almost hear Sam grind his teeth and it's clear that my non-committal answers are starting to piss him off. "Clay, just tell me. I promise that I won't judge. I've done things in my past that haven't exactly been legal, and when I search the database, I'm going to find out anyway."

He has a good point, but there's also the chance that the detective has nothing on me. Maybe he's just trying to spook me so I'll admit to shit that he can use against me. The sensible part of my brain tries to tell me that if the police really had anything, they wouldn't wait for me to go to the station. They'd be banging down the door with an arrest warrant so they could handcuff me and drag me to jail. None of that's happened though, just my little chat with the friendly detective, and that fills me with a bit of hope. Unfortunately, the confidence that brings isn't there, and that's why I need to tell Sam everything. "I killed him. I stalked him for a few weeks before following him and throwing him off a bridge. Now I think the police have a video of it and it could put me away for a long time."

"Oh, okay."

Sam's reaction isn't what I expect. I could understand fear or disgust, worry or even anger, but this is more like I just told him I drank the last of the milk. He doesn't say anything as he returns to his work on the large computer next to him. I try to keep up with what he's doing but the screens change rapidly, and the letters on the screen don't seem to make actual words. I thought Porter was good at this sort of thing, but Sam outshines him. It's like Sam actually talks to the computer in its own language, which I suppose is what he does, but seeing it in person is impressive. Grant always said that Sam was the best, and as much as it pisses me off to admit it, I think he might be right.

"Thank you."

Sam's fingers still for a fraction of a second before carrying on. He doesn't say anything to me but I know he heard me, and that's the important bit.

16

Sam

My mind's racing with everything that Clay just told me. He killed a man. Like, really honestly murdered a man. The funny thing is it doesn't make me scared of him, even though the fact should make me want him to leave. The only thing I can focus on is the need to find out if the police know anything so I can get rid of any evidence.

When he turned up at the door earlier, I honestly thought my time had come. He looked angry enough to rip my head from my shoulders but who could blame him? I could tell I was pissing him off when we were on the phone together, but that just made me do it more. Staring him down had been another story, and all my usual sarcasm had fled my brain. Especially when he started staring at me with heat in his eyes, and not the burning caused by anger. This was very different, and I didn't know what to do with it. Part of me wanted to close the distance between us, but there was still the worry that he would knock my head off if I tried. Instead, I prepared to ask him to leave, but then something happened. He backed off and asked for my help.

The whole situation threw me, and it took me a minute to recover, and when I did, my smart mouth came back online. Sarcasm is my default mode, and I thought that Clay could handle it, but something had changed. The look in his eyes told me that he was nearing the end of whatever patience he had. When he stormed out, I'd panicked, and even though I didn't want to think about why him leaving had me feeling like that, I took off after him to beg him to stay.

Now I have a hundred questions that I want to ask him, but I know he won't be receptive to them. So I focus on the software I'm writing to try and get past the firewall on the police database. I didn't expect it to be easy to get in, but it's going to take a little longer than I'd anticipated. Maybe they've finally hired someone who knows what they're doing to deal with their security. I swap between my laptop and my main computer, and I can feel Clay's gaze on me the whole time. I don't know if he's expecting me to explain everything I'm doing, but he's going to be disappointed if he is.

"You make that shit look so fucking easy. I don't think I've understood one thing you've done, and I thought I was good on the computer."

"You're probably good on the web, a lot of people are. But if it's not on Google, then you struggle." My words come out sounding snotty and dismissive, and I don't mean it that way. "That came out wrong–"

"No, you're right. I'm the bomb on the internet, but that shit," He points to the screen where I'm still typing away. "Yeah, not so much that."

My lips quirk up as I listen to him speak, enjoying it far too much. His voice is as deep as it was on the phone, but in person, there's a sexy huskiness. Even when he sounds happy, the rumble of his words vibrate over my spine and settle in my dick. Nothing compares to when he was angry though. Watching the colours swirl in his eyes as he tries to control his temper, and the full-on growl in his voice, yeah, that had made me hard in a dangerous situation. That's never happened before, and it was like my body was telling my brain that it wasn't really in danger, that the man in front of me was more bark than bite. But fuck, how I wanted him to bite me.

I cough when a moan builds in my chest, trying to dislodge the noise. The last thing I need is to let Clay know how much he turns me on, but he really does. In pictures he's gorgeous, but in person, there's a powerful energy that comes from him, and that does good things to my libido. All I can think about is how hard he would fuck me when the anger took over, and my arse keeps clenching in anticipation. It's going to have to keep daydreaming about how it feels though because nothing is going to happen with the huge, growly man, no matter how much fun it would be.

CLAY WALKS behind my chair again, and it takes everything in me not to turn and smack him. He has been pacing for what feels like hours, and it's doing my head in. Patience is obviously not one of his strong points, but he's going to have to get used to it because very little in this game happens quickly.

"Will you sit the fuck down." My patience finally runs out, and I bark at Clay, making him stop and stare at me. He gets a look on his face I can't identify before he lowers himself into his chair.

"Sorry. I'm not used to waiting so much on stuff."

That I don't believe for a second. "You're trying to tell me that you don't have to hang around on your cases?" I lean back against my chair and wait for his answer.

"That's different."

"How's that different?"

"Because I'm in control even though I'm waiting."

I chew on my bottom lip as I try to not let my smile out. He really is the control freak I had him pegged as, and asking for help must have driven him insane. "You really don't like not being in control, do you?"

"No. I don't give control to anyone."

Visions invade my brain without invitation, and I struggle not to reach down to rub my hand over my semi-hard cock. It's a difficult urge to avoid, especially when all I can see in my imagination is Clay handing over control to me. I can picture him on his knees in front of me as I feed my cock to him, guiding his mouth onto me as he takes me deep.

"Sam?"

"Huh?" I blink a few times before bringing my attention to Clay, who's looking at me strangely.

"What is that noise?"

I sit forward and finally notice the alert coming from one of my side monitors. I spin in my seat and turn it off, my stomach dropping when I see that it's showing movement from Damien. He's moved from London where I've been stalking his whereabouts for the last week, and he's now moving North towards Manchester. He's still nearly seven hours away from me, but the move has my nerves growing. I don't even know if it's him I'm tracking, because truth be told, I don't think he would be stupid enough to leave such a visible paper trail for me. That's the idea that's been niggling at the back of my head for the last few days. Damien isn't a stupid man, and he knows my skills. He wouldn't be so obvious with his movements unless he was trying to distract me from what he's actually doing.

"Did you get some news?"

I jump when Clay's speaks close to my ear. I got so stuck in my head I forgot he was there. I quickly close over the window because the last thing I need is for him to get all up in my business. No one needs to know what I'm running from, so I just need to get this job done and send Clay on his way so I can deal with it. There is a chance I might need to run again, and I don't want to deal with that with an audience.

"Sorry, no. Just another job I'm working on." Clay huffs and collapses back into his seat. I turn until I'm facing him and laugh when I see his pouty face. I didn't think it was possible for such an intimidating man to look like a stroppy teen.

"This is taking forever."

"Sometimes it does, Clay. There's nothing we can do until my programme finds a way into the system. It's a waiting game."

Another huff. I let myself look over Clay as he sits focused on the coding on the large monitor. He hasn't changed a lot since the picture I found of him was taken, but I can tell it's not a recent one because his hair is longer on top and the stubble from the picture is much thicker. Not quite a beard but more than designer stubble. The most glaring difference is the neck tattoo that runs from under the neck of his t-shirt up to behind his ear. It's a beautiful feather, and I swear it looks real, like an angel feather dropped from the sky and settled on his skin.

"You're staring." Clay turns to face me, and I can feel heat spread across my chest and up my neck.

"That's new." I point to his neck, and his hand drifts up to touch the ink. He seems to get lost in his head for a few moments before he's back with me, and when he is, I wish he would fade away again.

"It is. But how do you know?"

I don't think Clay wants to hear that I've spent far more time than could be considered normal staring at his photo because I'm sure he would think I was some weird stalker. I really fucking enjoyed looking at the picture though, and my dick approved whole-heartedly as well. I decide to go for a half-truth because from the look on his face, he'll know if I try to lie to him. "I stalked you, remember? You annoyed me by getting in the way, and I wanted to know who was messing with my shit." I wait for a response, wondering if he'll still think it's weird that I looked him up.

"Makes sense. If I had any way to find you other than a first name I probably would have done the same thing."

"You wouldn't have found anything." The words are out before I have a chance to think and I know I've peaked Clay's interest with them. I can see the colours in his eyes swirl as his brain works overtime, and I get to my feet before he can say anything. I have a quick look at the clock on my screen and see that it's nearly ten o'clock. I'm happy that it's late enough to kick Clay out without it being obvious I'm trying to get rid of him. I don't want to talk anymore tonight because I'm tired and that means I tend to say stupid shit. A good nights sleep is in order, and if I actually make it to bed for a change, that would be great. I'd made a promise to myself that I would make it to my room to sleep at night, and I haven't. I have made it the couch, which is still an improvement from sleeping over my desk.

"Look, nothing important is going to happen tonight no matter how hard you stare at the screen. Why don't you head home and come back in the morning? There'll probably be some news by then, and we'll both be rested and ready to work."

He looks like he's going to argue with me, but eventually, he stands. "Okay. I'll be back early if that's okay?"

I nod, not wanting to explain that I'm usually up with the sun in the morning. A good nights sleep for me is about five hours, and after that, the fear of someone approaching becomes too much to ignore. I lead him out into the hall and towards the front door. "If you honk in the morning I'll open the gates so you can park out front. I tend to leave them locked, it stops people trespassing." It's a lame excuse for being locked in, but if Clay doesn't believe me, he's polite enough not to mention it.

"Good night, Sam. And thank you again for helping me."

"You're welcome. I just hope I can do something for you." I look up at Clay, and we stare at each other for far longer than is polite. My hands itch to reach out and grab him so I can pull him to my mouth, but I behave, knowing that it would only turn out like Kelly all over again.

It's Clay that turns away first, and I watch him as he walks down the drive. It's only after he jumps over the gate at the end that I close the door and secure the locks. Once I'm alone, I let out the first deep breath since Clay arrived this afternoon. Holy shit. I'd spent the last five hours feeling like I was about to self-combust. Clay's presence is something I've never felt before, and it sent sparks along my nerves. It was like one wrong move, and I would be set alight, and only Clay would be able to extinguish the need inside me. Good god, this whole thing is going to go so badly.

I'VE RESISTED the urge to check my perimeter cameras as long as I can. Now it's nearly midnight, and I can't leave it any longer, or I'm going to climb out of my skin. No alarms have sounded, but still, I need to visually check to settle my growing nerves.

I scroll through the cameras set up at the back of the house first, zooming in on several dark areas so I can make them out clearly. That was one of the things I noticed first when I moved here. I was used to the city and the fact that it never got fully dark. Out here in the wilderness, it gets darker than I realised it could get. The night sky is full of stars, but none of that helps me see when I am panicking about what's out there. Winter is worse, but if Damien keeps getting closer, it looks like I won't have to worry about spending another one here.

The next camera I highlight is the one by the front gate, and when it appears on the screen, my heart nearly stops. There's a car sitting there in the darkening night, and my flight response is screaming for me to move. I'm just about to go full on panic mode when I take a second to really look at the vehicle. It's not actually a car like my fear had made me think, it's actually a truck. A dark coloured Ford Ranger.

Fucking Clay.

The fear changes instantly into dark fury as I race for my door. Why the fuck is he still here? Does he think he needs to watch me, so I don't run away, taking his secret with me? Does he think I can't look after myself?

I'm on autopilot as I unlock the door and run down the driveway. I'm so angry that I've forgotten I should be scared out in the open this late at night. All I can see is the arrogant arses truck as I race towards it. When I get to the gate, I climb over it, my eyes never leaving the dark windows of the truck. As soon as my feet hit the ground, I'm at the driver's side and pulling open the door. The overhead light comes on, and Clay jumps in his seat. "What the fuck are you doing, Clay?"

It takes me a moment to register what I'm seeing, but when I do, my anger fades quickly. Clay is blinking against the sudden brightness of the interior light, but it doesn't hide the fact that he's been sleeping. I look on his lap, and I see a small blanket covering his legs in an attempt to keep him warm. He seems as far removed from put together as I've ever seen anyone, and it's clear that he wasn't watching me from his position. "Are you sleeping in here?"

Clay rubs his hands over his face before a jaw-cracking yawn hits him.

"Clay?"

"What?" His voice is husky with sleep, but even that can't hide the frustration in his single word. I stare at him while I wonder why he's here.

"Why are you here? Why didn't you go home?"

"I live nine hours drive away."

I laugh before I think of keeping it in. His answer is so very him, but it also doesn't explain anything. "Then where are you staying?"

"I was at Niko's place, but he's too far away to travel to tonight."

Trying to get answers from Clay is like pulling teeth. It's like he needs to lead you around the houses before you get to your destination. "Hotel?"

"Full."

I blink at him like he's gone insane. He was planning on spending the whole night out here sleeping so he could come back in the morning. Why wouldn't he just tell me he had nowhere to go? As I ask myself the question, I already know the answer. Of course, Clay wouldn't mention needing help again, he's probably already filled his quota of helplessness for his entire lifetime. I step back from the door and lean my hands on my hips. "Get inside, Clay."

"What?"

"Get in the fucking house." I turn and start walking back to get inside. I hear Clay's feet hit the dirt before he shouts my name.

"Sam."

"Stop fighting me, just this once. I refuse to let you sleep out here in a bloody truck while I have a spare room. Now give me a few minutes to open the gate so you can park. Don't make me come out again." I climb the fence and storm up the driveway so I can unlock the gates. I can't believe he was out there all that time, asleep in his truck, while I was inside and didn't know. It shows that maybe I'm not as protected as I thought I was. If Clay can spend hours there without me noticing, it means that someone could sneak up on me at any time.

I stop that line of thinking when Clay appears at the front door looking more nervous than I thought possible. I glare at him before motioning him inside and locking the door behind him. I resist the urge to deadbolt the door, instead taking a deep breath before heading down the hall towards the spare room. I point out the bathroom on the way, and when I reach the room, I turn on the light, thankful that I changed the sheets once Grant left. "Make yourself at home and if you're up before me in the morning help yourself to anything in the kitchen. I don't usually sleep late, but just in case."

"Okay." Clay looks at the carpet and avoids looking at me.

"Well, I'll leave you to it. Good night, Clay." I reach the door, and I'm just pulling it closed behind me when he speaks.

"Thanks, Sam. For everything."

17

Sam

THE SMELL of bacon hits my nose as soon as I wake in the morning. I groan as I stretch, wondering what time it is. I finally made it to bed last night, and apparently, my body approved. For the first morning in nearly a year, I've woken up without my body screaming at me, but as I lie there my stomach lets me know that it's hungry. I give up the comfort and get out of bed, heading out into the hall and then the bathroom. I spend a few minutes having a piss and washing up, finally brushing my teeth before returning to my room to slip into some shorts and a t-shirt.

When I feel more presentable, I follow the amazing smell to the kitchen. When I step through the door, I freeze and stare. Clay has music on low, and he's cooking, his hips swaying slightly to the song. His jeans are tight against his arse and the vest he's wearing clings to his muscular body, creating the most erotic picture right here in my kitchen. *How is it possible for one guy to look so fucking perfect?* He looks like the universe did a poll of a hundred men to find out what they were looking for in a guy, and when they had the results, they made Clay. Muscles on top of muscles, a hard edge that causes shivers when it's turned on you, tattoos covering the smoothest skin, and an arse that you just want to bite.

Clay turns and finds my gaze over his shoulder, and it's only then that I realise that I've moaned out loud. I try to cover up the mistake by rubbing my stomach and moaning again. "Whatever you're making smells amazing." The raised eyebrow from Clay tells me he isn't buying what I'm trying to convince him of, but he's kind enough not to point it out.

"Thought I would make you breakfast to say thank you for letting me stay." He turns and puts a big plate of pancakes on the worktop behind him, right next to the biggest plate of bacon I've ever seen. Also on the counter is orange juice, a mixed fruit salad, and two large mugs of steaming coffee.

"Where did you find all this stuff?" I know for a fact that I didn't have half the stuff he needed to make this much food.

"I popped out this morning when I woke up. I didn't know how long you would sleep and I was hungry. You really didn't have any food in here."

"Yeah, I haven't been to the shop in a while."

Clay laughs as he hands me an empty plate. "Here, take what you want."

I take two huge fluffy pancakes and cover it with rasher after rasher of bacon, my mouth watering as I resist eating while still standing. "I don't have a table, I normally just eat in the living room on the couch."

Clay comes to stand in front of me, his hands full with his plate and coffee. "Then lead the way."

We take a few minutes to get comfortable, me on one side of the couch, my foot tucked under the opposite leg, so I'm aimed towards Clay. He sits on the other end, his plate leaning on his knees as he spears a piece of melon with his fork. I cut into the pancakes and take a huge bite, moaning as soon as the flavour hits my tongue. *Holy fuck.* These have to be some of the best pancakes I've ever tasted, and on the next forkful, I grab a piece of bacon before stuffing it into my mouth. I moan again because there's no way that I can hold in this much pleasure. I've been eating pre-packaged meals for so long that these taste like heaven.

I open my eyes to say thank you to Clay, but when I see him, he's sitting so still that I think there's something wrong. I wipe over my face in case there's something stuck to it, and my movements seem to pull Clay from his staring. He coughs before entirely focusing on the plate in front of him. He wriggles on the seat, and the sudden realisation hits me like a brick. Is Clay turned on? That thought has heat spreading through my body and straight to my cock. I lower my plate to my lap because with my thin gym shorts on, it's becoming undeniable that I have a growing problem. Clay's eyes flicker over at the movement, and when his cheeks heat I know, he's noticed my predicament. *Oh shit, could this get any worse?*

A knock at the door has me nearly jumping from my seat, and the fork falls from my hand and clatters on my plate noisily. Panic sets in before I can get control over it and I'm off the couch quickly. I put my plate on the table and rush to the front door. Bringing up the cameras on screen I select the one out front to see who's there. I don't know how someone got up to the house without me being alerted, but then I remember that Clay left this morning to go shopping. I'm not even sure how the hell he got the alarm system off, but I will deal with that problem once I know who's out there. I see a familiar car sitting next to Clay's truck, and even though my panic starts to ease, the dread stays at a high level. Kelly. *Why can't this guy take a hint?*

I groan and drop my head, willing Kelly just to go away. Heat behind me has me standing up straight, the feeling of Clay's body so close making my breath stutter in my chest. He feels like he's all around me even though there isn't a part of our bodies touching. I stand as still as I can manage because I have a feeling that any sudden movement could send Clay running.

"Who is that?" His breath ghosts over the skin of my ear. I close my eyes and bite hard onto my lip to stop a groan from forming.

"A mistake I made one night that won't go away."

"Female?"

It takes me a few beats to realise what Clay is asking. Wow, does he not know I'm gay? "Male."

He's quiet, too quiet, and I take the opportunity to turn so I can see him. We're still standing close, but there's no way for me to put any distance between us. "Is that a problem?"

"No." Clay still doesn't step back, and my eyes drop to his lips, the ones that are shining in such an enticing way. I lick my own lips, and this seems to make Clay realise how close he is. He takes a step back and runs his hand through his hair. "Anyway, do you want me to solve this problem for you?"

Solve this problem? "And how exactly would you do that?" I have to ask because at least one time he solved a problem, a man died.

Clays mouth rises on a huge smile, and I know that he's got a plan. "Just a yes or a no, Sam. Yes or no?"

I should say no, but the shit-eating grin pulls me in, and I suddenly want to see what he has planned. "Yes."

He claps his hands so suddenly I jump a little. He's still rubbing his hands together as he reaches the door and pauses. With a backwards wink in my direction, he opens the door. I stay hidden but find a better angle so I can see what's about to happen. Clay steps out onto the porch, crowding Kelly as he crosses his arms over his chest. "What?"

I see Kelly take a step back and I don't blame him. Clay's an intimidating figure when he's just chilling out, so to have him posturing angrily at you, that shit's scary. My mind goes back to yesterday when I was in the same position as Kelly is now, so I know how intimidated he must feel. The only benefit I had is at least I knew who Clay was.

"Um ... I'm here ... Is Sam here?" Kelly stutters over his words, and I feel like going to the door to stop this, but he won't take my subtle hints to leave me alone. This needs to happen for everyone's happiness or at least mine, and that's all that I care about. I thought he'd taken the hint at the petrol station, but apparently, I was wrong.

"He's still asleep." Clay unfolds his arms and leans against the doorframe, his hands going in his pockets. He looks more relaxed, like he's getting into his flow, but he's still as intimidating as shit. Silence grows between them, and I regret not being closer, so I could see the action more clearly.

"Could you get him?"

"No." Clay is going full on arsehole mode, and I wish it weren't such a turn on.

"Seriously. I don't know who you are but-"

"I'm the boyfriend." More silence at Clay's abrupt comment and even my own mouth drops open in shock.

"Boyfriend? But we–"

"I know what you did." More silence.

I lean around the corner, and my movement must catch Kelly's attention because he moves to the side to see past Clay. Shit, now I need to go to the door. I take my time to reach the men because I really don't want to join this party. When I get level with Clay, he looks at me, winking before putting his arm over my shoulder and bringing me in to lean against his side. My heart is already racing, but when he bends down to kiss my head, I nearly melt into a puddle on the ground.

"Morning, sleepy head."

I have to bite my lip to stop the laughter building inside from escaping. Hearing those words from Clay is just too funny. "Hey, Kelly. What are you doing here?"

Kelly's eyes flicker between Clay and me, almost like he's trying to work something out. "I was close, so I thought I would see how you were."

Clay's heat is burning into my side, and I chance a look up at him. He is watching me closely, mischief twinkling in his eyes. It's not something I thought I'd ever see on Clay and I take a moment to enjoy it. He looks good like this, with his edges softer, and I decide to play along with him. "I'm good. Clay has been entertaining me." I lean into Clays side, snuggling my nose into his neck. "That's why I slept so late."

Clay's hand tightens on my shoulder as I ease away from him. I shouldn't have gotten so close to him because it made my body notice way too many things that it hadn't paid attention to before. Like the way that Clay smells. I don't know what aftershave he wears, but it's mouthwatering. It has a freshness that makes me think of being outside, but I think it's the fact that it's mixed with Clay's own edible smell that makes it perfect. Then there's the stubble that rubbed against my jaw and made me want to lick him. My first thought was what it would feel like on my thighs as he blew me, but it quickly changed to the image of him kissing me while pushing inside my body.

"Oh, I just thought..." Thankfully Kelly doesn't finish that thought before he starts to back away.

I want to say something, but instead, I just watch him return to his car. I don't want to give him a lifeline to attach himself to, so silence is probably the best answer. His vehicle vanishes from sight a few minutes later, but Clay and I continue to stand there, our bodies pressed against each other. I should put distance between us, but I can't get myself to move. It feels like I'm on fire, like my whole body is an exposed nerve, and one wrong move could set me off. My dick is aching inside my shorts, and I want nothing more than to rub myself until I get relief.

After far too long Clay drops his arm from my shoulder, and even though I want to keep snuggled into his body, I step back.

"Well, I think that worked well."

Clay laughs, and I stare at him while he does. His whole face is relaxed, and for the first time, he doesn't look like a guy who could kill. Except he is that, and that thought sobers me. It reminds me why Clay is here, and it isn't so I can flirt and get fucked. With that in mind, I return to the living room and grab my plate. I eat a few more bites as I walk to the kitchen and put the plate in the sink. By the time I've grabbed a Red Bull from the fridge, Clay has joined me.

"I'm going to go check my computer to see if there's an update."

Clay just nods as I walk past him, escaping to my office and the safety of my computer.

"So how did you get started on all this?"

I look up from my screen at Clay's surprise question. We've been sitting quietly for about an hour while I worked my way through the open cases on the police database. I gained access to the police's server this morning, but it's taking a while for my computer to pick up the keywords I programmed in. I made sure that there was a selection of keywords that had to be present so that I didn't get overloaded with cases. I didn't use Clay or Paul's name as a search parameter in case it alerted someone to my presence. Now we're just waiting to get a hit that might help us. "It's always interested me, and I became really good at it."

"Oh come on, there has to be more to it than that. We all had hobbies growing up, but we didn't make a career out of it."

I spin my chair and throw my feet up on the arm of Clay's chair. He glares at them but doesn't say anything before returning his attention to me. I don't usually tell anyone how I got started with computers, but as Clay sits and waits, I think what the fuck. It's not like he'll be here in a few days, and there's nothing he can use against me. "I didn't have many friends growing up, so most of my time was spent alone. I was the nerd that no one wanted to hang with, but when I got online, I could be whoever I wanted to be. It started small with chat rooms and things, but soon I worked out how to see behind the rooms. That's when the real fun started."

"Real fun?"

I shouldn't admit to Clay about all the illegal things I did as a teen, but I suppose since we're currently searching to see if the police have evidence of him killing a man, my misdemeanours aren't that terrible. I won't tell him the incident that finally made me fight back against my bullies, but I won't hide what I did. "It was little things to begin with. Hacking into the school's system to mess with the people that bullied me. Changing grades and sending letters home to parents about their behaviour. Soon though it got bigger, and the more they hurt me, the more I fought back. I would make fake police reports and put an alert onto their cars. When it got really bad, I would get drugs delivered to their houses, and that led to one of them being arrested. That's when I stopped because it didn't matter how much I hated them, it wasn't right to destroy their lives on fake shit."

I wait for Clay's judgement, but it never comes. Instead, he peers deep into my eyes, and I feel like he is trying to see into my head. Clay is the kind of man who sees everything, no matter how much you try to hide it. I bite my lip when the silence grows, but what I want to do is hide from Clay's knowing gaze. "How bad did it get?"

The old ache of being rejected and tortured on a daily basis rises. The memories of being pushed in the hallways, of being cornered in the bathroom by a group of boys a lot bigger than me and crying on the floor after they all took turns to degrade me, of being spat on and beaten, and then the final act of cruelty after they pretended to be my friends. Clay doesn't need to know that I spent every day in fear that I might not make it home. A guy like Clay wouldn't understand being scared and alone, he wouldn't understand the pain of living waiting on the inevitable. "Just the usual. Kids making my life hell and making me love going home at night." I need to change the subject. "I'm gonna throw that question back at you. What made you get into the PI business?"

Clay is silent so long that I think he isn't going to answer, and when he does my stomach drops. "Gabe."

I didn't realise that there was someone special in Clay's life but the fact that this guy made him chose his career, well it tells me that he's important. It's like a bucket of cold water on my body, but it isn't a surprise that Clay has someone important. He's gorgeous and outgoing, being single would be strange.

"He kept me together in a difficult time. When I thought that there was nothing left in the world he told me to keep looking."

He sounds so sad as he speaks and I wonder what he's gone through in his life. Is it possible he's not had the amazing life I pictured for him? "He sounds special."

"He is. Meeting him changed my life for the better and he's the best friend anyone could ask for."

Best friend? Suddenly the name rings a bell. He's spoken about Gabe before, when he was talking about Paul. He also mentioned Gabe's girlfriend Rhys. I don't want to think about why that knowledge makes me feel better, but it does. The thick feeling of jealousy vanishes in a cloud of uneasiness. "It's good that you have that."

"Are you close to Grant?"

"Yes and no. I've known him a while but we've only met a couple of times. Most of our contact is done on the phone."

Clay laughs. "That conjures up a lot of inappropriate images. I'm thinking babe station."

"Wrong audience."

"Yeah, well I don't know any channels that gay men would watch. I'm a babe station kind of man." He laughs but my mind is racing.

I haven't spent much time thinking about Clay's sexuality, because why would I? But now it's confusing me. There have been a few moments when I thought he's been checking me out, and then he didn't have any problems holding me when Kelly was here. All that points to him being gay or bi, but the comment he just made puts him clearly in the straight box. There are so many questions I want to ask him, but none of them are appropriate.

18
Clay

Sam is staring at me, and I have the sudden urge to explain everything. When I mentioned watching Babe station, his body tightened. It's probably not something that most people would notice, but when you do my job, you learn quickly to read people closely. Like when he was talking about being at school, I could tell that he went through a hell of a lot more than he was admitting to me. Anger built inside when he dismissed what he went through as nothing, and I wanted to demand he tell me who'd made his life hell so I could track them down and show them how it feels to be bullied. Is that what he's hiding from now? Since I've arrived, I've seen panic colour his face at certain moments, but the most obvious time was when that guy, Kelly, turned up at the door. I thought Sam was going to have a full-on panic attack, and it told me that Sam was hiding from someone or something that's still out there. I thought initially that he was here because he didn't like being around people, but I can see there's a darker, possibly more dangerous, reason.

"Do you have a girlfriend?" I'm shocked by the question from Sam, but going by the look of horror on his face, he might be more shocked than I am. "Sorry, you don't need to answer that."

"No significant other." I don't know why I don't say girlfriend because the question is an obvious fishing expedition. I should just come out and tell Sam that I've only ever had girlfriends, that I'm straight and have never been attracted to men, but I can't get the words to form. They feel like lies even if they are the truth. I can't say attractive men haven't caught my attention because they have, but I haven't looked at a man the way I'm suddenly looking at Sam. I know he's noticed my stares, and it's becoming harder to hide my attraction. I don't understand it, but the way my body reacts when he gets close to me, that can't be hidden. Standing in front of Kelly with Sam in my arms felt natural, normal, it felt like fucking heaven. It's been a long time since someone caused my heart to race and palms to sweat, and never before has it been a man. Peoples sexualities have never been an issue for me, and I know that they can sometimes be very fluid things, but never has it been my own that I've questioned. Now I am.

"I swear talking to you is like pulling teeth." Sam laughs, and the sound of it vibrates over my skin.

There's just something about Sam that draws me to him. When he's feisty and sarcastic, I have this sudden need to show him who's the boss, to make him give in to me. Then there are the times when he's quiet, concentrating on the computer or what's going on in his head, and in those moments he's simply breathtaking. His body is slim but not in a way that makes him look like he works hard at it, he just looks like he's built that way. His hair is dark to the point of almost being black, and he alternates between slicking it back and letting it fall naturally across his forehead. I haven't worked out which one I like the most because both have their appeals. He has a habit of chewing on his thick bottom lip when he's concentrating on something, and it's not the first time I've seen a tiny spot of blood appearing without him noticing. It's things I usually notice when I find someone attractive, but it's always been on women. Now Sam has caught my attention, and I'm not sure what to do about it. "Sorry?"

"No, you aren't."

It's my turn to laugh. "You're right, I'm not."

"We have a lot of time to pass. How about a game?" He gets a wicked gleam in his eyes, and it intrigues me enough that I want to agree. I can't give in straight away though, not without some teasing.

"A game? Are we twelve?"

Sam sticks his tongue out at me, but it doesn't deter him. "Shut up. We can play a short version of twenty questions. We each get two questions, and then we swap."

"Ah, so we are twelve?"

Sam picks up the computer shaped stress ball from the desk and throws it at me. I laugh as I catch it easily, and nod at him.

"Fine, but I go first."

Sam looks wary, and it makes me even more eager to get started. I plan on going easy to begin with so I don't scare him off. This is the perfect opportunity to get to know Sam, and for some reason, that makes me happy. He motions for me to go ahead and I lean forward with my elbows on my knees. It brings me much closer to Sam, close enough that I can see his Adam's apple moving as he swallows. The movement catches my attention, and I have a sudden urge to feel it move under my tongue. *What would it feel like as it moved?*

"Are you forfeiting?"

I shake my head as I drag my attention away from Sam's neck. "Nice try. Question one. Favourite band?"

"Panic! At The Disco."

"Most embarrassing moment." This gets Sam chewing his lip as he looks at the ceiling.

"My first kiss. It was terrible."

Oh, he so isn't getting away with such little explanation, but before I can question him more, he takes over.

"Favourite food?"

I make a note to revisit his first kiss because I really want to know what happened. "Spicy chicken wings."

"I so had you pegged as a red meat man." His cheeks heat as he realises what he says, and I can't help but laugh at him.

* * *

We're still sitting in the same spot two hours later. We've stopped to eat, and Sam's had to do some things on the computer, but each time we've returned to this stupid game. It's been fun and the longer we play, the more risky the questions have become. It started gently with the usual things like favourite colour and holiday destination, but now it's getting more personal with questions about our jobs and friends.

"Have you ever done drugs?"

"Never." I don't go any further into my reasons. Watching my mum destroy herself with alcohol and antidepressants made sure that I stayed away from anything I might become addicted to. I still drink alcohol, but nothing stronger than that.

"Dream car?"

"The truck I have, just a bigger version. The F-150 Raptor is the ultimate." I almost moan when I envision the beast of my dreams. It's such a powerful machine, and I would give my left nut for one. "My turn. Do you have any siblings?"

"Um ... yeah."

It's not the open answers he's been giving me, and it piques my interest. Before I can dig deeper into his family, an alarm sounds from the computer next to him and he instantly turns to face it. He spends time working away on the keyboard and I forget all about our little game, thinking that something is finally happening. I try to follow what's appearing on the screen, but he's moving through the windows at lightning speed. I'm close to yelling at him to slow down when everything stills, and on the screen appears a picture of Paul.

My stomach churns as I stare at his face, the urge to kill him all over again spreading through me. He was always a smug fucker, and that shines through even from the picture. "That's him."

"Then I have the missing person file."

It feels like it's taken forever to find anything, but now that we have, I'm not sure I want to carry on. Sam turns to look at me, worrying his bottom lip as he waits for me to speak. "Can you see what's in it?"

He nods and focuses on the computer again. Reports appear along with evidence pictures, and I can see my own image on some of them. They've apparently taken stills from the CCTV near Paul's house, and the more that opens, the guiltier I start to look. "Shit. He really does have a lot."

"Sorry." Sam doesn't look at me as he continues to work, and a few moments later a video screen appears. I stare at it as I hold my breath.

This is the moment I'll finally see everything that detective Archer has on me, and it will tell me if I'm going to prison. "Do you want me to leave?"

I shake my head, and Sam presses the play button. It's grainy, but it's easy to make out my truck parked a few cars down from Paul's front door. Paul steps out of the building, and I feel the same anger that I felt that day. It's like watching a television programme unfolding in front of me, but I know what's about to happen. I know that I'm going to follow Paul down that alleyway, and a few minutes later I'm going to drag an unconscious Paul out and dump him in my truck.

Reaching out I grip Sam's wrist tightly. I can't speak but thankfully he understands what I'm trying to convey to him and he turns off the video. Bile is rising from my stomach because everything is about to change. The life that I've made for myself, the people who have become my family, I'm going to lose them all. When Gabe went away, he started to fade. It's like he gave up on everything and lost who he was. I don't want that to happen to me, but I don't know how to change anything.

"I'm so sorry, Clay. I..."

I clench my eyes closed against the tears that are building. I don't know if they are from anger or fear, but I know that I need to talk to Gabe. He's my lifeline and the only person I can speak to about these things. I'll need his help to sort shit out before I vanish. That's where this whole thing is leading. I need to leave before the police can get a hold of me, hide from everyone until they stop looking for me. If they can't find me, they can't send me to prison. Yeah, that's what I can do. I'm sure Niko would be able to help me become someone else. He's done it with himself and Corey.

"I need fresh air." I don't wait for a reply before getting off the chair in the stuffy room. I practically run for the front door needing to get outside. My chest is heaving by the time I get there, my lungs fighting against the panic building inside to try and fill. As soon as the cool breeze hit me I bend over and gulp in air.

I don't think before grabbing my phone and dialling Gabe. I need to hear his voice, let him talk me out of this panic attack. I rarely let anything get to me like this, but when I've slipped in the past, he's always managed to talk me away from the ledge. The phone rings in my ear as I collapse onto the top step, letting myself sag until I'm nearly doubled over.

"Hey, fucker. When you heading home?"

Even just the sound of Gabe's voice helps to ease a little of the fear that's attacking me. I want to talk to him, but I can't squeeze words past my tight throat. The only other time my emotions got the better of me was after my brother died. Gabe was the one to pick up the pieces and put me back together, and that was the day I swore I wouldn't let myself be controlled by emotions again.

"Clay? Are you there?"

Words still don't happen but the first sob escapes, and it's only the start of them.

"Shit. Clay, what's wrong? Talk to me."

I just can't calm down. My breathing has changed from being stuck in my chest to coming too fast. The sudden change is making my head spin, and I'm struggling to focus.

"Listen to me, brother. Listen to my voice and focus on it. I need you to slow your breathing down before you pass out. Take a deep breath and just keep listening to me."

I follow all his instructions, just letting his voice soothe my shattered nerves. He keeps up a constant monologue in my ear while I get my body back under control. I don't know how long he stays with me, but when the ringing in my ears fades entirely, he's still there, telling me to talk to him. I can finally breathe, but the tears are still falling unhindered down my cheeks. I scrub at them angrily, pissed off that I've let myself get into such a state. "Gabe."

"Welcome back. You scared me, Clay." I can hear the truth in his voice. He sounds strained, and I can't blame him. If he called me from some unknown location, sounding like I just did, I would have torn the world apart trying to get to him.

"Sorry."

"Talk to me."

I swore I wouldn't ever tell Gabe the truth. If he doesn't know what happened, he won't ever be involved in any trouble, but I can't keep this from him. I need to tell him. "I killed him."

There's silence, and I wish I had told him face to face so I could see his reaction. Will he hate me for taking care of Paul the only way I thought I could? "I know."

"I'm sorry. I just wanted-"

"Don't you fucking dare."

I go quiet at the anger in his words. Gabe doesn't often lose his cool, but when he does, he makes you stop and listen.

"I've always known what you did, and I don't think any less of you. You're my fucking hero, Clay. You did something I wasn't man enough to do. You made sure the woman I love is safe. I owe you my fucking life."

The tears that had stopped start to flow again. Relief floods my body when I realise I'm not going to lose Gabe from my life because without him my life is meaningless. It doesn't change the facts though. "The police know what I did, Gabe."

There's an audible gasp as my words hit Gabe and he realises what I'm telling him. Things are going to change, and not in a good way.

Sam

I watch Clay from the living room window as he speaks on the phone. When he rushed from the room, I'd followed him, worried about his sudden departure. Before he'd left, I'd seen the colour draining from his face, and I needed to make sure he was okay. I was so close to rushing to his side when I heard him hyperventilating, but I hesitated when I saw his phone coming out. Whoever was on the other end was yelling but not angrily, and whatever was being said was helping Clay calm down. When he finally started breathing properly, I moved to the window, but not before I heard his emotional confession. I could feel my own tears building with how lost he sounded.

Forcing myself away from the window I return to my office. I was always willing to help Clay with his problem, but seeing him break is giving me the determination to make sure everything is purged from the police's system. I need to do it in a way that leaves no links to me, and I need to make it look like a virus has attacked the whole network. If I go in and delete only the content from the one file, it'll be obvious what's been done. The plan is to clear out enough for it to look like system failure, but I also have to make sure I'm not getting rid of something important. The last thing I want is some evil prick getting away with something they did.

I start looking through some of the other files I'd highlighted. I need something small. Maybe some shoplifting or public drinking, anything that wouldn't put members of the public at risk. I run another search using a range of misdemeanours as search parameters, and it brings up a lot. They keep appearing on the screen, and I smile when I see how many there are. There are so many to choose from that I can make Clay's file disappearing look completely innocent. That's the important thing, making sure that no one suspects that this was an attack to help Clay. I can do it though, and I won't stop until I complete my task.

If I'm going to do this, I need to get supplies. Getting up from my chair I rush through to the kitchen to grab everything I need to get stuck into my task. Four cans of Redbull, a tub of red liquorice, and a packet of spearmint chewing gum later, and I'm heading back to my office to make some magic happen. As I step in through the door, I see Clay standing behind my seat, his hands in his pockets as he glares at the screen. He's more in control now, but his eyes are rimmed with red, making it obvious he's been crying. I ignore that though as I put my supplies on the desk because I'm sure he wouldn't want me to mention that fact.

"What are you doing?" He doesn't look at me as he speaks and I continue to set up around him.

"Getting ready to work." I get the layout on my desk perfect, so I'm not distracted once I get going. I'm not a neat freak by any stretch of the imagination, but once I start working on the computer, I need things a certain way.

"Work?"

"Yeah." I turn on my Sonos and press play, smiling as the first bars of This Is Gospel by Panic! At The Disco comes through it. This is my go-to playlist, and I can't work without it playing in the background. Hands grab me, and I'm spun until I'm facing Clay.

"What are you doing?"

I smirk, finally feeling like I'm in control of the situation. "Oh hun, I'm gonna make magic happen."

19

Sam

I LEAN BACK against the wall in the living room and stare at Clay's bedroom door. It's been two days since I started the task of infecting the police database, and tonight I watched as two hundred and forty-two files went corrupt. Everything that mentioned Clay was the first to be deleted, and it's all gone. He's in the clear. He can go home now without any risk from the police, and he plans to leave first thing in the morning.

I grab the bottle of tequila sitting next to my thigh and take another mouthful, hissing into the darkness when the liquid burns my throat. He went to his room earlier to get organised so he could leave first thing, and I've been sitting here hating the fact that's he's going to leave. Why wouldn't he though? There's nothing to keep him here any longer, and I can't think of a way to keep him here, not without making a fool of myself. I want to tell him that I want him, that he could stay another few days so I could taste his whole body, but I'm not sure how receptive he would be to that. He's all but told me he's straight, but I can't ignore the fact that there seems to be something between us, some sort of chemistry. Every time he gets close to me it's like there are sparks that ignite between us. It's been a living hell having him so close and not being allowed to touch him. *Holy shit.*

Every single brush against my body, every time he stood over me so that he breathed on my hyper-aware skin, and having his smell surround me in such close quarters, was both exciting and maddening.

Now he's all ready to leave, and I don't know how to make him stay. Honesty isn't going to work, and I dragged out the deleting job as long as I could. Realistically I could have finished the job within a day, but I was enjoying having Clay here. I spend so much time alone that his constant company helped me relax. I'm always so worried about Damien sneaking up on me, but with his size and skill, Clay made me feel safe. Also horny. I take another swig from the bottle and drop my head back against the wall.

The shower in the bathroom shuts off, and it brings my attention back to the fact that Clay is naked right now, his skin wet and glistening from the water washing over it. God, I bet he looks fucking amazing. What I would give to see his whole naked body just once. The clothes he wears make a perfect vision for a wet dream, but I know it would be nothing compared to him in the flesh. He has the most perfect arse, and I want to run my hand over it. The way his jeans mould to it as he moves makes my mouth water. And those tight muscle shirts –holy fuck they make me want to pin him down and lick him all over.

My eyes flash open from my sexual daydream as the bathroom door opens. Clay exits with just a towel around his waist and I see his bare chest for the first time. I nearly swallow my tongue as I get an eyeful of the most beautiful body I've ever seen, also the biggest. I've never been into men who are built, but Clay changes all that. He makes me think of all those guys you see at the gym, the ones who seem to spend their lives there, but I haven't seen him do anything to keep his figure. He hasn't worked out once and hasn't hinted at missing the gym. He seems relaxed with it, and that just makes it more attractive. His chest ripples as he moves and it's easy to see since his chest is pretty hair free. If he does have chest hair, I can't see it from this distance. His stomach looks solid but he doesn't have a six-pack, it seems more, I don't know ... just thick. I want to dig my fingers into it to see if it gives way under the pressure.

The bedroom door clicks closed, and I'm on my feet without actually planning it. I knock over the bottle of tequila, but I have enough of it in my system not to care. When I reach the door, I grab the handle but freeze. *What the hell am I doing?* It's a moment of clarity that I should pay attention to, but I ignore my inner voice and open the door.

Clay is standing in front of the dresser where his suitcase is sitting, grabbing a pair of boxers from it. He must hear me because he turns, and it takes everything in my slightly tequila hazed brain not to gape at him. His tattoos are like works of art, and I could spend hours looking at them.

"Sam?"

I look up, and when my eyes meet Clay's, I falter for the first time. This is such a bad idea. I shouldn't have come in here without his permission. I'm trying to convince myself to leave when Clay takes a few steps forward, close enough that I can feel the heat from his shower warmed body seep through my t-shirt.

"What do you want, Sam?" Is it just my imagination or is Clay's voice huskier than usual?

"I... um ..." I don't know what to say because all I can focus on is Clay's eyes getting darker. Those dark orbs flicker down to my lips, and I shudder at the move. I want him so fucking bad. He's so close, and I don't know what to do. The one thing going through my head is dropping to my knees to worship him, but I'm pretty sure he would freak the fuck out.

"Tell me. Be brave, Sam."

His words strengthen my nerve and when the corner of his mouth quirks up, I know that's his intention. *Is it possible that Clay wants me but doesn't want to admit it?* This leads to a whole new set of questions. Has he ever been with a guy before? Does he want to be with one now? There's only one way to find out, and as I stare at him intently, I'm glad that I have had some liquid courage. "Have you been with a guy before?"

His nostrils flare, and I know I've caught his attention fully.

"I don't think you have, but I think you want to. I think you want me, Clay. I just think you don't know what do with that." He doesn't disagree, and I nearly cheer in joy. If he'd told me he wasn't interested,

I would have backed off, but he's standing there with hooded eyes, and as I flick my gaze down his body, it's clear to see he has a pretty impressive erection behind the thin towel. I stare dumbly at it for far too long, and when Clay moves nervously, I shake my head. I have to build a plan, one that Clay will be willing to go with because I need this man like I need air.

I place my hand on his chest and put pressure on it until he moves. I aim him at the chair that's sitting in front of the window, and when we reach it, Clay lands on it heavily. He hasn't looked away from me, and it's giving me the confidence to keep going. If he were against any of this, or uncomfortable in any way, he wouldn't be going along with it as readily as he is. He's twice the size of me so making me stop would be easy.

Stroking my fingertips across his pecs, I almost melt into the floor. The muscles are hard, but the skin is so smooth and warm. I circle him until I'm standing behind him, and this gets my first nervous question from Clay.

"What are you doing, Sam?"

I kneel behind Clay, making sure I can work on his arms while speaking in his ear. I grab the tie back from the curtain beside me and secure one of Clay's wrists to the chair back. "I want you, but I know you aren't sure." I work to secure his second wrist to the chair. "This way you can pretend you had no option. You can tell yourself I forced you." His wrists are secure, but it wouldn't take more than a few good tugs for them to come free. I want him to feel like he has no choice but to sit there, but I don't want it to be that real. There's no doubt in my mind that he wants this, but tying him up against his will would be creepy.

Clay's body erupts in goosebumps, and I give in to my urge to taste him. I run my tongue along his shoulder and follow a path to his chest. His flavour explodes on my tongue, and I moan as I bite his nipple.

"Sam, god." Clay sounds like he's struggling to breathe and it spurs me on.

Finally fully in front of him, I slide my hands along his thighs until they touch his towel, and I add pressure until his legs open. When I have the space I'm looking for, I get to my knees in front of Clay and finally let myself look over him. He looks like Captain America on steroids, but not in an off-putting way. There's no getting around the fact that the guy is a fucking giant, but it looks good on him, like he was meant to look like that. His tattoos swirl around the dips of his muscles, emphasising their shape and highlighting his natural beauty. I don't have any tattoos, but if I ever wanted one, I wanted to see the guy who did Clay's.

"You really are a sexy fucker. God, I just want to spend hours exploring your body." I lean down and lick from his belly button to his nipple, moaning against his skin in pleasure. Clay's body is vibrating now, in what I hope is pleasure, but before I move this in a direction that there'll be no return from, I need to double check on Clay. "Are you okay?"

He doesn't speak, but he nods smoothly.

"Do you want me to carry on?" *Oh god, please say yes.*

When he nods again I almost fist pump the air, but instead, I run my finger along the edge of the towel where it sits on his stomach. When I reach the knot that holds it tied, I release it and brush the edges apart until it falls open on either side of Clay's thighs. Now I do groan, the noise deep and long as I eat up his body with my stare. "Jesus."

I can't tear my eyes from his achingly hard cock. It's sticking straight out in front of him, and if his words didn't convince me that he was into this, his erection would. My mouth waters as I stare at it because it looks fucking incredible. He isn't huge which is always a blessing, but he's thick, and I know he would stretch me to my limits.

"Sam, please."

I repeat Clay's words back to him, loving when his breath hitches. "What do you want, Clay? Be brave."

I can see the indecision in his eyes as he battles with his brain, but I won't carry on until he speaks. No matter how much I want to take his cock into my mouth, he needs to ask for it. I am willing to make this as easy for him as possible, but I refuse to be the only one admitting what they want.

"Touch me."

I smile as my body hums. This is it, the moment I've wanted since

I saw Clay storm down the driveway towards me. "With fucking pleasure." I don't even hesitate before running my tongue along the length of his cock, only to return my nose to the base of it to inhale his scent. I fill my nose with a smell that is pure man, letting my tongue sneak out to play with his balls.

"Fuck." Clay's word is punctuated with a thrust of his hips, and I ease him forward until he's sitting on the edge of the chair. The angle gives me better access to his balls, and I nuzzle into them before sucking one into my mouth. "Sam!"

I watch Clay as pleasure spreads over his face. He looks down at me in awe, and it makes me want to show him how good it can be. I don't know who's sucked his cock in the past but by the look he's giving me they have never done it right. Making sure he keeps eye contact with me, I let his ball ease from my mouth with a gentle pop, before using the flat of my tongue to lead a path to the crown of his dick. Precum coats my tongue before I reach the tip and the taste makes me lick harder. I want more of his cum, and there's only one way to get it. I take his tip gently, working my tongue around his crown before taking him deeper into my mouth.

"Fuck. Sam, oh god."

I fucking love that Clay is using my name so openly. It shows me he's fully aware who he's here with, and that he isn't trying to pretend I'm not a guy. I relax and ease down slowly until Clay's cock hits the back of my throat. Giving head is one of life's pleasures for me, and if I'm only going to get to do this once, I'm going to take my time and make sure it's fucking good. Groans of pleasure hit my ears as I slide off of him, only to drop quickly, so he's filling my mouth again.

My head is full of Clay as I continue to play with him, but I want more. Sliding my hands along his thighs, I grip his balls gently as I gag on his dick. The move has saliva sliding from my mouth and down to where my hands are holding him. I repeat the move a few times, watching as Clay's eyes glaze over. He looks thoroughly fucked already, and I've barely started. When my fingers are drenched with spit, I begin to rub them below his balls, slowly easing back towards his hole. I take my time to give him a chance to stop me, but when I brush my finger over the puckered flesh, he thrusts into my mouth as he yells. I gag loudly, blinking tears out of my eyes, but repeat the action to have him shoving deep again.

"I'm gonna come." Clay's voice sounds like gravel as he thrusts deep, his eyes glowing with lust and passion.

I ease away from his cock, but keep my finger pressed against his hole where I rub gently. His erection bobs in front of me, and I blow gently knowing how cold it will feel. After being in the warmth of my throat, the cool air will feel like ice.

"Fuck." Clay has been reduced to a few choice words now, and I take that as a badge of honour. When you can turn a man on so much, he forgets how to speak in full sentences, that means you're doing a fantastic job.

"You really are a work of art." I run my tongue over the top of his thigh, tracing the outline of a rose tattoo he has there. Clay licks his lips as he looks down at me and I want nothing more than to kiss him. I think that might be a line in the sand I shouldn't cross though, because kissing is more intimate than what we're doing, or at least I think it is. So no matter how much I want to feel his lips against mine, I entertain myself by returning to the blowjob. This time when I take him deep, I press harder against his arse, my eyes rolling as I feel his pucker twitching against my finger. He wants to let me in, he just doesn't want to want it. Not every guy likes arse play, but when I feel Clay pressing against my finger, I know he wants me inside.

Increasing my pace, I try to get Clay's attention away from his arse and squarely on his dick. If he relaxes I can get inside him and show him how good it feels. More pre-cum explodes on my tongue as I finally slip my finger inside him. Clay gasps, but he doesn't tell me to stop, so I press deeper, fucking him gently with the slim digit. His heat feels like fucking heaven around my finger, and my cock twitches inside my shorts with a need to be inside him. I try to focus, knowing I can come later once we're done. This moment is entirely about Clay.

"Sam."

I don't know if it's a plea or a warning, but either way, I want to taste Clay fully. I press my finger in deeper, brushing slightly against the Holy Grail inside his body. I know when I've found it because he thrusts without control into my mouth. I groan against the intrusion even though my jaw aches around his thickness. I'll be feeling Clay's stretch in my mouth for days to come, and that thought spurs me on.

"Sam. Shit, seriously. I'm gonna come if you don't stop."

I keep my eyes on his as I take him deeper, pressing against his prostate while I swallow around his crown. I'm not sure what action finishes his fight, but he roars as he thrusts into my throat, coming in thick streams against my tongue. I swallow as much as I can but feel some dripping from the corner of my mouth. I moan at his taste, the slight bitterness making my taste buds happy. I hate it when men are too sweet, and Clay is a perfect combination.

When he's finally finished, I slip my finger from his arse and kneel back on my feet. I wait for the panic and disgust to cross over Clay's face now that we're finished, but it never comes. Since he doesn't seem to be throwing a fit about getting out of his ties, I take another chance and stand in front of him. His eyes never leave me as I rub over my aching cock. There's a chance that he won't be happy watching me get my pleasure, but I'll keep going until he tells me to stop. Lowering my shorts until I can get my cock free, I grip my erection and wank slowly. Clay's focus doesn't drift, but his cheeks colour and he gets restless.

"Sam?"

This is it. This is the moment he explains it was all a mistake and it shouldn't have happened.

"Fucking untie me."

My heart drops in my chest. I tuck myself away, but instead of reaching around to untie him, I tell him how to get out. "Just tug hard."

He does just that, and I prepare for him to make his excuses. I need to leave before this becomes too embarrassing, but before I get a chance to move, he has me lifted against his body and my back hits the wall behind me.

20

Clay

FIRE IS SPREADING through my veins as I watch Sam pleasure himself in front of me. When he walked into the room earlier I had an idea why he was here, I just wasn't sure if I was going to go along with his plan. As soon as I got within touching distance, I knew that the pretence was gone. I wanted Sam with an urgency that I couldn't hide any longer. The first touch against my body and I knew there was no turning back. The way he played my body to perfection just gave me the most intense orgasm I've ever experienced, his finger inside me increasing every single feeling.

Watching him in front of me makes me need more. He's still fully clothed, and I want him stripped naked. I want to touch him like he did with me, but I can't with my arms tied to this fucking chair. It had been a smart idea from Sam. Making me feel that I didn't have a choice in tonight's events had made my brain quiet enough to let my body just feel. Now my mind and body are both on the same page, and I need out of these bonds so I can take what I want from Sam. "Sam?"

His hand slows on his cock, and he suddenly looks unsure. I hate seeing that on him. I want the confident guy who tied me to this chair. I want him to fight me for dominance because it will be all that sweeter when I win.

"Fucking untie me."

More doubt and his voice is quiet as he speaks. "Just tug hard."

I do as he tells me and the ties fall away almost instantly. I can't believe I was that close to being able to get free this whole time. Panic spreads through me as I see him start to turn away and instinct has me out of the chair, using my still naked body to manhandle Sam into the wall behind him. I growl as I feel him against me, but I don't spend too much time thinking about it. The only thought in my head is to claim Sam as mine. I'm not naïve enough to believe this will be anything more than just one night together, but that doesn't stop me from finally taking what I want.

Sam's doe eyes are on mine as he pants audibly, his pupils large with lust as he leans into me. I want to say so much but that all vanishes from my head when he licks his fucking lips. The wetness he leaves behind is as enticing as lip-gloss on women, and without thinking I lean forward and kiss him. He moans against my lips as he opens for me instantly. His taste explodes on my tongue, and I dive deeper, needing more of him. We wrestle for control with our tongues, and I fucking love that Sam isn't a passive participant. I want it rough with him. I want to feel it.

Grinding against his body feels like heaven, and it doesn't take long until my dick is back in the game, hardening against Sam's erection as he presses back into me. When oxygen becomes an issue, I separate our mouths but keep my lips on Sam. I trail them along his jaw, exploring the feeling of stubble against my lips. The roughness just heightens the whole experience, and I keep moving until I reach his neck. I've been fantasising about feeling his Adam's apple under my tongue and now is my chance to live out that fantasy. There's a gentle thud as Sam's head drops back and connects with the wall, and I use the extra space to explore.

I don't know how long I spend tasting Sam's skin, exploring the feel of it under my tongue, but my balls start to pull up with the friction from Sam's shorts where I'm grinding. I feel ready to explode again, and it's only then that I realise that Sam hasn't come at all. Easing back I stare into his eyes as I run my hands down his chest and grab the hem of his t-shirt. I want to see his body, no, I *need* to see it. Pulling the material up his body, I take my time undressing him, feeling like I'm unwrapping the most perfect present ever. With every inch of skin that's exposed my need grows. I'm so turned on, and I don't think I have ever felt this much need before. When his head reappears I throw the shirt away, not caring where it lands, and I brush my palms all over his slim body. He might not have a ton of muscle, but he feels firm under my skin. When I brush a finger over his nipple, it grows hard as a shudder spreads over his body.

"Clay, please."

Claiming his mouth again I continue my hand's journey south, pausing briefly when I reach the waistband of his shorts. Even after everything that's happened tonight, this feels like a huge step. This is the act that will confirm in my head that I am indeed attracted to a guy.

Sam draws back from me, his face gentle like he understands what I'm going through. "You don't need to do this. It's okay."

But it's not okay. I've wanted Sam since the first time I saw him. Actually, I think there was a part of me that wanted him the first time he cursed me out on the phone. He speaks to a deeper part of me, and my body doesn't care that he's male. "I know." With my mind made up, I slip my hand inside his waistband and slide them down over his hips. He's commando underneath, and it makes life so much easier. When his shorts slide to the floor, I let my eyes wander down to finally see what had been rubbing against me.

His hard-on looks painfully red and engorged, and when I give in to my need to touch him and wrap my hand around it, Sam groans loudly before dropping his head to my shoulder. The reaction spurs me on, and I slide my hand along his length, mesmerised by the way it feels in my palm. I've obviously wanked myself off, but this is beyond explanation. To feel another guy's cock in my hand is strange ... and so fucking amazing.

"You're killing me, Clay."

Soon I have Sam panting against my shoulder as I stroke him faster, and I flick a finger over his tip, using his precum to ease the motion. It might've taken me a while to admit how much I wanted Sam, but now I'm not hiding the fact I want to see him come. My own cock is leaking like it hasn't already come, and my eyes cross with Sam's next move.

He puts his hand over mine, but not before he grabs my cock and lines it up against his. We rub together between our joined hands, our mixed precum easing the way. Every time my tip rubs against Sam's prominent crown, I nearly come. This is too much sensation, but at the same time not enough. I want his taste in my mouth as we come together, but nothing in the world could get me to look away from our close cocks. The erotic way we fuck into our joined hands, our crowns appearing between our fingers before slipping inside again, it's going to star in my dirty dreams for the rest of my life.

"I'm gonna come, Clay. Fuck, it's just too good." As if to prove his point he bites my shoulder, and it's the end of my control.

I come with another roar, shooting all over our hands a few seconds before Sam joins me. His groans are the sexiest thing ever, and I wish I'd looked at his face to see his reaction.

The air stills between us but neither of us move, our warm cocoon keeping us from the outside world. Eventually, I need to move, but I don't go far, turning to grab the towel from the chair behind me. When I turn back and see Sam still leaning against the wall, I can't help but smile. He looks like he has been thoroughly fucked and I want to beat my chest with pride that I did that to him. Giving him pleasure is satisfying in the most primal way.

"You're staring." Sam smiles despite his words and I'm sure that he likes me staring at him.

"I am. And you make a pretty impressive sight."

This makes Sam's cheeks heat, and if I thought he looked perfect before, I was wrong. This is the vision that will haunt my dreams for years to come, and it will probably star in many erotic fantasies. I throw the towel at him after I've cleaned myself off, chuckling when his face screws up.

"Thanks, but you could have handed me a clean bit."

"You didn't complain a few minutes ago about having my cum in your hand."

More colour appears in Sam's cheek, and it takes all the restraint I have not to run a finger along his cheek. I want to keep touching him, get my fill of pleasure before I need to leave.

That though sobers my urges. Tonight is a one-time thing, and when I leave tomorrow, there'll be no coming back. The only chance I might have of seeing Sam again is if he ever turns up at Niko's place at the same time as me, and the chances of that are remote. No, common sense tells me that when I drive away in the morning, I won't see Sam again, and I don't want to dissect why that makes my chest ache.

"I should ...uh ..."

Sam's awkwardness is entirely out of character, and it makes my heart melt. I shake my head to stop with the stupid, soppy feelings. I need to remember that this was nothing but a good night to work off some built up frustrations. That's why my next action doesn't make any sort of sense, but it happens. Taking the towel from Sam's hand, I throw it in the corner where I can pick it up in the morning, and grab his now empty hand and drag him behind me. I pull the duvet back from the mattress and climb into bed, settling in the centre. Sam stands and stares at me, letting out a little gasp when I pull him into the bed beside me. Once he's settled, I drag the duvet over our cooling bodies, but I notice that he isn't close enough. He's lying rigidly next to me, and I think one wrong word from me, and he would sprint from the room. To make sure he can't escape, I wrap my arm around his shoulders and pull him into my chest. He's still tense for a few heartbeats, but soon he melts into me, and I sigh in pleasure.

Tonight is an escape from reality, and apparently I want to enjoy everything I don't usually indulge in. Take away the obvious fact that I just came with another man, the most disturbing thing is that I'm now cuddling with him. I'm more a fuck and duck type of guy, so wanting to lie here with Sam, without the urge to chew my arm off to get away, is really eye-opening.

"Are you trying not to freak?"

"Why would I freak?"

Sam's fingers start to brush over my chest. "Was I ..." He stops, and his fingers move faster until I place my hand on top of his, stilling his movements. "Was I the first?"

"I'm not a virgin, Sam."

He slips his hand out from under mine and slaps me gently on my chest. "I guessed that, you arse. I meant ..."

"Yeah. You're the first guy."

"And are you going to freak out?"

It's a fair question, and truthfully, I fully expected to. It's not like I suddenly moved to brunettes after a lifetime with blondes. This night should rattle me to the core because it changes who I am as a person. It changes everything I thought I knew about myself. I don't know if it's because I'm still in a post-orgasmic glow, or if deep down there was always the knowledge, but honestly, I'm just fucking happy that I had sex with Sam. "Was I that bad?"

His laughter is breathed over my skin and goosebumps spread at the chill. "No, idiot. It was ...fucking amazing."

I bury my nose into his hair and inhale. "I agree." Sam smells like man and sweat, and it's intoxicating. Silence descends on us, but it doesn't feel uncomfortable. It feels nice just being with Sam. Usually, I need to be on guard, making sure everyone is safe, but lying here tonight, I feel like I'm just a guy holding someone. It takes my mind back to the empty feeling I've been having the last few months, that feeling that I haven't been complete. I haven't felt that since I arrived at Sam's, and I just didn't realise it until this moment. I've laughed and joked with Sam, and it made me content to just be. He didn't expect anything from me, I don't have a front that I need to keep up, and it's damn relaxing. I hadn't realised how much energy it took to be strong, but letting Sam help rid me of a huge problem was liberating. It shows I don't have to do everything on my own, and I wish I could say that it will make me change my outlook on life. It won't though, but I can believe that it will as I lie here in a perfect little cocoon.

"It was nice having you here. Made a change from being on my own." Sam's voice nearly breaks my heart. He sounds much younger than his twenty-seven years, and his voice reflects exactly how I've been feeling. Lonely.

"Do you not have anyone here?"

"Closest person is Grant, but with his men keeping him company now, I don't think I'll be seeing him much."

I doubt that any of those men will be leaving the cabin any time soon. They need to spend time with each other so the obvious can be said. That they are all fucking crazy about each other. You can see it clearly when they look at each other. I don't know how a dynamic like that works, but since it isn't my life, it isn't my problem. "Do you not have a family?"

I feel Sam's body tighten against me and I know I'm about to open a can of worms that's difficult for him. That's if he answers at all. I've asked the question before, and he avoided it, covering up by doing something on his computer. It will be harder for him to hide this time, but it doesn't mean he won't try. Surprisingly, he answers, even if he doesn't go into details.

"I do. I have my parents, two brothers and a sister."

I wait for him to continue, but he goes quiet. If I want to know more, I'm going to have to ask. "Do they live close enough to see?"

"No. They still live near where I grew up down in England."

So he left his family behind to move here alone. He could have worked anywhere in his line of work, so why did he move so far away? "And you moved here on your own?"

More silence but I wait him out this time. "I needed to put distance between us. I needed … to be far away."

My mind races with all the reasons Sam would need to protect his family. Why is he basically hiding away in the highlands of Scotland where no one can find him? "Why?"

"Please, Clay." His voice is strained, and I know what he's asking me. He doesn't want to tell me his story, and no matter how much I wish he would, I won't push him. I know what it's like to have a story that you don't want to share, so I change the subject.

"Do you think the police will work out what you did?" When he'd told me his plan on how he was going to erase all the evidence against me, I was worried that it would end up getting him in trouble. I know all about electronic fingerprints, but when I mentioned it, Sam had laughed at me.

"They will see that things have gone missing, but they'll put it down to the virus that I planted. I linked it back to an email that an officer opened."

He makes it sound so easy, but god, I'm still not convinced. "And there's no way to link it back to you in any way?"

Sam moves from where he was lying, and I instantly miss his heat on my chest. That is until he leans over so he can look at me. He has a smile on his lips, and he's regained that cocky look. He runs a finger across my cheek, and I resist leaning into his touch. "I told you, sexy. I'm the best. There's no way that they can trace it back to me no matter how hard they try. I appreciate you worrying about me, but no police will be turning up at my door."

I can't help but laugh at his words. I love this side of Sam. It was the first thing that caught my attention, and it seems to rev my engine. "I'm just looking out for your welfare. I keep forgetting I'm looking at Mr Big."

It's Sam's turn to laugh, and he leans in closer to me. "Oh, call me that again." His body is fully on top of mine now, and I can feel my cock starting to pay attention. It's like I've become addicted to him and any time he touches me, I react. "Mr Big."

He kisses me gently, his tongue lazily swiping at my lips. I let him take control, just lying there and allowing him to have his way. He's kissing me like it's a Sunday morning and we woke up together with nowhere to be. This is what I imagined being with someone was like, I just know it's not something I am destined to have.

"I demand you call me that every time you speak to me."

"Hmmm." He's trying to hold a conversation, and all I want is for him to keep kissing me.

"Are you with me, Mr Wilson?" His voice is breathy, and he ruts against me. His skin is smooth and warm as it slides against mine, but there's just enough friction to make me want to combust.

"Yeah. I'm right here with you."

It's the last words spoken between us before a release induced sleep claims us.

21

Sam

I watch as Damien's goon grabs another bucket of water, and I brace myself for the ice-cold temperature that's about to hit me. I know they're doing everything they can to try and break me because Damien wants to humiliate me for daring to speak back. I don't understand why he's going to so much trouble when he could just kill me straight away, but I'd hoped his pride would take the lead over his common sense. When I picked a fight with him, I'd prayed he would want to get his revenge and thank god I'd been right about him. If he'd pulled a gun straight away and killed me, I'd never have gotten a chance to put my plan into action.

It wasn't much of a plan since I hadn't really had time to put together anything more than an escape route, but when I saw the first hints of what Damien had planned, I knew I needed to get out. I hadn't realised he'd actually taken a kid already, but when I saw Marc in Damien's office, I knew I had to work faster. Selling kids isn't something I want to be connected to in any way, and I refuse to allow Damien to keep doing it. My first job is to get Marc out of here, and then I can work on bringing down Damien's network of perverts.

The cold water splashes against me and I shudder at the freezing temperature. I inhale sharply at the shock, but I refuse to show any other reaction. I can tell the guy is getting bored of all this, especially since I've barely said a word since we arrived in this room. It's where I'd hoped I would be brought, the place where I set up my escape route.

"I've had enough." Footsteps follow the words, and when the large door bangs closed, I look up from the floor instantly.

Alone for the first time I spend a few minutes scoping out the room. I'd done all my planning from the blueprints I found on the computer mainframe, so I take time to familiarise myself in person. It's a stone room towards the back of Damien's property, and it's on a different security system to the rest of the house. The CCTV link is also separate from the main houses, and I rush over to the digital keypad to start working. I unclip the front of the keypad and rewire the screen, so a series of number appears. I'm about to input the code that will loop the CCTV feed when a banging sounds from around me. I look about, wondering where the noise is coming from. It isn't from the door, it seems to be coming from the air. I turn as the banging continues and I struggle to work out where it's coming from. There isn't one spot though. It seems to be coming from everywhere...

I COME AWAKE SLOWLY, and the banging is still happening. I'm so fucking hot, and it's only when I try to roll away from the heat source that I feel the large body I'm sharing a bed with. I'm confused for a fraction of a second until I focus fully, my eyes connecting with Clay's sleepy stare. He smiles at me, and my heart thumps harshly in my chest. Last night really happened.

I'm struggling with what to say when I hear the banging again. I sit bolt upright in my bed, my relaxed mood fleeing instantly.

"Someone really wants you." Clay's voice is rough with sleep, and I suddenly want to hear him moan in the same huskiness.

Another bang and I pull myself from my thoughts. The sane part of my head tells me that Damien wouldn't knock, but who else would be here? Fuck, would Kelly be stupid enough to come back?

"Sam. You might want to go answer that."

Fuck. I jump out of bed and scour the floor for something to put on. I have no idea where my shorts ended up last night, even though they shouldn't have travelled far from where they slipped down my legs. After throwing the gross towel to the other side of the room, I have to face the fact that they are gone. "Someone broke in and stole my shorts."

Clay laughs from behind me and hands me a pair I don't recognise. "Here, wear mine just now." He bends down to put on his own shorts as I rush out the door, tripping as I try to put mine on as I move.

My heart is pounding as I reach the door and everything in me tells me not to open it. I freeze with my hand on the handle, and it takes a few seconds for me to remember to breathe. I'm close to letting go of the handle when I hear a muttered *for fuck's sake* from the outside. I wilt in relief when I recognise the voice instantly and pull the door open.

"What the fuck are you doing here, Grant?"

Grant looks up from where he's trying to wipe coffee from the front of a leather jacket. That's obviously the source of his muttered curse, and the cup is now lying on its side on the ground, coffee spilling from it. "I was trying to bring you coffee, but that's not happening now." He glares at the offending cup before stepping over it and into the house. "I also came to make sure Clay hadn't killed you."

I laugh at his response. "Well lucky for you, since you're the arsehole who gave him my address."

He doesn't even look ashamed, his smirk brightening his eyes. "I felt you two meeting would be fun." Grant's eyes widen as he looks over my shoulder.

I follow his gaze and see Clay exit his room, his jogging bottoms hanging low around his hips, and he's running his hand through his messy hair. He looks thoroughly fucked, and my eyes feast on the delicious sight in front of me. I only realise what I'm doing when Grant coughs, bringing my attention back to him. When Grant skims his gaze over my body, I know he's guessed what happened here, and it wouldn't have taken too much effort to get there. I'm standing wearing shorts that are very obviously not mine. The fact that I have to hold them up with my hand is a dead giveaway. Add to that the bed head we're both sporting, and the very obvious bite marks on Clay's chest, and it would take a blind person not to put all the evidence together and come up with the fact we had sex.

"Morning, Grant."

Grant doesn't pull his eyes from mine as Clay speaks and I can almost hear the questions in his head. "Morning, Clay."

I need to put an end to this, and I do that by running away. "I'm going to get dressed." I nod before turning tail and getting the fuck out of there. As soon as I reach my room I slam the door behind me, leaning against it to prevent anyone from following me. I know no one will, but that thought is scary and one that won't go away. I don't need Grant's questions just yet, not until I have a moment to fully process everything myself. The truth is I hadn't planned on telling anyone what happened last night, but now that Grant knows there's no keeping it a secret. *Fuck.*

Banging my head on the door behind me, I take a few minutes to think about last night. Spending time with Clay had been mind-blowing, and the orgasms, well they made my eyes roll into my head. I hadn't seen it going the way it did. I totally thought that I was going to blow Clay and then leave so he wouldn't feel awkward, but when he pinned me to the wall and kissed me, I nearly came on the spot. He kissed like he acted, in total control. He took what he wanted, but that only made me want to give more. I would have done anything he asked of me after one kiss, but he seemed entirely focused on my pleasure.

God. The memory of his mouth and hands all over my body is making me hard again, and this so isn't the time for that. I push off the wall and rush to my dresser. I need to get back out there before Clay tells Grant things I don't want him to know. I may have sucked Clay's dick last night, but I'm not sure how talkative he is about shit like this. He seems like he doesn't let people know much about himself, but it could be different when it comes to his dick. *And what a lovely dick it is.*

Laughing at my own thoughts, I change out of Clay's shorts and into a pair of my own. I grab a t-shirt and slip it over my head, looking in the mirror as I run my fingers through my hair. Shit, there is no way to get control over that mess without a shower, so I give up trying. I sneak out of my room and into the bathroom, spending a few minutes brushing the funk from my teeth. When I can't put it off any longer, I head to the kitchen where I hear talking. Taking my time I look into the room before they notice me, watching the two men interact together.

Clay is leaning against the worktop, still topless, and he looks like he doesn't have a worry in the world. I keep waiting for him to freak out about last night, but so far he seems cool. Maybe when he goes home, it will happen, but he looks calm so far. I take a moment to get another eyeful of his impressive body while I can, but he must feel my stare and turns towards me.

"Hey."

I smile and enter the kitchen, making sure I keep my eyes away from Grant. That fucker has seen far too much already, and I'm not ready for him to start on me. "Did either of you want something to eat?" I head to the fridge and stick my head inside, scanning the pretty full shelves. Clay has made it his mission to make sure I eat, and he's been going to the store most days to build up my supplies. Now I can offer them a selection of breakfast foods, but I go with bacon and eggs.

"I'm going to go get some clothes on."

Crap. The silence grows after Clay leaves, and I can feel Grant's eyes burning into my back. I stand and close the door, finally turning to face my fate. "You have five minutes. Your time starts now."

"You had sex with Clay?" His voice comes out whispered, but I can hear him clearly. He looks intense, and as much as I want to mess with him, I think it's probably safer to tell him the truth.

"No, but we did ... stuff."

"Stuff? That's all I'm getting?"

"When you fuck Niko and Corey, who bottoms for who?"

Grant's cheeks burn with heat instantly, and his mouth gapes open. "I'm not telling you that."

I motion with my hands, telling him without words that's my point exactly.

"Fine, you win. I think you're being mean though."

I'm laughing when Clay comes back into the kitchen, and he looks between Grant and me. "Did I miss something?"

"Yeah, but it's probably for the best. Breakfast everyone?"

"Niko is about a day away from tying Corey to the bed so he can't get himself into trouble. Corey won't accept that he needs to heal and it's driving Niko insane." You can hear the affection in Grant's words, and it makes me happy that he seems to have found his place in life. He's found love with two men, both of whom he connects with, just in very different ways. I haven't seen them all together, but you can tell by the way he speaks about them differently that they both give him something individually that he needs. It genuinely sounds like he wouldn't feel complete if he was only with one of them, and that's intriguing. I always thought there was one person out there for you, the one that slotted into your heart and filled the missing pieces, but I was obviously wrong. Sometimes it's two people.

"Did you manage to see Drake while he was there?" It's the first I've been able to ask Grant about Drake, and considering the search for him was what brought everyone together, I hope he got to spend some time with him.

Grant smiles. "Yeah. We spent a lot of time just talking. I'm happy that he's safe, and he promised not to vanish on me again. It will be easier now that I'm living with Niko and Corey."

"You aren't going home? Back to the force?"

Grant plays with the napkin on the table in front of him. This is the first time he's looked unsure of anything since he arrived. "I can't leave. Everything I want is in that cabin, and if they'll have me, I'm staying."

I am so fucking happy for Grant. I have no doubt in my mind that Corey and Niko will keep him, and his happiness is all I want for him.

"I don't think there'll be much problem with that. I think if you tried to leave Niko would tie you to the bed next to Corey."

I laugh at Clay's words because they hit the mark perfectly. When Grant turned up at my door after leaving Niko, I could tell how much he was hurting. You don't hurt like that unless you're in love. Then hearing from Clay about how Niko had practically dragged Grant home with them, it shows the love that's there.

"You want to call and tell him to keep me?"

Grant and Clay banter back and forward for a few minutes and I enjoy watching him. Clay seems more relaxed today, and I want to think I helped with that.

An alarm sounds from my office, and I look towards it. I'm not searching for anything at the moment, so it's surprising. Clay looks towards me, watching, so I try to keep my body relaxed. He sees more than I'm comfortable with, and every time I panic he seems on the verge of asking questions. I ignore him, getting up from the table and heading to the door. "Why don't you both take your coffee to the living room? I'll just turn this off and join you."

I don't hang around as they start moving. I want to see what I'm being alerted to because now I'm away from Clay, my heart is beginning to race. The only thing that would set off an alert now is movement by Damien, and that always makes me panic. There hasn't been anything in the last few days, so I let myself become comfortable. Having Clay here helped to distract me too, but he's leaving today, and my mind will be filled with Damien again.

I sit at the desk and wheel myself to the laptop that's making the noise. I quiet it before reading through the notification, my heart nearly stopping when I make sense of what I'm seeing. Damien's credit card was used in the next town about thirty minutes ago. He's ten miles away. *Damien's here.* I roll back on the chair as my body goes numb, a cold sweat exploding all over my body. *Damien's close. That can't be a coincidence. He's coming for me.* I stand, but I don't know what to do. My mind has gone as numb as my body, and the fear is making me struggle to breathe. I rub my hands over my face in an attempt to clear the lightheaded feeling I have, but it doesn't help.

When I hear Grant laughing from the other room, it finally gets me thinking. I need to get Grant and Clay out of here before they're put at risk. If I'm quick, I can get them both far away from here before anything happens. Maybe I can leave with them after I purge my system so Damien won't be able to find anything.

This finally has me moving, and I rush into the hall. I don't care if they both think I'm crazy by making them leave so quickly as long as they go. That's the only important thing, getting them the fuck away. Movement on the security monitors by the door catches my attention, and I look at them, the blood in my veins turning to ice. There are three men out the front of the house. Two things register instantly. The first is the fact that the man in the middle is the one who has been giving me nightmares for months. The second is the other two men are pointing guns at the house.

I'm moving quicker than I thought possible. "Get down. Get the fuck down."

Clay and Grant turn to look at me instantly, the look of confusion clear on their faces, but they don't move. I won't reach them in time, so I just continue screaming, but it's too late. Even as I yell at them again to get down, the first sound of gunfire hits my ears. The noise is deafening, and I fall to the ground, covering my head as the room around me starts exploding where the bullets are hitting. The gunfire seems to go on for hours, even though I know it hasn't been, but when it stops, the room is eerily quiet. I risk looking up, and a sob escapes me when I see the bleeding body on the floor.

"No, no, no." I drag myself on my stomach towards Grant. This can't be happening, he can't be dead. When I reach him, I'm up on my knees instantly, my hands searching him to see where he was shot. "Grant, please talk to me." Hands on my face make me jump.

"Are you okay?" Clay's voice is rough, and I look up at him, needing to make sure he isn't hurt.

"Yes. Are you?"

He seems to deflate a little at my words, but he just nods briskly before his attention is on Grant. He checks him and Grant groans when his shoulder is pressed. Clay rips open his shirt, and I gasp when I see the blood covering Grant. There's a wound on his shoulder, and the blood is spilling from it freely.

"Oh god." The tears fall faster as the feeling of helplessness engulfs me. Grant can't die, he just can't.

"Sam?"

I can't look away from Grant, worried if I do he'll die. So I keep watching him until Clay growls out my name again.

"Sam."

I blink blankly at him, and he talks slowly to make sure I understand him. "I need you to press your hands here until I get something to stop the bleeding. Can you do that?"

I nod, and he takes my hands, placing them on Grant's skin, over the bullet wound. I press hard, and the blood seeps through my fingers. "Oh god." I keep repeating these two words, but I can't seem to get anything else out. When Clay says my name, I look away from the blood.

"Keep that pressed, and I will be right back."

I want to tell him not to leave me but I can't. He needs to save Grant and to do that he needs to get something to help. So I take a deep breath and nod, praying that the gunshots don't start again.

22

Clay

I HAVE no fucking idea what's going on, and I hate it. I'd been happily sitting in the living room with Grant when all hell broke loose. Now I'm tearing the bathroom apart searching for first aid supplies. Before starting under the sink, I grab my phone to call Niko. He needs to know that Grant is hurt, and I need help to get out of this situation. Someone's out there with a gun, and they don't care about hurting people.

My anger rises higher when I think about the fact that Sam has been hiding some really fucking dangerous secrets. I knew there was something he was hiding, a reason he left his family so far away, but I'd refused to push him for answers. That's my own stupid mistake. Maybe if I had forced him to speak to me, we wouldn't be in this situation now, or at least I would know what I was up against. Instead, I have my best friends boyfriend bleeding out on the living room floor and no idea who or how many people are outside. *Fuck*. I put my phone back in my pocket without making the call, needing to get back out to Grant.

Sam has no first aid supplies, so I grab a towel and rush back to the living room. All the colour has drained from Sam's face, and he looks close to passing out. He looks paler than Grant, but I can't ignore the fact that there's more blood spreading on the floor. I kneel next to Grant and get Sam to focus on me.

"I'm gonna need you to help me. I need to check if there's an exit wound."

"And if there is?" His voice is tight, and I can see he's barely holding onto his composure.

"If there is that's great. An exit wound means there's no bullet still inside him." I give him a small smile before removing his hands from Grant's shoulder. He lets me manoeuvre him easily, and I think shock is starting to set in. I want to pull him to my chest and hold him until he isn't scared anymore, but we need to get moving. "Okay, so you hold his chest there, and I will roll him towards you. You got him?"

Sam nods, and I roll Grant's body. He keeps him steady as I rip more of his t-shirt away, exposing the area I hope to see an exit wound, but there isn't one. "Fuck!"

"What? What's wrong?"

"There isn't an exit wound."

"What does that mean?" Sam's voice has gone higher pitched, and the panic is evident. I want to sugarcoat it to make him relax a bit, but I refuse to lie.

"It means the bullet is still inside him and probably causing damage."

Sam's hands falter, and I ease Grant back onto the floor. I look at the windows, acutely aware that I should be securing the house but I need to help Grant before I do. I want to ask Sam to deal with Grant, but I can't do that. There's no way that he would be able to handle it, but I need eyes on the outside, and he's the only person here.

"Sam. I need you to do something for me."

He blinks wide eyes at me, but he nods.

"I need you to go to the window and check outside. I need to know how many people are out there."

"Three."

"What?"

"There are three. Damien and two others."

So many questions that I don't have time to get answers to. The most important two are *who the fuck is Damien and what does he want?*

Those can be answered later though, once we are all safe. "Okay. I need you to go look where they are. I need to make sure that they aren't getting closer. Can you do that?"

He nods again but takes a few moments before he gets to his feet and walks slowly towards the cameras by the front door. That's another thing I chose to ignore. Why would he need such an impressive security system out here in the middle of nowhere? My mind told me it was because of the type of work he did. His equipment must be worth a small fortune, and I can imagine people would do anything to get their hands on the shit he knows. Is that what this is? Did he find out something about the wrong person?

None of that matter right now. I grab the towel and press firmly against the wound on Grant's shoulder. The bleeding won't slow, so I press harder, focusing on the towel to see if the bloodstain spreads. I pay close attention to Grant's chest because his breathing is becoming noisy. He sounds like he's trying to cough up something, the wetness obvious on every exhale. His chest appears to be inflating fully, but I hate the sounds that are coming from him. The last time I heard breathing like that was when Cameron had a collapsed lung after he had pneumonia. He ended up getting a chest drain inserted, and it had also been the beginning of the end. I shake my head to clear that thought, refusing to go down that path right now.

"Sam. I need you to talk to me."

I'm met with silence, and my head jerks up to look for him. He isn't by the bank of monitors like I expected him to be. "Sam?" I call out a little louder, but there's still nothing. I look around the room from my position on the floor, but it only takes me a few seconds to realise I'm alone. Did he go to call someone to get help? If he had why wouldn't he tell me?

Leaning back I look towards the front door, craning my neck until it's in view. The world drops away as I see it standing open, the bright sun clear through the space. *Oh god, what did Sam do?*

Sam

As soon as Clay asks me to check where Damien is I get to my feet. I watch him briefly while he works on Grant, and it's at that moment that I know what I need to do. I can't have either man suffering because of me, and I need to get help for Grant as soon as possible. I steel my back and walk to the front door, opening it as quietly as possible and stepping out into the bright sunshine.

Damien is still standing in the same spot on my driveway, and his smile is evil when he sees me walk down the stairs towards him. The men on either side of him move away slightly, flanking me from both sides as I get closer. I'm not sure what they expect me to do since they are all standing with guns and I'm unarmed.

"Ah, Mr Leighton. Just the man I was hoping to see. So good of you to join me."

"I didn't have much option. If you wanted to see me, maybe you shouldn't have tried to kill me." The attitude rolls off my tongue without choice because I refuse to let him get the better of me. He's probably going to kill me really soon, and I will not show him how much he's scared me.

"That was simply me knocking." His smirk makes me want to vomit, but I keep on my neutral mask. He takes a few steps towards me, and it takes everything in me not to step back. "I've missed you, Sam. How have things been?"

"Why are you here?" I need to move this on before Grant bleeds out. Hopefully, Clay has managed to stop the bleeding, but I can't risk wasting time on small talk. I was going to call an ambulance before I came out, but I was worried they would turn up while Damien was still here and the paramedics would get hurt.

"Why do you think?"

So many responses filter through my mind, but I go with the innocent act, not wanting to show my hand too clearly. "No idea, Damien. Why don't you tell me."

His smile fades, and his eyes turn dark and deadly. "You fucked up, Sam."

"Really?"

"Yeah. When you reported me to the police, you really should have made sure I didn't have another computer nerd at my disposal. I knew what you were doing long before you put the wheels in motion."

I stay outwardly calm, but my pulse has just spiked alarmingly. I should have guessed that Damien would have more than one hacker working for him, but I hadn't explored that avenue. That's probably why nothing has come of the files I sent to the police. Did he intercept them before they arrived, or did he clear out the system like I'd done for Clay? I'm cursing myself for not digging deeper, for not planting the information straight into their system as an ongoing investigation. I had put too much faith in them, and now I'm paying for my stupidity. "I have no idea what you mean."

"Sure you don't."

"Damien?"

My head spins towards Kelly's voice, and when I see him standing there, I want to scream at him to run. Then it registers that he just used Damien's name. A gush of air floods from me and I double over, grabbing my knees as the world starts to spin. I've been so fucking stupid. I let Kelly in and treated him nicely, and the whole time he's been keeping tabs on me for Damien.

"Ah, your little love interest is here."

I wipe the sweat from my forehead before standing up straight. Kelly has walked to stand closer to Damien, and it takes everything in me not to lunge for him. I want to grab him and take my frustrations out on his face, but I stay still, not wanting to rattle the goons behind me.

"I wasn't his love interest. He didn't ... he has a boyfriend." Kelly sounds so sad about that, and it's as confusing as hell. He acts as though he wasn't just doing his job, like he actually was trying to date me.

"That's right. You didn't do your job at all, did you?" That's all Damien says before he raises his gun and shoots Kelly in the head.

I yell in fright as Kelly drops to the ground, his body collapsing instantly. I can't look away from him, and my stomach churns as blood spreads from the wound in his forehead. His empty eyes stare at nothing, and I can no longer keep the contents of my stomach inside. I spin away from the sight of Kelly's body and vomit on the ground. The heaves wrack my body, and I feel like they may never stop. It feels as though my body is trying to expel everything it's seen over the last hour, and all the horrors and despair that I've witnessed ends up in a messy pool on the ground. I just don't feel any better when my stomach is empty.

"Right, let's get this show on the road. Sam, do you have any last words."

I pinch my eyes closed, saying a silent goodbye to my family. Wishing I could see them one last time but content in the knowledge that they're safe, and since they've already grieved for me, they won't know I'm finally gone. Taking a deep breath I open my eyes, refusing to meet my fate as a coward. If Damien is going to kill me, he'll do it while looking into my eyes.

He raises the gun and points it at my face. He looks far too happy for my liking, but why wouldn't he? He's won, and there's nothing I can do to fight back now. He will dispose of me and then go back to his old life of taking what he wants. That's what hurts the most, not the fact that I'm about to die, but knowing that after everything I lost to fight back against him, he can easily go back to the life he had before. He won't receive any punishment for hurting Marc or the others who will probably come afterwards.

"I hope the universe fucks with you. I know that I'm too late to do anything to you, but someone will one day, and I hope it really fucking hurts."

Damien laughs, and I brace myself for what's about to happen. I know it's going to hurt, I just hope that it's all over quickly like Kelly. There's movement on the edge of my vision, but before I have a chance to turn towards it, a huge body barrels out of nowhere and connects with Damien. There's enough force that Damien is lifted from the ground and moved back a few feet before being dropped. Damien manages to keep his feet and is instantly alert, his focus entirely on a really pissed off looking Clay.

My heart is racing as I watch what's unfolding in front of me, the feeling of helplessness building inside. I want to help Clay, but I don't know what to do. Clay rears his hand back and punches Damien in the face, loud enough that I hear the contact from my position, but it's not enough for him to drop the gun. It stuns him for several seconds, and it gives Clay enough time to look at me. "Go to Grant."

He doesn't wait for a response before turning away and grabbing Damien. Damien gets his senses back quickly, and since he's a fucking coward, he brings the gun up and smashes Clay in the side of the head. The move knocks Clay off balance but not enough for Damien to push him off. It does allow Damien to raise the gun again, this time pointing it straight at Clay. Clay knocks it to the side but it fires, and the bullet hits the ground near my feet. That gets me moving, but not inside like Clay wanted. Instead, I run over to the closest goon and search his now dead body for the gun he'd used. He has some sort of machine gun thing in his hand, but there's no way in hell I'll be able to make that work. I could probably handle a handgun since my brother taught me to shoot one of them, okay technically it was an air pistol, but I'm sure it's kind of the same.

I nearly yell in satisfaction when I find a small handgun tucked into the holster on the guy's chest. It takes a few attempts to get the clip open since my hands are shaking so badly, but eventually, I'm standing holding the gun. I pull the top of it back, hoping that I'm doing it the right way. I've seen them do this in the movies so it must be this way. When I feel confident in my abilities, I spin to find Damien on top of Clay. He still has the gun, but at least it isn't pointed at Clay any longer. Instead, he's using it to beat Clay's face, and as I see the blood dripping from the cut on Clay's cheek, I walk with determination until I have the gun in my hand pressed against Damien's head.

He stills instantly, fear becoming clear on his face.

"Sam?" Clay's voice is full of pain, but I don't look at him. I keep focused on Damien, my rage starting to build.

"I've spent the last eighteen months running from you. I gave up everything because I had to hide. I lost my family for you. I lost my life for you. And why? Because I refused to let you sell a little boy so some sick fuck could use him as a toy." I press the gun harder until the skin around the end of the barrel turns white. "But that little boy is back home, and he's happy. You didn't destroy him so I can live with my loss."

"Don't act like a martyr. You destroyed people's lives and didn't blink an eye. You can't pretend that you're better than me."

Damien's right. He's also very wrong. "I am better than you. I might have done some illegal things, but I never did the evil things that you had planned. He was only seven years old. The things they told you they were going to do to him ... you all deserve to go to hell. So I am better than you, and I would save Marc all over again if I had to."

Damien laughs, and the reaction throws me. I thought he might beg me not to kill him, maybe get angry and tell me to go to hell, but there's nothing funny about this. "You think he's the only little boy I've taken? Poor innocent, Sam."

"You've taken others?" I can barely get the words out as I envision all these boys, waiting to be molested by monsters.

"Not yet, but the plan is ready to be set into motion. You could have been a part of something big, Sam. You picked the wrong side."

Damien flinches like he's trying to turn and attack me, but Clay grabs the front of his jacket and keeps him in place. My next act comes naturally, and I barely think as I pull the trigger. I've never hurt anyone before, not even in a fight in school. I was more the run and hide type of guy, so I always managed to avoid any sort of conflict. I thought that I would feel more in this moment, but as I watch Damien flinch in Clay's grasp, his head flying to the side as the opposite side of his skull explodes, I don't feel anything. No anger, no fear, no shock. I'm numb as I watch his body fall to the side, Clay directing his fall, so he lands in the stones and dirt. Even as Clay takes the gun from my hand and wipes it on his shirt, throwing it towards the dead owner's body, I stand and stare at Damien.

"Sam?"

I blink back to reality as sirens fill the air. I don't know how long I've been out of it, but as reality rushes back in, so does the panic. "Grant?"

Doors slamming have me turning, and I watch as two paramedics rush into the house. I follow them instantly, begging out loud for Grant to be okay. The living room is a flurry of activity as the two men work on my injured friend. They quickly connect him to several monitors and put some cannulas in his hand.

"What happened?" The one with the blood pressure cuff asks without looking at us.

"He was shot."

"How long ago?"

I look at Clay for help. I don't know what time it is, and I can't get my brain to process anything properly. He wraps an arm around my shoulder before taking over the answers. "About forty minutes ago."

Nothing else is said before they scoop Grant up onto the stretcher and head for the ambulance. I follow them, needing to be with Grant. "Where are you taking him?"

"Belford." It's all they say before getting him inside the vehicle and taking off down the drive.

I stare after it. I'm confused why the police aren't here. There are four dead bodies in my driveway, and nothing was mentioned. I turn to look towards the bodies, only to find them hidden by the cars. Other than the evidence of a fight on Clay's face, Grant was the only visible proof something happened. "Are the police going to come?"

"I will call and report it, but the hospital will report Grant's gun wound. We need to let Niko and Corey know what happened."

"Am I going to go to jail?" Tears start falling at the thought. Clay pulls me into his strong arms, and I melt against his warm chest. Everything that's happened in the last hour hits me all at once, and I sob into his t-shirt, not sure if I will ever be able to stop.

"No, Sam, you won't go to prison. I won't let them take you."

23
Clay

I'M close to pacing a groove into the floor of the waiting room, but I can't force myself to sit down. We've been here for far too long waiting on news about Grant, and it won't be long until the shit hits the fan. I'm waiting for it to hit from all sides, I just don't know what will happen first. I called the police from my truck while we were driving to the hospital, and told them what they'd find at the cabin plus a brief rundown on what happened. I'd also explained we weren't running, that our friend had been shot in the incident, so we needed to go to the hospital. I didn't think there was any point hiding any facts from them since the hospital would report the incident anyway. I'm hoping the police won't turn up for us before we find out how Grant is, but then I don't think we'll be told anything until Corey and Niko get here. We aren't family so they might not give us any news.

Niko's the next problem that we're going to have to deal with. He'd been the first call I made, and it's a call I never want to have to repeat. Hearing his despair as he tried to grasp what I was saying, and then the rage as he started to understand, it was heartbreaking. He's been through so much in the last month, and I was only adding to his stress and pain. Dealing with the danger to Corey and now the possibility of losing Grant, I can just imagine how he's feeling. He'd hung up on me, so I don't know how he'll be when he arrives, and I need to be prepared.

My eyes flicker to Sam as I make another loop of the room. He's been sitting on the seat in the corner since we arrived. He's barely spoken since we left his house and I'm starting to worry about him. His attention is still on the floor, and even though I've tried to get him to speak a few times, he only nods or shakes his head. I want to get a nurse to check him over because I'm sure that he's in shock, but every time I mention it to him he just merely ignores me. I'll wait until the others get here so someone will be available for any news, but then I'm getting him help.

The automatic doors slide open, and I'm instantly alert as Niko and Corey enter the waiting room. Niko has his arms around a sobbing Corey, holding him close as Corey grips onto his shirt. I hear Sam move behind me and I glance over my shoulder to see him standing behind me. He looks stricken as he stares at both men, and I know that guilt is eating him up inside.

Niko looks up from Corey, and his red-rimmed eyes stare at me with a silent plea. He wants me to tell him everything is okay, that Grant will survive this, but I can't do that. I can't lie to him about something so important. His eyes change instantly when he glares over my shoulder towards Sam. The anger hardens his whole body, and he drops his arm from around Corey, moving quickly across the room. "You fucking bastard!" He reaches for Sam, but I grab him, dragging him away from his intended destination. He doesn't stop his abuse, pointing over my shoulder as he roars. "You put him in danger without him knowing. This is all on you. You killed the man I love."

I give him another shove, glaring at him as my own anger starts to take over. I understand Niko's pain, but hurting Sam won't change anything that's happened. "Don't!"

This gets Niko's attention.

"Don't you dare turn this on Sam. He didn't know Grant was coming, and he didn't know this would happen."

A sob from Niko. "But he did. He knew he was running from something. He put him in danger."

"Just like you did with Corey."

This takes the wind out of Niko's sails. I hate to talk to him like this, but he can't take his hurt out on Sam. Sam's only fault was not asking for help. A painful sob tears from Niko's chest and he collapses to a chair behind him. Corey is at his side instantly, holding him tight as he falls apart. I step back to give them space, not wanting to invade on their privacy.

I turn to check on Sam, only to find him gone.

* * *

I find Sam outside the hospital doors, leaning on one of the metal barriers. The night is cool, but Sam doesn't seem to care as he stands there in his shorts and t-shirt. I've noticed over the last week that it's one of his go-to outfits, and one I really love him in. Not that I don't think he looks fantastic in his black skinny jeans, the other staple part of his wardrobe, but this is more relaxed. I lean my arm on the barrier next to him but stay quiet. If he's looking for peace to think, then he can get it, but I'm not walking away. I'm scared that when the adrenaline wears off, he might collapse. Shock has a habit of doing that, and I've seen it far too many times to not worry about it now.

"When do you think they'll come?"

"Who?" I need to find out who he means. He could mean the police, but there's also a possibility that the guys we just killed aren't the only people after him. I want to ask him who they were and why he was hiding, but from the conversation that was screamed above my head when Sam was pointing the gun at the fuckers head, I can put enough together to realise it was really fucking wrong.

"The police."

The fact that he mentions the police makes me relax more. If he's worried about them, then the chances are that he killed the other danger to him. Damien. I'm sure that's the name I heard Kelly use before the guy put him down like a fucking animal. When I noticed Sam missing, I was fucking torn. I knew if I left Grant there was a chance he would bleed out, but not going after Sam was signing his death warrant. It was clear what he was trying to do. He was taking the attention away from who was in the cabin, away from Grant and me, and he put his own life on the line to do it. Leaving Sam on his own wasn't an option, so I used towels from the bathroom to tie a makeshift bandage around Grants shoulder, praying to fuck that it held long enough to get an ambulance there. That was my next job, and I'd given them the location but only mentioned an accident. Telling them that the wound was a gunshot wouldn't change the speed the paramedics would get there, but it would bring the police along with them.

Sneaking out the back of the house and around the side had been a practice in patience. Everything inside me was screaming to storm out the front door, but that would've only gotten everyone killed. I needed to swallow my emotions and pretend this was nothing but another job. Sam was a client, and I needed to get him out safely. When I was in a position where I could see what was happening, I was glad I had listened to common sense. It took time to place all the players in the game, but the most shocking one was Kelly. I hadn't seen anything in him other than a guy who wanted more from Sam than Sam was willing to give, and when Damien shot him in the head without blinking, that's when I knew I had to move quickly.

The two guys behind Sam had been easy to dispatch since their attention had been on the action in from of them, but Damien had moved quicker than I'd anticipated. When he lifted the gun to point at Sam, my heart had nearly stopped in my chest, and I'd been running before I'd formulated a solid plan. The ensuing fight should have been one I had the upper hand with, but when he coldcocked me with his gun, the fucker had made me see stars. How the fucker got me to the floor, I don't know, but I'd been fully aware of what was happening when Sam had pointed a gun at his head and started screaming. I just lay still and watched what unfolded, worried if I made any sudden movements that Sam would lose his foothold on the situation. Watching Sam trying to deal with his anger and pain had tested my patience because I wanted to take over, to protect him from what might need to happen. The biggest problem was I wasn't sure what outcome I wanted the most. The simple fact was the fucker needed to die, especially after Sam had mentioned selling kids, but I didn't want Sam to be the one to do it. I know what it's like to take a life and I didn't want that for him. You don't come back from something like that, and I knew it would live with him forever.

"Clay?" His voice is soft, but the pain in it pulls my attention, and I realise my mind drifted.

"I'm sure they'll be here soon."

"I just want to go home."

I stay quiet because I know the chances of him being allowed to go home anytime soon are slim, it's the reason I made sure to secure his office before we left. He locked down his computer system, making sure that no one could find anything on it without knowing where to look. The simple fact is, even if the police release him quickly, his house will be a crime scene for a long time. I've already contacted Porter so he can get me some accommodation close by. I'll need somewhere to take Sam when he's released, no matter how long it takes to get him out.

"Do you think I will go to prison?"

The pain in his voice is killing me slowly, and I take a step closer to him, so I'm leaning against his arm. "No. They'll see that we had no option. We did what we did to protect ourselves."

His head drops to my shoulder, and I feel his body hitch as he quietly cries. I stay silent and let him purge the fear he's feeling inside. When he quiets down, I wrap my arm around his shoulder, turning him and pulling him into my chest. He grips onto the front of my t-shirt and buries his nose into my body. The move feels natural, and in another lifetime I would work to make Sam mine. I'm not the kind of guy he needs. He deserves someone who can love with their whole heart and give him everything he needs. He deserves the love that my friends have found, and I don't think I'm that guy. With every part of me, I wish I was the man for him, I just don't know if I can change enough to make him love me.

"I'm sorry you're going to get into trouble because of me. I wish you'd just left me to deal with it."

I tilt Sam's head up so I can see his face clearly. "There was no way I was going to leave you to deal with that guy alone. I don't know what your story is, but I helped because I could. Don't worry about me, I can take care of myself."

Sam stares deep into my eyes, and I get lost in his gaze. The colour swirls as emotions flicker through them, and I want to lean in and kiss

Sam until he feels better. That's why I move back, putting enough distance between us that Sam's hands fall from my shirt.

"Why don't we go see how Grant's doing?"

He nods and follows me inside. We go up the lift in silence, and when we reach the floor where the surgical waiting room is located, Sam stops and looks in the opposite direction.

"I'm going to go to the bathroom before I come in."

I want to go with him because he looks like he's about to pass out from exhaustion. His skin is pale, even paler than before he'd gone outside, and dark circles are starting to appear around his eyes. He looks about five minutes away from collapsing on the ground, but I just nod and let him go himself. Sam's a grown man, and he isn't mine to prop up. I have and will do anything in my power to help him, but I'm not the guy who needs to give him the support he needs. He isn't my man.

As Sam vanishes around the corner, I head to the waiting room to see if there has been any news. There's a part of me that thinks no news is good news, but also the longer the surgery takes, the higher the chances of something being wrong are. Taking a deep breath, I walk in through the door and see Niko standing in front of the large window that looks out over the car park. Corey isn't in the room, and that surprises me. "Where's Corey?"

Niko doesn't turn before he speaks, his voice rough. "He went to call Drake."

I nod even though he can't see me, and head over to stand beside him. My heart hurts for Niko, and I hate this whole situation. He's been through so much pain in his life, and it's unfortunate that I seem to have witnessed most of it. I put my hands in my pockets and watch the darkening sky on the other side of the glass. I haven't thought about the time since we arrived at the hospital, but now I can see the stars I realise how late it must be. I probably don't have much time before the police turn up, and I'm shocked it's taken as long as it has.

"How bad was it?" Niko sounds flat, like his words have no emotion to them, and it worries me more than the previous anger.

"I don't know how to answer that, brother."

He finally turns to me, his eyes pleading with me and I feel a lump forming in my throat. "With the truth. You have never lied to me, Clay. Please don't start now."

"He was shot so it can't be great, and he didn't wake up before the ambulance arrived. But he was alive, and he's a fighter, Niko. He'll fight hard to come home with you."

A single tear falls unstopped down Niko's cheek. "I can't lose him. I just found him, he's half of my heart."

"We'll get him back. We won't lose him, baby." I turn to see Corey rushing to Niko's side and grabbing him into a hug.

I step away and give the men their privacy, but I keep watching them. Even as they separate and whisper to each other, I can't seem to drag my eyes away. It's like they're in their own little universe, their pain binding them together while they worry for the man they love. This is the other side of relationships I never learned about. I was shown that when times get hard, you run. You only think of yourself when the shit hits the fan. It's why I've spent my life just looking out for myself, so looking at these men sharing their grief is mesmerising.

"Hey." Sam's voice makes me jump slightly. I hadn't even noticed him arrive back, but then my attention had been in another place.

"Hey.' I finally turn away from the two men and focus on Sam. He has a little more colour in his cheeks now, and his hair is wet slightly around the edges like he's washed his face. The darkness is still around his eyes, but I think it would take a good twelve hours sleep to get rid of them. "You okay?"

He goes to answer me, but a voice from the door pulls everyone attention. "The family of Grant Morrison?"

Niko and Corey rush forward, the fear clear on their faces. "We're his family."

The doctor gives them a doubting look, and it's the first time I realise how their relationship must be complicated. In the everyday world, people wouldn't understand their love for each other. For them to have to always explain to people must drive them insane, especially in critical moments like this.

"I'm Mr Firth, and I'm the surgeon who operated on Mr Morrison. Would you like to come with me and I will explain everything."

Niko looks at me before shaking his head at the surgeon. "It's okay, they're family, and they can hear anything. Please just tell us, is he okay?"

The surgeon smiles at us before nodding his head. "Mr Morrison is in recovery, and he's doing fine."

Niko wilts before my eyes and he doubles over, grabbing his knees as he takes deeps breaths. Corey giggle sobs as he rubs a hand absently over Niko's back.

"He suffered a wound to the shoulder, but I managed to locate the bullet. It hadn't gone in too deep so it was easy to remove. It had caught a vein which needed to be repaired, but he will be fine."

"Holy fuck, he's okay." Niko speaks to the floor, but you can clearly hear the relief in his voice. I smile at the pure happiness I feel for my friend. It's about time the universe worked in his favour instead of trying to destroy everything he has. I look over my shoulder at Sam and see the tears falling freely down his cheeks. The relief is evident on his face, and I'm happy that he won't have the death of his friend on his hands as well as Damien's.

I want to go to Sam, to put my arms around him and tell him everything is going to be fine now, but before I can move there's more movement at the door. Sam goes as stiff as a board, and I don't have to turn to know who's there. I don't turn to confirm my suspicions before rushing to stand in front of Sam. His eyes are full of panic, and I see him struggling to breathe. Cupping his face in my hands, I stand directly in front of him, so I block his view of the police behind me.

"Look at me." I give him a moment to bring his attention to me before continuing. "Everything will be okay. I'll be right there with you the whole time. Just tell the truth, and there won't be any problems. You didn't do anything wrong, so you have nothing to worry about. Sam, do you understand?"

He nods, but I'm not sure he's heard everything I just said. It doesn't matter though because a shadow falls over my shoulder and I know my time with him is up.

"Mr Sam Leighton?"

Sam simply nods at the officer.

"We would like you to come with us in connection with an incident on your property. We have some questions for you."

"Is he under arrest?" I can't help but ask because I want to know what's happening before I contact Porter to get help. Porter will know who to get to help us if I can tell him the whole story.

"Not at the moment. We just want to have a chat."

I lean in and kiss Sam on the forehead, knowing that I'm giving off crazy mixed signals, but I need to give him all the comfort I can before he's taken away. "Go with them, but I'll be there soon."

Sam's head drops as he walks in between the two officers, and I'm glad that they haven't put him in cuffs. I'm also pleased that they haven't worked out my involvement yet, because I need time to call Porter. When he has all the details, I will turn myself into the police, but I need to get someone here to help Sam. There is nothing more important right now.

24

Sam

"So you knew Mr Howell before he turned up at your house?"

I stare at the police officer in front of me and wonder how many times I'm going to have to explain all this to him. I don't know if he's trying to get me to make a mistake by asking the same question a hundred different ways, but all it's doing is making me tired. I just want to go home, have a shower, and crawl into bed for eighteen hours. I want to hide from all this, but that's not going to happen for a long time. "I used to work for Damien so yes, I knew him before today."

"And what sort of work was that?"

"I'm a computer programmer, so IT is the best way to describe it."

"Let's not go with the best way, just explain what you did."

I take a deep breath before giving the answer I always use to explain what I do. It's the standard answer stating that I install online security and programming. I have a feeling that if the police go and search Damien's place, they won't find anything on his computers that will show I'm lying. I have no doubt in my mind that all Damien's illegal activity will be scrubbed from his computers already, probably passing onto the next in line before his body was cold. That's the shitty thing in that sort of world, it never stops. You think you've stopped someone, but all you do is create another six people who take over.

"Do you know why he came to your place today?"

"I took information about him and passed it on to the police. He wasn't happy and came to show me just how unhappy he was."

He looks at the notes in front of him, taking a few minutes to write something down. "You said this before, but there's no evidence that the police ever received the email you sent."

"I know. As I explained, Damien had someone hack into the server and remove the information. Go look up a missing kid by the name of Marc Collins. He went missing just over eighteen months ago, I was the one who found him and left him at the hospital."

The officer writes in his notes again, and I hope that he does actually search for Marc. If he looks at that case, he'll know I'm telling the truth about all this. "Why didn't you just go to the police with the information, why did you have to send it anonymously?"

"Because I would have died. Damien wouldn't have thought twice about sending someone after me, so I had to hide."

The officer nods and leans over to turn off the recorder. "I need to go check a few things. Do you want anything to drink or eat?"

I shake my head because I'm not sure my stomach can handle anything right now, not even the coffee I'm craving to keep myself awake. The officer leaves the room, and the silence is almost deafening. After spending the last few hours talking to one policeman after another, being alone now seems strange, and as my brain starts to drift back to the previous twenty-four hours, I wish the officer would come back and ask his stupid questions again. Being left alone with my thoughts isn't a good thing tonight.

My hands shake as they remember the feeling of pulling the trigger and putting a bullet into Damien's head. The sight of the side of his skull exploding as the bullet exited through it before he collapsed to the ground. Before today I hadn't seen anyone die, and now I've seen more than I ever wanted to. Watching Damien kill Kelly had been horrific, but taking a life was a thousand times worse. Even though I know I did the world a favour by killing Damien, that doesn't take away the guilt of actually doing it.

I close my eyes and force myself to think of something else. Like the fact that Grant is alive and likely to make a full recovery. When the surgeon came in and told Niko and Corey that the injury wasn't as severe as first thought, I felt the relief straight to my bones. Not only is Grant my friend, but he'd also been hurt because of me, and I will live with that forever. If he'd died, well I can't imagine what I would have done. Actually, I do, I would have let Niko do whatever he wanted to me since I'm sure he would've wanted to take my life as revenge. When he went for me in the hospital, I thought he was going to end me right there, but Clay had stepped in and stopped him. I'd wanted to tell Clay to move, to let Niko take his fear and worry out on me, but that would've only made me feel better. If what Grant said about Niko is right, he would have felt guilty after he had hurt me, and I didn't want him living with that. So I'm glad Clay had stepped in, at least for Niko's sake.

That thought leads me to the man who saved my life today, and when it does, I finally let my mind drift. He's been the happy spot in the last few days, and I'm more than happy to think about him. If I'm honest, he's been the best thing in my life in a very long time. Since I had to leave my family, my life has been filled with nothing but my work. Even Grant is only in my life because I helped him. Clay has brought some light into my dreary existence, and it's shit to know he's going to leave again. Spending the night with him was more than I ever imagined it could be, and as much as I tell myself that it was only a one-time thing, I can't stop my heart from racing when I think about the man who made my toes curl in pleasure. It wasn't just the sex though, it's been everything. The little touches, the way he looks at me when he thinks I can't see him, and the way he holds me when I'm about to fall apart, it's all addictive and leaves me craving more. I want something with Clay, but he's made it clear I can't have that. The only problem is that every time he comforts me, I fall for him a little bit more.

The door to the room opens, and the same officer walks in, dropping his file on the desk before taking a seat. He pushes a cup of water across the top of the table towards me before turning on the recorder. After stating the date and time for the tape, the officer takes a photo from his file and turns it towards me. It's a CCTV still of the night I dropped Marc at the hospital. It isn't a clear shot, but you can see what's happening in it. "So I checked into Marc's disappearance, and everything you said is confirmed by the statements."

For the first time since I arrived here, I can feel a glimmer of hope. Clay had told me that I would be fine if I stuck to the truth, and maybe he wasn't just trying to make me feel better. "I'm glad because it's the truth."

"Do you know the other two men that were found in the driveway?"

My stomach churns when I think about how many people died at my place. How many people's deaths I have on my hands. All this is my fault, and even though it was actually Clay that killed those men, he only did it because of me. "I don't know who they are. All I know is they work for Damien. I think one was called Mike, but I don't know." I feel bad that I didn't know these men, but then my common sense screams at me that that feeling is stupid. They were there to kill me, and they didn't care why.

He merely nods at me. "I need to ask about Mr Young."

Who the hell is Mr Young? "Who?"

"Mr Kelly Young. His body was found on your property along with Mr Howells."

My stomach drops when he mentions Kelly. I hadn't even known his last name, and he died in front of me. "I didn't know his last name."

"How did you know him?"

"He used to deliver my groceries."

I can understand the confusion on his face because I know everything about what went on and I still feel like none of it makes sense.

"I ordered my shopping online, and he would deliver it. I also had sex with him one time." I don't know if that parts essential, but Clay told me to be honest.

"Why was he at your house?"

"He knew Damien. When he arrived, he used Damien's name and said sorry that he failed. I take it that he was meant to be keeping an eye on me." I'm still in shock about that fact. I never would have guessed that Kelly had anything to do with everything I'd been hiding from. He just turned up one day smiling, and his sweet personality pulled me in. I wasn't looking for him to be part of my past and that was a mistake.

"So he was killed by?"

"Damien. He shot him in the head while I watched." My voice breaks and I take a deep breath so I don't lose it. I've already spent far too long crying over the whole situation, and I just want to get some control back.

"Do you know why?"

"No. Damien didn't exactly tell me before he did it." I grip the bridge of my nose and press, trying to ease the pressure building in my head. "Sorry, I'm just tired. He didn't say anything to me."

"Okay, so the gu-"

"Actually he did. He said Kelly failed him." I can't believe I forgot that he said that. Maybe I blocked it out because if he died because he had in fact failed Damien, that means Kelly's death is on me. I was the one who tried to ghost him before turning Clay on him. Oh god, I'm the reason that Kelly is dead.

I STEP out of the police station and into the bright morning light. It's just after eight o'clock, and I'm finally free to go home. Except I'm not because my cabin is still being treated as a crime scene and I can't return until the police are finished with it. Suddenly being free isn't as appealing as it was a second ago. *Where the fuck can I go?*

All the energy drains from my body until my legs are no longer able to keep me up, making me sink to the steps behind me. I spent hours in the station answering question after question, and my only thought was to get out, but now I regret it. I don't know anyone around here apart from Grant, but it's not like Niko and Corey are going to open their door for me. There's a good chance that both men will never forgive me, and I can't blame them. Why would anyone forgive the person that put their loved one in the direct line of danger without giving them a choice? I should have told Grant to stay away, but my loneliness had gotten the better of me. Now I'm going to lose him, and it will feel worse than it would have if he'd never become my friend.

Maybe this is the time to move on again, but this time I'll vanish completely. I have enough money in my account to live a few years without having to work, and by then everyone should have forgotten about me.

That sounds like the best option for everyone, but it doesn't help me right now. I need somewhere to go while I wait for the police to conclude their investigations because I'm not allowed to leave before then. They let me go today but told me that they would need me to come back to answer more questions. I could easily vanish before they want me to come back in, but the fear of them always looking for me would be too much to live with, so not an option. All that leaves me still sitting on concrete steps outside a police station with nowhere to go. I grab my phone from my pocket and start a search for local hotels. There are a few within a taxi ride from where I am, and I try to make an online booking.

A shadow over my legs makes me look up, and my heart skips a beat when I see Clay standing above me. He looks fucking gorgeous, and I hate him a little since I look like I've slept in my clothes for a week. "Hey."

I swallow down the lump that's built in my throat. Seeing him here is more than my emotions can cope with and I feel myself start to lose it. I don't want to break down, but I'm struggling to hold on. "Hey."

Clay's small smile is full of understanding, and when he holds his hand out towards me, I don't think before taking it and gripping on tight. He pulls me to my feet, and I follow behind him as he walks me around the side of the station and towards his truck. He doesn't say anything as he unlocks the door and opens it for me. I climb in and get comfortable as he takes his position in the driver's seat. When he's in, he hands me a small bag and a paper cup, the smell hitting me instantly. "Eat that."

I open the bag and inside there is a sausage and cheese bagel, and as soon as the aroma hits my nose, my stomach growls loudly. "Thank you." I devour the bagel as Clay starts the trucks and leaves the car park. I can't remember the last time I ate, but now that my nerves have settled a little I can feel every hour without food. Once I've finished I take a drink from the cup, sighing when the silky hot chocolate covers my tongue. I settle back into the seat more, the exhaustion hitting me hard as we drive along. The feel of the wheels vibrating over the road soothes me, and I struggle to keep my eyes open. Every blink gets longer, and before long it becomes harder to open my eyes. All too soon I give up trying and let sleep take me.

A hand gently shaking my shoulder startles me awake, and I sit up in panic, looking around frantically as I try to work out where I am. When I see Clay standing in the a few feet from the bed, the past day comes rushing back. I blink the sleepiness out of my eyes and look over Clay's shoulder. We are parked outside a house on a street I don't recognise.

"Let's get inside so you can get more sleep."

I look back at Clay, confused by what's happening. "Where are we?"

He takes my hand, and I automatically follow him until we reach the front door of the small house. I look over my shoulder and take in our surroundings. There are maybe another four houses on the street, and at the end of the dead end road, there's a field that's full of cows. "Clay, where are we?"

He opens the door but doesn't move to go inside. "I knew you wouldn't be able to go home so I managed to find somewhere you can stay temporarily. Don't worry, you'll be safe here."

I want to tell him that I'm not worried about my safety, not now that Damien is dead, but I just nod because talking seems too much like hard work. I need to have a shower and then sleep. "Okay."

Clay smiles, and it relaxes me even more. I don't want to think any more so I let him lead me into the house and down a dim hall towards doors at the end. He pushes the door open, and it leads us into a small bathroom. Towels are sitting on the side of the sink unit, and there's a smell of body wash in the air. It smells like Clay, and I take a deep breath, filling my lungs with the man that soothes my soul.

The sound of water fills the room and Clay cups my jaw, his thumb running gently over my cheek. "Take a hot shower, and I'll get you some clean clothes to wear when you get out. Take your time." He kisses me gently on the head before leaving the bathroom, and it takes all my energy not to follow him so he can just hold me. I need his strength to help keep myself together because I'm too tired to do it myself. I struggle with my t-shirt as I pull it off over my head, the material getting caught up on my head, making me curse at it before throwing it on the floor. I can feel the ball of emotion painfully in my chest, but I concentrate on keeping it there, knowing if I let it out there's a chance I won't get control again. My trainers and shorts follow my shirt into the corner, and I slip into the freestanding shower to let the hot water soothe me.

Closing my eyes, I stand directly under the water and let the flow hit the top of my head. The powerful spray massages my scalp, and as my body relaxes, the hold I had on my tears start to slip. Everything that's happened in the last eighteen months hits me like a fucking freight train, and I throw my hands out against the tiles in front of me to hold myself up. Tears stream down my face, the wetness mixing with the water from the shower and disappearing down my body.

How the fuck did I get here? My life growing up was great. I had a family that loves me, and my parents did everything they could to give me anything I asked for. We weren't rich or particularly well off, but our home was filled with love. My mum worked from home so she could be there for me and my two brothers and sister, and even after we were old enough to look after ourselves, she wouldn't let us come home after school to an empty house. It made our house popular with most of the kids in the street, especially since every day we came home there would be some sort of treat waiting for us.

My school days sucked, especially after I came out, but going home always felt safe. My family means everything to me, so to lose them entirely from my life has been the hardest thing I've ever experienced. I just want to hug my mum, have her take away all my nightmares the way she always did. And I want to meet my niece, to form a bond with her that will be unbroken for life. I need my dad to grip me by the shoulder and tell me that the world won't end because of one mistake.

A sob tears through my chest and I feel like I can't breathe. I can't get enough air into my lungs, and I feel like I'm drowning on my tears. Stepping back out of the water I try to calm down, but I can't get control, so I let it all out and hope that I will be able to stop at some point.

25

Clay

I PACE the floor outside the bathroom until I'm close to losing my fucking mind. Sam's taking far too long in there, and I'm starting to regret leaving him alone. Maybe I shouldn't have sent him for a shower because he looked half asleep, but I thought he would feel better going to bed clean and relaxed. Now I'm not so sure because what if he fell asleep in there? He could slip and hurt himself, and that will be on me because I left him alone.

Fuck it.

I knock gently on the door before easing it open. I wait for Sam to shout at me to get out, but when the sound of the shower is the only thing that reaches my ears, I open the door fully and slip inside. I don't know what I expect to find inside the room, but what greets me is Sam crying painfully, his chest heaving as he gulps in deep breaths. I don't even think as I strip off my clothes, my eyes never leaving Sam as I get naked and step into the shower behind him. I wrap my arms around his chest, pulling him tightly against my body and burying my nose into his neck. His fingers grip onto my arms like he needs that connection to survive.

"It's ok, Angel, just let go. I'm here." I brush my lips over his jaw as I speak, wanting to help him focus on something other than what's tearing him apart. I can only imagine what he's feeling because merely watching him is making me ache. I want to take away his pain, absorb it as my own, anything to make him smile again. I've never needed to sort something as much as I do now, and I've spent my life needing to fix everything around me. I'm the person who makes sure that everyone is safe and happy, but this feeling I have is soul deep. The need to fix this for Sam is a real thing, and I won't be able to rest until I take away his sorrow.

Sam shudders in my hold before turning to face me. He wraps his arms around my neck, his shaking body flush with mine. "Oh god, Clay. I want it to stop." His voice is raw and full of pain, and in this moment I will do anything he needs me to do.

"Tell me what you need, Sam. Anything."

Sam's arms loosen on my neck, and I worry, thinking he's about to leave me. He doesn't though, and when his lips brush across mine, I can feel my cock harden. I hate myself for being aroused when Sam is breaking, but his mouth on mine is more than I can handle. I try to put distance between us, but Sam keeps himself pressed against me. His next words don't help my erection problem. "Make me forget, Clay. Please." He grinds against me, and I groan at the friction.

"Sam."

It's the only thing I get out before Sam kisses me and I forget my protest. I shouldn't let him carry on while he's feeling so vulnerable, but I'm a fool and can't bring myself to stop him. I grip his arse and lift him, his legs instantly going around my waist. I turn us and pin him to the wall while kissing him passionately. The taste of him on my tongue is like fucking heaven, and I don't want to ever stop. He's like a fucking drug, and I've become addicted to him without realising.

Sam's mouth slips away from mine, and his tongue traces a path over my jaw until he reaches my neck. As soon as he gets there, he bites into my flesh, and I let out a cry as my hips grind into him harder. His fingers brush through my hair making me shudder, and my body comes alive when he grips the strands and jerks my head back. Pain spreads through my scalp and straight to my balls. I stagger backwards, but Sam doesn't release his grip. As soon as my foot hits the floor outside of the shower, I spin us until Sam is sitting on the sink unit.

It's only then that he lets go, and I instantly look at him. His eyes are red from his tears but there's no sadness, the only thing I can see is heat and lust burning in them.

I'm panting as I stand there staring at Sam. My conscience is telling me to walk away from him, to not take advantage of him when he's feeling so fragile, but as my eyes take in his sinful body and the need in his eyes, my body screams at me to take him and own him. Sam doesn't help my decision when he reaches down and strokes over his cock. I watch as he slowly runs his hand along his length before flicking his finger over the tip. He moans, and my fingers grip his thighs as I try to control myself. All bets are off when he lifts the finger he just wiped over his tip, the one now covered in precum, and sucks it into his mouth.

Kissing Sam becomes the only important thing on my mind as I lean forward and claim his mouth. His flavour explodes on my tongue, the saltiness instantly becoming a new favourite thing. I've tasted my own cum on the women I've been with, but that doesn't compare to the way Sam tastes. Our cocks rub together, and I can feel my balls pulling up as my orgasm starts to build. Being with Sam is becoming one of my favourite things, and he turns me on more than anyone else I've met. I can't seem to control myself when I get close to him, and he makes my body react with a simple look. The whole thing should worry me because never before have I wanted to be with a guy, but apparently, Sam is a game changer in every way. I would give him anything he asks for, and when I'm not as turned on as I am right now, that feeling might worry me.

"Clay." My name moaned against my lips makes my eyes roll in pleasure, and I thrust against Sam. There's a sound, but I ignore it, focusing instead on the feeling of my cock sliding against Sam's.

My eyes flash open a second later when something wet wraps around my erection. I look down to see Sam's glistening hand sliding over me. The feeling is fucking amazing, and I should ask what he's rubbing on me, but I don't care as long as he keeps doing it. His hand drops further until he's rubbing my balls, and my eyes widen when his hand turns, and he works on himself. I could watch Sam pleasure himself all day, and when he moans deep in his throat, I ease back so I can see his fingers. I nearly swallow my tongue when I look at them slipping inside his hole. He eases two of them in slowly, and I can't look away from the way his muscle stretches around them. Fucking hell, that's so fucking hot.

My whole body freezes when he slips from his body and back to my cock, pointing it down until my tip is pressed against him.

"Clay?"

I pull my focus away from his hand and up to his face. I have the urge to push forward because the heat from his body is almost searing against my tip, and the way he's looking at me isn't helping. I need to slow down though, I need to keep the control that's teetering on the edge, so I still my body.

"I want this. Please."

"Sam, I can't."

He leans forward and licks my bottom lip. "Can't because you don't want this, or can't because you think I'll regret it?" His tongue flicks out again, and my mind blinks out for a second.

"I don't want to hurt you." It's only one of my worries, but it's the main one at the moment. I do think Sam will regret this, but he's a grown man and can make his own choices.

"But do you want me?"

I ease forward slightly until I feel his hole pulse against my tip. One little push and I would be inside him, and there's nowhere else I want to be. "More than anything."

"Then I'm yours. I want this, Clay. I need this with you. Only you." His words should make me want to run away, but all they do is make me want to fucking claim him.

Only one thing is making me stall now, and it's not something I can overlook. "What about condoms?"

"I've never had sex without protection."

It's all I need to hear before I drop my head to Sam's and push forward. "I promise I'm safe." I thank Margaret in my head for making me go for a yearly medical because I know that I don't have anything that will put Sam at risk.

"Oh god." Sam pants as I push into him and it takes everything in me not to just surge forward. I've had anal before with women, and I know to go slow or risk hurting him. It's difficult though because every part of me wants to be joined fully with Sam. I want to be so deep inside him that I can't tell where I end and he starts.

Easing into him is more than I've ever experienced before, and I'm not just talking about his heat and how tight he is. It's something else, something I can feel deep in my chest. It's like the connection between us is linked to my heart, and it's completing a part of me I didn't know was missing. Thrusting the final few inches, I try to clear that thought from my head. *This is sex and nothing more.*

"Clay, oh fuck." Sam tilts his hips up, and I feel myself slipping even deeper. I still for several beats because if I don't, I'm going to come before I get a single thrust. I'm already on edge, and when Sam tightens around my cock even more, I dig my fingers into his hips. "You need to fuck me, Clay. Hard. Please."

My need takes over, and I do as Sam asks. My first few thrusts are easy, letting us both get used to me being inside him, but soon I'm picking up speed. I pound into Sam's body, keeping my eyes on him to make sure that he isn't in pain. The look on his face isn't one of pain, and when he urgently strokes his cock, I can see the pleasure clearly on his face.

"Sam." I want him to look at me. I have a need for him to know it's me that's inside him. I want him to know who's claiming him. He keeps his eyes connected with mine, and it only takes a few thrusts before my orgasm explodes out of me, making me roar with pleasure.

"Fuck. Clay, oh fuck." Sam's cry joins mine as he comes across his chest.

I collapse onto him, all my energy drained from my body. Sam wraps his arms around me, and I enjoy the moment.

SAM SNUGGLES INTO MY SIDE, and I tighten my arm around him. We're both in bed after getting cleaned up, and now we are snuggled under the covers and relaxed. Sam had tried to take the couch when we left the bathroom, but I threw him over my shoulder and carried him in here with me. There's no way he was sleeping anywhere but in my arms tonight. His fingers brush over my chest as we lie in silence, and the feeling is soothing. I want to talk about what just happened, but when I start speaking, that's not what comes out.

"I had a younger brother called Cameron."

Sam's fingers still but he doesn't move to look at me. "Had?"

I should stop talking. Only one person knows this part of my life, and that's just because he was there the day my life fell apart. For some reason I want to tell Sam about Cameron, I want to give him that part of me, so I keep talking, telling him about the incident that changed my life forever. "Cameron was five years younger than me, but from the day he was born, I knew I would do anything to protect him. He used to say I was his hero, but he was the amazing one. He was everything I wished I could be. Funny, smart, and so fucking kind. Even when the universe was kicking his arse, he only saw the good in it."

"He sounds amazing."

"You have no idea." I take a deep breath, steeling my nerve for what I'm about to tell him. "The day he died I lost the best part of me."

I can feel Sam start to move and I hold him tighter. I can't look at him while I tell him about Cameron, I can't see the pity. He must understand because he lies still. "What happened to him?"

"I grew up in a house that you wouldn't exactly call happy. I have no doubt that my mum loved me, but that wasn't enough. When I was ten, my mum found out my dad was cheating on her. I knew it wasn't the first time, but he'd never admitted to it before. It must have been serious with this woman because he left my mum and us, and he never looked back."

Sam is back to stroking his fingers over my chest, and for some strange reason, it makes it easier to tell him my story.

"Mum started drinking pretty soon after he left and it became my job to care for Cameron. It wasn't a hardship, but it's a lot for a ten-year-old. She disappeared into herself, so it was really only Cameron and me for a long time."

"I'm sorry you had to go through that. It must have been hard not having any parents to help."

I kiss the top of Sam's head, needing the extra connection for a brief moment. He doesn't sound like he pities me and that takes away some of my nerves. That is why I've never told anyone about my past, the pity would be too much for me to handle. I don't want anyone to look at me differently, I only want them to see the strong man I am today.

"It was what it was. I was too young to do anything to change it so I just did what I could. It wasn't difficult because Cameron was such a good kid, but it eventually started to drain me. I managed over a year before one of my teachers noticed a change in me." I let out a little humorous chuff, the memory of that day playing in my head. "Mr Wytock was the one who finally reported us to the family support group that worked with the school after I fell asleep in his class for about the tenth time. He'd asked me before if I was okay and I lied, telling him that I'd not been sleeping because my mum had been sick. When things didn't change after two months, he stopped asking and reported us." I go quiet because the next part of my story is where everything changes. It's the moment in my life that I will never be able to change, and the one that keeps guilt deep in my heart.

"Clay?" Sam wraps his arm tightly around my waist and leans his head on my chest, throwing his leg over mine. It makes me feel safe, like he's protecting me from the world. I've never felt that from anyone before, like I can hide behind them and the world won't be able to reach me. It feels different from all the times that Gabe or Niko have been there for me, this makes me feel more secure. "What happened?"

Pushing the thoughts of comfort and longing away, I continue to bare my soul to the man who's becoming important to me, even though I shouldn't let him. "I only left Cameron with my mum twice a week after school. I had extra math tutoring so one of the other parents would drop him off at the front door for me. It was Thursday, May fourteenth when the family support officer came to the door to ask my mum some questions. That's also the day she tried to run with my brother and drove her car into the side of a bridge."

"Shit, Clay. I'm so fucking sorry." I can hear the sorrow in his voice, but little does he know it only gets worse from here.

"My mum died in the crash instantly. My brother ... he was injured badly, and I thought I was going to lose him. It took a long time to get him back, but I did, for a few years at least."

Sam fights against my hold, and I let him go. He sits up and leans back against the headboard behind him. His thigh is pressed against my shoulder, and when his fingers start playing with my hair, I turn until my head is in his lap.

"He was paralysed from the chest down when he was just seven. I lost my mother at the age of twelve, and my dad was nowhere to be found. I ended up staying with my best friends mum until I was seventeen and I got the little money my mum had left me. Cameron went into full-time hospice care in a group home. He was happy, but I always felt guilty that I couldn't look after him anymore."

"You were just a kid, there was nothing you could do. You had already dealt with so much, Fuck, Clay, I don't know how you did it." It's the same thing that Gabe has told me a hundred times, but it doesn't ease the guilt that I couldn't do anything. I was Cameron's big brother, I should have always been there for him.

"Doesn't change how I feel. I wasn't there the day my mum drove drunk with him, and I wasn't able to care for him before I lost him." I close my eyes and concentrate on the feel of Sam's fingers in my hair. The pain that I usually feel when I think of Cameron isn't there this time. Thinking of what my mum did to him usually has my stomach tied up in knots and makes me want to reach for a bottle of something. Not tonight though, and I can't help but think the reason is Sam.

26

Sam

I WISH there was a light on in the room so I could see Clay where he's lying in my lap. This is the first time that he's opened up about his story, and it's more heartbreaking than I thought possible. My own story isn't one of dreams, but at least I know my family is out there and safe. "When did he die?"

I give Clay time to answer, letting him take as much time as he needs. With us being little more than strangers, I never imagined he would give me this window into his past, so I'm willing to just be here to listen to him. The night has flipped though, and after Clay giving me what I needed in the bathroom, he opened up and gave himself permission to share. Sleep was the only thing I thought would happen in here tonight, so when Clay started speaking, I knew I needed to listen. I have a feeling that he doesn't let many people into this part of his life.

"He died when he was thirteen. He got pneumonia after a chest drain, and he never recovered from that. It was just after I met Gabe and I'm glad he was with me. Without him, I'm not sure I'd be here today."

I'm suddenly very thankful to a man I've never met before. I can't imagine Clay going through all that on his own, losing his brother after everything else he had to suffer through. "I have two big brothers and a little sister. I haven't seen them in nearly two years, and that hurts like fuck. I can't imagine losing them though. I'm sorry, Clay. So sorry."

His fingers dig into the muscles on my thigh, and I scrape my fingernails over his scalp because it seems to soothe him. "Why did you leave your family?"

The darkness feels like a safety net around me, and I wonder if that's why Clay shared so much. It's the reason I want to tell him about Damien and everything he took from me. "I started working for Damien two years ago. It was just small stuff, to begin with, searching for stock leads or getting incriminating info on his competitors, but soon it got a bit more on the illegal side. I was hacking emails and skimming money from people's accounts. He always had an excuse for me doing the shit I did, so it made it feel less crappy."

Clay is silent for a moment, and the air feels tense. When he finally speaks, I'm glad it lightens the mood. "So little Sammy wasn't always a good boy?"

I scrub his hair, and I smile when I feel his shoulders rise and fall as a small laugh comes from him. It's the first time he's shown anything other than pain since he got into bed, and it's like a balm to my soul. Clay has been intense since the day I met him, but there was always a glint of something else in his eyes, like mischief trying not to be seen. If I could see him tonight, I know that shine would be missing, but maybe this laugh is the first step in him getting it back. "Shut up. I'm a badass, and you know it."

This gets a bigger laugh as he sits up, leaning back on the headboard next to me. He takes my hand and plays with my fingers. "I don't think you're a badass, but I do love your arse."

I knock my shoulder against his, my smile getting bigger at his compliment. Having a guy like Clay find me attractive is a serious fucking ego boost. He's so perfect with his muscles and tattoos that he could get any person in the world, man or woman. So having him here with me tonight? Yeah, definitely good for the confidence. "Glad you approve. Can I ask you how you got into the private investigator thing?"

Clay leans away, and I think I've asked him the wrong thing. A second later a small light comes on at the side of the bed, and I blink against the brightness. When he returns to his position, his heat seeps back into my arm. "When Cameron died I only had Gabe. He helped me organise a small funeral and stayed with me while I got back to work. He wouldn't let me disappear into myself, no matter how desperately I wanted it. We were having a drink in my record shop one day-"

"Sorry." I hold my hand up in front of Clay to stop him from talking. There's no way he's going to make a statement like that and not explain himself. "You owned a record shop? Like vinyl records? I didn't realise you were that old." One second I'm sitting teasing Clay, the next I'm moving through the air before my back connects with the mattress below me. Clay is on me instantly, his fingers tickling into my sides until I can barely breathe through my laughter. "I'm sorry. Stop, oh god."

He relents his attack, but he doesn't move away from me, instead leaning on his arm as he stays above me. "Yes, I owned a record shop. Cameron was obsessed with music and records, and he always spoke about owning a shop. When I was old enough to get my money from my mum's estate, there was only one thing I could do with it. It's actually how I met Gabe."

I reach up and brush a finger over Clay's cheek. "You really are a great big brother."

"Was."

"Are. You *are* a great big brother. You keep him alive by keeping his memories safe."

He kisses my palm but doesn't deny what I've just said. "Anyway, Gabe told me I needed to find my dad and tell him about Cameron. I didn't think he deserved it, but I listened. It took four months to find him, but I did it."

"What happened?"

Clay's gaze flickers away briefly, the memory obviously not a good one. "When I turned up at his door he told me to fuck off."

I'm pretty sure my eyebrows reach my fringe in shock. "He seriously said that to you? What a horrible fuck-"

Clay kisses me to stop the rant that I'm just about to start. I want to keep the anger building inside me, but his lips distract me from what I was trying to say. Unfortunately, he doesn't deepen the kiss like I want him to.

"He didn't say that exactly, but he may as well have. It finally showed me he wasn't worth my time, and it started my journey to what I do now. Gabe mentioned how I'd done well finding my dad and that I should do it for a living. The rest, as they say, is history."

I still want to explain my distaste at his useless excuse for a father, but I choose to keep quiet, so the relaxed atmosphere doesn't vanish.

"Your turn. I want to know more about what happened with Damien."

So much for keeping the pleasant feeling surrounding us. "I suppose it's only fair. One day while I was searching through Damien's files, the ones he thought were locked, I found a chat history about a boy who was for sale. It didn't take much digging to find out what he had planned, and I knew I couldn't stand back and let it happen. I rigged the security system to hack into it without a keycard, and set about getting the boy out."

Anger has darkened Clay's eyes, and I think if Damien weren't dead, Clay would go after him and kill him himself. "How did you get him out?" The words are ground out between clenched teeth, and I'm worried that he might crack them with the pressure.

"I stood up to Damien. I'd seen his reaction to others who pissed him off, and my plan needed him to put me in his outbuilding. I'd seen men go in there alive and come out in body bags. I knew if I got mouthy and refused to help he would send me there with his men."

"Please tell me you weren't hurt."

I don't want to carry on with this conversation. It won't take us anywhere good, and I've had a bad enough day. "Can we continue this later. I've spent hours telling the police all this, and I just want to forget for a while."

Clay looks like he's fully ready to argue, but when I lean up and kiss him, he sighs against my lips. "You win ... this time."

I smile, but it slips from my lips when Clay grinds his hardening cock against me. This is definitely a better option than speaking.

"Sam, you're going too fast."

I run away from Amber, hoping I can get to the park before she has a chance to catch up with my friends and me. My mum told me that I had to take her with me, but I'm sick of her always following me. Brogan and John never have to look after her, and I'm fourteen, I don't need my ten-year-old sister tagging along with my friends. I slow when I reach the edge of the grass, not wanting to look like a dweeb by my friends catching me running.

I wave when Jordan turns and sees me approach. "Seriously, dude. We thought you would never get here. You ready to bounce?"

I nod as I approach my group of friends, and when Lenny looks over my shoulder, he laughs. I know exactly what he sees, and I get pissed off at both Amber and my mum.

"You brought your sister?" Lenny keeps his laughter going and I turn to glare at my sister.

"Amber, go home. I'm going with my friends, and you can't come with me." I don't wait for her reply before I brush past her and head towards the forest. I know it's probably where we're heading so I don't wait for them as I storm away.

I'm so fucking sick of my mum making me look after my sister. I get that she works from home and it's difficult during the summer holidays with us all around, but that doesn't mean I'm her built-in babysitter. Brogan and John never have to stay at home to entertain Amber, and I don't know why I should have to. I want to go out with my friends, and I don't want some kid hanging around while I do it.

"You do know your dad is gonna beat your arse?" Lenny rushes to catch up with me and hands me a bottle of vodka.

I nod in agreement with Lenny, guilt chewing my insides at the picture I've painted of my dad. The truth is there isn't a gentler man in the whole world, but when these guys asked me to be part of their group I did shit to fit in. I've spent the last few years of school without any friends. Both my older brothers seem to have endless friends, and I'd hoped it would be the same for me. Instead, the rumours started quickly that I was gay and I became an instant target for the bullies. When Lenny, Jordan, Tommy, and Justin began talking to me, I thought all my Christmases had come at once. They weren't the coolest in the school, but they were respected enough that I lost the target that seemed to be painted on my back. So I changed who I was to be part of the gang. If you believe what my *parents say, my attitude has changed so much that they're worried about me. They don't understand what it's like to be a teenager in this day and age, so I ignore them.*

I take a long swig of the vodka before handing it back to Lenny. I duck under a few branches and go deeper into the trees. This is our go-to hang out area because no one bothers us since there's no path to the area. The small open space in the middle of several thorn bushes gives us privacy to smoke and drink. I jump over the trunk that leads us into the centre, taking the bottle from Tommy before I collapse onto the soft ground. "I am so sick of my parents. I swear they think I'm just here to babysit for them."

Tommy sits across from me, his feet touching mine as he settles in. I don't notice the look that passes between him and Justin, my attention entirely on drinking more vodka. I give the bottle to Jordan as I continue my ranting. "You don't see my brother's being told to stay in and watch her. I swear they think I don't have a life or something." The bottle is handed back to me, and if I'd been paying attention, I would have noticed that none of the other guy's had taken a drink.

Twenty minutes later my rant is long finished, and I now have the giggles. The vodka is hitting me hard, and I can't stop finding shit funny. No one else is laughing as much as I am, but I just think they haven't had enough to drink. I try to get to my knees but the world tilts sideways, and I grab the bush next to me to stop me from falling. The thorns dig into my palm, but I barely feel it in my haze. Tommy appears in front of me and takes my shoulders, keeping me steady. I smile at him, thinking he's a really great friend. I'm lucky to have met these guys.

When Tommy lets go of my shoulders, I notice that my hoodie is being lifted up my body. I raise my arms automatically, and my hoodie is slipped off over my head.

"Sam."

I look to the side of the clearing, confusion hitting me hard when Clay is standing there. Why's he here? I don't remember him from school, but he's here in front of us. "Clay?"

"You need to leave."

More confusion at his words and the world seems to blur around the edges of my vision. The hands on my body don't stop moving, and I want to tell them to give me a minute. I want to concentrate on what Clay's saying, and I can't do that with them undressing me. "What are you talking about?" *I blink, my eyes taking several seconds to open again, and when I do Clay is right in front of me, his hands on my cheeks.*

"You need to wake up, you're not safe here."

Not safe? I'm here with my friends so he must be wrong. "I'm safe."

"No, you're not, wake up, baby. Wake up now."

I SIT bolt upright in my bed, chills from the dream still spreading through my body. There's light shining in through the open curtains, and I focus on that, trying to chase away the darkness my dream has left. I haven't thought about that day in years, but apparently, my brain thinks I haven't dealt with enough shit the last few days. Thankfully I'd woken up before the part where the guys who I'd thought were my friends had stripped me naked and left me in the middle of the woods. Not before they'd written fag and queer all over my body in black sharpie and taken pictures. Those pictures had followed me for years as I finished school, my cock appearing every few months just when I'd thought things had settled down.

Scrubbing my hand over my face, I turn to sit on the edge of the mattress. Clay had been a surprising addition to the dream and one I'm thankful for. He had saved me from my own memories, and I won't be sorry about that. Even in my sleep, the guy is saving my arse. I look over my shoulder and see the other side of the bed is empty. It's not really a shock, and even though I don't expect to find him in the house, I get out of bed to look for him. I grab a pair of boxers as I walk past a small pile of clothes on the dresser, putting them on before starting my search. The house is silent, and I can feel how empty it is, but I continue through the rooms, seeing them for the first time since arriving. I'd been so out of it last night that I hadn't paid attention to my surroundings, and now I'm wondering how the hell he found this place.

The living room is furnished with quite old furniture, but it's clean and fresh, like it's not empty that often. My eyes drift over the pictures on the wall, the smiling family in the pictures looking happy. It's small but cosy, and the door attached leads to an even smaller kitchen. The units look like they're from the seventies but look like they have been well cared for. The whole house looks like something my grandparents would live in, which makes me wonder even more how Clay found it.

Finding every room void of the enormous guy I'm searching for isn't a shock. Truthfully, after last night I would've been more surprised to see him still here. Our one night together had been extended, and I need to just keep a hold of the fucking awesome memories. I head to the fridge to see if I can find anything to drink because water doesn't sound fun right now. A huge arsed smile appears on my lips when I open the door and see a shelf full of Red Bulls. I don't know when he managed to get these for me, but the fact that he did, makes my heart pitter patter like a fool. I notice a piece of paper on top of the supply, and I grab it along with a can. I open the tab and take a drink before putting it aside. My teeth bite into my bottom lip as I read the beautifully written note. Who would have thought that Clay had such perfect handwriting?

Morning, Mr Big,

Sorry I left without waking you, but you looked too beautiful to wake. Wow that sounded sappy. I want to thank you for all your help. Knowing I can go home because of you, well I wont ever forget that.

Thank you for listening to me last night. I've only shared that part of me with one other person, but knowing that you hold my secrets, it makes me happy. I wouldn't want anyone else to keep them for me. Know I will keep your secrets close to my heart. What we did, what you showed me, was earth shattering and fuck me, I don't think I will ever experience that with anyone else. I wont say thank you for that because then it feels less, feels like you did me a favour. I just hope to fuck you enjoyed it as much as I did.

I need to leave now and get back to my business. The police have all my statements but I will be back in a heartbeat if you need me for anything. A guy called Roy Black will be in touch with you soon. He's a lawyer who will help you, and he's the best. Let him help you and don't stress over anything. There is no way you are going to get into trouble for any of this. The house is yours until your cabin is released so get comfortable and treat it like your own.

If you need me, you know where I am.

Clay

27

Clay

I STARE at the guy standing at the bar and wish he was someone completely different. I've been back home for three weeks now and it's been the longest three weeks of my life. Leaving Sam lying in bed that morning had been the hardest thing I'd ever done, and I've regretted it every second since. There had been no other option other than leaving, but as I sat on the edge of the bed, watching Sam as he slept, the need inside had been hard to ignore. I've never wanted to be with anyone before but looking at Sam as he slept, I experienced longing for the first time. I wanted what Gabe had with Rhys, what Niko had with Corey and Grant, and I wanted that with Sam. I couldn't lie to myself about that any longer, and that's why I had to leave.

A bottle is waved in front of my face and I grab it before pulling my attention back to Gabe. I've seen him a few times since I came back but it's the first time we've been out for a night. I've been using work as an excuse not to see him but I couldn't put him off any longer without hurting his feelings. I want to pretend I've not been avoiding him, but I have. Gabe knows me too well and I knew he would see straight through me. One look and he would be able to tell that there was something bothering me.

"Thanks." I take a drink and my gaze flicks back over to the bar but the guy's gone.

"So, want to tell me why you're avoiding me?" Gabe leans onto the tabletop and glares at me.

"I'm not."

I'm met with an eye roll and I can tell he's already forming a plan to get me to talk. "Try again."

"I've been busy?"

"Nope, again." He motions with his hand that I should carry on.

"This is actually the third time we've been out, your old brain just doesn't remember."

His lip quirks up into a smirk but I'm under no illusion that he's about to let me off the hook. ""You're older than me, you fucker."

"Sorry, keep forgetting that." I try to buy myself some time, hoping that maybe Rhys will turn up and interrupt like she did the last time we were out.

"Clay, talk to me. There's been something bugging you for months, and it's only been worse since you came home. The last time I saw you like this …"

The worry is clearly seen on Gabe's face and I hate that I'm making him feel like this. "Was after my last run in with my dad." The time he's talking about is the night I met my dad in a pub. I'd been travelling for work and Gabe had come with me to keep me company, and thank fuck he had. Witnessing my dad being all romantic with some woman had me seeing red. Gabe had dragged me away before I'd approached him, but I'd been knocked off my game for a few weeks. This isn't the same though, because the guy who knocked me on my arse is the most amazing guy I've ever met.

"Yeah. And now I'm worried that he's been in touch."

I take a mouthful of beer to try and wet my drying mouth. I'm going to have to be brave and talk to Gabe, I just don't think it's going to be easy. "It's not my dad, you don't have to worry about that."

"Then what is it? Talk to me."

I moisten my mouth again before taking a deep breath. "I met someone."

"I figured you had."

"Why do you say that?"

He laughs as he shakes his head. "Because when I met Rhys I acted like a fucking tool too."

I join in with his laughter. He's telling so much truth right now and I can't help but feel amused. "True story. But I'm not planning on losing my shit and going to jail."

Gabe gives me the finger, but I can see the humour on his face. "So does she have a name?"

"Sam." I choose not to correct Gabe in his assumption of Sam's gender, not ready to admit just yet that he is in fact a guy.

"Tell me more."

God, what to tell? So much has happened and I don't know where to start. "I've been feeling … I don't know how to explain it. It's not exactly lonely, more like empty. Like I was missing something but I didn't know what. It started a few months ago and it's only steadily grown. Sam made that feeling disappear."

"Shit. I thought it was just some random woman you picked up."

"Give me a minute." I get up from the table and head to the bar. If I'm going to have this conversation with Gabe I'm going to need a lot more alcohol. Numbness might help me open up the way I need to.

Leaning on the bar I wait until Roxy heads in my direction. "Hey, beautiful. Can I have four Jaegers and four tequilas when you're ready?"

"Planning on being carried out of here tonight?" Her voice is husky, her terrible smoking habit evident as she speaks.

"Only if I'm lucky."

She winks and works to get my order for me. I grab the tray after I pay and return to the table, spending a few moments putting the glasses on the table and handing the tray back to Roxy. When I sit again, Gabe is looking at me with a serious expression.

He motions to the drinks in front of us. "That bad?"

"Worse." I pick up a Jaeger and down it, hissing as the alcohol burns my throat on its path. I follow it with a tequila shot before Gabe has a chance to drink one. With two drinks to settle my nerves, I open the floor to Gabe. "Right, ask away."

"What's she like?"

"Fucking perfect. Everything I never knew I needed, and they just get me. I can open up to them like no one else and I know they won't judge me. Did I mention really fucking hot? Dark hair, brown eyes, and an arse you just want to grab." A vision of Sam appears in my head and it's a struggle not to groan out loud.

"And is she into you?"

That's the question I don't want to ask myself. If I pretend that Sam doesn't want me then it's easy to stay away, pretend that he was using me to scratch an itch and nothing more. "I don't know."

"Where did you meet her?"

"They're a friend of Niko's boyfriend."

Gabe takes a tequila from the table and downs it but his glare never leaves me. He looks pissed off and I can't work out why. "You think you're so slick, don't you?"

Yeah, he's definitely pissed about something. "Usually, yeah. But I'm thinking there's something wrong this time."

He runs his tongue along the front of his teeth as his frustration builds. I can see it as he gets close to losing his shit, so I push a Jaeger towards him, and he grabs it, downing it in one. "You need a better memory, fucker."

"Either spit it out or drop the attitude."

"I know Sam's a guy."

The world feels like it stops rotating as Gabe stares at me. How the hell does he know about Sam being a guy? There's no way that I've …

I drop my head to the tabletop and groan. Of course he knows Sam's a guy, he isn't stupid. I spent hours bitching about Sam after he told me to back off. It makes sense that Gabe remembers that and has worked out the very obvious. God, how the fuck am I going to explain all this? Instead of trying to find words, I bang my head against the table. A hand drops onto the back of my head and Gabe strokes it through my hair.

"Stop being so dramatic."

I lift my head and glare at his far too happy face. "Why did you let me go on like that if you already knew?"

"Because it was fun." His face changes and he looks really serious. "Now do you want to really talk?"

"I don't know where to start." I glance at the tequila that's still on the table, my hand itching to grab it, but I leave it. Now I think about it, maybe being drunk isn't the time to try and make sense of it all. I think that's why I've been avoiding Gabe. He'll make me talk about what happened, and to do that I'm going to have to understand it all myself. I've been trying not to think too hard to make sense of what happened with Sam, because if I do, I might have to admit some things that I'm trying to hide from.

"How about we start with the biggie? A guy?"

"A guy." I give in to my urge and grab the tequila. I down it and stay quiet.

"That's new ...I think?"

"It is. He was the first ... only." I don't mention the fact that I don't want to be with any other guy because that's admitting something that I find confusing. If I'm just realizing now that I'm bisexual, shouldn't I want other men? I don't, I just want Sam. He's the only guy who has my attention, but if I'm honest with myself, I haven't looked at any women since he came into my life. So maybe it's not a sexuality problem, maybe it's a Sam problem?

"I have so much I want to ask but I don't know if it's insulting or not."

"Just ask them, brother. I doubt they're any different from anything I've been asking myself."

"Okay. Have you always been attracted to guys, because you've never mentioned anything."

I pick at the skin on my thumb while I think about what he's asking. This is the one question I know I can answer, but I don't know how to put my thoughts into words. "Yes, but never thought about it too much. You know how you see a guy and think they're hot-"

Gabe holds up his hands and I stop speaking. He shakes his head at me before speaking. "Dude, I don't find men hot."

"You know what I mean, like you think they have a great body and shit."

He scrunches up his face, and I'm starting to think I've missed something important. "Do you mean *'oh look at him, he's built like a brick shithouse'* type thing?"

That's not the way I've looked at them. I've noticed the way they filled out their clothes, but I also notice other things. Like how their arses look in jeans, or if their eyes draw me in. I thought this was normal, and since I was never going to do anything about it, I didn't think to mention it. I thought guys noticed that shit and just got on with life. Have I been missing this important fact about myself my whole fucking life? "Um ...yeah?"

Gabe laughs. A full on belly laugh that fills his eyes with tears. "You really didn't know, did you?"

I shake my head, feeling like the most oblivious fucker in the world.

"I hate to tell you, Clay, but I think you might like guys." Gabe is still smiling, and none of this looks like it's bothering him.

"You're not... I don't know. Disgusted?"

"What the fuck? Do you think I'm the kind of guy that would brush you off for who you fall for? I'm not a homophobe."

My cheeks heat in embarrassment. I should know that Gabe isn't the kind of guy who would turn his back on me. He isn't a judgmental kind of guy, and he's like my brother, so I shouldn't have judged him. "I'm sorry. Sam just has my head kinda fucked up. I'm not sure what I'm meant to do or think. I slept with a guy, and it wasn't confusing, it wasn't weird. It was fucking hot and the best night of my life. "

"None of it compared to anything else before? It felt like there was a fire in your skin that you couldn't put out? All you wanted to do was kiss him until neither of you could breathe?"

I know I should deny all of those things. It's obvious Gabe is trying to make some sort of point that I'm not going to like in the slightest. "No?"

The fucker laughs again, and I'm close to reaching over the table to smack him. He could at least pretend to be nice to me while he's pointing out everything I didn't know about myself. "Oh shit, you really like him. This is all too much. The great Clay Wilson has gone and fallen in love ... with a guy."

I give him the finger, but it doesn't stop him from carrying on.

"What happened to the guy who would never settle down? Remember no woman would ever get under your skin like Rhys did with me? Actually, I suppose you didn't lie about that one." He's having way too much fun with all this.

"I didn't act like this when you fell for Rhys."

"You fucking liar! You had so much fucking fun pointing out how attracted to her I was, even though I was working hard on denying it."

"You're welcome, by the way. But can I just say, I'm not falling for Sam." I want to get that point over clearly to Gabe. I might not have a clue about a lot of things at the moment, but that I'm sure of. I think.

"Tell me about him."

"He drives me fucking insane. He gets this attitude on him when he gets pissed off, and he could give anyone a run for their money."

"Including you?"

I smile at Gabe's question. I love when Sam gets pissed with me, and it takes everything in me not to kiss the attitude out of him. There's something about riling up Sam that makes my cock hard, and it became one of my favourite pastimes. "Including me."

"Oh shit, that smile," He points to my face. "Tells me more than those lies you're trying to give me."

I force the smile from my lips, so he has nothing to focus on. "It doesn't matter what you think. I'm here, and I doubt that I'll see him again."

"And how do you feel about that?"

What I should do is tell Gabe that the thought of not seeing Sam again is keeping me up at night. That I struggle through every second of the day not to call him and see how he is. I know he's back home since Porter got notice that the property I rented is empty again. I want to find out how he got on with the police, make sure he's sleeping okay, and I just want to hear his voice. I don't want to admit it to myself, but now I've had several drinks, I can't hide from the way I'm feeling. I have this need to connect with Sam because he settles my soul. I don't want to let anyone in, but I think I'm failing miserably. Sam is like a poison that's slowly spreading through my veins. Just instead of killing me, he's making me have feelings that I've always managed to hide from. He's making me want him, and to have him, I'm going to have to be honest about who I am. I just don't know if I'm strong enough to be that man.

I can't admit to any of this though, because if I build it up too much in my head, it will only hurt when I can't have him. "It is what it is. Some people aren't meant to be anything more than just an experience. And that's what Sam was. A really fucking great experience."

"That's really what you're going with?" Gabe doesn't look like he believes anything I'm saying, and since I'm having doubts myself, I can't blame him. But I need to lie to myself until I can forget about Sam.

"Yeah, because it's the truth."

"Well, I call bullshit, and I reserve the right to throw this moment in your face when you come to your senses."

"Hi."

I look to the side of me and see a stunning woman standing there. She's wearing a skintight pair of jeans that look like they've been sprayed on, and this little top that barely reaches her belly button. Her figure is banging with a tiny waist and sexy round hips, not to mention her tits that look like they could fill my hand with some left over. "Hey."

She bites her bottom lip and smiles sweetly at me, her eyes filled with lust and need. She's a fair bet for tonight, and I don't think I'll have to try very hard with her. "I was just wondering if you've seen my friend. She vanished and left me all alone."

A laugh comes from the other side of the table, and I turn to glare at Gabe. He smirks at me, and I can see the challenge in his eyes. He thinks I'm stuck on Sam, but I'll show him that what I said was the truth. Sam was nothing more than a one-time thing. Okay, a two-time thing but he doesn't know that. "What does she look like, maybe I could help you find her."

"She's gorgeous, but I think she might have left me here. Would you be able to help me find my way home?"

"Sorry, no can do. I'm out with my friend here, and I'm not leaving him. I could help you search the toilets if you would like?"

She bites her lip again before nodding. I grab my bottle of beer and take a long pull as I get up from my seat. I look to Gabe again, and the fucker still looks smug. Let's see how he looks after this. "Be right back."

"Oh, I'm sure you will be. Good luck."

I scrunch up my forehead in confusion but just ignore him, following the hot woman to the bathroom in the back. It's been a long time since I took someone back here, but maybe it's just what I need. A night with a hottie and Sam will be forgotten. Well, not forgotten, but he'll be only a pleasant memory, and I can get on with my life.

As soon as we reach the bathroom, I close the door behind us and use my body to crowd my company back against the door. I probably should ask her name, but since I'm not planning on talking, I don't really need it. I lean in, making sure I don't touch her body and put my hands on the wall behind her. I let my gaze drift down to her lips and when she licks them I wait for my cock to react. The stupid fucking thing isn't playing the game though. On the walk here I had tried to ignore the lack of erection, but now I'm this close, I can't pretend that it isn't a problem. I have a really sexy woman ready to fuck me, and I can't get hard. What the fuck? I haven't had sex since Sam, and I've spent so much time hard for him that I need relief. The orgasm he gave me rocked my world, but it won't keep me going forever.

I close my eyes and think of sexy things. I picture getting my cock sucked, and that helps until I realise I'm picturing Sam on his knees in front of me. "Fuck!"

I can feel the woman flinch next to me and I quickly open my eyes. She's looking at me like I've lost my mind and I can't blame her. I think I might just be losing it, and it's shitty that I have to admit that Gabe might be right. No matter how hard I try to deny it, Sam got under my skin, and I'm not sure how to get rid of him.

28

Sam

I PICK at the rip in my jeans and try not to look at the angry man next to me. The silence in the car is threatening to smother me, but I'm not planning on speaking any time soon. I have a feeling that pretending I'm not actually sitting here is the best course of action to avoid getting a black eye.

When Niko had turned up at my door this morning, I thought that was the moment he was going to get his revenge on me. There was no Clay to get between us and stop what was about to happen. Then he told me to get my coat and get in the fucking car. If it had been anyone else, I would have told him to go fuck himself, but truthfully, Niko scares the shit out of me. Grant fell for him so there must be a gentle side to him, but I only see the jagged edges of a dangerous looking guy. Damien thought he looked powerful but he wasn't, he always seemed like a wannabe bad guy. Niko is the real deal. He looks as though he wouldn't think twice about beating the crap out of someone, so that's why I got my jacket and followed him like he'd demanded.

I don't even know why I'm here, and every time I build up the courage to ask, I look towards him and bottle it. To say that Niko has a resting bitch face isn't quite right, it's more like a resting I will kill you face. The worry is that he's about to drive me somewhere secluded so he can bury me and my body won't ever be found.

"Grant asked me to come and get you. He knew you wouldn't come on your own."

I jump when he breaks the silence. I'm so worked up that something as simple as speaking makes me nearly leap out of the window. "Oh." After almost two hours of driving, that's the best response I can give to Niko. If he didn't hate me before, there's an excellent chance he will now.

"I'm sorry about the hospital. I was just scared. Actually, I was fucking petrified, and I took it out on you. I shouldn't have."

My heart is racing, and I don't know what to say. It's the most I've ever heard Niko say at one time, and it's an apology. "Um ...it's okay." I take a deep breath, determined to keep talking until I say what I've wanted to say for weeks now. "And I'm sorry. I shouldn't have become friends with Grant when I knew that someone was after me. It was the reason I was hiding ... it's just ... I liked Grant's company. I shouldn't have been selfish because it caused him to get hurt and I will never forgive myself. So yeah, I'm really sorry."

He looks over at me quickly before returning his attention back to the road in front of him. His thumbs tap on the steering wheel, and he looks like he's trying to work out what to say. All too soon he speaks, and I expect to get a mouthful of anger. I'm right, kind of. "I'm really fucking angry at you, just so you know."

I look down at my hands so he can yell at me and I don't need to look at him. "I'm sorry about Grant."

"Not about that. I'm angry because you were in trouble and didn't tell anyone. You could have come to us, and we would have helped you."

I turn to stare at him, a little shocked by what he's just said. "But you don't know me. I get Grant was a friend, but I couldn't bring you into my crap."

He looks over at me again, holding my gaze longer this time. "Did you help us when we needed it?"

"Yeah."

"Why?"

This conversation isn't getting any less confusing, and I keep feeling that I'm going to put my foot in it with the wrong answer. "Because Grant is my friend and he needed help. I help my friends."

Niko raises his eyebrows and what he's getting at finally becomes clear.

"None of you know me."

"Grant does, and that's enough for me. If you are friends with my man, then you are family, and we protect what's ours."

I drop my head and close my eyes, the tears building in them as he speaks. I want to believe that he means what he's saying, but he can't. As much as I want to belong somewhere again, I can't risk being hurt. It's the reason I haven't been in contact with my family even though Damien is gone. What if they are angry that I left without any notice and they don't want to know me now? I wouldn't survive being turned away by my family. "I've been looking after myself for a long time."

"And how did that work out for you? Grant could have died." His words aren't said with anger, but that doesn't mean they don't cut deep. I don't think he's trying to make me feel guilty but I do, and I will for the rest of my life. The first time I thought I had a true friend, one who didn't like me as a joke, and he could have lost his life for that friendship.

"I know, I'm sorry. If I could change it, I would."

"I'm not trying to make you feel bad. I'm trying to tell you that you're not alone."

I don't know what to say, and thankfully he's distracted by driving. He indicates and turns onto a one-track dirt road. I watch the trees as they go past, the nerves in my stomach increasing as I think about seeing Grant. I've only spoken to him once since he woke up in the hospital, and that was only just to make sure he was okay. I've been ghosting him since, hoping he would leave me to disappear from the world, but he won't give up. He's persistent enough that he sent his man to get me. Now I have the urge to open the car and run for it. Nothing good can come from this meeting, only more guilt and pain. Maybe this is Grant's opportunity to tell me how angry he is with me, to give me a piece of his mind before he throws me out. That's where my mind is even though nothing I know about Grant makes me really think he would do that. He's far too kind for his own good, and that's going to make this meeting hard.

The car stops and I finally look to the area in front of the car and see a large wooden cabin. It seems more modern than my own, and the trees around it make it more secluded. One of the specifications, when I was looking for somewhere to live, was the grounds were open so no one could sneak up on me, now I have an urge to plant hundreds of trees because this place is fantastic. It feels like you are in the middle of a forest even though there's a road only a few minutes away. I get out of the car, my eyes still scanning everything around me. The only sound is the birds and the rustling of the trees. Perfect.

"Come on. Grant won't wait for you long, and if he gets out of bed again, I'm gonna lose my shit." Niko heads towards the house, and I can't keep the smirk from my lips. Grant is obviously being a terrible patient for his men, and the fact doesn't shock me too much.

Just as I start to follow him, the front door opens, and Grant appears in the gap. I actually hear the growl that Niko emits, and he's moving faster towards his target.

"What did I tell you?" He grips Grant around the waist and Grant melts into his hold. I stop moving, letting the men have their moment.

"You told me to stay in bed, and then I told you I'm not broken so I would get up."

"Grant."

"Niko." There's a stare off for a few minutes, and it's only broken when Corey appears behind Grant, wrapping his arms around Grant and leaning over his shoulder to kiss Niko.

"I told you he would be pissed off." Corey's voice is gentle and sweet, the complete opposite of Niko.

"And I told you I would handle him."

Niko growls again, but quieter this time. "You were shot, beautiful. You need to rest because I refuse to lose you."

Grant presses his forehead to Niko's, closing his eyes as he speaks. "You didn't lose me. I'm here with you both, but you can't keep me wrapped up in cotton wool. You won't protect me that way, you'll only drive me insane." He kisses Niko's nose before turning towards me. "And you. I'm gonna kick your arse for ignoring me."

Corey and Niko both laugh, relieving the tension that was building between them all. It takes them a few minutes to let go of Grant, even though Corey keeps a hand on his lower back. The move is sweet and proves the pure love between these guys. I'm not sure how Grant managed it, but he really has found two men who love him deeply. I should be jealous because I can't even find one, but I'm just so fucking happy for him. I'm not sure how their relationship works, but it's not my place to know. Their dynamic is their business, and as long as they are all happy, then I'll support them wholeheartedly.

"Inside now." Grant doesn't give me an option to argue with him as his men help him back inside.

Not wanting to be left alone too long, I head in after them, following the noise until I find the three of them getting settled on the couch. Actually, that's a lie, two of them are fussing, and Grant is slapping their hands away.

"Stop now. I mean it." Corey leans in and kisses Grant on the top of the head while Niko glares at him. It doesn't faze Grant who sticks his tongue out at Niko, earning him a little smirk. He's definitely braver than I am because I would never act like that with Niko, but then I think back to Clay and how much I liked to push his buttons. I wonder if that's what Grant is doing. Does he get the same pleasure out of pissing Niko off as I do Clay?

"You, sit." Grant's voice drags me from my thoughts of Clay, and I find him pointing to the seat next to him. I do as I'm told, afraid that Niko will manhandle me if I upset Grant too much.

Niko finally leans in and kisses Grant the same as Corey did. "I'll go help Corey make coffee." Both men leave, and for the first time since Grant's accident, I'm alone with him.

"I want to give you a chance to explain yourself before I go apeshit. So you have five minutes to talk before I do."

I stare at him because I'm at a complete loss for words. He could have given me an hour to explain everything, and it wouldn't be enough time, so I'm not sure how he thinks I can do it in five minutes. "I'm sorry." I have so much to say, but those two words seem the only important ones at the moment. It also seems to piss Grant off, and he starts the rant that's obviously building inside him.

"Don't give me that sorry shit. You have nothing to be sorry for, and I will slap you if you say it again. Is that why you've been ghosting me?"

I go to answer, but he just keeps on speaking.

"Shit, you really are the smartest dumb fuck I know. None of what happened was your fault. I turned up unannounced, which is evident by the fact that I interrupted you and Clay – which we'll get back to by the way- and my timing sucked. I'm so fucking angry that you had something like that going on and didn't tell me. You spent months helping me with my problems, and you couldn't do the same. I thought we were friends, but maybe I was wrong. Ghosting me because you feel guilty is a shitty thing to do. I needed you, and you vanished."

By the time he's finished, I have tears in my eyes. The whole time I've only been thinking of myself, not once have I thought about how Grant was feeling. He's completely right, he's been through so much shit, and I left him to deal with it. I thought he would be fine with Corey and Niko, but I was wrong. "I'm sorry."

He picks up a pillow and throws it at me, hitting me square in the face. "Next time I'll endure the five minutes it takes to move and will hit you properly." He smirks before continuing. "Or I will call Niko. I'm sure he wouldn't mind doing it for me."

I place the pillow between us and return Grant's smile. "You would love that, wouldn't you? Watching me getting pummeled into the ground."

He laughs but quickly sobers. "You hurt my feelings, Sam. I thought we were friends?"

"We were ...are. Don't hit me, but I'm sorry. I didn't want you to be hurt, so I kept everything to myself. I thought I could handle it."

"By hiding forever?"

I pick at a small thread on the pillow, my nerves needing an outlet. "I knew I couldn't hide forever, but I thought you would leave once Niko and Cory were safe. I didn't expect you to stick around afterwards."

"Have you never had a real friend, Sam?"

My throat burns with emotion, and I struggle not to burst into tears. How fucking sad is it that I'm a grown man and I don't think

I've ever had a real friend, not one who would have my back through everything? "As pathetic as it sounds, no."

Grant moves and I see the pain clearly on his face. I sit forward ready to help him with what he needs, and I'm shocked when he uses his good arm to pull me into a hug. I'm so in shock that my whole body goes rigid, but only for a heartbeat before I relax into his hold. The last time I had human contact was Clay, and I didn't realise how much he'd made me crave more. I wrap my arms around Grant, making sure I don't hurt his shoulder, and just let him hold me. The world vanishes as he soothes me and I know that I nearly lost something really important. If Grant hadn't sent Niko to get me, I would have let this friendship vanish, and that would have been a tragedy.

Movement next to us makes me reluctantly put distance between us and I see Corey placing a tray with coffee on the table. Niko is sitting on the chair to Grant's left, and once he grabs his own cup, Corey sits on his knee.

"So what are we talking about?" This is the first time I've properly met Corey, and I think I could like him. He seems happy and light, and I've not had that in my life for a long time.

I look at Grant and wonder if he's going to keep telling me how stupid I am, but he gets an evil glint in his eye, and I know that something's about to happen. Something I'm not going to like. "We were just about to talk about the fact that Sam fucked Clay."

My eyes go wide, and my mouth drops open, the shock of Grant's words fully hitting me. The room goes deathly quiet, and when I chance a glance towards Corey and Niko, I see Niko with his cup frozen mid-way to his mouth. It's only then that I remember that Niko and Clay are friends, and it's obvious that Clay hasn't mentioned it to him. *Shit.* Is Clay embarrassed by what we did and is keeping it from everyone? Have I done something wrong by telling people, especially if I was a simple experiment? "I ...uh..."

"You slept with Clay?" I plan on not answering Niko's question, but I think the redness building on my face tells him the answer without words. "Well shit. Fucker kept that quiet."

Corey looks between us all, confusion evident on his face. "But you said Clay was straight."

Niko laughs, and it changes him completely. He loses that scary edge and I can see an entirely different man. "Oh, he is. Or so he thinks."

I drop my head and cover my face with my hands. I haven't actually admitted to anything, but that's not going to stop the truth from getting out. I just hope when Niko speaks to him, Clay isn't too angry with me. He never actually told me to keep it quiet, so I haven't done anything wrong.

"Oh. Ohhhhh." Corey must finally get what Niko's saying, and his eyes widen in shock. A second later he turns to look at me, a look of pride on his face. "Well done, Sam. Shit, that needs to go on your bio or something. I didn't think anyone could tame that guy. Is he as big down there as he is everywhere else?"

"Don't fucking answer that." Niko glares at Corey, but his words are entirely for me. I can't help but laugh when Corey's face turns super innocent.

"What? Like you don't want to know."

"I really, really don't. He's my friend and ... just no."

"I want to know." Grant gets in on the conversation, and I bite my tongue to stop more laughter. Niko looks like he's close to losing his shit and he gives up on talking to anyone but me.

"I suggest you don't answer either of these men. I will hurt you if you even hint anything about Clay's cock. Don't make me hurt you."

His words should make me shake in my seat, but his eyes don't hold the seriousness that his words do. I can tell that he really doesn't want to know anything about Clay's dick, but he's kidding about the physical violence.

I help the guy out because I get where he's coming from. I wouldn't want to know anything about what my friends were packing under their trousers. I appreciate that information like that isn't needed ... ever. I mimic locking my lips and throwing the key away.

"You ruin all my fun." Corey pouts, and it's cute.

Niko leans in and bites his bottom lip. "You know that's a lie."

Corey sighs at the move, and I look away, not sure I want to see what's happening. I'm comfortable watching them all being in love, but I'm not sure that's what this is about. When I meet Grant's eyes, I can tell I was right. He smirks, and I shake my head. "I'm with Niko. Some things don't need to be known."

This gets a laugh from all the men, and I relax back into the couch. They've all made me feel comfortable and wanted, and it's a feeling I haven't felt in a long time. I always feel like I'm putting people out, that they are tolerating me until I've used up my usefulness, but sitting here I feel accepted. It's at this moment that I decide they deserve my story. Grant was hurt because of it, and he needs to know why. "The guy who shot you, his name was Damien. Well, it was him or one of his men."

29

Sam

The room goes quiet again as three sets of eyes stare at me.

"I used to work for him, and he wasn't happy when I quit. I also took something that he wanted to keep."

"What did you take?" Niko's lost that soft edge he had a moment ago. I don't know if it's the memory of what happened to Grant or if it's the memory that I'd kept all this from them and put Grant in danger. Either way, I'm going to continue.

"A seven-year-old boy he was planning on selling."

Corey gasps, and it's the only sound until Niko whispers something to him and Corey gets up, moving to sit next to Grant. Niko starts pacing the floor, and I wonder if he's trying to control his anger. I get my answer a moment later when Niko lets out a curse.

"You got him out safely?" Grants voice is strained and tight. Corey wraps his arms around Grant and leans his chin on his shoulder.

The replay of getting Marc out of Damien's grasp flashes through my head, and my stomach tumbles even though it's already happened. I was so fucking scared, but I surprised myself by being able to get him out. The beating from Damien's henchman had been hard to endure, but I'd done it, just waiting for the right moment to put my plan into action. Hacking all the keypads in the property had been easy, and everything worked like I wanted it to so I was gone before anyone could come after me. "I got him out. He's safe and home again."

Grant's shoulders relax as the tension seeps from his body.

"How did you do it?" Niko is now sitting on the chair again, his elbows resting on his knees as he leans towards me. Grant takes my hand, and it encourages me to keep telling my story.

"When I saw all the files and emails about Marc I changed the codes to the keypads to each room. There wasn't a room in the whole property that didn't need a security code to enter. It made sure people couldn't get into places they weren't meant to go. For me, that was most of the house. I set it up so when I hacked one pad they would all lock to my code. All I had to do was get Damien angry enough that he would take me out to the back building." I take a deep breath remembering what happened behind those closed doors.

Grant squeezes my hand harder, and I use the connection with him to keep going.

"I knew if I pissed Damien off he would send me there, I'd seen it before. No one just stops working for him, they tend to disappear. I'd seen men go into that building and never come out."

"Shit, what did they do to you?" It's Corey that asks, his voice full of pain for me.

"Nothing too bad. I think they were just building up to the good stuff when I ran. A few beatings and some fun with water. Nothing that left permanent marks."

"Bastard. I swear if you hadn't killed him I would search him out and kill him for you." Niko's anger hasn't faded in the slightest, but at least he isn't feeling the need to pace.

"I got Marc away, and that was the important thing. The code change worked, and every door I went through I locked behind me, basically locking every person in the house. Finding Marc wasn't hard, but carrying him out was. He'd been drugged since he was taken and couldn't walk. It was a blessing though because when he woke up in the hospital, he didn't remember anything that had happened to him."

"And that's why Damien came after you?"

"That and I took all the evidence I could find and sent it to the police."

Grant smirks. "That's the Sam I know."

"I couldn't let him away with it, but I failed. He had someone searching for me, and when I sent the files, they got scrubbed. I kept waiting for a police investigation, but nothing happened."

"Shit. So you've been hiding all this time, and nothing had actually happened. You could have been having a life."

I shake my head at Grant's statement. "No, because Damien still wanted me. I had to hide from him so he wouldn't kill me. I said before, no one ever stops working for Damien. I had alerts set up for him, but he started a paper trail to lead me away from the fact he was close. I should have seen through it. I was so fucking stupid." I'll have to live my whole life knowing that I bought the wild goose chase so easily. I should have looked into it more and not taken it at face value. Of course he wouldn't want anyone to know where he actually was.

"You didn't know. None of this is on you."

"It is, Grant. It's all on me no matter what you say. I started all this in motion and then kept it to myself. You could have died."

"Shit, Sam. It was–"

"Sam." Niko interrupts Grant, and the tone of his voice has me turning to look at him instantly. "That night in the hospital I would have killed you if Clay hadn't got between us. I just wanted to rip you apart for putting Grant in danger. God, even thinking about him being shot now has my stomach wanting to empty." He closes his eyes briefly, takes a deep breath, and looks at me again. "But none of this is on you. Could you have done it differently? Yes, but we all do stupid things when we want to protect the ones we love." He gazes at Corey and Grant, and I wonder if he means the secrets he kept from Corey to try and keep him safe. "None of us blame you. Fuck, you saved a little kid, and that's the most important thing."

Grant squeezes my hand, and my attention is pulled to him. "I would take that bullet again if it kept that little boy safe. I give you permission to stop feeling guilty. It's done, and we're moving on. Got me?"

I go to argue, but Grant's glare stops the words before they tumble from my mouth. Corey laughs from behind him.

"It's better just to agree, Sam. Once Grant sets his mind to something there's no point arguing."

"When was the last time you went home?"

I look out at the tree line at the edge of Grant's back garden. We moved out here earlier to relax in the last of the day's warmth. Niko had fought with Grant trying to get him to go back to bed, but with a scowl on Grant's face, we ended up out here. "It's been a long time."

"Have you thought about going home now it's safe?"

I bite the inside of my cheek. I've been thinking about nothing else the past few days, but I still can't bring myself to go. "Yes and no. I'm scared to just turn up. What if they don't want to know me, what if it's been too long?"

"Sam, they're your family. They'll just be happy to have you home." His guilt trip does its trick, and I feel worse than I did before.

"I know, and I'll get in touch soon. I just need a minute to breathe. With all this police stuff and everything, it's been a lot."

"How is the police thing going?"

I groan loudly at the reminder of yet another dark spot in my life. I've spent the last few days trying not to look at my driveway because when I do, all I can see is Kelly and Damien's bodies. "I've been told that no charges are going to be brought against me at this time, but if they find anything that contradicts what I said, they may revisit the case."

"Even though you shot him? The cases I've seen involving firearms have been long and drawn out."

I keep forgetting about Grant's police background. I just see him here with Corey and Niko, enjoying life and recovering from his injury. Not that long ago he might have been the one to come to the hospital to get me. "The gun wasn't my property, so it was down to circumstance or something like that. I kinda stopped listening after they said there would be no charges and I could go home. I do remember them saying they had found some shit on Damien."

"What kind of shit?"

"I didn't ask, and they didn't tell. I think the less I know, the better. Distancing myself from all his crap is probably the best thing to do."

Grant screws up his face in what looks like pain and less than a minute later Niko appears at his side with painkillers and water. "Spying on me isn't nice."

Niko leans down and kisses Grant on the head. "Don't care. Take these or I'm dragging you inside to bed."

Grant wiggles his eyebrows, and I can't help but laugh at the suggestive move. "Well, that's not gonna make me take these. That punishment sounds quite pleasurable."

Niko growls, and I know that if I wasn't sitting here, there's a chance that Niko would indeed do as he threatened. Niko is definitely what I would call alpha, and it's not a surprise he's friends with Clay. Both men are so similar, and when I watch Niko interact with his men, I wonder if that's what being with Clay would be like. I don't want to admit that I think about being in a relationship with Clay, but I can't seem to stop my mind from going there most of the time.

The few hours that we spent in bed the night before he left were the most significant of my life. I told him things I'd never admitted to anyone before, but being in his arms felt safe. It felt right. There was a sense of belonging as he told me his own secrets, knowing he was sharing something important with me, something that few people know. Clay trusting me with that made my mind work overtime, hence the constant daydreaming about being with him. There's never been another guy that I've imagined being with, but I can see it so clearly with Clay. He's passionate and protective, and even when he gets angry, I never feared him. You can see that controlled power inside him, and that's so fucking hot. Knowing that he could let go at any second and no one could stop him. Not everyone would be turned on by that, but I am. *So damn much.*

"Sam?"

I blink a few times until I find Grant staring at me with a smirk.

"No point in asking where your head was."

I'm not sure what my giveaway was, but now that he's mentioned it, I know my blush is telling him he was right.

"You like him don't you?"

"Who?" I try for innocent, but I'm not sure Grant's buying it from the look on his face.

"Really? You're gonna play that game? Fine, I'll play along. Clay. The big, tattooed guy you fucked. You like him, don't you?"

I scrub my hands over my face and take a few moments to decide if I want to open this can of worms. Usually, I wouldn't but truthful, it would be great to get some advice. There's never been anyone in my life before now to share with, but I want Grant to be my friend, and maybe this is the way to start that relationship. "I really do, even though I know I shouldn't."

"Why not?"

"Because he's straight ... well, obviously not really. He's at least bi, but that's not the point. I was his first, and I might've been a way for him to taste and try before he made a decision. I mean, he left." I get a lump in my throat when I give a voice to the fear that's been bugging me since Clay left. He admitted he'd never been with a guy before me, but does that mean I was just convenient to test out his sexuality? Is he going home to sleep with other guys now, completely embracing the bisexual lifestyle?

"What did you just think of? I swear you went green."

"What if I was just an experiment, and he enjoyed it so he's going to go home and sleep with more men? God, I think I hate that more than him deciding he doesn't like men."

Grant laughs, and I can't help but hate him for getting pleasure from my discomfort. "Oh shit, you have it bad, my friend."

"I need a drink."

"Core?"

Corey appears instantly from inside the kitchen door like he was waiting there for Grant to need something. The way the men are hovering over Grant is sweet, even though I can imagine that I would hate it if it were me.

"Can you get Sam a beer?" He vanishes, and Grant shakes his head. "I swear those two need to get out of this house. I'm pretty sure they're convinced if I move I might die."

"They're worried. They love you."

Grant's eyes go soft, and he gets a dreamy look on his face. "I know, and I love them so fucking much. Didn't expect to find one guy who made me feel the way they do, never mind two."

A bottle of beer appears in my hand a moment later, and I thank Corey who vanishes inside again, even though I suspect he isn't too far away. "You're lucky. Hold on to this."

"With both fucking hands, Sam. With both fucking hands."

I take a drink, and we sit in silence. As it always does, my mind drifts back to Clay. I wonder what he's doing right now. The police said his statements were sufficient and they wouldn't need him to come to Scotland to be interviewed again. It means that he has no reason to come back, so seeing him again isn't likely to happen. Not unless he comes to visit Niko, but even if he did, would he tell me and maybe visit? The chances of him coming to see me are low, and that hurts more than it should. I've had a constant ache in my stomach since the morning I woke up without him, and as much as I want to tell myself it is nerves because of the whole Damien thing, I know it's not. There's a part of me that misses Clay being close. I barely know him, so I'm not sure how these feelings are possible, but that's where I am. The days we spent together are ingrained in me, and I want more. I want to laugh with him again, listening to his funny stories about the cases he works on. I don't think he knows how damn funny he is, but I could listen to him for hours without getting bored. Then there are the times he lets his passion for things show and it makes my cock hard. He gives everything a hundred percent, and that dedication is like a drug to me. I want that focus on me, but I know I will never have it.

"I miss him." The words come out without really thinking about them, and Grant smiles sadly at me.

"I know that feeling. Those few days without Niko and Core were the hardest of my life. You need to think hard and make some decisions."

"What decisions?"

"You need to decide if you want Clay, and not just for a little while. You need to think if you want him for as long as you can have him. I'm not talking about forever, because nothing is guaranteed, but for a long damn time."

I think about what Grant said. Do I want Clay for as long as he'll have me? Can I give him all my secrets so he can protect them along with his own? I picture spending every day with him, doing the mundane things that makes life boring, but the truth is, seeing myself do them with Clay makes them seem exciting. I want to curl up on the couch and watch movies after eating dinner together. I want to go to the supermarket and shop for the food we need or get bored doing housework together. I want all the things that couples take for granted and I want them with Clay.

"I want it all. I want forever if we can have it, and I'm willing to fight for it." I smile, the feeling of relief spreading through me and I feel relaxed for the first time in months. It's like finally admitting to myself that I have feelings for Clay has taken away a whole layer of worry. There are a lot of things happening that I can't control, but this thing with Clay, I can do something about that. He might not want me, and I might end up making a fool of myself, but I refuse to walk away without finding out. So many regrets fill my life, and I refuse to let Clay be one of them.

Grant's smile is huge, and he rubs his uninjured hand on his thigh. "I was hoping you would say that. Please tell me you have a plan, or you'll let me help you make one."

I shake my head. "I have no plan at all. This is the first time I'm actually admitting that I want him. I've been trying to convince myself that the whole thing was a one off and that the feelings I have should be ignored."

"Then I'm glad that you shared them with me. We need to make a plan though, and it's gonna have to be huge."

Grant looks far too excited at the idea of helping me win Clay over, but I'm happy I finally made him smile. Knowing that I put that look on his face makes handing over the reigns to him worth it. I just hope that he isn't going to make my life too traumatic in the near future.

30

Clay

"I CAN FOLLOW YOUR WIFE, Mr Robins, but I can't guarantee an outcome. I won't make any conclusion about what I find, I will only report the facts."

"I respect that, Mr Wilson. I only need you to give a rundown of where she goes during the day."

I look at Mr Robins across the table, and I'm not sure what I make of him. He's in his sixties and looks professional in his suit. Everything about him hints at him being a business owner, especially the relaxed, calm demeanour he shows. He's here to hire me to gather information on his wife, his much younger wife, and it's not a surprising job really. I would say that most of the men I have asking for my help are older husbands married to much younger wives. I try not to judge anyone or jump to conclusions about things, but after doing this for as many years as I have, I've seen a pattern emerge.

"Is there anything in particular you want me to concentrate on?"

He stares at me for several minutes, but I can see him thinking, like he's trying to make a decision. Finally, he speaks. "The people she's spending time with. I want to know if they're male or female, and I want pictures of who she sees."

It's the classic case of an older man suspecting his much younger, and hotter, wife is cheating. If I got paid every time I had to investigate this type of thing. Well, actually I do get paid, and most of my income comes from these types of cases. If people were happy in their marriages, then I wouldn't make enough to eat. Within my first year of being in business, about eighty percent of my jobs had been to follow cheating spouses. It only confirmed what my mum and dad had shown me growing up, that being married wasn't the dream it was meant to be. There may have been a time when marriage vows were important and people stuck to them, but now they're nothing more than a reason to have a party. Or at least that's what I thought before Gabe and Niko's relationships. I've watched Gabe and Niko both find the person -or people- who makes them happy, and the way they work at their relationship together, so neither one is more important than the other, makes me realise that maybe not all love is doomed. Just the majority of it.

That thought leads me, as it always does, back to Sam. He's been filling my head since the morning I left him asleep in bed. I thought walking away would be the end of it all, but it seemed to be only the start of my problems. I seem to be stuck in place, and I can't move forward. I've come to accept that the thoughts I've been having all these years about men aren't as universal as I thought, that maybe my attraction to them has always been there just under the surface, and all I needed was the right guy to push me to try. Not that it took Sam to push too hard, he just had to be close to me and my body was electrified. There was a connection that I couldn't explain, and even after I'd tasted him, experienced him, it wasn't enough. I don't think it will ever be enough.

"Fine. I have all the details I need, Mr Robins. If you speak to Margaret in the front office she'll get payment details from you. Reports will be available weekly, but if I have any major developments, then I'll be in contact sooner. Feel free to contact Margaret if you have any issues." I stand and hold my hand out to him, hoping he'll just leave so I can call Porter and get an update on the email he sent.

Thankfully he stands and grips my hand, shaking firmly before thanking me. "I hope to hear from you soon, Mr Wilson."

I walk around the table and open the door for Mr Robins. He

walks through and thanks me again. As soon as he vanishes around the corner and I know he's in Margaret's capable hands, I close the door and retake a seat behind my desk. I open up the email I'd been reading when Mr Robins arrived and read over it again. It contains three location reports for properties in Scotland. Another office had never been in my plans, but after speaking to Niko while up in Scotland, the idea came to me. He said it was going to be hard for him to get work since he can't exactly put Blue Diamond on his CV, and the idea started to brew of having him head up a second location.

I pick up the phone and dial Porter's number as I look over the report for the two-story property in Inverness. It's the closest large city to where Niko lives, and it seems the best area to move to.

"Hey, boss."

"Porter. I got the email with all the information."

"Any of it helpful?" Porter has been working on locations for about two weeks now, and I think I'm about ready to talk to Niko about my plans. If he isn't willing to get on board the whole thing, then it's a no go. I don't have the manpower to spare to open up a second office, and I'm not willing to let some stranger be in charge. Niko is the only man I trust, and I'm hoping if he's willing to work for me, then Grant might join him. Grant's experience in the police force would make him a great addition to my company, and I think he would be more than happy to work with Niko.

"I like the look of the old house in Inverness. Could you get more information on it? I need complete floor plans and any building regulations."

"You spoken to Niko yet?"

I'd shared all my plans with Porter because he's my right-hand man. I have a total of six men that work for me on a regular basis, but Porter is the one who they answer to. He has access to everything within the business, and I know that I can trust him with every part of it. I'm hoping that Niko will be another Porter, so I don't have to spend too much time away from this base. "Not yet, but I'm hoping if I have all the information to present to him, he won't say no."

Porter laughs, and the sound is deep, vibrating through the phone. "Like there's any chance he'll say no. You know that Niko is the perfect man for this, and he'll see that as well. Add in the lure of working with Grant, and we could be up and running in a few months."

I hope he's right. I don't want to drag this whole process out, and I already have some possible jobs lined up. If Niko agrees with the plan, then I can have him starting before the office is officially ready. As long as he has one decent room to work in, that will be enough. This I know from experience when I worked from home. "Get me that info, and I'll call him in the next few days. I'm sure that he's still fussing over Grant."

"How is he?"

"Grant? He's fine. He had the stitches out last week, and the doctor has signed him off. Won't stop Niko from being an overprotective fool." It's been nearly a month since Grant was shot, but the way that Niko speaks, you would think it happened only days ago. I know how scared he was, and I don't judge him for one single second for that, but Grant is completely healed now. I've spoken to Grant myself, and he told me that Niko is being an overprotective arse. He wasn't in any pain, and the wound was nothing more than a raised irritation.

"I wonder who that's like?" I don't like the laugh he lets out, and I ignore him, knowing he wants nothing more than to get an argument from me. He's right though, I understand what Niko's feeling because I'm just like him. When it comes to my family, no one is more protective.

There's a knock on my door, and I look towards it as Margaret pops her head around the edge. "Give me a second, Porter." I tilt the phone away from my mouth. "Everything okay, M?" I'm worried that there's a problem with Mr Robins.

"There is a detective Archer here to see you, Clay."

"Give me five and show him in."

She nods before closing the door behind her. I knew I would be seeing the detective again, but I didn't think it would take so long. I actually expected it as soon as I returned, once he noticed that his case file had suddenly vanished. As much as Sam said he made it look like a virus had corrupted the system, the fact that my records had disappeared had to raise suspicion. I just hope that Sam is as good as he claims and nothing can be traced back to me.

"I need to go, the police are here."

Porter pauses for a second, and I can hear the hundreds of questions that he wants to ask. "Is there anything I can do to help?" The edge of my lip quirks up as he attempts to sound casual.

"Not business related, so you're good."

"That's not what I asked."

My smile erupts full-blown at his comments. Porter is a bloody good colleague, and I'm lucky to have him, but it's more than that. Over the last few months we've become closer, and I can feel the friendship building. For a guy who doesn't like to let people into his life, I have a terrible habit of getting close to certain people. Apparently, friendships are okay if they're the kind of people I can call family. No acquaintance for me, if you are in my life, then it's forever.

My brain threatens to fill with Sam, the one person that I let go, even though I still get a dull ache in my chest when I think about him. It's like my body is trying to tell me that I shouldn't have walked away. Thankfully I've never let my body control my mind, even though this time it's only because of the distance between us. The truth is that if Sam was within reasonable driving distance, there's a good fucking chance I would have been at his doorstep by now. "Everything's fine. I just need you to get that info for me so I can get Niko on board."

We spend a few minutes saying goodbye, and just as I hang up, a knock on the door pulls my attention. I call out for detective Archer to come in. I stand as he makes his way into my office, trying to look as relaxed as possible. I have to pretend that as far as I know, the case against me is still ongoing and he hasn't hit any problems.

"Detective Archer. What can I do for you?"

I see his jaw twitch and I try to keep my face neutral. "I just had a few more follow up questions if you had a moment."

I nod and take a seat, wondering where the hell this is going. All the evidence is gone so I know that there is nothing he can pin on me. Statements might be retaken, but without any hard physical evidence, I will fight it tooth and nail. Sam checked through notes on the file and noted that there was no hard copy of the CCTV feed. They had digital and nothing else.

Detective Archer pulls a notepad from the inside of his jacket and spends a few moments reading over something. Suspecting that he's trying to rattle me, I lean back in my chair and look relaxed. There's nothing on me left, or at least I hope that's still the case. "I wanted to ask about what happened in Scotland."

"I'm not sure what you're talking about." I'm under no illusion on what he's trying to get me to talk about, but I refuse to give him anything. What happened at Sam's house is nothing to do with this fucker, and there's no way that I'm talking about it.

"The incident with," He looks at his book again. "Samuel Leighton."

"Is this in an official capacity, because I was told that my statement had been taken."

His twitching jaw is back, and I suspect that I'm not rolling over the way that he wants me to. If he wants to get the details of what happened, he's going to have to contact the police officers in charge. "You are a person of interest in a missing person case, and I'm asking about another death that you were witness to."

"And as I said, I have given my statement to the officer who was dealing with the situation. If I'm a person of interest does that mean I'm being arrested?" I need to know if he still has anything on me. I can only battle against being jailed for killing Paul if I know the details.

Detective Archer's eyes turn steely, and that's the moment I realise that Sam managed it. There's nothing left for this man to pin on me, and even though we both know I did it, he can't do a fucking thing about it. "I said a person of interest, not a suspect. The evidence I have points to you being one of the last people who saw Mr Clark."

"What evidence?"

Another twitch. "Just evidence. Back to the Scotland thing-"

"I've already told you that I'm not discussing that with you. I'm a really busy man, Detective Archer, so if there's a point to this visit could you get to it." I'm pushing him in the hopes that he will get angry enough to reveal his hand. One final hail Mary that if he still has something that can connect me with Paul, he'll show it.

"I had questions about Scotl-"

I get up from my seat and walk to the door. When I open it, I stand and wait for him to take the hint. "If you don't mind, I really need to get on. If you want to question me about what happened with Mr Leighton, please get the officer in charge to get in touch. I'll be more than happy to give an interview with the two of you present."

Detective Archer stands slowly, his eyes never leaving mine. His calm exterior doesn't hide the fire in his eyes, and I wonder how close he is to punching me. "That won't be necessary." He moves until he's standing level with me, his burning glare never leaving mine. He leans in slightly, his voice lowering so just I can hear him. "It's funny how people around you always die. You'll slip up one day, and when you do, I'll be there." He doesn't wait for a response before storming out of my office.

With the door barely closed behind him, I give in to my need to laugh. He might think that he's intimidating me, but it's obvious he's never met my friends or their friends. When I went to Scotland, it was the first time I'd met Ryden, Niko's old boss, and I can see why he was good in that sort of world. He's intimidating as fuck, and I have no problem admitting that. There's an underlying sense of danger to him, like a snake that's always ready to pounce when needed, and he would do it with a detachment that's creepy on a whole new level. Niko is a pussycat compared to Ryden, and Niko is pretty intimidating to most of the world. Nah, Mr detective doesn't rattle me in the slightest, not when I know the sort of men who have my back.

I CLOSE my computer down and get ready to leave for the night. I promised Rhys that I would stop spending the night in my office. She says she worries about me, so tonight I'll be having a drink with Gabe and Porter at Roxy's before heading home to get some work done there. I gather the files I need, knowing if Rhys knew what I was doing she would slap me across the back of the head, and put them on top of my laptop. I'm cheating a little, but Rhys didn't say I couldn't work from home, all she said was she didn't want me in the office all the time. This way I'm keeping her happy and getting the work I need done.

There's a gentle knock on my door, and I lift my head, surprised that someone's in the building. "Come in."

Margaret appears around the edge of the door.

"I thought you went home ages ago?"

She steps into the room and shrugs her shoulders. "I had something to catch up on. Are you ready to leave?"

I look at my desk to make sure I have everything before I nod. "Yeah. I'm heading out with Gabe and Porter."

"Try not to talk too much shop around Gabe. That poor boy must get bored to tears with you two." Margaret has a soft spot for Gabe, as most people do, and she treats him better than she treats me. My group of friends isn't exactly the friendliest looking bunch with their tattoos and muscles that rival some bodybuilders, but Margaret can see past all that and see the gentle hearts below. Not that any of us would admit to our softer sides, but we know they're there.

I hold up my hands trying to look as innocent as possible, but her smile tells me she isn't buying it. "Would we? It will be all talk about tattoos and hot women."

She looks at me funny, but it's brief, gone before I can really register it. "There's one more client here to see you if you can spare five minutes."

I look at the clock, noting that it's well after closing hours. "Get them to come back. It's late, and I want you to get home."

She takes another step into the office. "I think you should talk to this one. I have a feeling that it's important."

Okay, what the hell is going on here? Margaret is usually the first one to chase people away when they just turn up. She's a stickler for rules, and she isn't scared to point out to people that we have set times that they can visit. "Why?"

"Just speak to him. I will lock the front door once I leave, so you'll be free to talk." She doesn't even wait for me to agree to a meeting before she vanishes from my office, leaving my door standing wide open. I barely have time to stand before she's back, and she's not alone. "Mr Leighton, this is Mr Wilson, and he's going to help you."

My ears start to buzz as I stare at Sam standing in front of me.

31

Clay

SAM'S HERE? *Holy fuck*. He takes a step inside my office, and I don't know what to do. How do I react to this?

He takes a few more steps until he's standing on the opposite side of my desk. He holds out his hand to shake, but all I can do is stand and stare. He's wearing a dark blue suit, and it fits his body like a second skin. He has the jacket buttoned over a white shirt, and it makes his waist look fucking amazing. He doesn't have broad shoulders, but the shape of his body makes my mouth water. There's no denying my attraction to Sam, but that's not the bit that makes him dangerous. It's what he does to my heart that scares me. It's already beating like it wants to break out of my chest and rush to him.

"Mr Wilson."

I reach out and take his hand, not sure what the hell is going on. As soon as my skin connects with his, there's a zap through my entire body. It's like it's woken up for the first time in six weeks, for the first time since I walked away from Sam. "Mr Leighton." It's strange calling him by title, but since that's what he's calling me, I'm going to follow his lead. Something's going on here, and Sam is in charge. "Take a seat."

He undoes the button on his jacket to sit, and it takes everything in me not to moan at the sight before me. The shirt is fitted, and I can see the outline of his body clearly through the thin material. If he wore this outfit in the hope of driving me crazy, it's working. "I was told you might be the man to help me with my problem."

"Depends on the problem."

His gaze never drops from mine, and I can't help but get lost in it. "There's this guy I'm hoping you can help me locate. He left a few months ago, and I haven't been able to stop thinking about him since."

If I thought my heart had been beating erratically before, I was wrong. Now it feels like I've been running a fucking marathon. "Do you have any information on him?" There's very little doubt in my mind that he's talking about me, but there's also a tiny part of me that is worried he's met someone else.

"He lives around here. Thirty-four, two hundred and twenty pounds, six foot five ... a big guy who drives a huge truck, but it's not to compensate for anything."

His previous words repeated back to me make my lips twitch in humour. The day he'd called and bitched at me about investigating my own fucking case, that was the way he'd described me. That time he'd asked me if I was overcompensating, though. I suppose now he knows the truth, and the glint in his eye is unmistakable. "Sounds like a great guy."

"He is, but he sneaked out of bed like a coward. Didn't even hang around long enough to say goodbye."

"Maybe he had a good reason."

Sam shrugs his shoulders, but I can see a layer of hurt on him. I didn't think of how he would feel when I left, I just knew I had to get out of there before it became too hard to go. I'd let Sam into parts of my life that I close off to everyone, and I needed to get away to regroup. Figuring out why I told him had been my top priority, even if admitting why I'd told him made me want to run again. The simple truth was I told Sam because I wanted him to know. I needed him to see the real me, find out the things that make me the man I am.

"Either way, he left, and I want him back. I want you to find him for me, tell him that I'm waiting."

I'm lost for words. No one has ever chased me before, not in this way. Women are always happy to make it obvious that they want me, but Sam, he's going to a whole new level. He's telling me that he wants something more than a one-night fling.

He stands and panic surges through my body. I'm on my feet in mere seconds, and just as I'm about to run around the desk to grab him, he holds out a piece of paper. I take a deep breath to try and calm myself before taking the note. He keeps a hold of it, leaving the paper connecting us as I stare at him.

"If you find him, tell him to meet me here on Thursday. If he isn't there, I will know he doesn't want anything with me. But tell him I miss him." His smile is small but sad, and it cuts me to the core.

When he releases the paper, I stand and stare as he leaves my office. When I hear the front door close, all the energy drains from my body, and I collapse onto the chair. My mind is still clambering to catch up with everything that just happened, and if it weren't for the bit of paper in my hand, I would think that I'd only dreamt the whole thing. I look at the note in my hand and see an address on it, one I don't recognise. The urge to Google it nearly has me turning my computer on again, but I resist, instead gathering up my shit and leaving the office. I need to speak to Gabe before I tie myself in knots again over Sam. It would be too easy to let Sam go home without meeting him, but I have a feeling that it might finally break me completely.

"And he just turned up?"

I nod at Porter as I take a drink from the glass of Scotch in my hand. I've been explaining the whole Sam thing to him and Gabe, and I'm no further forward with knowing what to do. The note he gave me is burning a hole in my pocket like it wants me to go to him tonight.

"Wow. That guy has balls." Porter laughs before taking a drink from his own glass.

"What are you going to do?" Gabe is a bit more helpful, but he's the one I've been honest with about this whole thing. Porter only knows what I've told him tonight, and to give the guy some credit, he didn't bat an eyelid when I mentioned that I'd slept with a guy.

"I have no idea." There's no point in lying to Gabe, even though he looks at me as though the answer should be simple.

I'm just about to speak when a woman appears behind Porter and whispers something in his ear. He smiles as she continues, obviously only too happy to listen to what she's saying. When she saunters away, he slams back the last of his drink and gets up from the table. "Duty calls."

I laugh as I watch him follow his prey across the bar. That was me not that long ago, but I've tamed my ways recently. "I think that'll be the last we see of him tonight."

Gabe agrees, but his attention is on me again quickly. "What are you going to do about Sam?"

I scrub a hand over the back of my neck. Talking about this will be easier now that Porter's gone. I really like the guy, but Gabe knows me, he's seen me at my lowest points and didn't turn away. He's also the person's who's judgement I trust the most. I know he won't bullshit me, so when he speaks, I listen. "I honestly don't know. It's just all so fucking confusing. You know me, I don't do relationships."

Gabe looks at me with sympathy, and I fucking hate it. I point at his face, glaring at him so he knows I mean what I'm about to say. "Stop that. I don't need your fucking sympathy, Gabe. Don't do that shit to me."

"Sorry. I'm just pissed that this is the legacy your parents left you. Relationships don't destroy you. Trust me, I know. I thought that I was okay on my own, but with Rhys, I'm just more. I want that for you. I don't want you to be alone your whole life, not when there's someone out there for you."

"Who says there's someone out there for me?"

The sympathy leaves Gabe, and it leaves behind a disbelieving look. "Don't bullshit a bullshitter, brother. I wrote the book on trying to deny the fact I fell in love with someone. As much as we want to pretend that we have no feelings, the truth won't leave you. You know as much as I do that you have feelings for Sam, and the sooner you can admit it to yourself the better."

Gabe's right, but I hate that he is. I want to carry on my life without the complications that my mum and dad dealt with, but it looks like I'm going to be dragged into that without a choice. "I don't love him."

"I didn't say you loved him. I said you had feelings. Now what you need to decide is if you're willing to let him walk away while you pretend you don't care. Are you willing to lose him forever to save your pride?"

The thought of not seeing Sam again leaves a hollow ache in my chest. Seeing him in my office made all the feelings I was trying to deny resurface, and now I'm not sure I can fight against them, no matter how much I try. "I don't think I can let him walk away, but I don't know if I know how to keep him."

"You don't need to know. You just have to be willing to try. Go to him and take it from there. It's as simple as that."

Gabe makes it sound easy, but I know it's not. My mum and dad practically destroyed each other and I'm not willing to do that to Sam, or myself. "It's not that easy."

"It really is, my friend. If he's the one, then it will be simple. Will you argue and fight, hell yeah. But at the end of the day, it's completely worth it. If he really is the one that you're meant to be with, it'll work itself out. I think you once told me to get my head out of my arse when it came to Rhys, I'm returning the favour. I've seen you when you talk about Sam, and I can tell he means something to you. You light up when you speak about him, no matter how much you try to pretend you don't. Your parents should never have been together, they were toxic for each other. That doesn't mean that every relationship is the same. Do you think my relationship is toxic? What about Niko's?"

"Of course not." I don't want to have to explain to Gabe that his was the first relationship that made me think that all love wasn't toxic. They were honestly the first couple that didn't seem intent on destroying each other. Niko's relationship only added to the doubt about what I thought love was, and seeing him with both his men is unique but settling. To see the three of them interact is hypnotising, the flow that they seem to move around each other, like they can predict what each other will do, shows that maybe I was completely wrong. You can't fake feelings like that. Can you?

"Then stop fighting it and just be fucking happy. You won't lose your scary edge if you fall in love."

I give Gabe the finger, and all he does is laugh at me.

"Seriously though, why are you fighting it? And don't give me that shit about your past. I want a real reason. You've seen enough to prove that your parents were just fucked up."

"What if I decide to do this and I lose him? Not even because I'll fuck up ... which I will by the way. But what if I lose him like I lost Cameron? I don't know if I would survive that."

"Fuck, man. You can't live your life like that. Everyone dies, but that doesn't mean you should be alone. I thought we went through this already? You can't spend your life alone, so you don't hurt."

I wave to Roxy, and she nods, getting another round for Gabe and me. Talking about this always frays my nerves, but it feels worse tonight. Losing Cameron was the lowest point of my life. He was my everything for so long, even after he went into the care home. There wasn't a day that I didn't visit him with tales of what had happened in the record shop. He used to smile as he listened, excited to get little glimpses of the outside world. I'd initially thought that I would be able to look after him myself, but with all his medical needs, it wasn't possible. Being paralysed from the neck down left him vulnerable to infection and troubles with his breathing. Even at his young age, he could see how much I struggled, so he forced me to look for the care home he ended up in. He enjoyed living there, or at least that's what I like to tell myself.

"Clay? Stop fighting so hard. Allow yourself to be happy."

A lump of emotion sticks in my throat and I work hard to swallow it down. I want to give in to Sam, to spend the rest of my life with him. My eyes widen when the thought hits me. I want to spend the rest of my life with Sam? When did I decide that? "I want to spend the rest of my life with Sam." Saying the words out loud doesn't sound as scary as they should. Actually, if the truth were told, I feel lighter now that I've admitted to it. Is it possible that all my worry has come from the fact that I've been lying to myself?

Roxy puts our order in front of me, but I barely notice. The only thing filling my head is Sam. To know that he's come here to stake his claim is thrill-inducing. When I came out tonight, I wasn't sure what I wanted to do, but now everything is so clear. I'm going to go and meet Sam tomorrow and tell him that he's mine.

Gabe lifts his refilled glass and holds it out in front of him, and I touch my glass to his. "Here's to you finally going after what you want."

I smile at his toast, worry and happiness in equal measure warring inside me.

I WALK into Cameron's room and look at the empty bed, confusion spreading through me. There's no way that the nurses would let him leave his room, not with the way he's feeling. Last night when I saw him, he was still wired up to drips and machines, his infection leaving him weak and tired. Did he improve that much in the few hours since I saw him last?

Gabe walks in behind me, the confusion evident on his face as well. "Where is he?"

"I don't know. Did anyone say anything to you when you were coming in?" I look around the room, almost like I expect to find Cameron in a corner or something. His bed is unmade, but that's not unusual since he spends most of his day in it. His regular monitors are still next to his bed, but the new IV pumps are gone. They'd been using them the last few days to get more antibiotics into his system so he could try and fight his pneumonia better.

"I didn't see anyone. It's really quiet tonight." Now that Gabe mentions it, I realise that I didn't see anyone when I walked in either. The reception desk was unmanned, but since I'm a regular here, I just walked past to head to Cameron's room. I don't need to sign in since I'm his guardian, and it means I can come and go as I please within visiting hours.

A noise at the door has me turning, and I see Dr Kennedy walking into the room. She doesn't have the same smile that she usually greets me with and it just increases the uneasiness that's been steadily building inside. "Where's Cameron?" I swear she flinches when I mention his name and the sight makes my heart start to race.

"Clay."

"Where's my brother?"

She takes a step forward, her face full of pain. "Clay. Please-"

"Where the fuck is my brother?" My voice is booming, but I can't get control over myself. My brain is screaming at me to run, to get out of this room before she says something I don't want to hear.

"Clay. I'm so sorry. We did everything we could."

No. No. No.

I back away from her and don't stop until something at my back blocks my movements. This can't be happening. There's no way my little brother's dead.

My lungs struggle to inflate, and my head goes dizzy. I gasp quickly but it's not enough, I can't get enough air into my body. The pains in my ribcage pull my attention, and I grip at my chest to try an ease them, but it doesn't work. Nothing works. Oh god, my little brother is gone. He was the last part of my family, and I'll never see him again. I didn't get a chance to tell him he was my hero. Tell him how much I fucking loved him.

I don't know when I collapsed to the floor but Gabe speaking in my ear gets my attention. I'm wrapped up in his huge arms from behind, and he's holding me as I rock on the cold tiled floor.

"It's okay. Fuck, Clay. I'm so sorry. Shhh ... it's gonna be okay."

His words confirm the knowledge that I was trying to block out. I was trying to convince myself that I'd heard Dr Kennedy wrong, but I hadn't. "Oh god. He's gone. He's really fucking gone."

"I'm sorry."

I look up to find Dr Kennedy standing in front of me, tears falling down her cheeks. "What happened?"

She closes her eyes and takes a deep breath. If she's trying to appear unaffected by this whole situation she's failing. The pain in her is there to see. "We were taking him for a scan to check his lungs. He'd been struggling to breathe even with the increased oxygen. When he was in ... his heart stopped, and we failed to restart it. I'm sorry, Clay."

Cameron had died alone, and that fact guts me. A sob echoes through the quiet room and my warm cocoon tightens around me. Gabe's head is resting against the back of my head, and I'm so thankful he's here with me. Pain is lancing through my body, and I feel like I'll never recover from this, but Gabe being here is holding me together. I need to get a grip on myself. I need to be strong for Cameron and give him the final goodbye he deserves.

I GASP AWAKE IN BED, the sweat from the nightmare dripping over my body. Sitting up I wipe my face and run my hands through my hair. Fuck. It's been a long time since I dreamt of Cameron, especially the day he died. I've spent years building a wall around that memory so it couldn't haunt me, but tonight it was set free. It's the final proof I need that Sam has changed me, that he's opening up a part of me that I've tried to lock away, and it's going to happen without my control.

32

Sam

I FEEL like I could vomit. Like bend over and empty my stomach on the pavement kind of vomit. I don't think I've felt nerves like this in my whole life, and I've been in some nerve-wracking situations. When I called Gabe to ask him a favour, it had seemed like a good idea, but now that the time has come to cash in on it, I realise what a bad idea it was. People might think it's impulsive, but it's not. I've wanted to do this for a long time, but it's only now that I felt the courage to do it. I've made a lot of changes recently, and this is something to help mark that occasion.

I take a deep breath and push open the door to the tattoo studio that Gabe told me to come to. A little bell goes above the door, and a pretty blonde raises her head to look at me. Her smile is infectious, and it settles my nerves a little.

"Hey, how can I help you?" She stands but to be honest, it doesn't make her much taller than when she was sitting.

"Hi, I'm Sam. I have an appointment with Gabe."

Her eyes go wide, and she looks me up and down. "Oh, you're Sam?"

I flounder, not sure what to say to that. I don't know who this person is, but apparently, she knows about me.

"Rhys, don't harass the customers." I turn and see a huge tattooed guy heading my way. He isn't the size of Clay, but I'd also not pick a fight with him. He has visible tattoos covering both arms and a few peeking out of the neck of the fitted black t-shirt he's wearing. There's no mistaking that this is Gabe, not with Clay describing him perfectly. Big and scary looking, but with the kindest eyes you've ever seen. It was clear to see that Clay had a soft spot for Gabe when he spoke about him. "I'm Gabe."

I take his offered hand and smirk when I see him sizing me up. I'd expected it, especially since I'm not sure how flattering Clay would have been about me. "Sam."

"And I'm Rhys. I'm Gabe's better half." The blonde has come around the desk to stand next to Gabe. I smile as Gabe wraps an arm around her and kisses her head. The moment is brief as Gabe removes his arm and takes a few steps back, but even the few moments they were together showed their obvious connection. Clay told me how well Gabe and Rhys worked as a couple, and now that I've seen them together, I know that he was right. Sometimes you meet people and know they are a couple without being told, that's Gabe and Rhys.

"Come through." Gabe nods towards a door at the back of the reception area, and I follow him, trying not to notice how Rhys' eyes never leave me. "Ignore her. She has a thousand questions that Clay isn't willing to answer so she's hoping you will."

"Oh." It's all I can say, but at least I know that Clay has spoken about me to more than just Gabe. I wasn't sure if he would keep everything with me a complete secret, but when I'd called Gabe, he knew exactly who I was.

We enter a clean looking room with framed designs on the wall. There's a large black seat in the middle of the room, like the ones you get at the dentist, and the tray next to it holds things I don't want to pay attention to. It's evident that it's the tattoo machine, but there are also lotions and items that I can only imagine the reason for.

"Take a seat." Gabe pulls up a small stool on wheels, and I sit on the edge of the larger chair. "I've had a look at the design and made up a template." He pulls a sheet of paper out of a folder and hands it to me.

When I decided that I wanted to get a tattoo I wasn't sure exactly what I wanted. After talking to Gabe it seemed like I'd always known, I just needed him to get the idea out of my head. Now looking at his design, I'm not sure what to say. *It's fucking perfect.* The tree is artistic, and like nothing I've ever seen before. It feels kind of like I'm looking at it through the fog, but it's clear what it is. "Gabe. This is ... wow."

He smiles, and I can see how much he cares about his job. If everything he does looks like what he designed for me, then I'm surprised he doesn't have queues out the door every day. "Thanks. I tried to take everything you said and added to it." He points at the trunk, and it's the first time I notice the design in the bark. "I added the feather that you spoke about. Nothing too obvious, but you'll know it's there."

I develop a lump in my throat as I look at the obvious reminder of Clay. The feather tattoo on his neck is a reminder for his brother and something that is important to him. I wanted Clay to know that his loss won't ever be forgotten. I can't imagine losing one of my family members so young, and I'm willing to keep a part of Cameron with me forever. "Thank you. You don't think ... he won't be angry will he?" I've been worried that Clay will think it's weird that I'm remembering a guy that I've never met, that my tribute to his brother is overstepping a line that I shouldn't go past.

Gabe pulls up his sleeve and points to a small feather that's placed to the side of his wrist. "He wasn't angry at me."

"Yeah, but you're his friend. You mean something to him."

Gabe laughs, but I don't get the joke. "You don't have to worry about that." He turns and gets a spray bottle from his little table. "Ready to start?"

I'VE WATCHED Gabe work on my first ever tattoo for nearly two hours now. I was worried to begin with that the pain would be more than I could cope with, but it didn't take long for it to fade. Now looking at the beautiful tree on the inside of my forearm, I know that every second of discomfort was worth it.

"You okay? I've got a few more minutes of shading, and we should be done."

"I'm good."

He smiles before going back to work. We've spoken a little about nothing much, but we've mostly been quiet while he worked. It's not been uncomfortable though and watching Gabe work has kept my attention. He seems to get lost in the art as he draws it onto skin and it's like seeing magic happen. I know that sounds corny and lame, but it's the truth. I'm pretty sure that Gabe leaves a little part of himself in each tattoo he does, and his love for his craft is obvious to see. Now that I'm nearing the end of my tattoo I decide to ask the burning questions that have been floating around my head. "How's Clay?"

Another smile from Gabe as he puts the tattoo gun down and grabs the water spray. He covers the tattoo and uses a tissue to clean off the excess ink. "He's good. A little confused. Apparently, he's had a lot to think about recently."

I can feel my cheeks heat as I get what Gabe's trying to tell me. Clay has obviously confided in him about everything. "Oh. I'm sorry."

"Oh don't be sorry. It's about time someone came along and knocked him on his arse. Truthfully, I didn't expect it to be a guy."

More heat to my cheeks.

"He's been so closed off for years, determined not to let anyone in, that I thought he would spend his life alone. You just made him think about things a little differently."

"Or a lot differently."

Gabe's laugh is loud as he sits up and looks at me. "Yeah, a lot differently. How's that?"

I look at the finished product, and it's everything I had imagined a tattoo could be. "It's perfect." It doesn't express how much I love it, but it's the best I've got just now.

"Why not have a look in the mirror and then we'll get it covered. You need to keep the cover on for about an hour then take it off and clean it."

I nod and get up from the chair, walking to the huge mirror on the wall. My eyes are stuck on the tattoo as I twist my arm to get a better view. It's strange seeing ink on my skin, but it looks like it was made specifically for my arm. Which I suppose it was since Gabe drew it for me.

"Hey fuck head. Rhys tried to tell me you had a client, but your book is closed off-"

My eyes connect with Clay's in the mirror, and I freeze. He wasn't meant to know I was here, not until tomorrow when I see him. He seems just as shocked as I am, his huge body still filling the doorway.

"Clay." Gabe's voice cuts the silence but I don't look away from Clay, and his eyes are still firmly on me.

"Leave, Gabe." Clay's words spread over my skin, and it pebbles with pleasure.

"Clay-"

Clay finally breaks our staring competition as he focuses on Gabe. "I said leave."

I turn in place so I can see the friends talking, Gabe standing up to Clay in a powerful stare off. Part of me wants to beg Gabe to stay in the room as a buffer between Clay and me, but the other part is screaming at him to leave. With my heart racing, I'm more than ready to face Clay head on. Gabe looks at me like he's asking for permission to go, and when I nod slightly, he points at Clay.

"Don't be a dick." With those parting words to his friend, he leaves us alone, closing the door gently behind him.

The atmosphere in the room changes. Intensifies, and I'm tempted to leave right along with Gabe. Unfortunately, my feet are rebelling against me and refuse to move from their spot. I stretch my neck and unclench my fists, trying to fake the appearance of being relaxed. I don't want Clay to know how anxious I am in his presence, because none of it is fear, and all of it is because he's so close. Being in the same room is making my body go into overdrive, and I feel like I'm close to melting into a puddle of goo on the floor.

"What are you doing here?" The words sound like a growl, but from the heat in his gaze, I can tell it isn't through anger.

My throat feels thick, and I can't get words to form correctly, so I just hold out my arm and show him. I can feel the heat of his stare on my arm, and when a groan escapes his throat, I nearly come in my jeans. "You got Gabe to give you a tattoo?

"You told me he was the best."

His eyes come back to mine, and we stare at each other for several heartbeats before he looks at my arm again. He's silent as he inspects it, and when his hand comes up to his neck, I know he's seen the heart of my tattoo. "You got a feather?"

"I did."

"Why?"

Now is the time to be open and honest, and I hope that he doesn't hate me afterwards. "Because he's part of you. He deserves to be remembered. You deserve to have your memories shared."

He finally looks away from my arm, and when his gaze meets mine, I can see the emotions flicker across his face. When the colours in his eyes stop swirling, there is only one emotion present, and it makes my heart race as well as my dick hard. The heat and lust shine from his gaze, and as we stand there, his jaw tightens.

"Give me permission."

Confusion clouds my mind and I struggle to make sense of what he's saying. "What?"

"Give me fucking permission to touch you, Sam." Clay sounds like he's in pain and I can only imagine that if his dick is as hard as mine, there's a good chance he is.

My breath whooshes from me, and I stumble over my words. "Yes. God, yes."

The words are barely past my lips when he lunges at me. His hands grip my face, and with his huge body pressed against mine, my back hits the mirror, and I slide up it until I'm level with Clay's face. His mouth crashes onto mine, and everything vanishes except his kiss. He takes full control of me with his lips, and I relax into him, letting him lead the way. I'm just happy he's here, touching me like I wanted him to. I wasn't sure if he would turn up tomorrow as I asked, so having him in my arms is like I've finally found heaven.

I grip his hair in my fists and enjoy the growl vibrating through my chest from Clay's. His thigh eases between my legs, grinding against my aching cock as he thrusts against me. With my head spinning, I put some distance between our mouths. "Clay, stop."

He instantly freezes, and when I feel him start to back off, I grab him by the shoulders to keep him against me.

"No, don't move. Just slow down, or I'm gonna come in my jeans."

Clay's body relaxes as he laughs. "Is it bad that I kinda like the sound of that?"

I drop my head to his and close my eyes, just enjoying being with him, surrounded by his smell. "Yes, it's bad. I'm the one who would have to walk past your best friend with a wet patch."

His hands massage my neck, the gentle touch electrifying my skin. "I fucking missed you."

With four simple words, Clay opens my heart and becomes a permanent fixture. Wherever this thing goes, he'll always be with me, no matter how much I try to fight it. It's a simple admission but one I thought he'd fight until I had to bang his head against a wall. I had a whole elaborate plan to convince him that he needed to give me a chance, and here he is, giving in before I have a chance to do any of it. He's thrown me, and I feel adrift, needing him to anchor me again. "What do we do now?"

"You came after me, what was your plan?"

"I was going to pester you until you took pity on me."

The smile never leaves his lips, but Clay steps back to put some distance between us. The cold air hitting my body makes me want to reach out and wrap myself around his chest. I feel better when he grips my hand. Pulling me back to the chair I just spent hours on. When I'm sitting, he takes Gabe's seat, going into the drawer and pulling out some cling and tape. "Arm." I place my arm on his leg, and he starts covering my new tattoo. "What was at the address you asked me to come to?"

My stomach tumbles now, because there's no escaping what I've done. Things have changed in the weeks since I last saw Clay. The case with Damien is officially closed, the police deciding that it was nothing more than a matter of self-defence. I'd still worried for weeks that they would turn up at the door and tell me they'd changed their mind, but after giving them all the information I'd kept on Damien, I'd been convinced they were happier to investigate him and his clients. That was when I decided I needed to do something with my life. I was sick of hiding from the world, and I also wanted the chance to go after

Clay. Now everything I've done seems silly, and I'm not sure I want to tell Clay.

"Sam, what's there?" His eyes look away from my arm, and his gaze makes the words tumble from my mouth.

"It's my new house."

Clays eyes widen, but then a huge smile appears. "You moved here? Seriously?"

I look away before nodding my head, suddenly feeling very much like a stalker. Clay's finger under my chin makes me raise my head until I meet his gaze.

"I'm so fucking happy about that. I like you close ... fuck, I love you close."

My stomach is still a tangle of nerves, but his happiness is helping a little. "I thought it would be easier to win you over if I didn't have an eight-hour drive to get to you."

Clay leans in and kisses me, but this time it's gentler. There's still the same passion as before, but this time the need is tempered like he wants to tell me something important. "So much easier." His words are murmured against my lips before he claims them again. His tongue slips into my mouth, and I gently bite it, causing him to groan loudly. I've always been in control when it came to partners, but with Clay today, I'm happy to take a back seat and let him lead. I allow him to take what he wants from me, only too happy to follow him anywhere.

All too soon the kiss ends, but the tingle against my lips reminds me that Clay was there. I struggle to open my eyes because the dreamy feelings are making me want to float away. It's that thought that has me finally opening them with a laugh. Clay looks at me strangely, and I have to let him in on the joke. "With the thoughts running through my head just now I'm surprised there aren't cartoon lovebirds above my head."

Just as he's about to answer there's a knock on the door. Gabe opens the door a crack but doesn't look inside. "Is everyone alive ... and dressed?"

Clay stands and kisses me on the head before going to the door. He pulls the door open, and Gabe nearly falls on his face. "You're an arsehole."

Gabe enters the room, his eyes trained firmly on me, telling me that I'd been his main worry. "Everything okay?"

"Of course it is. What did you think I was going to do to him?" Clay sounds annoyed as he comes to sit next to me on the chair, his heat seeping through my clothes and into my skin. I want to rub myself against him, but I refrain, not wanting to look desperate in front of Gabe.

"I know you, Clay. There was a good chance I'd come in here, and Sam would be crying, or you'd have him pinned to the wall while you fucked him."

My cheeks burn with embarrassment, but neither of the men seems to notice. I can't believe that Gabe just said that while I was sitting here, and not to mention the fact that Clay doesn't deny either of the scenarios. "I'm sitting right here you know."

Gabe and Clay look at each other and burst out laughing. I would be pissed off if Clay didn't pull me close to him, kissing my temple as his hand rubs my back. "Sorry, beautiful. All I can do is apologise for my friend."

I don't know if Clay is aware of what he just called me, but while butterflies erupt in my stomach, Gabe's face softens, and he looks really fucking happy. He apparently caught the name, and he's more than happy that Clay let it slip.

"How about we all go out for a drink? I have no more customers tonight, and Rhys can close up then meet us."

Clay stays quiet, his gaze firmly on me while he waits for me to answer. As much as I want to drag Clay back to my place by the hair, I think it's important that he sees I'm willing to be part of his life. When I left Scotland, it was to start a new life here, or at least to become a part of Clay's if he would have me. I want to start a new life, and I hope that Clay wants to be part of it. "I think drinks sound great."

Clay gets up and grabs me by the hand, pulling me until I'm standing in front of him. "Prepare yourself, Sam. This could get interesting."

Now I'm not so sure a night out was a good idea.

33

Clay

If someone had told me a week ago that I'd be sitting in Roxy's with Sam I would have called them a liar. Never would I have imagined that he'd be pressed against my side, letting his leg brush over mine again and again. Every whisper of his jeans against mine sends an electric current to my balls, and it's taking all my control not to drag him to the toilet to get a taste of him. I don't think I've ever been turned on by anyone as much as I am by Sam, and it's taking a lesson in patience to stay in my seat.

Sam laughs at Gabe's stories about the shit I used to get up to, and when he turns to look at me, I feel another part of the wall around my heart chip away. He looks so fucking happy, and I need to keep that look on his face as much as possible. "You seriously puked on a baby?"

I realise that I've missed the whole conversation between Gabe and Sam, his leg obviously distracting me more than I thought. "You told him that? Fuck you, Gabe."

Gabe's laughter tells me he has no guilt about letting that particularly embarrassing story out, and I make a silent vow to pay him back. "What? He asked for the funniest story I have of you and that's it. It wasn't my fault you puked on that baby and then ran away."

I glare at my possible ex-best friend before explaining the real story to Sam. "What he isn't telling you is that it was a grown man dressed as a baby. We got invited to a friends party, and we didn't realise what sort of party. Let's just say there are some bizarre ways that people get off. I'm not one to judge, but when that guy shit in the nappy he was wearing, I was done."

Sam's face turns a little green as he listens to my description. "I'm pretty sure I would have puked too."

"Definitely." I whisper that against his lips when I give in to the urge to kiss him. It's the first affection I've shown him since we left Virgin Ink, and where I thought it might cause some panic inside me, it actually settles me. I mean to keep the kiss brief, but when Sam opens his lips and licks his tongue against mine, I have no option but to deepen it. I grip the back of his neck to make sure he doesn't back away, but his fingers digging into my thigh makes me think he isn't going anywhere. Fuck me, I could kiss him all day, and it wouldn't be enough. I've never really been a fan of kissing, but with Sam, it feels different. The scrape of his stubble against mine and the softness of his full lips, it's addictive.

A cough reminds me that we're sitting in the middle of a bar with Gabe, and when I break apart from Sam, I notice that Gabe isn't alone any more. Rhys is sitting on his knee, her eyes wide as she watches us. To be fair, she isn't the only person watching us, and it suddenly becomes a little awkward to be the centre of attention. "Close your mouth, Rhys."

She laughs, and I'm worried about what's about to come out of the aforementioned mouth. "That's freaking weird ... but also really hot."

Gabe covers her mouth with his hand, but I can still see the happiness shining in her eyes. "I'm sorry about her. But I have to say she's right, that was weird. I'm used to sucking face with women, and Sam's not one of those."

I want to tell them both to shut up before they make things awkward, but Sam's laughter interrupts me. I face him and give him a questioning look.

"Sorry, but it is kinda funny. You better get used to people being shocked unless you lied about me being the first guy?"

"Oh no, he didn't lie about that. I swear there was never an inkling that he liked men, not by the number of women he whored around with. I thought he was trying to get through every woman in the City."

My stomach sours at Rhys' words and Sam's silence only makes me feel worse. Rhys must realise that she's said something wrong and her smile vanishes. "Shit. I didn't mean–"

Gabe covers her mouth again and stands, making her stand along with him. "Okay my little big mouth, why don't we go and get some drinks?" He gives me a sympathetic smile before leaving me alone with Sam.

The silence continues and it fucking kills me. I finally decided that I don't want to be alone, that there is someone out there for me, and I fuck it up with my past. There's no way for me to change what I've done, and if Sam has a problem with it, it's maybe better we find out now. "I can't change the past, Sam. I've been with a lot of women, and truthfully, I'm not ashamed of it."

Sam's head spins to look at me. "Shit, no. That's not ..." He lowers his head as he goes quiet again.

"It's just you and me here. You can tell me anything."

He looks at me, his eyes a little sad as he chews his bottom lip. "Have you been ... you know ... since me?"

Suddenly his worry makes a little more sense. He wants to know if I returned to my loose ways after I left his bed. "One."

"Oh." The sadness increases, and it takes everything in me not to reach out and touch him. I won't start this relationship with lies, but he'll listen, so he doesn't get the wrong idea.

"I was so frustrated with myself. I wasn't sure what I was feeling for you, and I needed to prove to myself that I didn't want you. But fuck me, it was a disaster."

This gets Sam's attention, and he leans in a little. "Really?"

"Yeah, like huge disaster." I point to the door that leads to the toilets at the back of the bar. "I took her in the toilet back there with every intention of fucking her." He follows my finger, his face heating as he bites his lip harder. I wish I knew what he was thinking. Is he jealous or does he hate the story?

"Did you?" His voice is soft and a little breathy, anticipation clear.

I lean in getting closer to his ear, my cheek brushing over his as I place my lips next to his ear. "I couldn't. For the life of me, I couldn't get hard, not until I thought about you. I don't know what you did to me, Sam, but nothing gets me hard except you."

I feel the rush of air against my cheek, and I smile in satisfaction. I don't want him to doubt what is between us, and it's time for him to understand that I want him more than anyone before him.

"I don't know what label I should pin to myself, but I'm past caring. The only thing I know is that it doesn't matter who it is, man or woman, no one turns me on. Only you. You're the only one I think about, the only one I fantasise about while I rub my dick." He's the only one I think about as I do a lot of things, but I leave him with the filthy images in his head. There's plenty of time to let him into the rest of the details later. He'll find out soon enough how much I want him in my life, for everything.

"Clay."

That's what I wanted to hear. The breathy moan of my name that I've missed almost every second since the last time I was with him. "But see I have a problem."

"What?"

I can't help but smirk. "I don't know if I couldn't get hard because it wasn't you, or was it possibly the fact I was in the bathroom?" I know for a fact the reason was one hundred percent because it wasn't Sam, but that doesn't stop me from issuing my challenge. "I wonder if there's a way to test out which one it was?"

I lean back, and I'm met with Sam's eyes that are on fire. I can see the lust burning deep inside him, and it's my turn to let out a gasp.

He doesn't even speak as he gets up from his chair and heads towards the toilet. I glance towards Gabe to let him know we will be back, but he's watching what's happening already. I nod towards the bathroom, and he shakes his head at me before smiling. I would deny what's about to occur, but I don't want to. I'm hoping I'm about to fuck Sam in there and I don't care who knows it.

I follow quickly, worried that I've got it wrong when I can't see Sam in front of me anymore. I push the door open and slip inside. I'm barely through the door fully when I'm grabbed and pinned against it. Sam's body presses against mine as he claims my mouth. I've never been the kind of guy who let someone else take control, but with Sam, I love when his dominant side comes out. It's like the night he finally took what he wanted, tying me to the chair so I couldn't move. Nothing has revved my engine quite as much as that did, and as he leads the kiss, I melt against him in pleasure.

Chasing his tongue when he tries to back off, I keep us connected as his hand's fumble with my jeans. I moan when he gets the zip down and finally gives my hard on some space. I've spent the whole night hard, so the relief is fucking amazing.

"Looks like it's not the bathroom." I groan when his fingers wrap around the front of my cock through my boxers. He strokes me roughly, the slight pain making my toes curl.

"Baby, I've been hard the whole fucking night. I told you, I just need to be near you to be turned on." Another groan and his fingers play along the elastic of my underwear. He's teasing, and I don't know if I want him to stop or do it more. With Sam, I'm always torn between instant gratification and making it last forever. Both sound the perfect ending when he touches me. When his finger dips beneath the material and brushes against my wet tip my patience vanishes. I take over and spin us until it's his back that hits the door. I reach down to make sure it's locked because what I'm about to do, I don't want any witnesses.

"Get your cock out. Show me."

Sam's eyes never leave mine as he does as he's told. His tongue flicks out to wet his lips as he lowers his zip painfully slowly. He's testing my patience again, and I fucking love it. He always pushes me to get a reaction, and the twisted side of me wants him to push harder, make me do shit I would never dream of. When I hear the rustle of fabric, I let my gaze drift lower, my mouth watering when I see his hard cock standing proud against his stomach. Never in my life did I think I would ever see an erection and think that I needed to taste it, but like with everything else, Sam is the exception. Every part of him calls to me, and his hard-on is no different.

Dropping to my knees, I reach out and finally touch him. His gasp is sexy as fuck and I stroke him to get more noises from him. When I lick the precum from his tip I groan, the taste exploding on my tongue. It's the first taste of Sam, and I think I could become addicted. I never did blow him when we were together, and I've spent so much time regretting it. Not knowing what it felt like to have him in my mouth was going to be a regret that followed me forever. Now I'm going to rectify that mistake.

"Clay, you don't have to. I know–"

Another lick to Sam's cock silences him. "I know. I want to more than you might understand. I've spent too long wondering how it would feel." I suck his tip into my mouth, and more precum explodes on my tongue. I close my eyes and enjoy the feeling of his cock. The softness of his skin on my tongue is surprising. I expected him to be hard in my mouth, but he's not. It feels a bit like silk slipping over metal, and the feeling is addictive. So are the noises that are escaping Sam, and it's those that make me take him deeper. I focus all my efforts on making this good for Sam, drawing up on everything that I enjoy when I'm being blown. I have a lot to learn, but I can try my hardest to make it as good as I can.

"Fuck, Clay. Oh god."

I open my eyes and look up the length of Sam's body. His head is dropped back against the wall, the length of his neck on show. I'm tempted to stop what I'm doing so I can lick that skin, but when he tangles his hands into my hair and looks at me, there's no way that I can stop. His hips move, thrusting his cock into my mouth, but not too deeply. He's being gentle, and I need to make him break apart. I want him to lose control and take what he wants. I want to make him shatter.

I drop my hands from his thighs and grip them behind my back. I don't lose his gaze, and when I relax my jaw in invitation, he understands. He slides in deeper but stops when I gag. Frustration comes out of nowhere, and I press forward until I choke on his cock. He grips my hair and pulls me off his erection.

"Clay, stop."

"No." I fight against his hold, and the pain in my scalp makes my whole body come alive. I swallow his dick, tears building in my eyes as I struggle to breathe. The feeling is fucking exhilarating, and I take him deeper. The pain in my head increases and I finally look up at

Sam's. He's close to snapping. I can see it clearly on his face. One more push and I'll get what I want, what we both want. Bracing myself I relax my throat, trying my hardest to take him the whole way down. It's clear it works when Sam's eyes darken, making him look so fucking hot. He's always sexy, but seeing this side of him makes my heart stutter.

"You tell me to stop if you need me to."

I nod slightly and grip my fingers tighter behind my back when Sam finally gives in to his need. He starts gently, brushing the back of my throat as I get used to his presence. On the third thrust, he pushes deeper until he blocks my airway. He holds himself in there as tears slide from the corner of my eyes. He watches me carefully, but he doesn't need to. I'm burning with need for him, and I want him to take this. He finally pulls back, and I gasp in air to fill my lungs.

"You are so fucking perfect. God, I want to fuck that mouth." That sounds like a great plan to me, so I smirk at him and open my mouth. Thankfully he takes the invitation that I'm giving him, and he starts to use my mouth the way he wants. He alternates between filling my mouth fully and running his tip along my lips.

I can feel my cock drip down my thigh, and I give in to my own need, gripping my cock and pumping hard. The action makes Sam thrust harder, and it takes only a few slides of my hand before my orgasm is building to a point that I can't turn back from. Sam has a full hold of my head as he thrusts into my mouth and I can tell he's close. I use my free hand to slide a finger behind his balls and over his tight hole. With the first brush of my finger, Sam explodes over my tongue. I have a moment of indecision as his cum fills my mouth, but the need to swallow comes quickly. I drink everything he gives me, and as he shudders above me, I explode over my hand.

I drop his now spent dick as I yell out in pleasure, and it's only when he kisses me on a laugh, that I realise how loud I'd been. If anyone was walking past the bathroom, there's no doubt that they would now know what was happening in here. I let Sam manhandle me to standing, and I use the sink behind me to lean against. My legs are struggling to keep me upright, but when Sam leans his body against mine, I feel more secure.

"Again I say, I don't think it's the bathroom." Sam wiggles his eyebrows, and I can't help but give a weak laugh.

"I didn't think it was, but it was the only way I could think of getting you in here." I kiss his nose and contemplate lying on the floor for a nap. The orgasms I've had over the last few months can't compare to this one. Every one of them has been brought about by my hand, but having Sam's cock in my mouth just made it better. Being with Sam, giving him pleasure, makes everything better.

"You saying I'm that predictable?"

"I was hoping. Fuck, that was amazing." I cough and groan at the slight pain in my throat.

"Sorry." Sam looks a little ashamed, and there's no fucking way he's thinking anything other than great thoughts about what happened.

"Don't fucking do it. What you just did ... fucking mind-blowing. I wanted it, and I'm ecstatic that you finally gave it to me."

"It was your first time. I should have let you go slowly."

"Sam, I'm a grown man. This will only work if you let me decide what I want. There's going to be a whole shit ton of stuff I haven't done, that doesn't mean I don't want them." I grip his face, only remembering far too late that I have a palm covered in drying cum. I can see the moment that Sam realises the same thing as his nose screws up.

"You just covered me in cum didn't you?"

I suck my lips into my mouth to try and stop the laugh that is building quickly inside me.

"I hate you."

I lean forward and kiss his lips, keeping my hands firmly in place so I don't spread the stickiness. "No, you don't."

He sighs against my lips. "No, I don't."

34

Clay

MY STOMACH IS full of butterflies as I park outside Niko's cabin. I haven't been back to see him in months, but I needed to talk to him about the new office. He's already agreed to run the Scotland base for me, but I haven't broached the subject of hiring Grant yet. I wanted to make sure he was over his protective streak before I brought it up, knowing that he was struggling after what had happened to both his men. It's also why I'm here now, thinking it's probably better to have this conversation face to face. Ultimately it will be Grant's decision, but I don't want Niko to believe I went behind his back.

"You look like you're gonna vomit."

I turn to Sam who's in the passenger seat of my truck and give him a small smile. *Four months.* That's how long it's been since Sam called me to curse me out, and my life has changed so much since then. We've only been official for a few weeks now, but it's felt like a whirlwind. Like the perfect fucking storm. It's difficult to remember what life was like without Sam in it, but I'm okay with that. "I'm good."

He reaches out and squeezes my hand before getting out of the truck. He's barely on the ground when Grant appears at the front door. Sam rushes towards him and the two friends embrace. Sam had explained what happened after Grant had been shot, that he'd avoided him until Grant had sent Niko after him, and I'm glad that Grant hadn't let him escape. Sam's never had a real friend, and he's missed out. I'm not exactly the most open and welcoming person in the world, but the friends I have kept me sane. Gabe is like a brother, and I wouldn't be half the man I am without him. He doesn't think twice about calling me out on my bullshit, keeping me from making some huge mistakes. Niko and Porter are becoming just as important, and I hope that they feel the same about me. They are more than just friends and work colleagues. They're family.

I follow Sam out and head slowly towards where him and Grant are standing talking. I don't want to interrupt their moment, but Sam turns and holds out a hand to me. This is the first time I will be showing Grant, Niko, and Corey that I'm with Sam. After numerous calls to Niko, they're well aware that I'm in a relationship with Sam, but knowing and seeing are two different things. Niko had a lot to say about the whole situation, his humour evident the entire time, but the bastard won't miss his chance now to take the piss face to face. I'll take it all though, and I'll do it with a smile on my face. Niko's shit is done with love, and being with Sam is worth every single word he throws at me. So I wrap my arm around Sam's shoulder, smiling when he tucks his body in close to mine.

Grant smiles as he looks between us, but before he can say anything, Corey and Niko appear behind him. Corey seems to take everything in his stride, but when Niko looks at Sam and me standing arm in arm, a shit-eating grin appears on his face. Yeah, he's going to have way too much fun with this.

"Come in you guys. I just pulled some carrot cake from the oven." Corey grabs Niko by the hand and pulls him in the front door, but Niko keeps looking over his shoulder, his eyes firmly on me as he's dragged inside.

"Have fun with Niko." Sam's voice is full of humour, and I tickle his side. He squirms before escaping my fingers, rushing into the house ahead of me. It leaves me walking next to Grant, and when he slows, I match his pace.

"He looks happy. Thank you for that."

"No need to thank me. His happiness is important to me, but

honestly, it's all him. He makes me want to love him and it's easy to do."

Grant bumps against my arm. "Who knew what a big softy you are."

I growl at him but can't deny that he's right. Sam has brought out a gentler side to me, but he can also bring out the animal like no one else. One filthy smile in my direction is all it takes for me to pounce and pleasure him until he's screaming my name. We haven't had sex since we got together, waiting for the right time to take that step again, but all it's done is made me more imaginative in other ways. "Bite me."

"I would, but I like Sam as my friend, so will leave that to him." He laughs again, and I have the sneaky suspicion that there'll be a lot of laughter today at my expense.

When I reach the kitchen where everyone has assembled, I see Sam laughing with Corey as they try to decorate the carrot cake. He looks relaxed and happy, and that's when I decide I don't care how much teasing I have to take. Let Niko have his fun. I'll put up with the worst he can throw at me to keep Sam smiling like that. It's strange how quickly I've gone from not having to worry about how others felt, to a deep down need to keep Sam happy.

"It's strange, isn't it?" Niko comes to stand close to me as he watches Sam and Corey together.

"What is?"

Grant appears at Niko's side long enough to kiss him before heading over to join the other two. He wraps his arms around Corey's waist and is rewarded with some cream cheese frosting on his nose.

"Them." He nods towards our men. "That we fought so long to deny our feelings and now we would jump into a fire for them."

He's so fucking right. All that time I wasted trying to pretend that I didn't want Sam, and now I would fight to the death to keep him. "Sorry if I didn't realise how much you were hurting when Corey vanished. I didn't know."

"Don't stress it, brother. You kept your head, and that's what I needed. We got him home, and that's the only important thing."

I look at Niko and see the love shining from his gaze as he

watches his men fight over the spatula, both of them wearing more frosting than is on the cake. I turn and find my own man, and he must feel my stare because he looks at me. I wink at him, and he blows me a kiss. "You got a minute, Niko. Got some things I want to discuss with you."

He nods before leading me towards his office. I take a seat in front of his desk and get comfortable while he walks to his cabinet.

"Drink?"

When I nod, he pours me a glass of Scotch, taking a seat next to me.

"What's up?"

"I needed to talk to you about the business."

"Everything okay? I'm still ready to open next week. I've got the first lot of client meetings booked for Thursday."

I take a drink and try to buy myself some time. I need to approach this in the right way, or Niko will shut me down before I get to explain everything. "Yeah still set for next week. You know I'm leaving it in your capable hands. Porter will arrive on Tuesday to help you get the final bits and bobs organised. Sam will get the computer system set up in the next few days so it'll be linked to our system. Thought it would be easier that way."

"I want to thank you again. I don't know what I would have done for a job if you hadn't offered me this. I owe you one."

Okay, maybe this is the way into this conversation I was waiting for. "Well, if you mean that."

"That sounds a little scary." Niko puts his glass on the desk and leans an elbow on the wood. I take a deep breath and jump straight in.

"From the enquiries that we've had, it's clear you're going to be busy. I want to take on another full time member of staff. He's trained for this sort of thing, and I think you would work well with him."

Niko's eyes scrunch up, and he still looks worried, like he's waiting on the downside. Always said this guy was smart. "But?"

I hold up a finger and get up from my chair, going to the door and opening it. When it's fully opened, I shout Grant's name, refusing to look at Niko. I'm going with the theory that if I don't look at him, he won't punch me. I'm playing with fire, but it's kind of exciting.

"Yeah?" Grant appears in the door, and I motion for him to come into the office.

"Clay." Niko's voice is loud, but there's no anger, just a wariness that if I were sensible, I would acknowledge.

Grant's eyes flicker between us, and he looks really fucking confused. I don't plan on dragging this out, so I jump straight in and offer him the job I hope he takes.

"I want to offer you a job. Niko is going to need another investigator in the office, and I think you would be perfect." I don't know what I expected from Grant, but laughter wasn't the one I would have expected. When I don't laugh along with him, he stops, his eyes opening wide.

"Shit, you're serious?"

Now I'm the one who's confused. "Yeah, why wouldn't I be serious?"

"Fuck, Clay. Did you pay attention when we were looking for Corey?"

Okay, so now I know what he's talking about. Yeah, he was worse than useless, but I don't judge him for that. "You know there's a reason that people don't look for their loved ones, right? You can't be objective when there are so many emotions involved. You could have been in the police for thirty plus years and would've been hopeless in that situation. Niko wasn't as helpful as he probably thinks he was."

"Hey!"

I smirk at Niko's reaction, but again, I don't turn to look at him.

"It's okay, babe, I thought you did well."

I snort laugh at the soothing tone that Grant uses for Niko. If there was a way to make a man feel less than a total alpha, it was the tone Grant just used. Add in the kiss that he blows and I find I'm having too much fun.

"So how about it? I want you and Niko to run my Scottish office together."

Grant rubs his tongue along the edge of his teeth as he looks over my shoulder at Niko. "What do you think?"

"Totally up to you, Grant. I think that Core might be happy if you are around to keep me in check though."

I look over my shoulder at Niko. He's taking this better than I thought he would and I'm wondering why. I thought I would have to fight to get him to work with Grant, especially after him being shot. "Who are you and what have you done with Niko?"

"Fuck off. I have no problems working with Grant, especially since I'll be his boss and get to assign the cases I want him to have."

"Oh fuck." Grant shakes his head before grabbing Niko by the front of his shirt. He drags him close enough that their noses brush against each other. "Don't be a dick with this or you'll be punished. You aren't the only one who knows how to tie a decent knot." He backs off instantly, looking at me while Niko struggles with a response. "I would love to take a job with your company. I can't wait to get started." Grant doesn't say anything else as he leaves the room.

I smirk as I retake my seat, watching Niko as he stares after Grant. "Should I get Sam and leave? You look like there's somewhere else you'd rather be."

"Fuck off." Niko tries to rearrange his dick discreetly, and I burst out laughing. I have complete sympathy for him. I still have that problem when I'm around Sam. He glowers as he takes his seat again, downing the small amount of Scotch left in his glass. "You could have given me a heads up, by the way."

"Wasn't willing to let you argue about it. Grant is a grown man and doesn't need your permission to take the job. I know how you get, overprotectiveness is in your blood."

"I wouldn't have stopped him." At least he has the decency to look guilty since he's lying like fuck.

"Doesn't matter. I think you two will make a great team."

He nods in agreement before silence falls over us. It's obvious he has something he wants to say, but I refuse to ask. No way am I going to give him an easy way to start this conversation. It only takes a few minutes for the need to get the better of him. "So are we ever gonna talk about it?"

"Talk about what?" I'm only playing dumb with him because there is only one thing that I know he'll want to talk about. I spent most of our phone calls trying to change the subject so we could focus on the business. I knew that he would have so many questions about Sam, but I wanted to have them face to face and not over a phone. I wanted to see his face, and I wanted him to be able to see mine. I wanted him to see the truth in my words, so he would know how much Sam means to me.

"About the fact that you're in a relationship."

"Is it that much of a shock?"

"Well if you remember that you're dating a guy, then yeah."

I've gone through this conversation with Gabe and Porter, and even though both guys were cool with my choices, they did have questions for me. The funniest reaction was Roxy. Maybe I should have broken it to her before I approached Sam at the bar and kissed his breath away, but I hadn't seen him all day, and he was the only thing on my mind. Her chin had almost hit the floor of the bar at the shock. "It kinda took me by surprise as well."

"Have you always liked guys? I swear I would have bet money on you being straight as fuck."

"I've always noticed men, but I thought that was normal, or at least I convinced myself that it was. There have been a couple of guys that I've had a serious attraction to, but nothing like with Sam. He's just ... mine."

"Are you happy?"

I think about my life with Sam. Everything we do together seems to be my new favourite thing to do, even if it's as simple as cleaning our places together. I always imagined that the every day mundane things would drive me crazy in a relationship, but it's those things that make me love him more. It just feels real. "So fucking happy."

"Do you think he's the one?"

"I know he is. I don't know if he's aware, but I'm never letting him go." My need for Sam gets worse every day, and when he smiles at me, I want to beat my fucking chest. He's the one thing I wasn't looking for, and he's the one thing I can't live without now.

Movement at the door grabs my attention, and when I look behind Niko, I see Sam standing there with a gentle smile on his face. He doesn't say anything as he comes and sits on my lap. He gently kisses my lips, nothing more than a brush of his lips against mine. "I don't want you to let go. I'll be yours forever if you'll have me. Promise you won't let go."

I close my eyes and drop my head against Sam's, my arms tightening around his waist. "I promise not to let go. I might fuck up a lot, but I'll always come back to you, Sam. You are my everything."

"I love you, Clay."

"Oh, fuck." It's the first time he's ever told me that and my chest aches as his words fill my heart. This is why people do it. This is why they fall in love. I've spent most of my life running from anything that resembled a feeling, and all I was doing was missing the most incredible and awe-inspiring experiences of my life. To know that I might've gone my whole life without knowing true love makes me want to knock myself over the head. My parents did a number on me, and they had the entire thing so fucking wrong. Love doesn't destroy you. It makes you. If you find the right person it changes you, but for the better. Sam has completed parts of me that I didn't know I was missing, and I hope that he feels the same. This is it for me. He is it. If I die tomorrow, I'll know that life couldn't have been better.

"I want to move in with you, Clay. Say I can."

And just like that, Sam proves that just when I think things can't be improved on, he does it. We've only been dating a few weeks officially, getting to know each other properly, but it's been enough time. I know that I love Sam and moving in together makes sense. I want to wake up with him in my arms every morning and make love to him at night before we fall asleep together. Coming home to him after a day at work feels like perfection, and there's nothing that would ever convince me to say no. "Yes, and as soon as possible. I want you in my bed, our bed, every single night. I want fucking everything with you."

My mum and dad spent my childhood showing me that love wasn't like they showed in the movies. I'd been told how much it destroys you, leaving you broken and shattered, but they were wrong. So very fucking wrong. Love is the one thing that makes this life worthwhile, it's the one thing that makes sense. My only regret is that my brother isn't here to meet Sam, but I know he's watching me with a smile on his face. He'd always told me that love would come along when I least expected it, but he was a kid, so I just nodded to keep him happy. Who knew that he was right all along? Maybe he's the reason I found Sam. Perhaps he's been looking out for me this whole time? It's the only reason I can explain finding Sam when I wasn't looking.

I thread my hands through Sam's hair, holding him tightly against me. I don't care why he's here, I only care that he is. I've had an ache in my chest for a while now, and I've finally worked out what it is. It's the wall around my heart crashing down, the bricks landing with a thud one by one. Sam did that for me, and there is no more hiding from it. I love him so fucking much, but this isn't the time to tell him. I'm only ever going to tell one man that I love him, and I need him to believe it. I don't want him to think I said it as a reaction to his declaration. I want the words to mean something, because I love Sam, and I always will.

35

Sam

I KICK the box inside the cupboard and slam the door before it can fall out again. My task had been emptying all the spare room boxes, but there were just so many of them. I've now decided that if I hide them, Clay will never know and everything will be okay. I didn't realise that moving house would be so tiring. The last time I did it most of my stuff was still in boxes and unpacking had been low on my list of things to do. When I asked Clay if I could move in with him, all my belongings were still packed away, but when we returned from Scotland, and we brought them here, Clay had insisted that I unpack.

"All done?"

I turn to see Clay standing just inside the door of the room, a massive smile on his face. I spread my arms and turn a full circle. "Look ... no more boxes."

He nods before approaching me, but when I think he's going to hug me, he opens the closet behind me, and the boxes land with a thud on the floor. "All done, yeah?"

I drop my head to his shoulder and feel it rise and fall with his laughter. "There are just so many. It's never-ending. How about we bin it all, there's nothing important."

Clay kisses my head and wraps his arms around my shoulders. "If it was important enough to pack up and bring, we're keeping it. This is our house, and I refuse just to have my shit here."

I hate it when he says sweet stuff like that. Now I'm going to have to empty the fucking boxes.

"How about a break? I need to make a few calls for a case, but you could pop out and get us something nice for dinner. Grab a bottle of wine too, and we'll make a night of it."

Okay, so that's sound so much better than unpacking, so I nod before he changes his mind. "A romantic night in? I think that sounds like a great plan." I'm suddenly hoping tonight might be the night. It's been nearly a month, and Clay won't have sex with me. He says that we need to connect on other levels before we take that step again, and I think he's being a jerk. Well not really, but if I get any more turned on I think I might die. The other things we're doing have been mind-blowing, but I need to feel him inside me. I need that connection again.

"It does. So you get us something to eat, and I will get finished up. It's Friday night so we have nowhere to be tomorrow." He eases me back so he can see my face. "Actually, why don't you get enough food for the whole weekend." He winks before leaving me standing in the middle of the room with an instant boner. He is so good at shit like that. He just has to say a few words, and I'm turned on, so to hint that we are spending the weekend together, well of course that's going to excite me.

I look at the boxes behind me and decide that they can wait. The only thing I need to do now is go and get some food for my man and me because I'm all for the plan on not leaving the house this weekend.

Clay

I knew I had him as soon I mentioned buying food for the weekend. He's been pushing to reconnect again, but I've had this plan. Its been the hardest thing I've ever done to deny Sam what he wants, but I needed tonight to happen. I'm not much of a planner when it comes to romance, but for Sam, I was willing to try. Okay, so maybe calling tonight's plan romance is pushing it a little, but I don't think Sam will complain in the slightest.

I take a seat at my desk and pretend to be working in case Sam appears. Telling him I had some calls was a lie, but he might have asked for company if he knew I wasn't busy, and I need some time alone. I have a lot of shit to get sorted before he arrives back, I just need to get him to leave first. I'm starting to get angsty when I hear Sam shout goodbye and a few seconds later the front door closes with a gentle thud. I force myself to stay seated until I hear his car leave the driveway, but as soon as the wheels hit the road, I'm out my seat and getting to work. I race through to our bedroom and grab the supplies I stashed in there earlier. My time is limited, and I need to be ready for him arriving home.

I HEAR Sam's car pull into the driveway and I lean back against the wall to wait. The front door opens and closes before Sam makes his way to the kitchen. I know it won't be long before he comes looking for me, and I'll be right here waiting on him.

The wait feels like forever, but finally, I hear his footsteps heading down the hall towards me. He'll probably stop in the office first, but he'll find it empty. My heart is racing, worry starting to spread through me. I hadn't doubted what I had planned, but now thinking about it while I hide in our bedroom, I wonder if he'll like it.

"Clay?" When Sam shouts out to me, I know that the wait is over and I can't change my mind now. I need to see it through, stick to what I organised and have faith he'll love it.

A shadow falls over the carpet in front of me, and I know that Sam is standing in the doorway. I purposely kept the small lamp on in the hallway while the bedroom is dark, all so I could see him, but he can't see me.

"Clay?" Another step and his body appears around the edge of the door, but I'm still hidden in the shadows behind the open door. When Sam has stepped fully into the room, I push the door so it closes behind him, surrounding us in complete darkness. "Holy fuck. Please tell me that's you, Clay?"

I take a few steps towards him, using his voice to guide me. I reach out and cup his face, feeling him relax into my hold. He knows it's me without any words, and that is a thrill. "It's me, beautiful."

"What's going on?" Sam's voice is quiet, almost like he's scared to make too much noise in the darkness.

I don't answer his question, but I do turn his body until he's facing away from me. When I think he's facing the headboard, I take the little remote control from my pocket and press the button. The whole area above the bed lights up with tiny lights, rivalling any Christmas tree. Sam gasps and his hand comes up to cover his mouth. "Do you still want a romantic night?"

Sam nods, and I press the second button on the remote and the light start flashing, creating a twinkling masterpiece. Done with the remote, I throw it onto the carpet and finally touch my man.

I lean my body into his back as I bury my nose into his neck. He always smells so fucking good, and I can never get enough of him. I want his scent in my nose all day, but I haven't found a way to do it other than making Sam stay with me all the time. Sam grinds his arse against me, and I moan with pleasure. He is trying to tempt me like all those other times, but little does he know that he isn't leaving this room tonight until I fuck him. "You are the most amazing man I've ever met."

Sam sighs and leans his head on my shoulder. I use the move to kiss his neck, smiling against the skin when he leans away to give me better access. His throat is so fucking smooth, and I spend time enjoying the feeling. As my lips happily work, my hand's stroke over his body, removing clothes as they move. I want him naked against me, and I want it now. It doesn't take long until he's standing there entirely stripped, and as soon as he is, I press against him until he takes the hint and moves forward. When Sam is directly in front of the bed, I push on his shoulders and let my eyes devour him as he gets onto his knees on the mattress.

"Fuck me, Sam. You are fucking gorgeous. I haven't seen anyone as perfect as you."

I see his skin flush even under the limited lights, and when he buries his face into the duvet, I can't resist smacking his arse. He yelps, but when his back arches I know he's enjoyed it.

"Move up towards the headboard. You'll find two straps on the pillows. Hold on to them until I join you." I bite my lip and wait for Sam's response. Our whole relationship has been a tug of war for dominance, but tonight I want to be in control, but I need Sam to let me. I wait for him to tell me to fuck off, and I sigh in relief when he slowly crawls into position. When he grabs the restraints I fitted to the bed legs, I grip my rock hard cock. There is nothing hotter than Sam having an attitude, but watching him give in to me, well that shit is fucking irresistible.

I strip quickly because the need to get inside Sam is becoming too much. I need to feel him around my body so I can tell him a few important things. That's my plan tonight. I'm going to drive him to the point of insanity, and then I'm going to tell him everything. When I'm as naked as Sam is, I kneel on the bed and slowly make my way towards Sam's head. I grip his wrists and tie the restraint around them, loving the sound of Sam panting in excitement. I lean down until my lips are at his ear. "Now it's your turn to be tied up."

Goosebumps erupt over Sam's skin, and he turns unfocused eyes to me. He's already so turned on, and I growl in pleasure. He looks so fucking delicious right now, and it's taking every ounce of control I have not to pin him to the bed and take him. Stay with the plan, Clay. Don't let him distract you.

I move back to the end of the bed, using my hands to tilt Sam's arse so I can see everything that I want on display. The last time I had sex with Sam, it was in a haze. He had been breaking apart, and I'd done what I could to hold him together. It had been amazing, but I hadn't been able to explore the way I wanted to. Tonight I'm going to change that, and Sam is just going to have to let me. Reaching over the edge of the bed I grab the tube of lube I left there. I don't hesitate before unclicking the top and pouring the cold liquid onto Sam's arse. He flinches before tilting his arse in my direction more. My eyes don't leave him as I close the tube and throw it on the bed. The slick liquid makes a slow path between his cheeks and I decide to help it on its way.

Gripping his arse in my large hands, I massage the pert muscles, loving the redness that appears on Sams skin.

"Oh god, Clay. Baby, please."

I don't know what Sam is pleading for, but when I slip my finger into his crack and across his puckered hole, he nearly leaps from the bed. I don't let it deter me, and I use my free hand to hold his hip while I explore. I'm fascinated by the way his puckered muscles clench when I run my fingertip over it, only to relax and open slightly like an invite. My mouth waters at the sight, and I make a mental note to taste Sam here another night. Not tonight, tonight I want to get inside him. "Shit. I want inside you so badly, Sam. I'm so close to coming already."

"Stop talking then. Just do it, I want to feel you."

I would smirk at how desperate he sounds, but since I match his need, I don't find it funny.

"Please, Clay. I've waited so long. I need you, so fucking much." Sam's hands grip around the restraint, his fingers going white at the tension.

I fumble with the tube of lube, covering my aching cock with liquid before pressing against Sam's hole. My common sense tells me I need to prepare him more. I need to fill him with fingers before I fill him with my cock, but I don't have the patience. "I should slow down." I say the words out loud to try and get my body to listen, but then Sam presses back against me, and I slip inside him for the first time in weeks. I watch as he bucks his hips and my dick slips from his body, only for him to ease back again, making me disappear inside him. The whole scene is erotic and sensual, and it only takes a few more thrusts for my orgasm to threaten to hit me.

Grabbing Sam's hips, I still his movement. I gave him his fun, but now its time for me to take over. I've pictured this in my head so many times, and I refuse to get distracted by his hotness. Buried deep inside him, I lean over his body so I can reach the restraints. I fumble with the clips, but soon I have Sam's wrists free. It won't be for long, but he doesn't know that. Using the small amount of restraint still attached, I ease Sam upright until his back is pressed against my chest. My cock throbs inside him but I try to ignore it as I bend Sam's arms behind my back and connect his wrists with the clips on his restraints.

"Clay." My name is panted into my ear as Sam struggles against being captive.

"Shhh, baby. Just relax and feel." I roll my hips, getting as deep as I can inside Sam's body. He tightens around me, and I bite his shoulder. With his arms tight around me, it restricts my movement, but that only makes the whole thing better. Being so close and feeling him inside and out is perfect, and exactly what I need for the next part of my plan.

Sam moves as much as his position allows him, but I use my hands to still him. I look down the length of his body and see his dick pointing straight out in front of him, hard and aching as it glistens in the light. The temptation is too much, and I run a finger along him, flicking over the tip when I get there. A full body shudder goes through Sam, and his restrained hands dig into my arse.

"Clay, please move. I need to come."

Widening my thighs, I tilt my body until Sam can no longer move. He is being held captive on my cock, and I fucking love it. I am fully in control, and I don't plan on losing the advantage. "Look at you. I love it when you're desperate for me."

I run my hands over his chest, stopping briefly to tease his nipples to soft peaks. His hole tightens around my cock and my eyes cross with pleasure. "I love it when your body tightens around me."

Sam tries to free his arms again but soon gives up his fight. It's like he realises he has no say in what's happening, so he relaxes against me and prepares for the journey.

"I love it when you give in to me."

Sam shudders again when I slide my palms below his belly button. I make sure I don't touch his hard on, and when I stroke the soft skin of his groin, he moans low and long. It is like fucking music to my ears, but also sends me closer to coming. I've barely moved inside him, but my body doesn't seem to care. I need to move this along before it's too late.

"I love it when you kiss me."

I lick along his neck while I continue to stroke over his body.

"I love it when I wake up holding you."

My teeth graze against his skin.

"I love having you here all the time."

Sam is shaking in my hold, and I know this is the moment. I am only a few seconds away from coming, and I think Sam might be at the same point. The whole experience is heady. Being inside his body at the same time as his head is just where I want to be.

I ease slowly out of his body as I stroke my hand over his erection. I thrust into him, and the angle is perfect. Sam cries out in pleasure as my balls hit his arse. Fuck me. It's so fucking good. I repeat the move a few more times, and my orgasm tingles in my balls. I'm only going to last a few moments longer before I finally mark Sam as completely mine.

"I love you, Sam. I love you so fucking much."

Sam explodes as soon as my declaration of love leaves my lips, and he covers my hand with cum. His hole tightens around me, and the last tendrils of control vanish. I come with a growl, filling Sam completely.

It takes a few minutes for the world to come back to me and I start to worry that I've shot my brain into Sam. His hands tugging against me finally has me moving, releasing the clips on Sam's wrists. As soon as he's free, he spins and tackles me. I groan when my softening cock slips from his body, but it's cut off as I tumble onto the mattress.

"That was a shitty move." Sam is trying to sound pissed off, but his shining eyes show he's lying.

"Did you not like it?"

"I fucking loved it, just like I love you. But seriously?"

My brain is still slow, and I can't catch up. "What?"

"You tell me you love me when I can't see you? I wanted to see your face." Sam suddenly looks a little sad, so I cup his face and pull him entirely on top of me. I gaze at him, fully absorbing how fucking gorgeous he looks. This guy is mine, and I still struggle to believe that on a daily basis. He is everything I never knew I needed, and I don't know how I lived without him. Life before Sam was good, but life with Sam is fucking perfect. I love this man more than I thought possible, and I don't plan on letting him go.

"I love you Samuel Leighton, and I think I always have."

EPILOGUE

Sam

I WIPE my hands on my jeans as I stare at the house at the end of the street. I've been sitting in Clay's truck for about twenty minutes now, unable to move. I know I should just open the door and walk up to the front door, but it's proving harder than I'd anticipated.

"Hey, beautiful."

I turn to look at Clay in the driver's seat. I expected him to have said something before now, but he's been patient. "Yeah?"

"Are you gonna go in? I don't mind waiting, but I'm scared someone will call the police on us." He smiles and my heart races. Even after eight months, seeing Clay looking at me like that makes me want to melt. I'm not sure I'll ever get over the fact that this guy is mine.

I take a deep breath and put my hand on the handle, finally ready to do this. I keep my eyes on the house as I open the door and step out of the truck. I hear Clay's door close a minute before I feel his presence at my back. He doesn't touch me, but knowing he's there gives me a confidence boost. "I need to do this."

Clay kisses the back of my head, his lips lingering for a few moments before the connection is broken. "You got this, sexy."

I take another deep breath and start a slow walk towards my parent's house, my stomach threatening to get rid of the little bit of breakfast I managed to force down this morning. Damien has been gone nearly a year, but this is the first of me building up the courage to get in contact with my family. Most people would have called first, made sure they wouldn't get a door slammed in their face, but I wanted the chance to see them one last time in case they turned me away. That's the fear that I can't get over. What if I've been gone too long and they don't want to know me now? Everyone has told me that's not going to happen, but my mind always goes to the dark place. God, I don't know what I'll do if they tell me to go away. It happened to Clay with his dad, but he is so much stronger than I am. Maybe it would be better if I turn around and live with the dream that my family is out there and missing me?

I don't turn around though and, as the house gets closer, I wipe my hands on my jeans again. I feel like my heart is trying to beat through my chest, but I concentrate on putting one foot in front of the other. When I reach the front gate, I pause, and when Clay puts his hand on my lower back, I want to hug him to say thank you for supporting me. If I had had to do this on my own, I would have driven away without even parking. I crack my neck and open the gate, determined to walk to the door and knock finally. When my hand connects with the wood, I struggle not to run away. Shit, I shouldn't feel this nervous going to see my own parents. This is my mum and dad who love me. There's no reason to think they will be anything other than relieved and excited to see me. There's just that part of me inside that doubts everything.

The door opens in front of me, and I see my mum for the first time in nearly three years. She looks older than the last time I saw her, her hair slightly greyer, and a few more lines on her face, but she's still the most beautiful woman I know. She freezes completely, her eyes widening to the point they look like they might pop from her head. "Angelo. Angelo!" She screams my dad's name before rushing down the steps and grabbing me into a hug. As soon as her arms wrap around my waist, I feel the tears running down my cheeks. "Oh, my baby boy. You're alive, and here. Oh god, I thought you were dead." Her words are punctuated with sobs, but she doesn't let me go.

"Rose, what's wrong?"

I open my eyes and see my dad standing at the top of the steps, his face mirroring my mums from a few minutes ago.

"Samuel? Is that really you?"

There is no chance to answer before he barrels down the steps and wraps my mum and me in his arms. His grip is fierce, and I close my eyes, feeling like I'm ten years old again. I feel safe like I always did growing up. Even when the world outside my front door got close to destroying me, inside these four walls, I felt protected. My dad would have fought the world if he needed to keep us safe.

I can hear both my parents murmuring things to me, but I can't make any of them out. Not until my mum eases us apart and cups my face with her soft hands. She stares at me like she can't quite believe that I'm here. "I thought you were dead." Her voice breaks as she speaks and I hate that I've caused this much pain to my family. I need to tell them what happened and that I left to keep them safe, but first, there's someone important I want them to meet.

I ease out of their arms and hold my hand out for Clay. He's been standing quietly behind me as I reconnected with my parents, but now I want him with me. He takes my hand, and I drag him into the group. "Mum, dad. I want you to meet Clay. This is … this is the guy I love."

Clays eyes burn with love as he smiles at me. We have been through so much together, but those words still make my breath leave my lungs. I've never met anyone like Clay before, and I doubt that there's anyone else like him out there. He is strong and fierce, but also gentle and passionate. He fought so hard to deny that he was worthy of my love, but there was no way I was giving in. After everything he's been through, all the pain in his life, I am only too willing to show him how good it can be. He thinks that he was unworthy of love, but he is so fucking wrong. I've never met a man who deserved it more, and I'm humbled daily that he chose me for the job of being his.

I drag my gaze away, knowing if I don't I'll get lost in his eyes, and this is not the time for that. That's a habit I've been trying to gain control over, but when those hypnotic colours swirl in his irises, I just can't look away.

Instead, I look at my parents, at their wary faces, and realise that I have a lot of explaining to do. They have missed three years of my life, and so much has happened. They deserve my story, and now is the time to give it to them. "Can I come in? I need to tell you some things."

THE END

ACKNOWLEDGMENTS

There are always so many people I want to thank when I finish a book, because those are the people who make all this happen. The support I get astounds me every day, and I truly love everyone.

Claire: you know why...always!

Claudia and Mildred: You ladies...I owe you so much! You pushed and checked and supported...and you were basically my cheerleaders when I needed it. I can't repay what you've done, just know how grateful I am <3

Marie: The scary one...you know I love you...and your truffles!

Michele: Thank you for reading my words and making sure they are fit for release. I love you.

My betas - Jax and Tina: Without you this would probably still be a huge mess...so thank you!

To my Minxes: You all help me pimp and are there to listen to my crazy ramblings...and also state the hotness when I need it. I love my little group, and I'm so glad you are all on this journey with me.

To everyone who has been waiting on this story for so long, I hope it was worth the wait. Clay spent so long hiding his story, I just didn't know that he was waiting for Sam.

ABOUT THE AUTHOR

For more information on T.a. McKay

www.authortamckay.com
tamckayauthor@gmail.com

ALSO BY T.A. MCKAY

Leaving Marks series:

Leaving His Mark - Out now

Leaving Her Mark - Out now

Hard To Love series:

Worth The Fight - Out now

Make Me Trust - Out now

This Isn't Me - Out now

Undercover series:

Undercover - Out now

Unsuspected - Out now

Clay -Out now

Standalone Novels:

Someone To Hear Me - Out now

Rescue Me -Out now

Coming Soon:

Satan's Crush

Maxed Out

Printed in Poland
by Amazon Fulfillment
Poland Sp. z o.o., Wrocław